RHONDA PARRISH ANTHOLOGIES

Available Now

A IS FOR APOCALYPSE

B IS FOR BROKEN

C IS FOR CHIMERA

D IS FOR DINOSAUR

E IS FOR EVIL

F IS FOR FAIRY

FAE

CORVIDAE

SCARECROW

SIRENS

EQUUS

MRS. CLAUS: NOT THE FAIRY TALE THEY SAY

TESSERACTS TWENTY-ONE: NEVERTHELESS

METASTASIS

NITEBLADE MAGAZINE

FIRE: DEMONS, DRAGONS AND DJINNS

EARTH: GIANTS, GOLEMS AND GARGOYLES

GRIMM, GRIT AND GASOLINE

Coming Soon

HEAR ME ROAR

SWASHBUCKLING CATS: NINE LIVES ON THE SEVEN SEAS

D IS FOR DINOSAUR

Book 4 of the Alphabet Anthologies

Edited by Rhonda Parrish

Poise and Pen Publishing

EDMONTON, ALBERTA

www.poiseandpen.com

Publisher's Note: This is a work of fiction. Names, characters, places, and incidents are a product of the author's imagination. Locales and public names are sometimes used for atmospheric purposes. Any resemblance to actual people, living or dead, or to businesses, companies, events, institutions, or locales is completely coincidental.

Book Layout © 2014 BookDesignTemplates.com
Edited by Rhonda Parrish
Cover art by Janice Blaine
Cover design by Jonathan C. Parrish

D is for Dinosaur / Rhonda Parrish.—2nd ed.
ISBN 978-1-988233-15-4 (Physical)
ISBN 978-1-988233-16-1 (Electronic)

Note From The Anthologist

This isn't an introduction, not in the traditional sense, but I wanted a word with you before you dive into this anthology.

Usually, when I put together an anthology a great deal of thought and care goes into choosing which order to place the stories. With the anthologies in this series that task is taken away from me because the most logical way to order the stories is alphabetically. Usually that works out just fine but this time RNG was not in my favour and arranging the stories in *D is for Dinosaur* alphabetically resulted in stories with similar themes, tones or voices appearing side-by-side more than once.

If you're the kind of reader that doesn't bother then by all means read this book from front to back. However, if you'd rather not read two similar stories in a row I suggest mixing up the order in which you consume these.

I haven't got a suggested reading order for you (because creating one of those would set a precedent I'd feel obligated to follow throughout the rest of this series) but I do encourage you to try something different. Read all the vowels before you start on the consonants, or chose the stories that spell out your full name and read them before going back to devour the rest, for example. If you discover a particularly awesome reading order and share it with me I will pass the word on to others via my mailing list and social media.

Above all else, enjoy!

Rhonda Parrish
Editor

CONTENTS

A — Michael M. Jones 8

B — Simon Kewin 19

C — Brittany Warman 31

D — C.S. MacCath 35

E — Gary B. Phillips 61

F — L.S. Johnson..75

G — Suzanne J. Willis..103

H — Megan Engelhardt 119

I — Michael Fosburg 123

J — Jeanne Kramer-Smyth 137

K — Pete Aldin..157

L — Alexandra Seidel...161

M — Michael B. Tager 171

N — KV Taylor 185

O — Amanda C. Davis 191

P — Beth Cato 195

Q — Lynn Hardaker 203

R — Sara Cleto 217

S — Jonathan C. Parrish 223

T — Samantha Kymmell-Harvey 225

U — Michael Kellar..237

V — Cory Cone 247

W — Hal J. Friesen...259

X — BD Wilson..285

Y — Andrew Bourelle 316

Z — Laura VanArendonk Baugh......................................339

Michael M. Jones

Tanith Murray is always angry. Not the cool sort of angry that comes with superpowers, because at least then she could save the world and feel like she was making a difference. No, the shitty kind of angry involving lots of yelling and slamming doors and hitting walls. The sort of angry where everything sets her off, from burned toast to an accidental bump in the hallway at school. The sort that always ends with bruised and bleeding knuckles.

She hates being sixteen and half-white, half-black and not fitting in with either race. She hates being poor, she hates being unattractive, unpopular, unloved. She hates the way she doesn't fit in with her family. She hates the way everyone else seems so confident, so accomplished, the way they have their shit together when she doesn't. She sees the world through the red haze of perpetual fury, stomping around like Godzilla and people scatter out of her way. She hasn't hurt anyone yet, but everyone knows it's a matter of time until punched walls become punched people, or worse.

At night, when she's tossing and turning in the too-hard, too-small bed tucked into what used to be a storage space in the basement until she demanded she not have to share a room with her little sister, she dreams of something ancient and reptilian. It squirms inside her, restless and hungry.

In her dreams, Tanith rips at her skin, tearing away big flaky chunks to reveal green scales underneath. She picks and shreds and soon there's nothing but a pile of Tanith-skin, of clothes and hair and everything that makes her *her*. Oh, and the dinosaur. There's a dinosaur standing where Tanith used to be. It's human-sized, whip-thin, built for speed and meanness all scales and tail and teeth, radiating menace and hunger.

Oh, she knows that supposedly dinosaurs had feathers and weren't really green, or whatever, but Dinah, as she thinks of her dino-self, doesn't give a shit about scientific accuracy, she's something dredged up from the foulest part of Tanith's psyche, anger made real, and in her dreams, Dinah runs free.

Tanith dreams of loping through the empty streets and back alleys, of knocking over garbage cans and plunging through hedges. She feels the cracked pavement under her feet, hears the click-clacking of talons as she runs. She lifts her snout to the sky and sniffs, simultaneously attracted and repelled by the nighttime odors of a city only half-asleep. She chases small animals that cross her path, driven by the need to hunt and kill and eat, and the impulses carry her until sunrise. She never sees any people.

Every time Tanith wakes to find herself in bed, clothes intact, mouth free of the taste of blood, she's both relieved and disappointed. She's taken to scanning the news for reports of monsters or missing animals, and isn't sure how she feels when nothing turns up. Dinah is so real, it's almost a shame that she only exists in dreams.

Tanith used to have friends at school, a small gaggle of outsiders like herself, the ones who didn't belong to any one group and the ones comfortable with crossing boundaries. But when Tanith's constant sulking and insults got to be too much they all had other places to be, other cliques to join. One by one, they stopped hanging out with her, until she was a pack of one.

Maybe they sensed Dinah, knew she was a predator and they were prey.

Or maybe they just didn't want to deal with her bullshit.

Hell, even she doesn't like herself that much. Apart from terrorizing the city in her dreams, Tanith's only joy is running. That doesn't need skill, it just requires stamina and the ability to put one foot in front of another until you've gone from point A to point B and maybe back to the beginning again. She's not particularly fast, and she doesn't care where she's going but she can run for hours—around the track, through the parks, along the streets. She's not running from anything, not running to anywhere, but the constant pounding of feet, the inhalation and exhalation, the burning of muscles—they chip away at her anger, so she can fall into a state of quiet calm. When she runs, she's totally Zen.

And then one Tuesday early in March, as she's running around the track after school, someone joins her. Not someone she knows well. Daisy Gray. A junior. Part of that artsy crowd. Has lots of friends. Laughs a lot. Probably always has the right answers in class.

Tanith's never spent any time with her but now here she is, matching Tanith's pace like it's not a thing. She's a head taller, all long pale limbs and flying blond ponytail, and Tanith's irrationally jealous because Daisy's gorgeous and makes this look easy. Like the bitch doesn't even sweat or get tired. Daisy doesn't say anything. She just runs alongside Tanith, speeding up or slowing down as necessary, even when Tanith breaks into a sprint to try and ditch her.

When they're done, Tanith's exhausted and pissed, and Daisy just gives her this innocent smile before jogging away in a different direction. Tanith's like... what the fuck just happened, and she stalks home, confused and angry. That night Dinah, is extra aggressive, roaming the streets like she can find a way out if she looks hard enough.

Tanith sees Daisy in school, but they don't even acknowledge each other. Like yesterday never happened. And afterwards, instead of heading to the track, Tanith breaks left, goes to the fitness trails in Van der Bleek Park where she can be alone.

Only halfway through the first lap, Daisy appears next to her. Matches her speed, and the two run side by side. There's no way Tanith's going to let this interloper get to her, no way she's going to admit defeat, so she keeps running and tries very hard to pretend that Daisy's not there. That she can't feel the other girl's presence, can't hear her breathing or the sound of her footsteps. She ignores how they're basically in sync.

What the hell kind of game is Daisy trying to play with her? She doesn't even *know* Daisy, so what is this? Some kind of hazing?

She runs until she's exhausted, and they still haven't exchanged a single word. Which is odd. Tanith usually has lots of words for that which annoys her. Three older brothers taught her an astounding amount of profanity at an early age, and she's mastered words as a weapon, because she knows that if she gets into a fight, a real fight, she's just going to lose her shit and get stomped. She's angry, not stupid. She should be telling Daisy to fuck off, already. She should be demanding answers, or threatening to shove Daisy's head up her ass.

But no, this whole Daisy thing leaves her unsettled; when the other girl departs, Tanith wanders home in something of a head-scratching daze. That night, her dinosaur prowls restlessly, looking for something in the darkness but not finding it.

This repeats for the rest of the week. No matter where she goes to run, there's Daisy. And impossibly, they still haven't spoken to each other. Not at school, not on the track, not in the park. It's like they coexist without acknowledging one another, save when they accidentally lock eyes. Then it's a smile on Daisy's part, an increasingly-perplexed glare on Tanith's.

She wants to feel violated. After all, Daisy's invading her space, getting all up in her business...but at the same time, she's not that bad.

After a week of this, Tanith's resigned to the fact that Daisy's going to show up and keep her company and maybe she doesn't hate it.

At night, though, her dinosaur is riled up like a motherfucker, roaring at thin air, knocking over trash cans, racing down empty streets like a toddler on speed. Tanith's sleep is fitful, unsatisfying. Everything feels off-kilter, and she can't get it together to snap and snarl at people like usual. She spends her days in sullen silence, and when she does talk, it's without the usual bite in her tone.

Finally, she's had enough. It's Wednesday and after she and Daisy have run through the park for a while, she speaks. "What the fuck is this?"

Daisy doesn't respond.

"Is this some sort of stalking thing, because it's really fucking weird."

Nothing.

"Is this a dyke thing, because you're not my type and I've seen you sucking face with guys."

Not a damn thing.

"Why won't you leave me alone, Goddamit?" Tanith hears the whine in her voice and hates it—*hates* it. She's not whiny.

Daisy come to a halt, so suddenly that Tanith's about a dozen steps ahead before she realizes something's happened. This is the part where she should keep going. Ditch the bitch. But she stumbles to a stop as well, and just stares at Daisy. She folds her arms.

"Do you really want to be alone?" asks Daisy. She's not judging, there's nothing but honest curiosity in her voice.

This is the first time anyone's actually asked Tanith what she wants in she can't remember how long. It's always been "Do this…or else. Don't do that…or else." Parents who expect her to obey them when they're not ignoring her. Brothers who don't want her around. Teachers who've long since run out of fucks to give.

Finally, she just shrugs, jerks her head in a gesture Daisy's free to interpret however she wants, and takes off down the trail again at her usual steady pace. A minute passes, then Tanith feels the familiar presence at her side. It makes her smile inside. Just a tiny bit. But that warmth tickles her heart. It's surprising. Her dinosaur stirs grumpily deep within, as though disturbed in its sleep. But Tanith wills it to chill out, and it does.

Tanith and Daisy are silent for the rest of the run, and they part ways without any further discussion. But now that Tanith is pretty sure it's not a stalker thing or a lesbian thing or a weird prank, she's not so uncomfortable. She tries a friendly nod, the sort of thing that suggests "I don't hate you at the moment," and stalks away before she can see how Daisy responds.

They encounter each other in the cafeteria at school the next day, and Tanith is caught by surprise, so much that she just stares at Daisy, at a loss for words. Christ, it's been so long since she'd had a friendly conversation that she forgets how it goes. She's so much better at telling people to get the fuck out of her way, or just shoving past them, and she's used to throwing insults rather than greetings, and....

"Hey," says Daisy casually.

"Hey," says Tanith, like there's a damn echo.

And that's that. They go their separate ways, Daisy to join the artsy kids at their table full of color and laughter, and Tanith to her corner of solitude, where she hides behind a glare and some math homework due next period.

When Daisy doesn't show up on time for their run that afternoon, Tanith starts working herself into a royal pissyfit, her anger quickly ramping from annoyed to incandescent. She knew this would happen as soon as she let her guard down and started to care about someone else. Abandoned. Let down. This was probably that bitch Daisy's intention all along. Build her up, throw her away.

She channels her fury into her legs, picking up the pace until she's practically sprinting, and she can pretend that the wind in her face is making her cry. If she's fast enough, she can outrace her feelings.

Deep inside, her dinosaur stretches, roars, shakes the cage of her heart. It wants to be free. She wants to unleash it.

Then Daisy's beside her, and for once she doesn't look all put-together and chill. She's frazzled and breathing hard and Tanith understands it's from trying to catch her. Good. She forces the pace a while longer before dialing it back to a more sedate speed. She studiously ignores Daisy, of course.

"Alvarez caught me before I could escape. She wanted to talk about my final paper for European History." It's not an apology. Tanith would probably have tripped Daisy for apologizing. She's okay with the explanation. They continue on in their usual silence, and when they're done, Tanith pauses a moment. Words struggle to be free, but she's not sure they're the right ones. So instead she dismisses her friend—wait, friend? When did *that* happen? —with a nod.

That night, she falls asleep still trying to sort through her confusion. Why? Why is Daisy doing this? Why is Tanith okay with it? The confusion carries over to Dinah the dinosaur, far less aggressive than usual as she stalks the dream streets, frequently pausing to sniff the air and roar as if expecting a response.

It takes Tanith several more days before she finally lets herself take the next—irrevocable—step. After the run, she says, in a voice more accustomed to harshness than shyness, "I need a drink."

Daisy's smile almost blinds her. And that's how they end up sharing a park bench with cold bottles of water purchased from a vending machine, a bag of barbecue corn chips between them. That was Daisy's idea, but she offered to share without a second thought. It gives them both something to crunch on while the heavy silence settles around them.

"Why?" asks Tanith at last.

"Because you're not the only one with a dinosaur inside her," says Daisy blithely. She eats a corn chip, washes it down with a swig of water.

The *fuck*. Tanith just stares at her. Tries to drill into that pretty blonde head with her laser vision of doom. Fails.

"I call mine Sue. After the T-rex skeleton in the Museum of Natural History in Chicago."

The *double* fuck.

"When I was little, I used to wish I could turn into her, and stomp around and eat everyone who was mean to my dads," says Daisy. "I wanted to terrorize everyone who didn't understand that love is love. I was always so scared that something would happen to my family, and I wanted to be big and strong and fierce enough to protect them." She shrugged. "I was *really* anxious as a kid."

Tanith silently digests this information. Feels bad for the dyke comment she made the other day. She thinks about saying something, but when she meets Daisy's eyes, she realizes that it doesn't matter to the other girl. Not like that. So she grabs some corn chips instead.

Daisy smiles. "Then I let Sue do the work. I figured out just what frightened me, and I turned her loose on them in my dreams. And eventually, I realized I wasn't so scared anymore. I mean, it's not that simple but that's the gist. It also helps that I met good people, the sort who loved and accepted my whole family, and I realized the world didn't have to be terrifying." Shrug. "It's horrible at times, but it has lots of good points."

Huh. Tanith tilts her head. Is Daisy for real? She seems sincere. "But I don't have your problem," she says at last.

"I know. You're a total rage-monster. But why? What's bugging you?"

Tanith is all set to answer. Or to tell Daisy to mind her own fucking business. Or to just storm off. That moment of decision lasts an eternity; finally, she gets to her feet with a need to move.

"People!" she bursts out, like someone lanced a boil and all the pus and nasty stuff escaped. She throws up her hands, and a lifetime of frustration spills out. But as she's airing all of her petty grievances and frustrations, she hears herself and realizes just how little most of it really means. How she's let all the little stuff fester until it filled her and driven everyone away because that way they can't let her down. And as she realizes this, she trails off. She stares away from Daisy because she doesn't want to see pity or scorn on the other girl's face.

Her dinosaur is throwing itself against the bars of her heart again. She wishes she could vanish into herself, and let Dinah take over. Dinah doesn't care, Dinah's a ferocious monster that doesn't take shit from anyone, and Dinah *definitely* isn't a whiny bitch.

There's a hand on her shoulder. It's Daisy, of course. It's comforting, and Tanith can't remember the last time anyone touched her like that. Like they care. She shrugs the hand off, and immediately regrets it. She goes dead still, still not able to turn around. That's okay: Daisy hugs her from behind, and this time Tanith accepts it. She closes her eyes so the tears won't leak out, and leans back against her friend, taking deep, shuddering breaths. They remain like that for a few minutes until Tanith's got control of herself. She pushes away, grumpily. Whirls to glare at Daisy, who's just doing that thing of hers. The tall, quiet, patient blonde thing. "I gotta go," Tanith says. And Daisy lets her.

But something in what Daisy said sticks with her, and that night, when Tanith tears her skin off and becomes Dinah the dinosaur, she thinks about her anger and everything that pisses her off, and how she can use her dino-self to deal with it. And just like that, as if someone flipped a switch, her dreamscape is populated with grotesque representations of everyone she knows, everyone who has ever pissed her off. Classmates, teachers, family.

And she hunts the fuck out of them. Chases them down. Tears them into bloody gibbets. Swallows them whole. Goes full-on Jurassic Park on her family. It's a beautiful night-long orgy of destruction, and in the morning, when Tanith wakes, she feels good. In control. Like she's finally conquered some small part of whatever's been eating away at her all these years. She smiles at herself in the mirror, and for the first time in years, it's not tinged with distaste or self-loathing. Her parents seem smaller, less... significant. Her little sister is less annoying.

When Tanith and Daisy get together for their run, it's in silence as always. That is, until Tanith mutters a quiet "Thanks" out of the blue, and Daisy replies, "You're welcome." A whole conversation condensed into three words. And later, when they're chilling on a bench and sharing corn chips again, Tanith says, "Dinah. Her name is Dinah." And Daisy nods. She gets it.

"So how'd you know?" Tanith asks her.

"It's just a feel," replies Daisy. "Something in the eyes. In the way you move. I knew you were like me. Sometimes people just have dinosaurs in them, I guess. It's not like there's a Wikipedia entry or Facebook group for it."

"Huh." Tanith has a handful of chips. "So why'd you bother with me?"

"Why not? You were hurting. I knew I could help. You just needed someone who understood you."

Tanith nods. She feels weirdly empty now that so much of the anger has drained out of her. Adrift. Awkward. That, of course, starts to annoy her, but she takes a deep breath, tries to find her new calm.

"You don't have to be alone at lunch," says Daisy. "The others, they're pretty cool. As long as you're not a total bitch, they'd be okay if you joined us."

Tanith frowns a little, and mulls it over. "Maybe," she finally allows. "My people skills are for shit at the moment."

"Take your time."

Just as she's getting up from the bench, Tanith has a different thought. "Hey. The dream thing. The dino thing. Are we all separate, or do you think there's overlap?"

That stumps Daisy, and she's quiet for a while. "No clue."

"Well if it's possible... you and Sue can come visit." She takes the bag of chips, upends the crumbs into her mouth, and wanders off.

A week later, Tanith finally decides to join Daisy and the artsy types at their table. It turns out that when she's not busy being angry, she's pretty damn funny, able to produce biting impersonations of their least favorite teachers. Years of hate-fueled observation have given her a gift for pinpointing the stupid and absurd, the flaws and imperfections. When she uses her powers to make friends instead of drive people away, it feels so much better. The awkwardness fades quickly.

She and Daisy still run almost every day, but it's no longer the only thing which gives her relief from a world determined to press her buttons. It's more a thing they do because it feels right.

And when, one night, Dinah is joined by Sue, the two dinos rampage happily in a dreamscape made up of fears and insecurities, conquering their inner demons one tasty morsel at a time.

Tanith Murray isn't so angry anymore.

A is for Angry

Simon Kewin

Sometimes, in her dreams, Brontë became a dinosaur.

If she'd been given a choice in the matter she'd have gone for a flying lizard, some flapping proto-bird soaring over steaming primeval swamps aloof from the carnage below. Or, failing that, one of the vast herbivores that lumbered untroubled across the plains or waded through the lakes, too large to be a target.

That was her approach to life: rise above. It worked. Most of the time.

But, no, when she dreamed she was a raptor, a predator, sinking her dagger teeth into the smooth flanks of her fleeing prey, their blood spurting into her eyes and the air filled with the panicked, dying roars of their last thrashing moments.

It troubled her a little to have such dreams. It troubled her more that she found them so very satisfying.

"Brontë, are you up yet?"

She mumbled a reply to her mother. It was understandable she'd fantasize about being a *T. Rex*, or a *T. Regina*, anyway. Who wouldn't? One of her father's pet names for her as a child had been Brontësaurus, but there wasn't actually much fun in being a creature that was basically a cow the size of a building. Although, being stepped on by a giant like a Brontosaurus had to be fairly fatal, too.

"Brontë, you'll miss the bus!"

She slouched downstairs to sit at the breakfast table, sipping tea while waiting for her fifteen-year old brain to start working. She was not a morning person. She scrolled through messages on her iPhone but couldn't make much sense of any of them. The kitchen reeked of bacon, the smell enough to put her off her toast. Being the only vegetarian in the house had its difficulties but secretly she was pleased, too. She didn't feel hungry, her stomach already a fizzing cauldron of anxiety. The nausea of the smell would be her excuse.

"So what subjects have you got today?"

Her mother often tried to engage her in conversation over breakfast. It wasn't like Brontë meant to be rude or uncommunicative. It just came out that way. She often listened to herself, the way she spoke, with stark dismay. Why couldn't she be nice? "Don't know. English I think."

That was usually enough to please her mother. The great works of literature were her mother's *thing*. She wrote novels of searing emotional honesty that were loved by those that read them but which sold next to nothing. The passion explained the name Brontë had been given. Given or lumbered with. No one could ever manage the umlaut. Still, it could have been worse, she could have been branded *Woolf* or *Plath* or something.

"Ah, wonderful," said her mother, almost closing her eyes in delighted anticipation. "I envy you, truly."

You wouldn't, thought Brontë. *Not if you knew the truth.*

Her tormentors met her at the school gates, a pack of them that opened to engulf her like the jaws of some huge predator.

She'd never understood why they hated her. Okay, she was different. Fay, dreamy Brontë. Ethereal Brontë who never fought back. She was stick-thin, delicate, her bones slight. Perhaps that was all it was. They laughed at her, saying she was really a boy, she was still a kid. They delighted in emphasizing the swell of their breasts to her, explaining she'd have some of her own one day, when she grew up.

The irony was they spent much of their time wishing they were thinner while Brontë stayed as she was however much she ate. She sometimes wished for a few more curves, and more than once she'd eaten until she was sick. It had made no difference; she was what she was.

She tried to push through the throng. Rise above. But Lois, the ring-leader—beautiful, rich, popular Lois; cruel-eyed, vicious Lois—barred her way. Try as she might, Brontë wasn't strong enough to force the taller girl aside.

They'd been friends once, the best of friends, when they were young. They'd played together. Played pop singers, played princesses, played dinosaurs. But things changed. For a year now Lois had made Brontë's life a misery.

Lois laughed. "Let's give the poor starved girl some food. Hold her hands."

The other girls in the gang, content to follow orders, grabbed Brontë and pinned her arms to her side. Brontë struggled but wasn't strong enough to fight off so many. Chelsea, perhaps the nicest of them, or the least worst, spoke up. "Come on, leave her alone. She's not doing us any harm."

Lois pretended to be concerned. "But she'll fade away if we don't feed her." She'd taken out some food from her own lunch bag: a grey, floppy slice of chicken. "Open up and eat."

"Lois, leave her," said Chelsea. "You know she's a vegetarian."

"But once she tastes this she'll realise what she's been missing, won't she? She'll thank us. Hold her head still." Brontë clenched her lips shut while Lois tried to force the wedge of flesh into her mouth. She felt the rubbery touch of it on her lips.

"What's going on here? Leave that girl alone."

Mr. Porter, who taught her history, was striding over, face red, teeth bared as he shouted. Lois and the others backed off, but only a short way, reluctant to yield their pray to the newcomer.

Brontë stood alone for a moment, caught between the girls and Mr. Porter. No one liked him. There were whispered rumours about what happen to girls who were summoned alone to his eyrie on the third floor. Brontë was tempted, briefly, to toss Lois to him, tell him some story to get her revenge, but she held her tongue. Her tormentor was small-minded and cruel, but even *she* didn't deserve Mr. Porter.

"They weren't troubling me," said Brontë. "We were just messing around."

Mr. Porter looked like he was going to pursue the matter for a moment, his bulging eyes casting from Brontë to the others but then, with only a wordless exhalation, he strode away. Before Lois and her gang could regroup Brontë left too, heading up the grey stone steps for her classroom. Her hunters could ambush her anywhere about the school, but she was generally safe in a lesson, under the gaze of one or other of their teachers.

But as she walked away, something clicked into place in her mind. Enough was enough. She wasn't going to put up with Lois and the others any more. Who did they think they were? It was time she started paying attention to those troubling dreams. She was one against many but there had to be a way. A means of fighting back.

That lesson, she barely paid attention as her English teacher rattled on about Lady Macbeth. Plans for what she would do took shape in Brontë's mind.

The following day, a Saturday, she went into battle. Time to stop being the prey and become the predator. The prospect filled her stomach with bubbling acid, but it thrilled her, too. She could do this. She *wanted* to do this.

She put on her retro Marc Bolan tee-shirt. Most likely no one would get the joke, but it amused her. Her mother studied her with narrowed eyes as she slipped out of the house but didn't say anything. Lois liked to hang out with her pack at the local shopping centre but Brontë would make sure she was there first and confront the other girl when she was alone. She hadn't mapped out exactly what she was going to do but she wanted to scare Lois. She'd rehearsed several speeches in her mind and she knew a few jujitsu moves from a half-hearted attempt to learn self-defence a year back. One way or another she would put a stop to Lois's attacks.

But Lois strode into the shining shopping centre already surrounded by her friends and the thought of tackling them all was too much. Brontë spent the day stalking her quarry, watching them across the heads of hurrying shoppers or through store windows. Lois was never alone, her entourage always around her.

Finally her chance came late in the day, as Lois and Chelsea and the rest were bidding their farewells. The others were all laden down with bags but Lois, perhaps disdainful of everything the shops had to offer, had bought nothing. She carried only the plain handbag she'd arrived with. She stepped alone onto the bus that would take her to the sweet, leafy greenery of the country village her family lived in. Fortunately, Lois climbed to the upper floor of the double-decker, and Brontë was able to slip unnoticed onto the lower.

Lois left the bus as it squealed to a halt at the single stop in her village. Brontë waited as long as she dared for Lois to put a few paces of distance between her and the bus, then followed. It was already getting dark and ornate iron streetlamps cast pools of light among the trees. Lois walked towards the lines of huge houses and mansions that sat quietly behind their high fences.

Brontë didn't have much time. Once Lois reached the gates of her family home her chance to confront her would be lost. She was about to run after Lois to catch her up but then Lois stopped unexpectedly. She glanced around, and there was something furtive in it, something guilty, that made Brontë stop and hide in the shadows of a hedge.

Lois looked through the railings at one house in particular, a white wedding-cake of a place, ornate interiors visible through high windows, gardens immaculate, but instead of going inside she took a rolled-up jacket from her bag and slipped it on, throwing the hood over her head. Which seemed odd: why put a coat on just as you reached home?

Then, with another glance around, Lois walked away from the house. She crossed the road and retraced her steps towards the bus stop and the centre of the village.

Brontë held her breath as Lois neared. Fortunately there were no near streetlights and Lois had her gaze cast down. Brontë let Lois pass then, puzzled, resumed her hunt.

Back at the stop, Lois waited for a bus going in the opposite direction, back into the city. There was something defeated in the way she sat slumped on the nearby bench. Brontë stayed back, watching to see what Lois was doing.

Twenty minutes later another bus arrived, windows bright in the gathering gloom. Lois rose and climbed on, moving more slowly than she had. Once again she took the top deck and once again Brontë followed. The bus rattled off. The lights inside made it hard to see what they were passing. Brontë pressed her forehead to the cold, vibrating glass and watched as leafy lanes gave way to the first familiar tendrils of urban sprawl. Soon they were rushing past the tightly-packed houses and tenements that clustered around the edges of the city. Then, at a stop still several miles outside, Lois came down the narrow, twisting stairs from the upper deck and left the bus. Once again leaving as much gap as she dared, Brontë followed.

They were in a part of the city she didn't know well. A part of the city you never went *to*, only hurried *through*, car windows tightly closed. Fires, open fires, burned on squares of wasteland and people gathered around them for warmth.

Lois, walking by them all as if they were the most normal thing in the world, crossed a broken wasteland of rubble towards a teetering construction of boards and corrugated iron sheets leaning against the leg of a motorway flyover. The traffic streaming by overhead was an unceasing roar.

Brontë paused, unsure of herself, all her former resolve gone. She no longer felt like a hunter. She was alone, vulnerable. She imagined eyes watching her from the shadows all around. Predators' eyes. There probably wouldn't be another bus for at least half an hour to whisk her away to safety. She should never have set out on this craziness.

The weird thing was the only person she knew there, who was any sort of friend, was Lois. Brontë resumed walking, keeping out of sight but getting close enough to Lois to see what was happening. What was the other girl doing here? What was going on? It made no sense.

Lois walked up to the ramshackle hovel and, ducking, called through a low opening that was the nearest thing there was to a door. Then she disappeared inside, perhaps hearing some response out of Brontë's earshot. Brontë crept closer. If someone did attack her, some gang or crazy, that broken hovel was suddenly her only refuge. She shivered. It was fully dark now, although the lights from the motorway up above cast everything in a constant glow.

An older woman approached from a different direction, and Brontë shrank back into the shadows of another of the motorway's supports. The newcomer looked a little like an older version of Lois: the same red hair, the same swaying way of walking. This time Brontë heard the muffled response from within the hovel at the woman's call. Clearly whoever lived there had agreed some system so that they knew it was a friend approaching.

It was precisely then that Brontë's phone rang, probably her mother calling, the bright, chirpy pop tune loud in the echoing space beneath the road. Brontë stepped backwards three, four paces, finally intending to flee to the road and the bus stop.

She was too slow.

Lois, the older woman, and a boy Brontë vaguely recognized as Lois's younger brother emerged as one. The older woman carried a length of wood, as if used to defending her family and in that moment Brontë understood. This was Lois's home. This was where she lived. Not one of those grand houses in the country, but here, in the eternal daylight of this urban wasteland.

"Brontë. What are you doing here?" Lois's voice was a mixture of unusual notes. Confusion. Shame. Fear. Brontë wanted to step backwards, run, but she couldn't. Instead she stepped closer, wary, and replied. "I... I followed you. I came to confront you. To tell you what I felt about you."

The words sounded suddenly ridiculous. She thought Lois was going to leap to the attack, filled with anger at being followed but instead she looked down at the muddy ground. "Go on then," said Lois, her voice low. "Tell me. Tell me what you like. Because there's nothing you can say that's any worse than what I tell myself every day."

Here was Brontë's chance. She could do exactly as Lois said. Now Brontë had power over the girl who had so tormented her.

But no, she wouldn't. This wasn't her. She wouldn't be prey and she wouldn't be predator either. She didn't want to be any sort of damned dinosaur.

"You should have explained," said Brontë. "You should have said."

Defiance sparked across Lois's face. "Really? You think that would have helped? You think that would even be possible?"

"Look, I'm sorry," said Brontë. "I should never have followed you. I didn't understand how things were for you."

"So now you do."

"Yes."

Lois didn't look Brontë in the eye. From the scowl on the other girl's face, Brontë could see that Lois didn't want her understanding, her sympathy. Lois's mother placed a protective hand on the girl's shoulder.

"It's okay," said Lois over her shoulder. "She isn't going to harm us." But it was clear from Lois's expression that she didn't believe it at all; that she was very worried indeed about what Brontë might now do or say.

Saying nothing more, all thoughts of revenge gone, Brontë turned and walked away.

The following Monday at the school gates, Lois and the others were there. Lois didn't move and kept her gaze cast down as Brontë approached and the others, taking their lead, did the same, letting her pass. Chelsea, leaving the group, ran to catch up with her.

"Hey. Are you okay?"

"Sure," said Brontë.

"I heard what happened."

"She told you?"

"It was hard to get much out of her. She would only say, 'Brontë saw us.'"

"So you know about her?"

"A few of us know. If everyone found out it would kill her."

"I don't see why."

"It just would. That's the way she is. I mean, she lost everything."

"She could have told me. I wouldn't have cared."

"She's ashamed."

"I know."

"So are you going to tell everyone?"

Brontë couldn't resist a smile. "Don't think I'm not tempted. What happened to her exactly?"

"Her parents' business went bankrupt and they split up and lost their house and ended up where they are. It doesn't excuse how she behaves, I know, but it sort of explains it."

Brontë walked in silence for a moment before replying. "It's not my secret. It's up to Lois who knows and who doesn't. But I wish she'd just told me."

Chelsea studied Brontë for a moment, then nodded. "You know they're all secretly jealous of you, don't you? Lois and the others. And, I mean, me, too, I guess."

"Because I'm so skinny?"

"Because you're always *you*."

Her mother had taught her that. Whatever else, be yourself. She'd written whole novels that could be reduced to that one sentence. "Who else would I be?"

"They're so afraid of being singled out they're just happy when it's someone else. You threaten their whole approach to life."

"That's pretty stupid."

"Yeah. I know. But that'll stop now, I think. Listen, want to grab some food before lessons?"

She was hungry. She could murder a good breakfast. She glanced back at Lois, who still wasn't looking her way. She didn't know if they could ever be close again. Perhaps not. Or, perhaps. Things changed. Brontë thought for a moment, then relented with a shrug of her shoulders. "Sure. That would be good."

Chelsea hooked her arm through Brontë's and the two walked together to the canteen.

That night she dreamed again. This time she wasn't a gore-splattered carnivore, nor a plodding diplodocus stamping through the mud on tree-trunk legs. She wasn't a heavily-armoured stegosaurus, hide so thick that nothing could penetrate. She wasn't even a pterosaur, flapping through the sky above the carnage, croaking from her saw-toothed mouth.

Instead she was a dragonfly, a true giant of the Carboniferous, her clattering buzz filling the sky. Her stained glass window wings caught the dazzling light and broke it into a million rainbows.

She danced through the air and nothing could harm her. She was delicate and she was beautiful and the whole world was hers.

B is for Brontëaurus

Brittany Warman

PROLOGUE

My teachers were the wind and the rain, the grass and the trees. Our mother whispered for us to listen to them carefully, told us that they were always speaking, that only they knew the most profound truths of existence, and that only they could help us fly. When she left to find food for us, we would argue and cry but try our best to listen too. Safe in the broken pot where our parents built our nest, safe from the wide world below us, we would often tell each other stories. We imagined what the river hoped for and where the sun went each night. We dreamed and the stories helped us understand, helped us see ourselves as we once were, our true selves, a truth so enormous we couldn't really understand it at all. But the stories did help and the wind would ruffle our feathers as if it was pleased.

Each night, when the sun went down and we were warm against her feathers, our mother would sing her own prayers to the earth. We would try to listen, try to hear as she heard, but what I remember most is her soft night-song.

THE PROFESSION OF FAITH

We believe in the ancient ones, the spirits of the earth,

Creators of all that surrounds us and guides us.
We believe in the lessons of the forests and the seas.
We believe our people once ruled this world, that we were the first
chosen–
We believe that the bones of our ancestors sing beneath the ground,
Sing long and loud, long and loud,
That we were once huge and powerful and free from fear.
We believe the ancient ones have placed our spirits into these small
bodies
To teach us, to humble us, to show their love for us.
We believe they will come again to judge us, to see us fly.
We believe in bravery.
We believe we will be chosen to lead again.

THE CELEBRATION OF THE MYSTERY

We grew, we flew, we left the nest. Mother turned into a memory and
I have forgotten the names of my brothers and sisters. The wind
guides my life, taking me from place to place, danger to danger. In my
heart I try to hold our truths, I try to be brave. When the cats pounce I
hold our truths. When food is scarce I hold our truths. I imagine what
it would be like to be bigger than the cats and the rulers, bigger than
their cars and their houses, bigger than the consistent fear that
dominates my days and forces my vigilance at night. I am so much
more than I appear.

PRAYER

Oh ancient ones—teach me to be brave, to be strong. Though I am
little and insignificant now to so many, help me to remember my
people were once huge and glorious. Help me to remember what my
heart never truly forgets—that we once roamed the earth, its sole
rulers, our feet crushing the ground with the slow, deliberate
movements of gods. That the trees would bow to our hunger, that we
once crushed those who hunt us now. Help me be grateful I can still

look down on the earth from lofty heights, that I am still free. Though I am changed in form, though I am small, my spirit is the spirit of my ancestors. I am massive. I sing.

C is for Catechism

C.S. MacCath

Have this in mind, oh princes

do not forget it.

Who could conquer Tenochtitlan?

Who could shake the foundation of heaven?

7-Atl (1-)Calli 11-Tecpatl:

A good day for purification by battle, a bad day for rest.

Her name is Alejandra Maria Yaotl, and she is desperate to squat here, in this ribbon of grass between armies, to defecate. But her knees do not permit squatting, and she knows the desperation is only a great, killing mass in her bowels making demands of the failing body it consumes from the inside out, a little more every day. So she walks; strands of white hair blowing about her eyes, bent spine unable to straighten, papery hand gripping the rough wooden knob of a cane.

The punishing sun shines down on a spill of engine oil, a pool of chlorophyll, a gob of intestine crushed into the soil. Behind is a shuttle with a weeping grandson at the helm. Ahead are the towering gates of a city-state that teaches its people how to perform it, a grand theatre of violence caked in the blood of its sacrificial victims, the place where she will die one way or another.

To Minsky Prime, she is 01100100 01101001 01101110 01101111 01110011 01100001 01110101 01110010, the same designation he has given to all her people because they refuse the transcendence of technology, preferring instead to live in plain, fleshly bodies. His army defends her passage to the left; a host of boxy metal torsos bristling with automatic weapons atop bare human legs. It is a ridiculous construction undermined by a blow to the knees, but these half-sentient soldiers are not designed for effectiveness. They exist for show, a prideful display of craftsmanship designed by a transhuman demigod who long ago surrendered his body and exists now only as data.

Minsky Prime does not care that the Speaker of the city-state goes too far. He only wants the machine that sends New Tenochtitlan's jaguar and eagle knights into the pasts of other places, where they make war on the lost settlements and isolated tribes of old Urth and from where they collect the sacrifices cast down from the Great Temple in such staggering numbers.

To Autochthōn Gaea, she is a vision of pointed teeth, a roaring in the ears, a pungency of scales, a tongue tasting the afternoon air, a heavy footfall in the distance. It is the sensory translation of Minsky Prime's designation and a joke at Alejandra's expense. Her army defends the right with a whipping of poisonous vines attached to photosynthetic warriors, a cloud of toxic mushroom spores pouring out of humanoid mouths. Ageless and voluptuous, she wears a living suit of armor that scatters thorns wherever she walks. Her city-state is ever green, a place of perpetual Spring where the women are always fertile, the men always potent. Autochthōn Gaea does care for the old Urth but in the way a master of thieves might care for an orphan. The machine does not matter. The sacrifices do not matter. Only the double helix does in all its exploitable diversity. This, she would preserve.

Jaguar and eagle knights meet Alejandra's defenders with fang, beak and claw. They are furred and feathered; changed by the theatre they inhabit into caricatures of their antecedents, brutal chimeras of man and beast. Jaguars hunt Minsky's host with macuahuitls. Eagles cast javelins down at Gaea's warriors with atlatls. Cultivated hatred curves the lips of their grinning mouths, turns the weapons in their hands toward excruciation. They are a single, faceted ruby shining under that punishing sun; red, hard, and flawless.

Alejandra's shoes are slick with oil and blood, clotted with chlorophyll and offal. Her cane sinks into the ground, sticks, pulls free with a sucking sound. There had been a spread at the shuttle port; corn tortillas, beans, and squash, all soaked in human blood, garnished with a human heart. She had known to expect this, but the Speaker could not frighten her with food. Tortillas were ground corn clinging to the hands, the pop and sizzle of hot oil, the chatter of family chopping peppers and tomatoes. Beans and squash were a cool rain falling in the garden, a bounty gathered into a frayed skirt. No. The Speaker had only reminded her of the reason she had come. Now every step is a prayer for the dead and a promise to the living.

The gates open. Nanomachines, like a swarm of gnats, look for carbon dioxide in front of her face, ride oxygen into her lungs, shake hands with her nervous system. They are the servants of New Tenochtitlan's AI; Keeper of the city-state, neutral voice in her mind:

"By his own decree, whoever tempers the Speaker in a duel of the challenger's choice shall send him to travel with Huitzilopochtli, eat of his heart, and take his place."

Alejandra does not want his place. She wants him dead and the city-state abandoned. The Keeper knows this now and does not care.

The Speaker waits above her on a stair of solid gold. He is magnetic in the way of all transhuman demigods; archons of living myth whose domains are the constructs of collective consciousness made manifest, whose sycophants dream in cultural archetypes and rave in the glossolalia of ancient tongues. His body is a fabricated thing of too-perfect beauty; smooth brown flesh draped in a cloak of hummingbird skins, prominent cheek bones, obsidian eyes under heavy brows, long black hair caked in blood like the city-state itself. Arms spread wide, voice like a thunderclap, he greets her. "A cousin of Quetzalcoatl arrives at the gates of New Tenochtitlan!" Jaguar and eagle knights stop mid-slaughter to stare. "You smell sick, Little Dinosaur. Have you come to offer yourself in the chalk and feathers of sacrifice?"

Alejandra has no strength for banter and no patience for theatre. Bile floods her throat from a stomach twisted with nausea. "I'm here for the duel your Keeper spoke of in my mind."

The Speaker's eyes brighten with humor. "What weapon do you bring to temper me, Little Dinosaur, the macuahuitl? Or is it the atlatl you prefer?"

Nearby, a clutch of eagle knights erupts in derisive laughter.

"I'm not amused with you." Alejandra grits her teeth on the urge to vomit, swallows hard. "What you're doing here is evil; twisting a history that isn't yours, making sociopaths with it, murdering innocent people from the old Urth." She pauses to breathe, leans on the cane with a jaundiced hand. "I've come to make you answer for all of that. Words, they are my weapons."

"Philosophy! Excellent." The Speaker smiles. His teeth are white and square. "You have the welcome of my home until the moment I cut the precious eagle cactus fruit from your chest."

Autochthōn Gaea joins them on the stairs, trailing thorns. Her breasts, belly, and hips are round as a mouth fallen open in ecstasy, and her skin subverts the enemy with heady pheromones. A creamy hand drifts over the battlefield. *"Plant Frangipani now."* The suggestion is telepathic. *"It loves the blood."*

"You are an Oleander blossom; lovely and lethal." The Speaker catches her palm and kisses it. "How fortunate we've all agreed not to depose one another. He glances at Alejandra. "And what an interesting proxy!"

"Isn't she a specimen? Will you send me her bowels if she dies? I've never seen a cancer I didn't create." Gaea's lips droop in a moue. *"But she does have a point. You go too far."*

The largest of Minsky's constructions mounts the steps with a dancer's grace and folds open. There is nothing inside but a bald, thick-lipped head attached to a nutrient tank. Its voice is wet and strangled. "NT's AI did a drive-by download of softwarily magical shield-crashing malware when it received my Head of State creds. You might be good at spacetime machines, but your security is fucktastically out of date." The legs pivot to point the mouth at Alejandra. "We got you here, now hurry up and do the rest before you crap out. Ha! Crap out." The head pauses, blinks. "Fossilized dinosaur shit is called coprolite."

Alejandra cannot muster a reply, faints in front of him, must be carried to a guest house where she sleeps through the night.

8-Itzcuintli (1-)Calli 11-Tecpatl:

A good day for being trustworthy, a bad day for trusting others with questionable intent.

In the morning, her back is wet with bloody diarrhea, but there is no pain. Bare feet swing out of the bed onto cool, jade tiles. A breeze blows white gauze curtains into the room. There is a slave girl waiting, pale and silent as a moon, who guides her toward a deep, fragrant bath. The child's hands are so gentle and her face so sweet that Alejandra wants to gather her up and flee, to save one life at least. But this is not an option. Save them all or lose them all, these are the only paths ahead.

Jaguar knights bring a simple, untainted breakfast she cannot stomach and escort her by shuttle to the heart of the city-state. Draped across the tiny planet like a vault of the underworld, New Tenochtitlan is proud in its temples, industrious in its streets, quiet in its flowery gardens. As with its predecessor, it is divided into quarters that evoke Quetzalcoatl's house of worship; the Gold Abode of the East and its shining stairs, the Turquoise Abode of the West and its spacetime gate, the Silver Abode of the South and its verdant miles of farmland, the Red Shell Abode of the North, where the Keeper makes men and women into warrior chimeras. At the center of it all rises the Great Temple, where heartless bodies are cast from the summit day and night, so many the stones are forever stained with their blood.

At the top of that temple, four priests in feather headdress pin the limbs of a Gaean warrior to a rough-hewn altar. He is naked, and his poisonous vines have been pruned. The wounds ooze chlorophyll. He is screaming when Alejandra arrives; eyes bulging, chest open as a cave. New Tenochtitlan's Speaker towers above him; green heart beating in one hand, thick obsidian knife in the other. The scream fades. The heart stops. The warrior's body is hauled forward and cast down the stairs.

Alejandra clutches the buttons of her blue cotton frock and watches him tumble, lifts her gaze to the Speaker's hands.

He comes to her sweating from exertion, animated as if he has just received some necessary drug. A priest hurries to his side with a broad bowl in both arms, heavy with green hearts. The Speaker lays the last of them atop the others.

"They travel with Huitzilopochtli now." He faces the midday sun, turns a shoulder into the light. His hummingbird cloak shimmers with color.

The four priests on the temple summit stretch their lips into savage smiles.

Alejandra sees this, frowns, pokes him in the side with her cane. "You don't believe that any more than I do. It's just a folktale, and you're just a pomposo fraud with too many machines. If they all disappeared, would you fall over dead? I think so."

The Speaker bares his teeth, exhales in a slow release of sudden fury. "Myth has power, and ritual is a performance art." Dead-eyed calm falls over his face. "Let us agree upon terms, Little Dinosaur."

"My name is Señora Yaotl."

"Just so, but to the rest of the human species, your people are dinosaurs in need of a mass extinction event."

Alejandra thinks of her grandson and the pretty, brown-eyed girl he wants to marry. "That's what you're going to do, isn't it? When the past is so empty the present starts to shift like a pile of salt, you're going to come after my home, my family. Well, not while I'm breathing. Not while I can stand and spit in your face."

The Speaker tilts to one side, wipes chlorophyll over blood in the trophy of his hair. Sunlight gleams on the gold plugs in his earlobes. "You're dying of a disease my people will never contract but call me evil. You've abandoned your ancestral heritage but rebuke me for claiming it. You know nothing about my knights but accuse me of 'making sociopaths'. You've never been through the spacetime gate but criticize what I do beyond it." A priest arrives with a steaming towel. The Speaker finishes cleaning his arms. "Very well. I will debate with you the merits of civilized violence over the colonized peace of your fatuous condemnation. Let the Keeper itself decide whose logic is better."

There is music far below, beneath the clouds; a cacophony of drums, bells, and trumpets.

In Alejandra's mind, the Keeper of New Tenochtitlan stirs, vast and impassive. *"Do you accept a three-round structure for this duel? Yes/No"*

She responds without speaking. *"Sí."*

The Speaker nods.

"You both accept a three-round structure for this duel."

"Wait." It is like falling into a well, like nearly drowning as she had almost done in childhood. A memory comes of chattering teeth and a voice gone faint from screaming. Alejandra points at the

Speaker. "You didn't answer my question, and also, how am I to know the Keeper can be trusted? It's *your* machine."

"No I didn't, and you don't have the luxury of trust." He slaps her hard across the face, points at her crumpled body on the stone summit floor. "And also, never touch my body disrespectfully again."

The music nears, and there is lamentation under it. Two lines of slaves crest the clouds in a jerky semblance of dance. Some wear plumage in their hair. Others carry fans. Many are forced to play instruments. All are lately arrived from the spacetime gate; dressed in antiquated clothes, pleading in forgotten tongues. Above, eagle knights chivvy them forward with wing and claw, enjoying the sport.

Alejandra stares at the stains on her shoes, remembers the slave girl weeping over them, cracked pink knuckles clutching a scrub brush. They shared no language but kindness exchanged; soap and dignity for an old woman's failing body, salve and comfort for a terrified child. How she misses that child right now. "So, the pomposo fraud will hit me, but he won't kill me just yet. That's useful to know. Maybe this duel *does* mean something to him." Spitting blood, she struggles to stand, gripping her cane. "Why are they here, the slaves?"

The Speaker suppresses a scowl and flourishes a hand gilded with patterned nanofilaments. "You challenged me for the right to rule, and my people want to see that occasion marked." The stones reverberate with his voice. Butterfly cameras come and capture the flutter of his cloak in a warm breeze. "Half will go to Huitzilopochtli, and half will go home, according to the winner of each round."

Twenty slaves arrive at the summit to gawk at the Speaker, his feathered-bedecked priests, the altar they do not clean. The music stops, but the lamentation does not. So jaguar knights move among them and shred the lips of the loudest with sharp claws.

Alejandra hobbles toward a portly, middle-aged woman, clasps her hand. "So you will force me to participate in this monstruoso thing you do."

"I'm not forcing you to do anything." The Speaker shrugs, but his eyes are alight with guile. "Go lie down on the altar, and I'll send them all home right now."

The air is heavy, like water in the lungs. Alejandra cannot breathe it until the middle-aged woman touches her bruising cheek with a cool hand. She gasps. "You know I can't do that."

"I also know what you want to do with my home." The Speaker poses for the cameras and the crowd gathering on the ground; an exquisite demigod towering over a broken old woman in the final days of her life. "But before I surrender it to a mewling descendant of the mighty Aztecs, I will make certain your hands are bloody as my hair."

"Only if I lose." Alejandra's voice rings from the stones like the prayer of a weary girl trapped in a well.

The Speaker laughs down at her.

The Keeper pronounces the duel commenced; neutral voice sounding in the mind and over the city-state. *"Speaker Cuauhtémoc the Second champions the civilized violence of New Tenochtitlan. Alejandra Maria Yaotl challenges it. Polemists, make your first arguments."*

An eagle knight swoops in, lands on the summit, folds dun wings. White plumed head, eyes of black and gold, his humanity is a vestigial thing, an appendix that no longer serves any purpose.

"This is Aeton, who came from Olympus on Aphrodite Terra, Venus." The Speaker gestures at the knight, who bows low, wingtips brushing a pool of chlorophyll. "Vasiliás Ares gave him to me. Do you know who that is?"

"The warrior king of the inner planets." It is not possible to stand unmoved so near an eagle knight. Alejandra's heart beats like a frightened rabbit's, and still she longs to touch his feathers.

"Said I like killing too much." Aeton's words are guttural, slurred, punctuated by the click of a yellow beak. "Not true. Just don't like anything else."

"So it is with them all." The Speaker's gilded fingers shape a window in the air. Images pass rapidly through it of jaguar and eagle knights, so many they blur together. "I do not make sociopaths, Little Dinosaur. I rescue them from across the Confederation, and in so doing, I rescue the rest of humanity *from* them."

"Modern humanity, such as it is, and only for now." Alejandra cuts in. "Let us be clear. The past is not safe from them."

A shimmering gesture closes the window. The Speaker squares his shoulders, brow lifted in the triumph of a trickster springing a trap. "Aeton bought his wings with twenty rapists from all over the old Urth's history. Snatched them up before they did any harm. Tell me, are the women they would have abused safer because of my eagle knight? Such is my argument."

"So this woman is a rapist?" Alejandra lifts their clasped hands into the air, teeters with sudden vertigo, lowers them. "And all the people who live here were born somewhere else, killers from the womb in need of rescue? Hmph. You call me the Little Dinosaur, but you can't figure out how to cure them with all these magnífico machines? How sad."

Aeton cocks his head, peers at the middle-aged woman with a predatory eye. "Accused her husband's mistresses of witchcraft. Let two women burn for it."

"Are you her judge?" Alejandra lifts her chin, fronting defiance. The vertigo strengthens; because she has not eaten, because of the medication she took to prevent pain and nausea.

"Don't care about judging. Care about hunting. Predators mostly." Aeton folds claw-tipped arms across his chest, leans backward off the summit, soars away.

"Do you need to lie down, Little Dinosaur?" The Speaker's sudden concern is all syrup and deceit. "You look unstable."

A deliberate choice of words. Alejandra snorts, closes her eyes. "I am well enough to hear the answers to my questions, or would you rather just hit me again?"

The Speaker waits a long time to reply. When he does, his words are precise, impassioned. "I have spoken for New Tenochtitlan many hundreds of years. Most of my people are the children of its founders. They expect this life and hold the values it requires. But they are also the finest scientists anywhere and the finest doctors. They are poets, musicians, artisans, dancers, the best in all the known worlds, who understand the need for violence and let their own blood often in the service of the gods." Another pause and a rustle of fabric. The tap of pacing sandals. "Your ancestors built the theatre we emulate here. Is it not a more honest thing than the colonized peace Cortés and his army forced upon the Aztecs?"

Alejandra releases a heavy sigh, shoulder muscles sagging, and looks up at the pomposo fraud who has just lost his argument. The vertigo recedes leaving exhaustion in its wake. A flock of four-winged birds soars across the Great Temple summit, too bright and strange to be Mesoamerican recreations. Natives of this world, perhaps? She imagines their little grandchildren nesting in the ruins of this place.

The Speaker clears his throat.

"Lo siento." She moves away from the middle-aged woman. Butterfly cameras flit overhead. " But I don't understand what you mean by 'colonized peace'. It's been fifteen hundred years since Tenochtitlan fell. My people aren't colonized anymore, and we're certainly not always at peace. But I will tell you that my ancestors, they outgrew human sacrifice. You have been fetishizing the same period of history for generations, and you don't age. So of course the people born here think you can't die, and of course they also think violence is normal. But is it more honest than the life you believe I have?" A thick haze of copal resin rises in the air from a pair of tall censers near the altar. Alejandra blinks, coughs, continues. "Well, it doesn't matter, really. You invade the past. Cortés invaded Tenochtitlan. You capture slaves and pretend to worship ancient gods with human sacrifice. Cortés colonized the Aztecs with Spanish men and smallpox. It's the same thing, inflicting the will of one people upon another, and it's wrong. If some benefit comes to your victims, that's a mercy, but don't excuse the evil you do with the good."

For a moment, Alejandra believes she has overestimated the strength of her response. The Speaker's four priests come in chlorophyll-spattered tabards and drag the middle-aged woman toward the altar. One loses a fistful of headdress feathers to her flailing hands; they flutter to rest on the temple floor in a weak breeze that no longer mitigates the heat. But the Keeper of the city-state proclaims Alejandra the victor, an echo in the stones of the proclamation it has already made in her mind.

Even so, jaguar knights are marching the wrong line of slaves back down the stairs. Priests are forcing the wrong victim into the shape of a human star atop the altar. The Speaker's lips are twisting into a strange expression of cunning as he abandons the duel for the copal smoke and obsidian knives of sacrifice.

Alejandra hobbles after, hand outstretched toward the woman, who bellows like a cow in an abattoir. "You said the slaves assigned to the winner could go home! She was standing with me! And the people behind her, they were standing with me also!"

One of those people jumps off the temple stairs, black coat like a broken wing as he plummets toward a better death than the one awaiting him on the summit. An eagle knight dives after, catches the man, hauls him back.

"That isn't what I said." The Speaker's voice is quiet under the shrieking of the slaves and the gabble of the woman who is wetting herself now. He takes the knife from the altar table and slices her garments in two, exposing breasts of uneven size and a belly lined with stretch marks. His expression relaxes into rapture. "You can still take her place if you want."

Alejandra finally collapses in a clatter of wooden cane and fragile bones. "I see what you're doing here," she quavers with the last of her unspent stamina. "Yesterday, it was only killing, but you want me to think that today it is killing because of me. No. This is *your* sin, and you can choose not to commit it. I have a grandson to protect. It's just..." She pauses, grieving for the naked woman staring up at the knife poised above her body. "I don't understand why you're killing *her* if *I* won this round."

And then she does.

The Speaker did not offer to die in the case of his overthrow. He asked to be tempered. Gaea did not surrender her warriors because they lost, but because they won. And now this middle-aged woman is a proxy for Alejandra's victory.

She does not need to defeat the Speaker. She needs to let him win, because only the worthy are fit to travel with Huitzilopochtli.

The knife descends, and the damp chlorophyll on the altar streaks with blood.

9-Ozomahtli (1-)Calli 11-Tecpatl:

A good day for lightheartedness, a bad day for seriousness.

It rains all night; a downpour smelling of sulphur and iron, a native ecosystem spitting at its alien veneer. Alejandra lies awake and listens to water sluice from the roof, breathing in the defiance of this tiny, alien world. The pale slave girl sleeps at her feet, waking often to offer broth, medicine, a blanket, anything her hands might make or do to give comfort. They spend the precious coin of the darkness thus; dozing by turns, sharing cups of thin soup, dosing and taking drugs that include a steroid injection now. The end is near, very near indeed, and Alejandra knows she cannot continue the duel without it.

Minsky Prime and Autochthōn Gaea wait in orbit for New Tenochtitlan to stand or fall. At least Gaea must have known, should have warned her that only the worthy were sacrificed here and that winning would not be simple as losing to the Speaker. Any person might do that, but few could replace a sociopathic demigod, who would not surrender his throne to a mediocre mind no matter how well the Keeper sculpted the body that housed it. So if the resolution of the duel was not in victory or defeat, where was it? This is the question that plagues Alejandra's thoughts while the steroid lends its fleeting strength to her flesh.

In the morning, jaguar knights bring a silk gown patterned with small, feathered serpents - an unsubtle nod to the Speaker's epithet - and a floating divan outfitted with plush pillows. Alejandra checks her pride and accepts them both, grateful for a change of clothes and a respite from the cane. They take her to the Coacalco, an open temple of sulphur-and-iron-stained marble where statues of foreign deities rest in carved wall niches. The Speaker meets her there and introduces them as the gods of conquered peoples brought here to live as captives.

Alejandra rides by his side on the divan, relieved there is no blood in this place except in the Speaker's hair and the handprint bruise on her own cheek. Even yesterday's crippling heat has given way to scattered showers greening a garden bright with blossoms.

"I know why you sacrificed those people yesterday." She shifts among the pillows, spreads the silk over her calves.

They stop to inspect a gold elephant statue with too many arms. The Speaker smiles. "The gods give us life, and so we must nourish them in return with the finest gifts we have to offer."

"If this were a physical duel, what would happen if I lost?" Sunlight creeps across the temple walls, finds and warms Alejandra's feet.

"I would kill you on the battlefield and not before the gods." The Speaker licks his thumb, rubs a smudge of dirt from the elephant's trunk.

"How many times have *you* lost?"

"I never lose."

Alejandra watches the flex of perfect muscle under his cloak, under his skin, and believes this. "So it's a trick. Nobody can take this place from you in a fight. But did you ever expect a duel of wits, I wonder?"

"It isn't a trick." The Speaker lays a long, brown hand upon the divan. Dark hair brushes the upholstery. Blood flecks stick to the heavy fabric. "It is a challenge within a challenge within a challenge. Those who duel me to win do not understand the gods. Those who lose out of cleverness do not understand New Tenochtitlan. No duelist has ever understood me. Perhaps you will."

Alejandra lifts her gaze to the absolute blackness of his eyes. "Will you really lay down on that altar and let me kill you?"

A bead of sweat falls from the Speaker's brow, lands on her gown, darkens the silk. "Only if you promise to eat of my heart and take my place before you parcel my home out to Minsky and Gaea. Will you do that, Señora Yaotl?"

A faint memory of her grandson surfaces, hovering like a face above the water line. Alejandra gulps and grips the cushions on either side of her body. "I would do anything for my family."

The Speaker's brow lifts, and it is charming, boyish. He leans forward, kisses her mouth before she can protest. His tongue tastes of cayenne and cocoa. "If you were a healthier woman, I would invite you into my bed. It would be good to make love before one of us gives the other to the gods."

Alejandra slaps him, the feeble gesture of an old woman. It does not leave a bruise.

Later they come to a shaded dais overlooking an arena facing south. Around it, citizens of the city-state gather like hummingbirds themselves; brightly colored, suffuse with the life they have stolen from others. The Speaker sits on a marble bench, gestures for Alejandra to hover beside him.

Two young men stride from either side of the field toward the center. Like human songs they are, like gods themselves. Clad in fine woven cloth and gold bracelets, they are graceful in the way of young warriors, exquisite in the way of the Speaker himself.

"They were slaves once." He takes an orange from the bowl between them, digs fingers into its flesh. "Now they are vessels of

Tezcatlipoca - he of the smoke and mirrors - and one will die today as a god might die, of his own free will, an example to my people."

The warrior from the east is at least eight feet tall, a giant by any measure, with eyes like sapphires and a long beard the color of corn silk. He bows before Alejandra, pulls an obsidian plug from his earlobe, places it in her hand. The warrior from the west is wiry and small; tight rows of black braids, sinewy arms and legs, hip bones visible through his flesh. He offers a turquoise plug to the Speaker, who accepts it as he might a token of favor from Tezcatlipoca himself.

The Keeper speaks in Alejandra's mind, in the marble of the temple, in the risers about the arena, in the earth itself. *"Alejandra Maria Yaotl has won the first round, and her sacrifices nourish the gods now. Two rounds remain. Polemists, make your second arguments."*

"You are my people." The Speaker stands and spreads his arms amidst a butterfly kaleidoscope of cameras, hummingbird cloak flowing over his back like a shower of sun-struck water. The crowd cheers. "Together we decide what is right and what is wrong, and we have decided upon a culture of civilized violence. This means we all must volunteer ourselves in sacrifice, and we do, letting our blood to feed the gods so the sun might travel above us forever." He steps down from the dais, takes an obsidian knife from his loincloth, cuts across his forearm. Blood drips onto the ground. *I am one of you*, the gesture says. *We are the same.* "Is this not the foundation of society, that a community decides these things? Does the Little Dinosaur believe we have no right to free will?"

The warrior from the west flourishes a wooden flute, begins to play in agreement. Music pierces the day; sweeter than oranges, lighter than a wisp of cloud. It sounds in the heavens. It sounds in the earth. To everywhere it travels until the Turquoise Abode of the West adorns itself in glad reply. Stained glass murals appear in the windows. Precious inlay covers the streets. The quarter performs for the man, who performs for the demigod who enslaved him.

The crowd sits rapt until the flute falls silent and then roars its approval like a horde of jaguar knights. The Speaker returns to his seat. "How do you answer, Little Dinosaur?"

Alejandra cannot rise or play the crowd, does not have its favor in any case. So she does what can be done from a divan, draped in silk that both covers and insults her, while the sun begins to set above the shade-covered dais. She speaks the truth as her people understand it.

"No, not every person has a right to free will." The crowd interrupts with raucous castigation. Alejandra waits for it to ebb as the drugs in her blood do the same. "We take it from the sick of mind when he harms himself. We take it from the criminal when he harms another person. We go to war with invaders to prevent colonization." The urge to sleep lies heavy on her voice, in her bones. She sighs and sits up. "So a community decides to do a thing. That does not make the thing correct, and it does not mean another community stands aside if it is harmful. Just men and women must intervene to stop injustice. This is my answer."

The warrior from the east spreads his arms and turns in a circle, swinging a pair of macuahuitls above his head. He dances war; bare feet pounding the earth, chest muscles bunching, throat roaring a challenge until the Gold Abode of the East quakes in fear. Doors clatter. Bricks crumble away from buildings. The sky and street darken, hiding from the countenance of this perfect warrior god, this other face of Tezcatlipoca.

But as he finishes, Alejandra sees her mistake.

Yesterday she argued it was wrong for one people to inflict its collective will upon another. Now she has contradicted that argument. The Speaker sees it too, and soon the Keeper declares his victory to the vessels of Tezcatlipoca and the crowd, ending the round.

In a fit of incongruous rage, the blond giant casts his weapons down and storms away. The wiry musician plucks his token from the Speaker's palm and reinserts it, bowing low with arms outstretched.

Two beautiful women lead him from the field, gauzy dresses clinging to the contours of their breasts, entertainments for a god about to die.

"A perfect thing happens now." The Speaker looks down at Alejandra, and there is nothing of the blood-soaked punisher in him. There is only the rapture of belief, black and shining as the blond giant's token still resting in her hand.

Alejandra gasps, epiphany opening the Speaker like a knife wound to the chest. What she sees there is impossible as the rage of a brainwashed warrior slave who gets to keep his life another day. "It's real to you; the gods, the sacrifices, the things you tell these people. You're not a fraud at all. You *want* to die."

"No, Little Dinosaur. I want to be tempered, and then I want to travel with Huitzilopochtli, but only after a worthy successor comes to stand in my place." The Speaker gazes out over the now-empty arena, watches the sun begin to dip below the horizon. "If you should take the precious eagle cactus fruit from my chest, remember that I think you are that person."

At dusk, Alejandra hovers near the base of the Great Temple. She is empty of medicine, food, and strength, weary in a way that welcomes death, wonders if it will come before the Speaker's proxy offers up his body to the people who already have his mind.

It does not.

He arrives, flower-bedecked, finery abandoned for a cotton loincloth. A flute sits in the hip of that garment as it had in the afternoon. When his high-arched foot touches the bottom stair, he pulls it free, breaks it in two, casts the halves at the crowd gathered there.

He is smiling.

At the summit, above the clouds, the proxy reaches for the priests, embraces them as brothers, lies down upon that altar where a middle-aged woman wetted herself. The Speaker greets him, a transhuman demigod to a vessel of Tezcatlipoca. Alejandra does not, cannot protest the flute-broken thing about to happen to this man who would fight her intervention, and so she is silent as the death coming for them both.

The knife descends, flaying a perfect abdomen from breast to belly. The Speaker reaches in, cracks a cage of white bone, removes a still-beating heart.

Blood sprays from the proxy's mouth, drowns a sigh of ecstasy, paints the rictus of his smile in red.

10-Malinalli (1-)Calli 11-Tecpatl:

A good day for those who are suppressed, a bad day for their suppressors.

Alejandra dreams of conquered gods, cayenne and cocoa, blood in the hair, blood on the stones. Two moons rise, one after the other. The pale slave girl wakes her for medication, whispers comfort in that sibilate tongue, but there is pressure in the bowels, pressure on the heart. Alejandra groans with the pain of it, slips under in that well of the mind, sinks to the bottom.

The Keeper of New Tenochtitlan speaks to her there as if from above.

"You are comatose. Do you wish to be revived? Yes/No"

"Sí."

"There is a <78% chance you will die in the next three hours. Do you wish for me to keep you alive until the end of the duel? Yes/No"

Alejandra's lizard brain does not hesitate, forces her to reach up for the Keeper.

"Sí, por favor. Sí."

In the morning, she is well. The pale slave girl is absent, but both the frock and silk are draped over the bureau, clean. She reaches for one, pauses.

"...Not while I'm breathing. Not while I can stand and spit in your face."

Reaches for the other, pauses.

"...if you should take the precious eagle cactus fruit from my chest, remember that I think you are that person."

Chooses a garment, tries not to think of it as a choice.

"...Do you wish for me to keep you alive..."

She knows how to win now; lose today and consign the Speaker's allotted slaves to death. But what of New Tenochtitlan's jaguar and eagle knights? What of its sociopathic citizens? They would disperse throughout the present if she shut the city-state down. Where would they go? Who would they murder? How much violence would they teach?

"...I do not make sociopaths...I rescue them from across the Confederation, and in so doing, I rescue the rest of humanity from them."

Jaguar knights come; tails flicking about, whiskers twitching in a cool morning breeze and bring a breakfast Alejandra devours in front of them, standing, spine and knees both straight. *I could take his place*, she thinks, licking orange pulp from her fingers, *wean the city-state from its appetite for blood. A controlled decline would be safer for my family, my people, and I could live.* The food settles, warm and nourishing, in a belly that stretches around it without discomfort.

I could live.

They take her to the Turquoise Abode of the West, there to see the spacetime gate, where slaves are brought from the past to serve the present and to die. At best a blue distortion of air, the city-state moves around it on feet and paws and wings and engines. Through the translucent haze at its heart, a cluster of young men and women are coming away from a crumbling cityscape. Some are tattooed. Most are too thin. They would pay the price for controlled decline and so would thousands like them for at least three generations.

They would also, she observes, *pay the price for my own life.*

Upon the Great Temple summit, the Speaker has no greeting for Alejandra, but gazes down the stairs like a man about to do a sorrowful thing. The priests behind him light censers, position the knife, try not to weep. Butterfly cameras flit above them all, bright under a blue sky.

A faint wailing begins to rise, small and terrible, from the cloud cover below.

Alejandra recognizes the sound, chokes on the horrified protest lodged in her throat, and shakes her head, mouthing "No, no, no…"

"They are little paper streamers, and their tears are a gift to Tlaloc in exchange for the rain." The Speaker continues to gaze down; mild as a madman, certain as nightfall. "It is very sad, but the rain must come."

Alejandra turns away from the stairs, hands up in a warding gesture, and remembers the offer he made two days ago. *I could forfeit the duel.* She faces the stairs again, imagines a knife splitting her flesh. *Nobody has to die but me.*

Only two children crest the clouds, hauled aloft by a jaguar knight each. Nearest the Speaker, nails ripped from her fingers to force those tears, is the pale slave girl.

The jaguar knight gripping her wrist goes to stand with his demigod, who turns away from the summit's edge to wipe her cheek with a long thumb.

"Good." He smiles down at the child as if she has given him a sweet.

A flock of four-winged birds flies overhead, warbling to one another about the sun, or the wind, or the needs of flying creatures. Alejandra closes her eyes and for a moment is one of them. *Sweet girl, I should have fled with you in the beginning.*

The moment passes, and the other jaguar knight is so close she can smell his fur. The little boy limping beside him is brown as her grandson's son might be in a better future, one without New Tenochtitlan. His hands are not mutilated, but he hobbles on legs broken long ago and left to heal badly. Alejandra wonders if the wounds were deliberate, wonders this even as she sees what the

Speaker is doing, even as the pale slave girl is permitted to fling herself at the old woman's knees.

"Alejandra Maria Yaotl and Speaker Cuauhtémoc the Second have nourished the gods with their sacrifices." As before, the flat voice of the Keeper sounds in her mind and over the city-state. *"This round will decide the duel. Polemists, make your final arguments."*

The Speaker says only one word.

"Choose."

Choose to forfeit the duel, set both children free, and die. Choose the little boy who looks like her grandson's son and die. Choose the pale slave girl who has shown her such kindness and live, claim the city-state, do with it as she sees fit. Choose the collective wisdom of a people the Speaker will soon enslave, or choose the collective sociopathy of the enslavers. Choose colonized peace or civilized violence.

Choose.

Alejandra stares at the altar until she is sun-blind, remembering ground corn clinging to the hands, the pop and sizzle of hot oil, the chatter of family chopping peppers and tomatoes. Silent tears stream down her face, and if they could bring the rain, it would never stop. The pale slave girl settles, warm and full of trust, against her body. *Save them all or lose them all, indeed. What a foolish old woman I was.*

She grips the girl by the shoulders and pushes her back toward the Speaker.

Eyes wide and dark as wells, the child looks up at the old woman, unable for a moment to believe, and then believing, unable to voice the betrayal rising with the bile that pours from her mouth.

The Speaker's expression breaks like a sun through clouds. He receives the girl into firm hands, and she is screaming, blood-sticky fingers reaching out to no one for protection that will not come. Alejandra follows her to the altar, refusing to abandon this child who will buy the lives of so many others, refusing to look away from the wounds on her fingers and the deeper wound on her face. The pale slave girl reaches out again, plucks at her sleeve, begs for life in that soft, sibilate tongue.

"Perdóname, por favor. Perdóname." Alejandra says to a child who can neither understand nor forgive. One weathered hand comes down to cover her eyes. The other reaches up to join the clasped hands of the Speaker around the knife.

"Is it sharp?" she asks him, foolish old woman to pomposo demigod.

"They always are," he answers, and the knife descends as the Keeper of New Tenochtitlan pronounces Alejandra the victor.

Behind them, a small brown boy sits on the summit stair and sobs with relief.

11-Acatl (1-)Calli 11-Tecpatl:

Acatl is the scepter of authority which is hollow. A good day to seek justice, a bad day to act against others.

A pale yellow sun climbs the sky on a cloudless day, nearing zenith, and Speaker Cuauhtémoc the Second comes to the Great Temple to die as a god dies. White flower petals fall upon him from above, cast by fat-fisted children who will watch his sacrifice, who watch every sacrifice. On the street, grieving men and women pierce their flesh with obsidian shards and dance before him, raining blood upon the petaled cobblestones.

Butterfly cameras alight on a dried blood and chlorophyll trophy of matted hair. One bare foot comes to rest on the bottom stair, bloody petals clinging to the toes. In a flourish, he sweeps a cloak of hummingbird skins above his head and rips it in two. He is smiling, face wet with the tears of a demigod in love with his own death.

Alejandra knows what must be done, feels it in the rustle of silk upon skin, the Keeper's support of a body that should have failed, the death of the righteous woman she had been four days ago. Gilded nanofilaments pattern her own hands now, and from stone to spacetime gate the city-state awaits the command of its new Speaker.

"Alejandra the First." Cuauhtémoc the Second completes his ascent, names her as a father might name a child. "Or would you prefer an Aztec eponym? Atotoztli was a founder of…"

"New Tenochtitlan is not your concern anymore and neither am I." Alejandra dismisses the window she drew in the air to watch him ascend.

"Be careful, Speaker." He raises a black brow, gestures at the feather-bedecked priests and the crowd below. "They would have killed you in the beginning without my offer of welcome, and they might yet kill you after I am dead."

She gestures at the altar, an abyss in the brown eyes that stare up into his. Her voice is flat. "Go lie down if you intend to die."

"Remember that my sacrifice needs to be different from the others." Cuauhtémoc the Second stares back into that abyss, ignoring her bitterness, teaching slaughter as if he were not the object of the lesson. "Take my precious eagle cactus fruit and eat of it while it beats. These people should see it in your hands and in your mouth as I depart." He turns away, lies down upon the red stain left behind by his victims. "Give the rest to Huitzilopochtli."

Alejandra goes to him, picks up the obsidian knife to test its edge, does not reply. A dead righteous woman still lies upon her tongue, behind her teeth. She wants to show him the corpse. *I have a grandson to protect.*

"Take my place, Little Dinosaur. Don't abandon my people. Don't let my home fall to ruin." He pleads with her, filling the silence. Four priests pin his limbs, obeying even now the sociopath who gave them purpose. "Save your life. Save your family. Rule."

Alejandra watches uncertainty grow in him as the Keeper grows in her, shaping what Cuauhtémoc the Second is not anymore, New Tenochtitlan's key, its voice, its demigod. Her gilded hands raise the knife above his heart, and the pendulum between the old and the new falls to nadir.

Dinosaur. Of course they call me that; Minsky, Gaea, him. I was never human to them because they do not recall what humanity is. Perhaps there is something in this, a place to work back from. She feels it in the muscles of her face like the toothy grin of a predator, under the feathered serpent silk like a promise of scales, in her bones like the marrow of the monster she is becoming. The Keeper responds, mapping nanomachines to flesh the way it does for every jaguar and eagle knight, sculpting the body it has already invaded and healed.

The knife plummets.

Cuauhtémoc the Second grunts but does not cry out, eyes fixed upon the widening jaw of the woman above him. Brown flesh splits around obsidian, drawn down his abdomen by hands that are pebbled with scales now. Blood pours from the old Speaker's belly as plumage bursts from the new Speaker's brow. The gray of the summit stones, the black of the knife, the pale yellow of the sun grow more brilliant with each blink of her nictitating membranes. Roaring, roaring, roaring the grief she will never be able to speak, Alejandra reaches in, cracks Cuauhtémoc the Second's ribcage like the soft shell of a crab, and peers down at the beating heart of the demigod who smiles up at her still.

"Beautiful." He gurgles the word, mouth awash in red.

The priests on the summit gape at her in awe. Silence falls across the quarters of the mourning city-state. The pendulum begins to rise again.

Minsky Prime and Autochthōn Gaea will be hoping to hear from the proxy they fashioned out of a frightened old woman. Alejandra thinks of the proxy she was forced to make of a child when they both might have brought an end to this violence long ago. A silent command to the Keeper sends a volley of missiles to both orbiting ships, and a gesture draws the window she uses to watch them bloom with fire and break apart.

On the altar, Cuauhtémoc the Second groans, delirious with pain.

The Speaker looks down as though she has forgotten he was there. "You're still alive. Qué interesante."

She thinks of a faraway grandson and his children, who are safe from her subjects now, and of the people who will lie beneath her knife in the generations to come.

She thinks of Huitzilopochtli, Tezcatlipoca, and Tlaloc, whose worship demands such sacrifices.

She thinks of herself and holds the memory of a pale slave girl like a talisman and scourge against the loss of her vanishing humanity.

"People of the city-state, hear me!" Butterfly cameras come to flit above her head. The temple stones reverberate with her voice. "I am Alejandra the First, Speaker of New Tenochtitlan, Cousin of Quetzalcoatl!" One clawed hand reaches in, plucks Cuauhtémoc the Second's precious eagle cactus fruit, and holds it up, still beating.

"You shall have no other gods before me," she growls, and swallows it whole.

D is for Duel

Author's Notes:

The poem excerpt that introduces this story was found in Pre-Columbian Literatures of Mexico by Miguel León-Portilla on Page 87.

The Aztec and Maya Calendar, found at www.azteccalendar.com, is protected under a Creative Commons Attribution-NonCommercial-ShareAlike 2.5 license. Excerpts are abbreviated from the original.

Gary B. Phillips

EXPOSURE

The act of allowing light to strike a light-sensitive surface.

"Your reputation precedes you," Martina said. I think she was one of the scientists, but couldn't be sure. They had led me into the hot little room and introduced me to a dozen scientists, three PR drones, and six lawyers, all on the other side of a long table. Standard intimidation tactic, but I've spent hours in the dead of winter within feet of a hungry Siberian tiger so that didn't faze me. Besides, when you've been in this business for as long as I have all the assholes tend to bleed together.

I wasn't sure if she was referring to my work or everything else. Didn't really care. I had always lived my life with the idea that every bit of exposure helped, good or bad.

The balding man who had introduced himself as Alvarez, the lead scientist. He shuffled through my portfolio, peering down at it through his bifocals.

"Your work," he said. "It does speak for itself. As for everything else-"

"Let's not get into that," Martina said. "Let's focus on his work."

The rest of them murmured amongst themselves.

"What makes you think you can do this job?" Alvarez asked.

As if my work spread out before them didn't speak volumes. Is a picture worth a thousand words or isn't it? The Pulitzer, the National Geographic issues dedicated to my work, the worldwide acclaim, and mansion that came with it all. The bastards had already made me sign my life away before I could even talk to them and it still wasn't good enough?

"I'm not doing it for me," I said.

They scoffed at this as if I had ruined their little circle jerk.

"Exactly, you're doing it for us," Martina said, with a warm smile. I don't know why she kept trying to defend me when it was clear they all hated me, but I chose to keep my mouth shut.

Alvarez spoke again. "You must understand the importance of this project. This is how I will show my creation to the world. All the work you've done in the past, as impressive as it is, will mean nothing after this. You will capture the world's imagination with these photographs. Your name will go down in the history books."

An impressive speech, no doubt the same one he had given to every other photographer that had been in this seat. They asked a few more questions before abruptly ending the interview.

"We'll be in touch," they said.

None of them stood up to shake my hand. I grabbed my portfolio and shoved it into my bag. Wrenched off my tie before I had even gotten out of the room. I had almost escaped the building when Martina caught up with me.

"I'm sorry," she said. "They're critical of everyone. You must understand how important this is."

I wanted to be home, or better yet, find a bar and drink it all away. The job didn't matter anymore, but in the back of my mind there was my little girl and the light in her eyes. It would have mattered to her. I forced a smile.

"Of course," I said.

"As a kid I think I had every National Geographic you had ever been published in. I was obsessed. My parents bought me all three volumes of *America, Undressed* for Christmas when I was fourteen."

"First editions?"

"Yes. Still have them."

"Probably worth a small fortune now."

"Doesn't matter," she said. "I'll never part with them. My mother thought for sure that I would be a photographer, but your wildlife photography inspired me in a different way. I wanted to save the endangered animals. Ended up going into Genomics which led me here. I owe it all to you."

"Probably a good choice," I said. "Photography is one percent taking pretty pictures and ninety-nine percent dealing with douchebags. Present company excluded."

She laughed and hugged me.

"Thank you," she said. "I'm fighting for you."

"They're not," I said.

"You're the best for the job. I know it."

"Am I? My eyesight is shit. My hands can barely hold the camera without shaking."

She waved her hand dismissively. "That's why they have tripods."

I laughed. First laugh in too long and it burned at my throat. I could really use that drink.

"Every shit-grinning photographer in the world wants this job," I said. "They want their shot to make their mark, to do what I've done. They want to make history, as your boss says. He'll balk at my price or my attitude or hate the tie I chose to wear today. They'll fight me every step of the way... But I'll give you the best goddamn photograph of a dinosaur in the world."

APERTURE

The mechanism that controls how much light passes through a lens and onto film.

I was a wealthy man. My work had been published in National Geographic, my exhibits toured the world, and made me a mint. I thought I had it all. And then Olivia was born and she showed me, as only a child can, how poor I had really been. The truth was, I didn't have shit before I had her.

Ten perfect fingers and toes and the light in her eyes when she smiled at me, and that was all it took to bring me to my knees. As if my slate had been wiped clean. She was my aperture.

Like every kid in the world she loved dinosaurs. Even at four months old her tiny hand grasped the soft blue felt blanket with the smiling dinosaurs on it that my sister had given to her while explaining that "dinosaurs were for girls too." I had never understood our culture's fascination with the extinct monsters. Those oversized lizards, or birds, or whatever they were had never appealed to my own lizard-bird brain. Olivia, though, she loved them and by the transitive property so did I.

Martina called me three days after the interview. I had stayed in Seattle to imbibe at my favorite watering hole. I stepped out of the darkened bar and into the drizzling rain to take her call.

"We've awarded you the contract," she said, with a pause that sounded a little too uncomfortable for my taste. I waited for the other shoe to drop. There's always another shoe. "There is some bad news."

"Lay it on me."

"They don't believe you can do the job. They've hired another photographer as backup."

I wasn't surprised. I laughed and told her to wish the other photographers good luck.

The next morning I boarded a plane to San Francisco. I had been staying with my sister and working on a new project that would show the hypocrisy of the city; the new tech that had turned the Golden City into a hub for the hottest businesses and the geniuses that flocked there while bleeding the city of its true people. The pictures came easy, on each street corner. A mentally ill homeless person begging for change next to a Tesla. That sort of thing.

Even with the new project, and the chance at helping to show the world a dinosaur, I still only thought about Olivia and how I could make her proud, do her right. Assuming I didn't fuck it all up. She would want all the details about how they made a real, live dinosaur. Alvarez had tried to explain it, but even with his simple high-level overview it was pure science fiction wankery to me. Impressive as it all was they needed me to help tell their story. The funny thing about photographers though, is that we're the world's best liars. What you see in the photograph is not the truth. There's always a real story and it's usually just off-frame. The picture of the starving child and the waiting vulture is one story, but there's another story we may never know. Sometimes it ends with one end of a hose taped to a truck's exhaust and the other end going through a rolled-up window until it's all over at thirty-three years old.

SHUTTER SPEED

The mechanism that controls the length of time that the film is exposed to light.

I touched down in San Francisco International just as the sun was coming up glinting off the buildings and turning the fog snow white like a blanket draped across the bay. I Uber'd to my sister's house, told her the good news, and was back at the airport three hours later. I packed light: My camera and trusty old Canon 50mm lens, a telephoto lens that I had no intention of using but brought for show. A few standard bounce boards, white, gold, and silver. An on-camera fill flash. And a couple of cheap disposable cameras for Olivia's approval.

The other photographers would likely be picking quality prime telephoto lenses so they could just stand back and click a button. Easy mode. That wasn't my style. I wasn't going to taking a fucking Olan Mills portrait.

Life moves so fast. I used to tell people that's why God gave us such fast shutters, but that was a long time ago and I haven't been a believer in a long time.

A fast shutter allowed humanity to see things that we were never meant to. Pause time, freeze a hummingbird in mid-air. Hell, photography itself was just another way for man to try and ward off death, to allow ourselves to live forever. That fight was a struggle as old as time. You can't live forever, though, I knew that all too well.

Olivia had been another reminder of my own mortality. She learned to walk at six months old. She never cared for crawling, just pulled herself up on our ratty couch and started walking as fast she could until she reached the edge of the couch and tumbled back down. After that I chased her around the house every day snapping pictures of her laughing, chasing the cat, and generally just being the cutest thing I've ever seen.

Capturing a dinosaur would be so much easier than Olivia at three, tearing through the house on one of her juicebox-fueled benders. It was hard work keeping up with her but she brought me so much joy. The beauties that I had captured of the animal kingdom paled next to her smile as wide as a canyon, deep sea blue eyes, and golden sunkissed hair. I didn't know beauty until I saw her, and my photographs have been lauded as the most beautiful in the world.

FILTERS

A mechanism used to modify the image.

The subtle use of a filter can change the color or contrast of an image. Reshape what the viewer sees. I only brought a polarizing filter to protect my lens. Sure, it had the added benefit of filtering out any pesky reflections, but unless the dino was made of glass I didn't think that would be a problem. Filters are just another way to change the story, to tell a lie, which I had never had any interest in with my photographs.

Filters had saved my lenses from dozens of falls and brushes with death thanks to Olivia's wandering fingers. It was always cheaper to let a cheap filter take the brunt of damage than a lens that cost the price of a used car.

When she was born I promised myself I would never let her touch my prize cameras, the ones that gave me my living. Of course, any parent can tell you what happened next. It didn't take Olivia long to turn the tables on me and start chasing me around the house with my own camera, snapping blurry photos of me. Our house was filled with the photos she took. First, just pictures of my feet as she chased me. Slowly her framing and patience got better and one day she ran in from playing outside to tell me she'd taken her first picture of a butterfly on a flower after waiting ten minutes for it to land next to her.

The photos she took were as honest as it got. The truth of the world was inside the frame of the picture, not hidden away like in so many professional photos. Nothing was filtered out when she had the camera. She waited patiently for the perfect moment with one eye open outside the frame to find the truth of the story, that emotional moment when life coalesced in that perfect way it did so rarely. She taught me everything I knew about making true art.

I tried to emulate her, but could never get rid of those bad habits, the hidden truth that was always just outside of the frame—editors and lawyers always have their say. The hidden truth was that he had chased that vulture away from the starving child, but it didn't matter, because the world only believed what they saw in the finished product.

LIGHT

And Photographers said, Let there be light: and there was light.

A lot of photographers will bring bounce cards and lights wherever they go. Even at the golden hour, they've always got a crew hauling equipment, whatever they can do to make their shot more perfect. Sunlight is all I ever needed.

My daughter had been the source of light in my life through the dark times. I had spent too long in hell, photographing the atrocities of mother nature and mankind alike and then drowning myself in a bottle. That was before Olivia. After she was born I got clean because she was always waiting for me when I came home, arms outstretched to hug my legs.

The plane touched down in Buenos Aires. They told us it would be a five hour drive from there to our destination. I hadn't spent more than half an hour in a car in fifteen years and I damned well didn't want to start now. I offered to charter a helicopter, but they just told me to shut up and get in.

I tried to sleep, but the narrow two-way roads freaked me out, and I was wide awake, trying not to pay attention to how fast we were going and how close the cars in the other lane were.

The sky was stormy and the clouds blotted out the stars. The only light was from the cars and it wasn't enough to give me comfort. The terror of it all made my thoughts turn to Olivia and that eerily similar night so many years ago.

It had been so fucking dark on that road. We had been driving from a shoot in San Francisco back home to Los Angeles.

She was in the backseat screeching like a dinosaur and begging me to drive past home and take her to Cabazon Dinosaurs. I was tired and already uncomfortable with having brought her along, hoping she hadn't annoyed my client too much, but happy enough with the work I had done. We were on the part of the California 99 that is only two lanes, one north and one south.

The semi drifted into my lane and I swerved to avoid it. My tires hit dirt and we fishtailed. Then I lost control and we slammed back into the eighteen wheeler.

I remember the sound of the screeching tires, the exploding glass, my own voice calling the driver an asshole again and again, but most of all I remember the way Olivia screamed, louder than the crash itself.

When we finally stopped spinning the world had grown black around us. The dome light had busted and I couldn't see anything. There were no freeway lights but I was pretty sure we had ended up a ways off the road. I looked back at my daughter and saw her face in the passing light of the cars that didn't bother to stop. Her face was black, like it was sucking in the light and my brain couldn't understand why, couldn't process it. Finally it clicked.

It was blood.

I scrambled out of the car. The semi that had hit us was nowhere to be seen and the road had grown dark again without any passing cars. I stumbled to the back of the car, crunching on gravel and broken glass and ignoring the pain in my leg. I opened the door and reached for her.

She was silent. Still clutching her favorite blanket, the one with the happy dinosaurs on it and looking up at me with fearful eyes that pleaded with me to help her. There was so much blood and I could see it pouring from the mess of her head, thick and dark.

"Let me see the blanket, baby," I said.

I gently took the blanket from her, pressed it against her head and watched the black blood spread to each little smiling t-rex until one by one they all slipped into the darkness.

Sirens whined in the distance. She was still silent, not even a cry from her lips and that was all I really wanted, to hear her sob and say my name and ask for me. I reached over her and grabbed the cheap disposable camera that she always carried with her in an attempt to be more like me. There was no light, no possible way to get a good picture, but I took the photo anyway. My little girl with a dark blanket draped around her head like a funeral shawl and the light in her eyes almost gone... almost gone...

THE SHOT

They put us up in a couple of shitty villas. *Villa miseria*, the locals called them. Colorful blocks stacked on top of each other like a child's discarded building blocks out. After we get settled the lawyers brought us large binders. The contracts. NDAs, threatening language, the works. When we would be allowed to photograph them, the kind of lighting conditions, f-stops, allowed equipment, the 9:00 am start time, how many photographs we must take, required angles for each shot, strict limits on post work, it went on and on for a thousand fucking pages. I gave it only the most cursory of glances, not because I didn't read my contracts like a hawk, but because I had seen it all before. I still signed.

Martina was there and greeted me with a hug. She introduced me to Robert, the lead photographer that was my "backup". He had a team of three assistants. They invited me to dinner and I didn't want to go, but I wanted to show Martina that I could be a team player.

"Hell, I'll buy your drinks," Robert said.

How could I say no?

True to his word he bought all the drinks.

"Not that I'm going to steal your ideas, because we've already planned our shoot," Robert said. "But how do you plan to setup your shot? I'd love to hear more about your process."

I was already half a dozen cervezas in and feeling bold. "The process," I said, with a laugh. "That's all schoolbook theoretical fuckery if you can't hold the camera and press the damn button at the right time. That's all that matters. Did you tell the story you wanted to? Will your children be proud of you?"

"I guess we'll see how that works out for you tomorrow," Robert said.

"Do you have children?" Martina asked.

"No."

I woke to birdsong and the mother of all hangovers. I had no idea how I had even gotten back to my room. Martina wasn't in bed with me so I figured I hadn't made too many mistakes, until I checked the clock and saw that it was 10:32 am.

Fuck! I had overslept and missed the call time. Missed the entire shoot.

I threw my gear together and was out the door in five minutes, cursing Robert who I was convinced got me dead drunk on purpose.

I was at the location within another ten minutes. Robert and his crew are already packing up and he gave me the biggest shit-eating grin in the world.

"Where's the dinosaur?" I asked him.

"Just inside that fence, but they're putting him away now."

Inside the fence were four security personnel with guns moving into the foliage. The entrance was closed but not locked so I slipped inside and sprinted past the armed drones. They were yelling at me, threatening to shoot me dead. It wasn't the first time I've had angry men pointing guns at me and yelling to put down my camera and back off. Fuck 'em.

The creature was tiny. No bigger than a wolf but looked more like a giant chicken, feathers and all. The feathers were more vivid than anything you would see on a farm chicken though—deep hues of blue and green that didn't look like anything nature could produce. Where there weren't feathers there were scales. It was watching me with knowing eyes and sharp teeth. Me. The guy stuck between the guns and a dinosaur.

My camera was around my neck but it was the disposable in my pocket that I reached for. I pulled it out slow and steady so as not to draw too much attention to it. I was just a few feet from the feathered creature and I shot from the hip, clicking the plastic button on the disposable camera. Three pictures before pocketing it. Then I took the rest of the pictures with the real camera, put my hands up, and walked back toward the angry men with their big guns.

ACCLAIM

In my office there were two pictures. One of them had been there for fifteen years and was, in my opinion, the best shot I had ever taken. It was the picture of Olivia on the dark road. The last photograph of her because I couldn't bear to take one of her body in the casket.

The other, the picture on my desk, does not officially exist. Breach of contract, maybe the ugliest sentence in the English language, especially when delivered by a smug lawyer. They confiscated everything after my stunt in the dinosaur cage. Destroyed my equipment and laughed about it. I'm pretty sure I saw Martina cry. But they hadn't found the disposable camera. It had three shots on it, two of them completely unusable blurs of pretty colors. The last picture turned out though. It was a grainy, out of focus, and poorly framed shot of the dinosaur. Looked like a bad bit of CGI from the early 90s.

People ask why I did what I did. Threw away a perfectly good job. Ruined my name and business in one fell swoop.

Something they don't teach you in school is knowing your audience—where acclaim really comes from. Alvarez said my audience was the world. I had been hearing that from men like him for years, but that's where they were wrong. My audience, since the day she was born, was Olivia and I guarantee she would have loved that picture.

E is for Exposure

L.S. Johnson

To tell my story, I must begin with Robert.

Though he was raised in the same small town in Virginia as myself, I only knew Robert by sight until he returned from Japan, a dashing veteran of a noble conflict. I was swept off my feet—the moreso for I had never set foot outside our town. Robert seemed so worldly, older and wiser than his peers, and at the dance held in his honor I was the first in line vying for his attention. I wanted him badly, and I got him; I also got the surprise of a pregnancy despite my precautions. And thus do the impulses of desire shape our lives for years to come.

I had no family to speak of, other than the elderly aunt who had raised me, for my parents had died when I was very small—my mother from illness, and my father from a subsequent suicide. Thus I had no one to advise me on what to do, who could have guided me towards adoption, or even a doctor. Instead I simply told Robert, and after he cursed my stupidity and foolishness he reluctantly offered to marry me, and I accepted.

In public, Robert was affable and friendly, though a little coarse and prone to drink. In private there was the world, and there was Robert's world, and the latter was infinitely better. The residents of our town shared a conviction that we were better than our county neighbors, more proper, more right; in Robert this belief was magnified a hundredfold. Any deviation from his viewpoint was cause for derision, or even outright rage. I know now that I became small with him, that I buried away the Carol I had been, and instead shaped myself around his looming presence.

I miscarried soon after our wedding, and that coupled with my subsequent inability to conceive upset Robert badly. As time passed he came to view my infertility as one of many ways I was undermining him. If I forgot to do something he asked, it was evidence of the small regard I held him in. If I expressed concern for him, I thought of him as little more than a child. If I left him alone I was ignoring him, and perhaps I would be happier without him. The latter sentiment was a bait I might have risen to, save I had never worked anywhere other than our local market, and I had no family or friends to turn to.

I'm not sure when exactly he began to hit me. There were a few slaps during arguments, and I believed him when he apologized. But the slaps became more numerous, and then one night he shoved me so hard I fell... if I look back now there were dozens of moments, spread out over years, that snowballed into what we became: the lack of children, the promotion of a junior employee over him, the death of his father. Each loss making Robert a little more short-tempered, a little more bitter in his outlook. These are the things you never read about in women's magazines: how violence can creep into a marriage, until you can't quite remember a time without it.

It was around this time that he discovered the first book about the Sereideas. What began as an idle read one weekend soon became an overriding interest, and just as quickly an obsession. At first I could not fathom what it was about this particular conspiracy that so piqued his imagination, save that it was of a grander scale than, say, communists running America. To declare God Himself a tale, while these snake-people were real—

But you probably have not heard of them, for you are an intelligent, reasonable person. Those who believe in these creatures say there was never a God, only a Serpent, who left behind descendants upon the earth to cultivate it. Much as one might coax forest into farmland, or breed a herd from a handful of cattle, so the Sereideas moved through the world, creating religions as mere smokescreens while encouraging us to multiply. The proof, for Robert, lay in the cleverness of casting their own dark god as the villain of the tale, which allowed them to work in the shadows for millennia.

I could not understand what about this ridiculous story kept him up at night, poring over mildewed volumes that he ordered from every corner of the earth, taking careful and precise notes long after I had gone to bed. I could only watch, bewildered, as he first befriended other theorists, then one by one dismissed them as being too limited in their outlook. Soon there were other, deeper changes: he stopped fuming about the juniors promoted over him, our childlessness, the figure he cut in our small community; he seemed to stop thinking about me at all. His knowledge filled him with a kind of smug, silent certainty, the likes of which I had never seen before.

It was only after he had run out of correspondents that he began to explain himself to me, in the form of rambling lectures that I smiled and nodded at, though I wavered between boredom and dread. And then, at last, he told me.

He was not only convinced these beings had existed. He believed he alone had found the secret location of their ancestral home, filled with centuries' worth of their accumulated wealth—a treasure he was determined to take for himself.

In the weeks leading up to our trip, I became what I perhaps had been to Robert all along: a servant. No more pretense of a partnership, or of any romantic inclinations. I fulfilled his endless shopping lists and made arrangements per his precise instructions. Even our one last coupling—I cannot in any way call it lovemaking—felt like some kind of perfunctory task being accomplished, a necessary release ticked off between finalizing our lodgings and garaging the car.

By the time we embarked I was exhausted. As we caught the bus to Washington, then endured the long, grueling flight to London, my exhaustion gave way first to shock, then a new kind of grief. Never before had I been to a city, any city. Everywhere I saw people who looked different, spoke differently, dressed in fashions I hadn't known were legal much less acceptable. They smoked and drank openly, they kissed and groped in public while I blushed on their behalf. I saw trim women in suits going to work, long-haired men minding small children with no mother in sight. And the music—! Loud, nerve-jangling, full of howling and wailing, yet it made my feet tap even as I struggled to understand it. Some sea change had happened between the war and our journey, one that had missed our small corner of the world. It was as if everyone had signed up for a kind of life, a freer life, that I hadn't even known existed.

We landed in London and took a series of small, grimy trains north, punctuating our journey with brief stays in equally small, grimy rooms. As the landscape became more bleak we changed to a bus, and another, until at last we reached the Scottish coast. I had thought these villages would feel more familiar, but even here the world was changing. Girls strolled along the footpaths in scandalously short dresses; a group of men dressed in a blinding array of colors handed out flowers to us. I saw Robert eyeing the girls, but when a bare-chested man tried to give me some kind of card he seized my arm and jerked me away.

"Stop making a fool of yourself, Carol," he said in my ear. "You're old enough to be his mother. It's disgusting."

He had said worse to me in our time together. Yet something about hearing those words, in the face of so much ease and freedom, made me aware as I never had been of just how many years I had lost to our unhappy marriage.

We took rooms in a little pub, and dined that night in its restaurant. Even then, hours later, I could hardly raise my eyes for the grief I felt. It took all I had to force down my soup and keep up some pretense of calm. Robert, however, was clearly feeling pleased with the world. He ate his fill of fish and potatoes, washing it down with several pints of ale.

As we ate, his head kept jerking around, as if listening to the other conversations, though they were barely murmurs to my ears. At last he peered at me. "What did you say?"

I shook my head, uneasy at the edge in his voice. "I didn't say anything."

He seemed about to say more, but instead downed his pint. When he spoke again his voice was loud. "We're nearly there," he said. "Tomorrow we'll rent a boat and I'll prove I'm right once and for all. They say it's all a myth, a fairy tale. But they can't fool me." As he looked for the waitress, gesturing for another pint, I saw there were flecks of food in his beard, yet he was usually meticulous in his appearance.

"I know they think I'm just another idiot," he continued, leaning forward and lowering his voice to a stage whisper. "Just another asshole who'll putter around the islands before giving up. Just another nutjob." He leaned back, smiling grimly. "Boy, are they in for a surprise."

When our waitress brought over his pint he asked, in a terrible imitation of the local accent, "Can ye tell me, hen, where we can hire a boat to Ormrey?"

"Ormrey, sir? Don't you mean the Orkneys?" She glanced pityingly at me as she spoke. "There's no such place as Ormrey, but there are many nice places to visit in the Orkneys. For those you can hire a boat at the waterfront, or catch one of the ferries."

Robert smiled at her. "Of course you're right, love. There's no such place." As soon as she moved away, though, he grabbed my hand, crushing my fingers until I whimpered in pain. "See?" he hissed. "See?"

"I see," I said, but could say nothing more, for I was on the verge of tears. How had it come to this, that I was here on the edge of the world, chained to this mad, cruel man?

"There is such a place," he breathed. "I know it, Carol. I can see it, in here." As he tapped his forehead he rose, glaring down at me from his full height, his other hand still crushing mine. "I know how little you think of me," he spat out, and I flinched. "But I'm no ordinary man, Carol. I've got greatness in me, and I'm gonna prove it to you. I'm gonna outwit the devil himself, just you wait." He gave my hand a last squeeze, cracking my knuckles, before he released me at last. "Just you wait," he repeated, and turned and stumbled heavily to the bar.

It was some time before I was able to coax a half-stupefied Robert up to our rooms. As I struggled to balance him while unlocking the door he began groping me, squeezing my breasts and crotch. I maneuvered him onto the narrow bed only to be pulled down under him, pinned helplessly beneath his weight while he sloppily kissed me. The taste of his mouth made my stomach heave. When I tried to push him off he wrenched my hands aside, grinding against me and mumbling under his breath *I'm coming...* and then he slowly sank down on top of me. It could only have been a few minutes, yet it felt like an eternity before I heard him snore. With some effort I extricated myself from him, trembling and hollow, and slipped out of the room. By the time I reached the doors of the pub I was nearly running.

Despite it being late spring the air was cold and damp. It was the darkest hour of the night, with not a light to be seen save for the streetlights. I stumbled along the promenade, weeping fitfully, my stomach roiling. What would happen when we found no mysterious island, no treasure? The prospect seemed to promise a fit of rage I had not yet seen in him. I knew he would make it out to be my fault; he might well kill me. The thought of dying so violently, so painfully, made me collapse into outright sobbing.

Before me the dark ocean crashed relentlessly against the rocky shore, and I realized that I could end it all right there. No one would see me, no one would be able to stop me. It would be cold, I would be frightened at first... but nothing compared to what I believed awaited me should I step onto that boat.

I clutched the railing of the promenade and tried to see if there was a way down, or if I needed to climb over and lower myself onto the rocks...

Just then I heard a faint popping noise, followed by a cry. Far down the promenade something flickered beneath the streetlights. I watched as a tall, slight figure came barreling towards me. Some ten yards away he stopped, seemingly arrested by the sight of me, then turned and ran inland, his pale face flashing as he looked frantically one way and another before diving between the houses.

As he ran, something fell from his pocket onto the road.

I hurried to where he had been, thinking perhaps he had dropped his wallet. I could at least leave it someplace safe, I could at least make my last act on earth one of helping a stranger.

But the thing in the road was not a wallet. It was a gun, and the muzzle was still warm to the touch.

At   that   moment,   my   plans   changed   completely.

Back in the safety of our bathroom I inspected the weapon. It was a small pistol, light and comfortable in my hand, even able to fit in my pocket; clean and well-oiled, every mechanism moving smoothly.

There were still five bullets in the clip.

Robert, I knew, would insist on us sailing alone, lest someone try to take his precious treasure. And if he happened to have an accident? The locals already knew him to be a foolish drunk. It seemed doubtful that they would waste a moment investigating his death, especially if there was no body to be examined.

It felt... possible, and it was that very feeling that made me quake inside. How many times had I wished for something like this, something that could just make him go away forever? Yet now that I held such a thing in my hand it seemed monstrous; it *was* monstrous, it was murder. Yet hadn't I just been contemplating suicide?

It was with these uneasy thoughts chasing each other that I put the pistol in my knapsack. Perhaps I wouldn't do anything; perhaps I would turn it on myself. But at least I had some protection should Robert's behavior escalate. Or so I told myself.

It was early morning when I awoke, but Robert was already gone. From our window I glimpsed him far along the promenade, talking with a man in overalls and rubber boots. As I watched, Robert counted out many bills and handed them over, then shook the man's hand.

Today, then.

I dressed swiftly, checking my knapsack twice. The pistol was real, loaded, and well-hidden. In the mirror I could not meet my own eyes. Today, then. Everything would change today, for good or ill.

Robert returned, his feet heavy on the stairs, and I met him with a smile, but he looked me over with such a searching expression that I began to panic. He knew, he had searched my knapsack and he knew...

"I've found us a boat," he finally said, in the tone I had come to think of as Stern Father. "Now you're going to do exactly what I say from here on out, Carol. I only have one chance at this, I can't have any mistakes. Otherwise, hen, poppet, love? You'll be paying me back for the rest of your goddamn life."

I nodded, keeping the smile on my face, but a small, angry voice said, "or maybe *you're* going to pay *me*." Robert didn't react, but instead started to gather up his things; only then did I realize the voice came from inside me, that its anger was mine.

There was a moment, that morning, when everything felt ... not good, but not terrible either. When everything felt neutral, balanced. Perhaps it was that, occupied with steering the boat, Robert had little cause to speak, and thus I could pretend we were as we appeared: an adventurous, middle-aged couple indulging in an off-beat holiday.

Or perhaps it was that both sea and sky were the same color that morning, a slate grey, so that it was all but impossible to see a horizon, where one element ended and the next began. Just a soothing infinity of nothingness.

Too, there was something about those islands. Vast, rocky slabs jutting from the water, their tops fuzzy with a pale green: they were like nothing I had ever seen. As stark as the landscape was, it wasn't jarring like the young people we had seen, but rather welcoming in its timelessness. Had I my way we would have brought a picnic, and visited several of the islands. But one look at Robert's face was enough to remind me that we were not here for pleasure. This was the culmination of all his years of obsession.

As we passed what seemed to be the last of the islands he slowed the boat and stepped out of the cabin, checking our location against his maps, muttering to himself as he worked out calculations. "It should be here," he said aloud. And then, as if addressing the island itself, "where are you? I'm close, I'm nearly there..."

My stomach clenched and I reached for the knapsack. "It must be nearby," I offered, trying to sound cheerful. "Perhaps we should go back to that last island? That rise would let you see for a good distance around."

"You don't navigate by sight, you idiot," he retorted. "You navigate by coordinates." When I started to speak again, he shouted, "just shut up, Carol! I can't think for your damn whining."

I reached into my knapsack, letting my fingers close around the handle of the pistol. A single shot, and then I could push him off, his boots would act like weights...

But he suddenly jerked upright, peering into the distance, his lips parting slightly. I looked, but there was only the water and the sky, the gloomy clouds of a piece with the whole grey expanse—

only as I let my eyes become unfocused I realized that there was a texture in one area, a strange density. I looked at Robert again. He had a pair of binoculars out now, scanning the horizon, his lips curving into a smile that did nothing to ease my dread.

"Right on the goddamned money," he said.

He started the boat with such a rush that I nearly fell off. As the boat skipped over the increasingly choppy water I saw that my eyes had not deceived me. The texture coalesced into another rocky island, only this one was much darker, seemingly in a perpetual shadow while its fellows were dappled with light. The sheer face of the island was of a piece with the gray water and gray sky, and nothing seemed to grow atop it save for a few skeletal shrubs clinging to the lowest edges.

"That's it!" Robert roared over the engine. "That's it! Tell me that doesn't exist!"

I curled my lips over my teeth, trying to smile but feeling more like a frightened animal. The water seemed to swirl around Ormrey, if indeed Ormrey it was. The boat lurched as if caught in a storm, though the sky remained unchanged. As Robert turned the boat to follow the island's outline we came upon an inlet of sorts. It was here that he steered the boat, and my fear began to blossom into outright terror. What if he wrecked the boat, what if it sank here? Who would find us? We were miles from the last inhabited island, with barely enough supplies for a day trip. I didn't even know if the boat had a flare, or anything to start a fire, or—

The boat scraped something as it entered the inlet and I cried out, a shriek of pure fright. Robert, upon hearing me, began laughing—a wild cackling that I had never heard him make before, that reverberated off the rocks around us and sent a flock of dark grey seabirds aloft.

After our rough entrance, however, the inlet proved calm. Robert slowed the boat, still sniggering to himself, and I tried to relax by studying this new landscape. What kind of rock was this, and why was it so markedly different from the other islands? What were those birds, seemingly neither gull nor raven but some odd mixture of the two?

We wound through what felt almost like a canyon at times, until at last the inlet began to widen, and the rocky walls sloped downward. Peering ahead, I saw we were entering a misty area, almost like a tiny bay, a hollow navel in this belly of land.

And then I saw the pilings jutting from the water, and my stomach clenched again.

"See?" cried Robert. "You're my witness, Carol!"

How was it that someone could inhabit this godforsaken rock? And then it struck me in its simplicity: however crazy it seemed, this was private land. The locals didn't encourage visitors not because of some strange conspiracy, but because it was trespassing. We were trespassing. The owner was probably some wealthy recluse, ready to shoot us on sight.

Robert steered the boat towards the pilings. On one was a weathered sign: *Private Keep Out*. He pointed to it, laughing. "As if that's going to work," he declared. "I've come too far, baby. Too damn far."

As Robert lashed the boat close, I found myself envisioning different outcomes to this day. Perhaps we would be shot, and all my worries would be over. Perhaps God would be kind, and Robert would be shot first, giving me a chance to plead for my life. Perhaps the owner would simply call the police and we would go to jail, and that seemed the most pleasant outcome of all: food, shelter, other women to talk to.

"Carol!" I blinked and Robert was in front of me, angry once more. "Goddamnit, get off your ass and get to work. This isn't a vacation."

We had brought our knapsacks, stuffed with our raincoats and a couple of sandwiches, but then Robert lifted one of the benches, revealing a tent, two sleeping bags, and a large flashlight. I realized I was gaping, and forced myself to look away. When had he made these arrangements? Did he expect us to stay here overnight?

"Let's get moving," he said, slapping my shoulder. "We're wasting the fucking day."

My jaw dropped open. The *fucking* day? Robert *never* swore. Even in his worst furies he had never used the f-word. I felt like I should say something, before we left the boat, but I could think of nothing. Robert had already snatched up a sleeping bag and the flashlight and was climbing off the boat, leaving me to struggle with the tent as well as my own sleeping bag. It took some doing to get everything off the boat and onto the narrow strip of shoreline, then to figure out how to carry it all; it left ample time for my shock to turn into outright panic.

Overnight, on this distant rock? We only had two sandwiches, we didn't even have water. How did he expect us to survive?

I trudged up what had once been a path, but was now weeded over. The sun was starting to drop from its height: past noon already. The path was steep, winding upwards into the heart of the island, and I plodded wearily along its track. So lost was I in managing the equipment that I was well round the bend in the path before I saw it.

Before me rose a castle. Not the crumbling ruins we had glimpsed in our journey north; this was a castle out of a movie, intact, nearly pristine. The stone, though weathered, was solid and undamaged. The windows were boarded over with whole planks, nailed together and bolted to the stone; the roofs were smooth expanses of metal. The only real sign of decay was the weeded-over path, a ribbon of green-tangled gravel that ran right up to the arched gateway.

Which was open.

I hesitated, only to glimpse movement inside, and slowly entered. Robert was standing in the middle of a kind of courtyard, knapsack, sleeping bag, and flashlight piled at his feet, his arms spread wide.

"I'm here!" he suddenly bellowed. "I'm here!"

The hairs on the back of my neck rose as his voice echoed off the walls *here here here*. "Robert," I said, but couldn't think of what I might say without risk of agitating him further.

Everything's going to change." I wasn't sure if he was speaking to me; he seemed to be addressing the sky, or the castle itself. "We can have whatever we want, do whatever we please. Everything changes now." He turned around, twitching as if he had expected to see someone else. "Put it down," he said more brusquely, gesturing to my full arms. "We need to start looking before it gets dark."

"Looking for what?" I slowly let my burdens drop. My shoulders screamed in pain, my hands were striped red where handles and straps had dug into my flesh.

"The cellars," he said impatiently. "Haven't you heard a word I've said?" Before I could speak he suddenly slapped me. I cried out in pain, nearly falling to my knees as my whole face lit on fire. When I tried to straighten he hit me once more, sending me skidding to the ground. Gravel cut into my hands and knees.

"I am so fucking sick of that look," he said, his voice thick in his throat. "That goddamn look. You think I'm crazy, don't you? Your crazy failure of a husband. But that's going to change, starting now." He leaned over, catching my eye. "Now shut up and follow me."

I rose slowly, flinching lest he lash out at me again, barely able to see for the burning pain. He was already consulting yet another hand-drawn map. Slowly I hunched over my knapsack, pretending to check inside it while I tried to calm myself. I was terrified lest my tears provoke him to more, I was terrified to follow him, I was terrified to spend another minute in his company—

and then my hand closed over the pistol, and I felt an iciness wash over me, a nervelessness that was a welcome antidote to my tears. I moved the gun to my jacket pocket and wiped my eyes.

"I'm ready," I said.

We entered the castle through a moss-streaked wooden door whose hinges opened smoothly. If Robert noticed, he made no sign. Once inside we found ourselves in a great hall, the kind that would have once been filled with cheering knights and serving wenches. The hall was empty and dusty, like returning to a vacation home after a long winter. For a moment I forgot all about Robert, forgot even about the small weight in my pocket, so taken was I with the space. One wall was lined with tall, arched windows, their leaded glass neatly removed to reveal even lines of wooden boards; through the gaps between streamed the thin afternoon sunlight. A few boards had come undone, revealing in strips the endless churning sea. The wind whistled as it caught at the openings.

Above the vast fireplace before me was some kind of painting, directly on the stone, showing a tree adorned with faded symbols. Behind me, over the door we had entered, was another painting, of a cross like the ones on hospitals, only entwined with many snakes instead of the usual two.

None of it spoke of some ancient, long-perished race: the colors seemed too fresh, the images too distinct. Yet Robert was oblivious to everything save his map. He had already crossed to the far side of the room and was working open a wooden door beside the fireplace.

"She's this way," he called over his shoulder.

His voice snapped me out of my reverie. *That goddamn look.* If I shot him here the report might carry out to sea. Instead I followed him into a dim, narrow hallway.

Opening another door, he revealed a staircase spiraling down into darkness, and I wondered at his sureness. How could he have mapped the castle so exactly just from books? As I followed him down the stairs I could hear him muttering, "I'm coming, I'm coming..." the way one might if a visitor were leaning on your doorbell. Save that I doubted there was anything for him to be going to. This castle seemed stripped of anything of value, and it was only a matter of time before Robert realized it.

I tightened my grip on the pistol.

We descended into a damp darkness, our way lit only by the cone of light from the flashlight. At the base of the stairs we moved through an archway and found ourselves in an open space, cool and black. The light picked up stone columns at regular intervals, the skeletal remains of what looked like racks lining one wall—

and at the far end, across from us, a large, barred door of scarred wood, its edges outlined in molten metal.

Robert made a small noise in his throat and rushed forward, forgetting completely about me. The light danced over the wood as he felt along the metal seam, then tried to prise free the bar. After a few minutes he began kicking and punching at the door, flinging himself at it in a futile paroxysm of rage.

Those fists and boots, striking me.

At last he fell to his hands and knees, focusing the flashlight on the bottom edge of the door: the light revealed a thin space between door and floor that Robert pressed his face to. "I'm coming," he said. "I'm here, I'm coming."

"Who are you talking to?" I blurted out.

He ignored me, clawing and gouging at the crack, trying to work his fingers under the door as he whispered into the narrow space.

"Robert," I said again. He sounded on the verge of tears, and I felt a bitter pity then for this man, reduced to scraping like an animal, his whole being so taken with whatever lay behind the door.

I felt pity, but I also wanted no more of it.

Suddenly he turned to me, rising up on his knees and holding out his hands: his fingers were coated in blood, his knuckles split and his fingernails hanging. His eyes were glistening with tears. "Do something!" he screamed. "Do something, you stupid, worthless cunt! Do something or I'll feed you to—"

I raised the pistol and fired.

Robert jerked back against the door, then fell to the ground. Around us the shot echoed, ringing out against the stone like some terrible tolling bell.

I fired twice, then a third time, until he was perfectly still, until he was just a thing at last. I couldn't even see his face anymore... and then it was as if all sensation rushed back into my body: suddenly I was trembling and heaving, my stomach emptying itself and my icy hands opening of their own accord. The pistol tumbled to the stone and I dropped to my knees beside it.

As I knelt there, collecting myself, I felt my pants becoming wet: a thin rivulet of blood had reached my knees, following the cracks in the stone. More was pooling around Robert's body, seeping under the barred door that was now pocked with bullet holes. Instinctively I began crawling backwards, seizing the pistol and raising it before me though there was nothing left of Robert but so much dead flesh.

It was done and I was free. Why then did I feel so sick, so terrified?

It was then that I heard a faint, pattering sound. At first I thought it was rodents, which made me laugh bitterly: what a fitting witness to it all. The sound, however, became louder, more distinct. Not the sound of feet, but of something... moist, like lips smacking. I reached the bottom of the stairs, unable to take my eyes off Robert's body still framed by the light of the flashlight, but there was no hint of movement. Still the sound persisted, becoming an insistent lapping, as if something were *licking*...

A thump suddenly echoed through the space, and another. I nearly fired again, pointing the pistol at every shadow, but there was nothing, nothing—until my eyes focused on the barred door.

The thump came again, and the door trembled. A flurry of scraping followed, as if long nails were being dragged over the wood, as if something were looking for a crack, a seam, any way to get out.

And then a long, thin finger emerged from one of the bullet holes in the door, curling around to stroke experimentally at the wood with a clawlike fingernail.

I turned and threw myself headlong up the dark stairs, stumbling in my haste, cracking knee and chin on the stone edges as I blindly ran upwards. At the top I didn't pause but kept running out into the open courtyard and the foggy, damp twilight, out of the castle and back down the path. I couldn't see more than a few feet in front of me; silently I prayed I was on the right path back to the boat. The ground, at least, was sloping downward, but I kept skidding on the dry earth and twisting my ankles on hidden divots and rocks. My pace slowed to an awkward trot, and my mind finally caught up with my panicked instinct.

The sounds that had so frightened me seemed smaller and more foolish with every step. Clearly there had been an animal behind the door, eager to get at Robert's corpse. There was probably another way into that space, and some creature had smelled supper and acted accordingly, and here I was stumbling around in the dark like an idiot.

And not even a free idiot. Robert was dead, but I wasn't free yet. If I made my way back to shore now, with our things missing as well as my husband, I would need a plausible explanation that wouldn't provoke a search party. I began turning over possibilities in my mind: he had fallen off the cliffs, perhaps, while exploring? Gone back to the boat in the night and slipped, struck his head—I could put an artful smear of blood somewhere?

At last I reached our boat and climbed on board, still debating possibilities. No matter what, I couldn't go back out to sea in the foggy darkness; it was best to wait for morning. Instead I huddled in the little cabin, my mind churning. So we had landed, we went exploring, somehow Robert became lost... or...

Somewhere a branch snapped.

I froze, listening. Another snap, closer this time. The boat had a spotlight on it; I found the switch and turned it on, bathing the shoreline in light.

A woman stood there, her face half-obscured by a mane of thick, tangled black hair, her torso strangely lumpish. For a moment I thought it some insane prank, or perhaps she was just mad, for she seemed to be wearing a leotard made of sequins and carrying a stick. She blinked, raising an arm to shield her eyes, and it was then that my blood ran cold.

They were not sequins, but scales. In her raised hand she clutched not a stick but a human forearm, wrenched off at the elbow like a chicken wing. Slowly she lowered her arm now, still blinking, and idly sucked on the raw edge of the torn limb, studying me much as I was gaping at her.

The sight of her suckling the bloodied stump ran through me like a jolt. It seemed horrifyingly primitive, a savagery that filled me with terror. I jerked into the driver's seat and seized the wheel, reaching for the ignition, I would take my chances on the sea—

The key was missing.

A clamor of thoughts filled my mind: The key was in Robert's pocket; I was going to die; I had risked everything for nothing. I burst into tears as I realized my fate, babbling prayers for mercy and forgiveness.

But when I next looked up, the woman was gone. A sweep of the light showed no movement; everything was still once more.

I spent some time huddled in the belly of the boat, trying helplessly to make sense of the wiring, why didn't they teach you to hotwire vehicles in school? For that matter, why didn't they teach you to avoid legends of snake-people, or how to distinguish a bastard from a kind man?

The futile exercise, however, calmed me. I knew where the key was, and in truth I had no other option. A thorough search turned up a second flashlight, though nothing else of use. But I still had the pistol, with two precious bullets left.

Taking a deep breath and whispering one last prayer, I turned off the boat light and climbed back onto the shore.

Back up the path. The slightest noise made me jump. I was torn between craving the light of the flashlight and knowing I dared not advertise myself. She had seen me; why hadn't she come closer? Now I regretted not paying more attention to Robert's ramblings. Even the most fantastical description would have been better than the ignorance I felt.

The courtyard was still empty and echoing, save that *she* had torn our equipment to shreds, scattering pieces in a wide circle. With a wary look around I inspected the remains of the knapsacks, hoping against hope Robert might have stashed the keys inside—but I knew in my heart that his paranoia would never allow for such possibilities.

I stepped back inside the great hall. That I could smell blood even here, so far from the cellar? For a moment my nerve failed me, and I considered just sitting down and waiting to die. Yet I was suddenly filled with the memory of my mother's last days, for the hospital had smelled like this, damp and cool and bloody. Remembering my mother, when I had pushed her from my mind for years, was strangely comforting. Perhaps at least I would see her soon.

It was this thought that propelled me across the hall.

As I reached the top of the stairs, I realized just how utterly lonely I had been for so long. I had lost what little family I had before I married, and my few friends soon after; my entire world had become focused on surviving Robert. That it should come to this, now—I no longer felt any anger, or fear for that matter. I just felt tired.

I wanted to go home, wherever home might be, whatever world it was in.

I turned on the flashlight and gripped it as best I could while still keeping the pistol steady in front of me. The stairs seemed more numerous than I remembered. Had Robert and I taken so long to descend? I felt as if I were entering the very bowels of the earth.

At last the smell... thickened. I can't describe it any other way: it coated the inside of my mouth as if it were I who had been suckling at a torn limb.

There was still the lump of Robert by the door. The door itself, however, had changed. A board had been snapped in half, creating a jagged opening just large enough for a body to pass through. Even from a distance I could see how thick the wood was, yet it was snapped like it was no more than a twig. The sight made me feel faint with terror, for how could such a thing be possible? Who could do such a thing?

I hurried to Robert's body, only to quail again. I had seen the arm, but I was unprepared for what it represented. The whole of his corpse was bitten and torn, as if worked over by a pack of wild dogs. Everywhere was blood and muscle and bone, the shiny curves of organs, the malodorous contents of his stomach splashed freely over his torso—

I turned away, heaving once more, though I had nothing left to vomit. When at last I had control of myself I steeled my nerve and began teasing through the sodden layers. Exploratory pressing turned up the jagged shape of the key, but it took longer to find the opening of the pocket, then press my fingers inside. All was soft and wet; with every movement I seemed to force more liquids free, setting my nostrils on fire with their biting odors.

At last I drew forth the key. I rose at once and started for the stairs, but as I reached the first step I realized something was coming down. A weight was hitting each step, slowly and steadily, and between each thud came the whispering of a dry, scaly body sliding along the walls.

I looked one way and another, but there was no place to hide—no niches, no other openings. Nothing save for the vast, barred door.

I slid through the narrow opening, the rough edges scraping at my body, and at once I knew I had made a terrible mistake. The room was a prison, designed to keep something far stronger than myself from escaping. Manacles hung from rings in the wall, broken and rusting. The floor was pounded earth dotted with soft, flocked patches—what I realized were the dessicated corpses of rats. Moonlight was just visible at the end of a narrow shaft far overhead, a tiny channel that seemed to rise forever.

She was coming and I had nowhere to run. I would die a far worse death than Robert had.

I turned off the flashlight but kept it clutched in my hand as I raised the pistol, aiming for the door. And then I waited.

And waited.

I could hear her moving around outside, hear the sticky slap of flesh on stone as she did something to Robert's corpse. She was making a steady vibrating noise; it took me a moment to realize she was humming, though the sound had no music in it.

At last the gap in the door seemed to blot, and I heard that strange whispering sound again as she pushed her way inside. And then her silhouette rose before me.

With a cry I turned on the flashlight, revealing her completely: at once female and serpent, with a body painted in scales, twin lines of nipples running down her lumpish chest, and solidly dark eyes that gleamed behind shimmering lids. She opened her mouth, baring long, sharp fangs. I fired the pistol once, then twice, hitting her squarely in the chest each time.

The creature only stood there, seeming to almost grin at me. She looked down at her chest where dark liquid was streaming from the wounds. Casually she poked a finger into one of the holes, scraping and digging, until at last she held up a glistening bullet between her webbed fingers.

My terrified, exhausted mind could take no more. I screamed, again and again, squeezing the trigger fruitlessly. She flicked away the bullet and moved towards me, flexing her jaw as if in anticipation. I backed up until I struck the wall, my feet scraping for purchase on the rats. When she touched my face her skin was dry and cool and abrasive.

The shimmering lids raised, revealing black, bottomless eyes split with gold.

"*Nee-creh tech-ne*," the creature said then.

The sounds were foreign and guttural, her throat snapping over the consonants. Yet I had a glimmer of hope, for a creature that could fashion a kind of language might be reasoned with—

but then she ripped open my shirt and sank her teeth into my chest. I shrieked with the excruciating pain, sobbing and pummeling her head with the butt of my pistol. I could feel my blood rushing to that one blinding point, I could feel her sucking the very life out of me—

and then everything gave way to a blissful absence, and mercifully
I knew nothing more.

When I awoke it was to sunlight torching my eyelids. I sat upright
with a gasp, waving my now-empty hands in front of me, unable at
first to understand where I was or that I was still alive. My flailing
fists collided with hard metal and wood. I tried to crawl... somewhere,
only to crash into obstacles until finally I found myself huddled in the
cabin of the boat.

For that's where I was: safely on board, with no savage creature in
sight. That she existed, however, was written in the caked blood on
my chest, the bruises that coalesced where I should have been marked
by her teeth; it was written in the dried blood on my hands, the muck
caking my shoes, the key in my pocket.

The *key*. I looked around warily, but the little inlet was as quiet as
when we first arrived. I started the boat and began working it back the
way we had come. I drove blindly, twisting the wheel with little
thought, my stomach aching with renewed panic. All I could think
was to get out, get away, before *she* came back.

At last I got the boat turned about and racing for the choppy waters
that marked the start of the sea. Only then could I finally take stock of
myself. I was fairly certain I was in some state of shock, for my fear
was giving way to a remote, airy neutrality. I had murdered my
husband and nearly been murdered in turn; I had escaped some kind of
prehistoric, serpentine woman; I was returning with no husband and
an unbelievable story. I knew all this, yet I could not make the pieces
form a coherent account of the past twenty-four hours.

As I drifted into calmer waters, a dense fog settled about me. The
sun disappeared, giving way instead to a glaring, filtered glow. I had
no sense of where I was or what direction I should be heading, and in

truth I couldn't bring myself to care. I felt scraped hollow, so fragile that a tap would make me shatter.

It was some time before I heard the baying of a horn in the distance. I opened my mouth to call a reply, but all that came out was a croak, not unlike the guttural utterances of the creature. I scooped up some water and gargled, then called out a clearer hail. It was answered with a cry and the human sound brought tears to my eyes.

At last a fishing boat loomed out of the mist. It was only when I saw the three men peering down at me that I remembered my torn clothing and tucked my ripped shirt closed. When I waved to them, however, they only stared impassively at me.

"You're the wife of the fellow who rented the boat," one finally said, raising his voice above the wind. "The one looking for Ormrey."

"Yes," I said. "Please, I have no idea where I am. If I could follow you back to shore—"

"Where is he, then?" the man interrupted.

"There was an accident," I said.

Still they just stared at me. Another man whispered in the ear of the one who had addressed me, and he nodded.

"I think my husband drowned," I continued, trying to make my mind work faster. "I have no idea where I am. Please help me. All I want to do is get back to shore, I need to report what happened."

"No," the man said.

The single word was like a slap; I even flinched at it, could feel my face burning.

"I don't know what you did," he continued, "or how far you two took this. But you're pale as chalk and he's gone, and I know the taint when I see it." He turned to his friend. "Shoot a hole in her and let's get back. We need to call a meeting at once."

"What?" I leaned forward as one of the men raised a shotgun. "Wait! What are you doing? You can't just—you can't just sink me!"

"Yes, we can." The man shrugged. "Sorry, hen."

"You—" I struggled for words, for the sudden, blinding rage I felt. "You stupid bastards," I finally gasped. "You think you know! You think you know everything! You think you can just judge me? You don't know anything!"

The man ignored my outburst, taking careful aim at the stern of the boat, angling until he found just the right trajectory—

and then a dark shape rose up behind him and with a mighty swing clubbed him in the head with the anchor. He dropped like a stone. The creature leaned down and wrenched and twisted and when she stood again his head dangled from her hand like something out of myth.

I ran to the controls of the boat as the other two men screamed. I heard the scuffling on the deck, heard the shotgun go off as I threw the throttle all the way and sailed into the fog. Behind me I heard a splash and one of the men crying for me to come back. And then there was another   splash;   and   then   there   was   nothing.

I did not stop until I saw the lights of the village harbor, and then I paused only for darkness, to steer the boat back and tie it at the far end of the promenade. Like a thief I snuck back into our rooms, gathering up our things as silently as I could and slinging myself out the window. I changed clothes behind a bus stop as the first light of dawn broke over the hills, and when a bus came down the road I boarded it as if I did so every day.

Through it all I felt consumed by fever, though my forehead stayed perfectly cool.

I did not stop. I changed buses until I reached a large city. I went straight to the first pawnshop I saw and gave them everything I had of value—my jewelry, Robert's watch, his clothes and wallet. All I had left of him were his notebook and passport. With the money I went to the airport and bought the cheapest ticket I could get to America.

Once I landed it was another round of bus rides until, at last, I was home.

During the journey I barely slept, for every time I closed my eyes her face loomed before me. Each dream seemed to reveal new details: the slight wave in her coarse black hair, the hints of orange and green in her scales, how her teeth seemed to drop lower in her jaw just before she bit me. It was only when I was back home and had Robert's library before me that I found his rough dictionary and managed to piece together her words to me: nikrà tekne.

Little offspring. Little *daughter*.

In the town library they carry the major papers from abroad, and it was there that I learned of a strange series of incidents in the village where we had stayed: a fishing boat with its hands lost, a farm broken into and its livestock slaughtered, a couple brutally murdered on the main road that led inland.

I knew, then, that she had made land. How much further might she go? If all that Robert's books said was true, she had lived for centuries, perhaps millenia.

She may well find me, unless I find her first.

It was on the airplane that my strange fever became something... else. It began merely as a sense of longing: I wanted to touch everyone near me, just to feel their warmth, their flesh. I put it down to guilt, a need for forgiveness. In the days that followed, however, I soon understood it was nothing of the sort. This was no emotional need, nothing that could be solved with psychotherapy or pills. This was a hunger for human heat, that quickly became a hunger for flesh and blood.

Food has become... unpleasant, save for the rarest of meats. I find myself watching people now—watching the veins pulsing in their necks, the way their muscles flex and cord when they move. I imagine myself biting into them, as she bit into me.

I must learn how to control it, or God help me, to sate it.

Sometimes, after I've dreamed her, I wonder if I somehow created her—conjured her from my pain and frustration. How often did I long for something that would simply make Robert disappear? But then I feel her teeth in my chest again, I see her swing the anchor with brutal, practiced ease. No one woman's anguish could engender such barbarity, or so I want to believe.

Robert's books call her Denèter. They say she was a queen who went mad, who couldn't adapt to civilization. The others humored her until it no longer suited them, and then they locked her away.

I know all about being unable to adapt, and being locked away.

They called her Denèter, like the goddess, but more and more I find myself thinking of her as *ana*: mother. As I will address her, should I find her again.

—*Carol Jean Lamb, née Harlow, May 14, 1967*

F is for Females of the Species

Suzanne J. Willis

Death came the first time in a shower of stars. Clumps of angry white light fell to the earth, burning and pocking the land. The ground thundered as the dinosaurs who had ruled for eons ran and fell. Scale and skin and claw flashed under the raining stars, giants cowering under Lightning's hand. Their roars no longer the sound of the hunt, but the hunted.

Everywhere lay the carcasses of the giants. Survivors picked over their remains, groaning and shrieking at their loss.

Winter came and winter stayed, snow falling first like ash and then in bitter icicles. The few who were left lay down by the bones that scythed up from the earth and became bones themselves.

Those who remained found shelter in the high caves, far from the deadlands. There, they saw out the long winter, their wings taking them where the heavy footfalls of the others could not. The future whispered through their hollow bones, "come, come". Time snaked alongside it, singing "fly, fly"...

Far from the caves, on the cold coasts, stromatolites became the storytellers, the history keepers, as motionless as rocks, and shaped like them, too. They waited, patient as time, as the dinosaurs that were left huddled in caves or found refuge by their wings or their gills.

Washed by sand, tided by the ocean, the storytellers took in the path of the stars and the slow march of the land. They were strong enough to withstand the passing of time, these colonies of tiny beasts banded together as a whole. They saw, but did not feel. They knew without sorrow. Perhaps this is why they live forever, heavy with the infinite music of history, of possibility.

Then, in the time of in-between, as the earth moved and the skies spat fire and icy rain, they breathed out. The planet greened and calmed. It rested.

The remains of the dead shifted and turned and embedded themselves in the rock and layers of time. Memories opalised into jewelled ammonite, blazing auroras in their infinite spaces. Bones to gembones, teeming with life. Here was old magic.

The storytellers began to breathe in again, a breath that would last for thousands of years.

Everywhere, the earth and the skies, the lakes and the seas, told of the in-between creatures who were waking up. In its constant advance and retreat, the ocean brought tales of armoured fish, big as mountains, doing battle in the deep trenches. The wind brought with it griffinflies, with wings of diaphanous light and eyes that saw a thousand fold .

Shells turned to ammonite and eggs turned to opal, long buried under ice, warmed and began to crack. Beaks and horns and damp feathers poked through into the sunlight. They were like the old dinosaurs, yet not, with their gembones and dreams centuries deep. Their incubation was long enough to give them sentience as well as life. The dinosaurs of in-between—the dinodre. The guardians of cities to come.

Roasted tomato hearts were the dinodre Pax's favourite food. He watched them growing over the summer, on the vines that lined perimeter walls of his city, Atrainum. When they ripened from spring green to the dark, purple-red of human hearts they were ready to harvest. He walked past them now, in the early morning, sniffing delicately at this one and that one. Not quite ready yet.

When the time came, Abby and Evres would collect the fruit, roast it in the great ovens, then pull the flesh away and set it to boil for winter sauce. As the two children chosen as his companions for their lifetime, they were supposed to bring the discarded hearts to Pax on beaten silver trays, an offering to him as the city's guardian. But he preferred to sit with them as they worked, letting the ocean air salt the hearts before he munched them, still warm, in great mouthfuls. They tasted smoky and drew up memories of creatures yet to come: like him, but with immense wings, breathing fire embered in their own deep hearts.

It also called the past and thoughts of his triceratops ancestors to mind. He was smaller than them, finer and more nimble, and he had a touch of avian in him, as well—his gembones had seen to that. That morning, though, he thought of the past. The ancestors seemed to call to him and uneasiness picked at him.

He paused, pressed the moon-silver horn on his forehead to the earth, felt the vines pushing upwards, the nutrients flowing to the fruit. Beyond that, he sensed the earth under the city and the people as they moved through it. Nothing spoke of danger, but Pax was uneasy all the same.

He shook the feeling away, closing his eyes and turning his face towards the rising sun. It is just because the council is soon, he thought and he didn't like leaving his city, even for something as vital as the Council of The Thirteen. But he would be back before harvest—the thousandth for him and Atrainum.

Behind him, he felt the city waking, its stone laneways and houses curling up the gentle slope of the mountainside as though it grew out of the land itself. Pax lifted his head, sniffing the air: beneath the smell of salt and low-tide seaweed drying on rocks was the scent of the dinosaurs of the great cold. The gliders. The ones whose ancestors had endured and who now ran the obsidian cities in the impenetrable mountains of the interior. They smelled of death and the wars they wrought a thousand and one years ago.

Pax began to walk again, toward the sea shore.Once he reached it, he stood facing the ocean. The fringed limbs protruding from his shoulder blades twitched, itching for the flight that his descendants would know. It was not for him, though, to fly to the obsidian cities. All the same, thoughts of them made him restless.

Pax listened to the avian chatter that the sweeping sea wind brought with it. The image of them swam before Pax, sharp and decisive. Dinosaurs with beady eyes and clawed wings that spanned the length of five men, end to end, gliding from the mountaintop keeps. They were not of jewelled bones, like Pax and his kin. They had a want for –

"Pax! Pax!" Abby and Evres were laughing as they ran towards him. "You've a tomato vine growing from your back."

Evres guided Abby's hand to feel the vine sprouting from between the hard plates on Pax's right flank. His touch was soft and curious as he learned to see the world through his hands rather than his eyes. Abby's wonder at learning what the eye didn't immediately see—the raised veins of the leaves, the tiny hairs lining the stem, the soft pulse of a white bud about to bloom—was apparent.

"What else do you feel, Abby?" Evres asked.

Abby pressed his hand flat against Pax's armour, fingertips lightly tracing the outline of the plates; the fragile, exposed skin around his eyes; the moonlight-silver horn, warm with morning sunlight. Abby frowned. "Worry, I think. And something that is very like cold, cold ore and...covetousness. Old feelings and not Pax's. Except the worry. Am I right?"

Pax nudged Abby gently and nodded to Evres. "You are. It might be time, I think, for us to consult with the storytellers."

The storytellers—great stromatolites, some as tall as the women who danced the sunset rites of the city—lived in the little cove at the base of the cliff. They had been there from the beginning of time.

The dinodre were patient enough to know their language, to listen for their quiet, slow rhythms. It had been a great effort on Pax's behalf, however, to slow Evres and Abby down enough to learn their moods. That morning, as the tide receded, they lay themselves down with Pax before the storytellers, slowing their breathing and turning their mind to the rhythm of the waves so they might better listen. A murmuring became a whisper then a creaking voice that sounded not unlike the voices of the old women who told tales around the fireside at night.

And of the ones who had survived the great cold? They skulked in the shadows and the caves. They took the cold inside them, diamond-hard and fiercely-bladed. Like hunger, it made them want.

Not for them the gembones with burgeoning life and creation. Nor a thousand year city whose foundations the awoken ones had sung into existence. They had no need for the storykeepers living on the shore or the history-making rivers that had carved their way through the earth, cold with glacial-time.

They bred throughout the great freeze, unexpectedly tender with the fledglings that hatched from leathery eggs. By day, teaching them the cold and the hunger. By night, stretching their great wings as shelter and willing survival into their slow heartbeats.

Just as they had been taught, the young ate the elders when they died. Theirs was not a world that could afford waste. Longing laid itself down inside them, generation after generation. Then the dinodre awoke and the cities were built and for the gliders, existence was no longer enough. The power to create, to form the world, should belong to them.

Evres and Abby stood, brushing the damp sand from their arms. "What does that mean for us, Pax?" Evres asked.

Abby spoke first. "I think it means...danger?"

Pax longed for just another year, perhaps, even another month, to keep Atrainum safe. To keep Evres and Abby from an uncertain future. He kept his voice even as he answered. "More than that, Abby. It means war."

For the first time in centuries, the Council of The Thirteen was a war council.

Twice a year, Pax and his twelve kin tided towards the sacred plains, where golden grass grew high and the shards of the opalised shells from which they had hatched lay beneath the earth. Autumn hung from the trees like a cape and frost had begun to touch the edges of the nearby lake.

The thirteen dinodre stood in a circle among the granite boulders limned in moss. Used to the freezing northern climes, his sister Aietha stayed in the water, neck arched upward like the branch of a great tree.

Then there were his three brothers from the west, whose cities were immense and fast-paced, full of traders and mercenaries and new inventions of metal and gears and airships. The three were the lithe descendants of nothosaurs, fluid of movement, the light rippling over their serpentine bodies and spindly legs.

His sisters from the south were bolder in colour and form, a rudeness of life against the pale plains. Their cities held secrets and, as guardians and secret-keepers, they made Pax think less of descendants and more of ghosts.

Pax was the only one from the east, Atrainum the first city that the sun hit each day. His people the watchers of the storykeepers, full of music and stories of their own telling. The kin bowed solemnly to one another and began to speak, one by one, in grunts and guttural snarls, the language of the ancestors. Matters were grave and Pax not the only one to fear the gliders, to know that they were seeking the creation that lived in the ammonite and gembones.

"But the ammonite is the foundation of our cities! If they succeed, it will end them..." Aietha's voice was watery and sad.

"And if they don't get it from the cities, they will get it from us." Pax shivered. He had no doubt that the gliders would cut them open and mine them for the beginnings of life that existed inside them.

All the kin grew quiet under the setting sun. Although they had planned for war before, those were wars between humans, defending their cities from the threats of other lands. The dinodre were guardians, not soldiers.

Aietha swung her tail, splashing the water in the gathering darkness. Pax nudged her gently with his snout and she lowered her head to his, her forehead to his silver horn. They closed their eyes, the touch of scale on armoured flesh sparking a future, shared memory between them. The kin grouped together in pairs and trios, the air thrumming with electrical impulses that would be felt back in their respective cities as a long, newborn breath. Skin to scale to starpoint armour they stood, as the smell of damp earth, salted air, the old ice of winter lands washed them fresh.

In the space of a slow, shared heartbeat, Pax thought of Atrainum, the central courtyards of its homes open to the sky to collect rain in pools, dark with slippery eels. Of its murals and mosaics that travellers came from far and wide to see, marvelling at the histories cavorting on the walls. Of its people: of Abby and Evres, devoted to one another and to him.

Aietha's city began to open up before him, in the ragged, lake-bound mountains of the north. Her people wore heavy furs and pulled silver from deep inside the mountains, for swords and jewels and the chains of punishment sent to far-off destinations.

Pax glimpsed Yvette, hair hanging in wild curls down her back, casting off her furs and swimming naked through the winter waters to take Aietha her offerings. The cold ran through him, just as the salt air of his coast washed over Aietha. Far away, Pax felt Abby and Evres shiver.

The vision deepened and the sky darkened to indigo, not quite black enough for the stars. A thousand shadows alighted from the obsidian cities that were scattered along the bleak, bitter coasts. They spread their toughened wings, gliding towards the thirteen cities. They clacked their great, toothed beaks, their hunger palpable in the evening air.

Pax found himself looking down, as though he was a rider on their backs. The warm eastern air scanned past him, the waves crashed in foamy white horses riding to the shore. Then...the stench of smoke, of charred flesh rose up toward him. Below, where his beautiful city of stories and song and sweet people should be was devastation.

Stones tumbled in incomprehensible piles where houses once stood. The streets had been ripped up, the foundations gouged away. No ammonite-light shone from below but the sky was awash with gliders glowing with it as they flew from the ruins of Atrainum. Bodies piled on the beach and in destroyed laneways, their limbs poking out at strange angles from beneath the rubble. He lurched, sickened, and he ached with loss as the image washed away.

On the plain, howls rent the air. Pax collapsed to the ground, panting. Aietha thrashed her tail, smashing it into the water. After a while, the sounds of misery calmed and only the rustling of the golden grasses in the wind disturbed the night. Pax called softly for Aietha and she swam to the edge of the lake, laid her head on the grass next to him.

"The future is not solid. Is there nothing we can do to save the ammonite?"

"We cannot win this war," he said "but there might be another way..."

The rest of the council rose as Pax turned and looked toward the crescent moon, in the direction of the deadlands. "We are at the end of the thousand year rule. Our only way onward is to ensure that they die out, evolve into something beyond what they are now, and the only way we can ensure that is to keep the ammonite from them."

He shuddered again at the bleak emptiness that awaited if the gliders managed to take the ammonite. There was nothing in the future, only a great maw of time, with no movement, no life. Just silence and interminable space. It would be death the second time, but with no survivors, no more beginnings, only a final end.

He outlined his plan to his kin.

"But it is such a sacrifice, Pax." Aietha broke the horrified pause after he had finished.

"Do any of you see another way?" His kin were silent in response.

"When I remember the future," he replied "this is the only path that I see towards it. All others are broken and gone." That one bright point fluttered before him, like vine leaves skittering in the breeze. Like feathers on updrafts, wheeling toward the vertiginous blue.

Arriving home, Pax marvelled at how late autumn had overtaken Atrainum. He stood on the cliff edge, looking down. Thin skeins of silver smoke rose from the chimneys, and the trees and creepers had turned vivid red and crisp copper. It was as though the city slowly smouldered and Pax was reminded again of the creatures to come who would hold fire in their belly. The light was golden and a taste of winter chill blew in from the ocean. He had loved this place for a thousand years and felt the lives of all the inhabitants as though they were his own lives. He had watched as they found music, buried in the foundations of the city and as the musicologists had dug it out, coaxing it into the city above. Stories washed in on the tides and each of his companions over the years had learned the language of the storytellers on the shore, so they could pass on their tales. He would not fail his beloved city that even now called to him in the same way he had heard lovers whispering to one another in the cold hours before dawn.

In the cove below the cliff, a tiny figure sat on the sand, waves washing over his feet. He was gesturing angrily toward the storytellers. Making his way down the cliff, the voice, high-pitched and full of fear, became familiar.

Evres. Pax lay down on the sand, gently touched his forehead to Evres' shoulder. The boy was crying, great heaving sobs. He slumped down next to Pax, who murmured a soothing song to him, its rhythm matched to the waves. Wiping away the tears, he tried to calm his breathing, his voice shaking as he spoke. "They took Abby."

Pax had no need to ask who, and had no doubt that the companions in each of the thirteen cities had been subjected to the same fate.

"Why would they take him, Pax? He'll be so scared..." Evres scrubbed at his face, clearly exhausted.

"They want something from us, Evres. They want the ammonite upon which the city was built, the gembones belonging to me and my kin."

Evres laid his hand on Pax's shoulder as the storytellers whispered, the soldier-crabs scuttling over them and the sharp, sleek blue-eels twined around them.

"Why?" Evres asked.

"They are of the old world, before the great cold, and they remember the time when their kind ruled. Their memory traps them in the past, like the insects trapped in the amber lining the walls of the great hall. The ammonite is power—the power to create and the power to rule."

"I want Abby back, Pax, can't we just give them the ammonite?" Sadness and worry set his mouth grimly and for a moment, Pax envied him. For Evres, this was simply about reuniting with Abby. It was simply about love, unweighted by history or future or wars between those who acted as though they were gods.

"We will get him back, I promise you."

The waves shushed across the shore as the storytellers murmured on, unperturbed. Behind them, the city sighed itself awake and new songs unfurled from the opaline firestones resting deep beneath it. For the first time in his thousand years, Pax could not tell if they were songs of celebration or the dirges of darkness.

The exchange was set for sunrise the next day.

Pax and Evres stood at the upper gates of the city—silver gates sent as gifts from the people of Aietha's city, centuries before, that glittered in light or in gloom. They were flanked by two great pillars, etched with images of the guardians of all thirteen cities. Evres ran his trembling hands across the stone. On Pax's orders, everyone else in the city was locked tightly away in their homes, although not one of them slept. It was unnaturally quiet, with only the breaking waves and a shushing of wind across cobbled lanes to break the morning.

Pax felt them before he saw them. He and Evres turned to the north as hundreds of shadows skimmed silently across the sky as it paled to dawn. Updrafts caught under their wings and they circled upwards before diving down toward the coastline. There was nothing joyous in their flight. Only determination. As they drew closer and lower, their thick talons reminded Pax of hunting knives, the click of their beaks of the marching of time.

Evres pressed close to Pax as the gliders landed on the rocky outcrops of the cliffs, the roofs of the houses, the corners of the laneways. They were storms wrapped in flesh, contained by hollow bones. In their stillness, they seethed. The foundations of Atrainum shivered, an echoing cry of the thirteen cities in which other gliders were landing at that same moment.

The largest of them, eyes the pale milk of cataracts and skin like a folded, faded cloak, stepped forward, beak snapping and rasping in the old language. There was a cry from above as another dangled something over the sheer cliff face. Pax's guts churned.

"Abby!" Evres cried, holding tightly onto Pax's shoulder.

Pax threw his head back and bellowed. Then he lowered his horn, its silver tip gleaming and sharp. The old glider cocked his head then motioned with his beak to Abby. Pax nodded and Evres pulled out the whorled ammonite Pax had entrusted him with earlier. He held it in front of him, turning it this way and that—the colours glowed, pulling in the light so that shadows danced and leapt around Evres' hands.

On the shoreline, the storytellers began to breathe out again.

Faster than Pax thought possible, the glider holding Abby flew down to them and dropped him at Pax's feet. Abby stood, wrapping his arms around Pax's neck, then Evres'. Reunited again, the three stood for a moment, not caring for the menace surrounding them. Pax remembered trayfuls of tomato hearts; teaching Abby the secrets that lay inside the whorls of a giant conch shell; listening to Evres sing the histories of the fossils lying in green, undersea caves.

Evres whispered to Abby, then placed the ammonite between Pax's forelegs. The gliders rustled their wings and clacked their beaks, shifting their weight impatiently. Abby frowned and whispered back to Evres in a murmur like the language of the storytellers.

"Will you trust me?" Pax asked Evres and Abby.

Abby laid his hand on the delicate, unarmoured skin between Pax's eyes. "Always and forever," they replied, then turned and walked through the gate, towards the city square. The sound of their footfalls faded away as Pax stepped back and bowed to the gnarled, old glider. It rushed forward, waddling on its stumpy legs as the others cawed.

Leaning forward, it nudged the ammonite with its beak, then picked it up between its broken teeth. The jewelled colours glittered in its maw, diamond-bright and dangerous.

Silence and a moment in which Pax saw the future twisting and turning. As the old one began to crush the ammonite between its teeth, Pax ran forward, head lowered, and caught it on the end of his horn, tearing through its belly and tossing it into the air. The fossil flew from its beak, shattering on the ground. Fury unleashed, the others flew forward in a great flapping of wings. They ignored their dying elder and frantically pecked at the mineral shards glittering on the ground. Squabbling among themselves and fighting for their prize.

The sky filled with shadows. Gliders in their hundreds were soaring towards Pax's city to begin a war that he and his kin couldn't possibly win. There were simply too many of them and they were too determined. Those on the ground before Pax, who had greedily gobbled up the broken ammonite were frozen with wings outstretched, beaks opened wide. They had turned to ashy rock, the breeze tugging at their edges and breaking them apart, scattering them towards the shoreline.

Pax raised his head and roared, an ululating cry that came from his bones and echoed through the city, wound its way downward. Far below, the foundations of the city began to shift, the ground steadily shaking as the city broke away from the mountain.

The gliders dived towards Pax, towards his city as it slipped towards the ocean. He fended off wave after wave, impaling them on his moonlight-silver horn that reddened with their blood, tossing them into the air. The crack of breaking bodies as they smashed into the earth mingled with their angry cawing. But they kept coming, so many, too many, flocking over him. Their talons tore at the plates that armoured his back, their beaks searching for vulnerable, unprotected flesh. He whimpered as they opened a gash in his side.

Atrainum slid toward the ocean, but its people were silent—no cries of fear rang out, even though the noise was fearsome and parts of the city crumbled and fell. In the midst of his battle, Pax's heart lifted. They trusted him still. The gliders slowed their assault, their prey weakened by his wounds and they scrabbled through the remains of their kin, searching for the elusive ammonite they had come to claim.

Pax turned his back on them and followed Atrainum towards the shore, slowly limping on injured legs. Blood poured from the wound in his left side. He walked on, as the ocean drew back then rushed forward toward the city like a long-lost lover. The fear of the people was palpable, then, as the ocean consumed his thousand-year city. It flooded the streets and poured through the windows as the seabed welcomed the foundations that dug themselves deep down through the coral and the sand and the rocky underbed.

The future flickered before him, turned like autumn leaves, sparked lightly as moonlight on shale shores. The air shivered and the weight of past and future fell away. His almost-wings twitched in the ocean winds and his shape became fluid, the edges of him being pulled, amorphous and malleable. The future sung through his bones as he laid down, snout between his forelegs, looking down through the shallows to his thousand year city, now lying below.

It was limned in an aurora of light, scarfing through the water, as quick as schooling fish. He breathed in and the light filled him, the ocean lapping at this feet. His shaped expanded, pulled by the breeze. The memory of the giants of the sea filled him and he grew bigger, dwarfing the gliders that were now retreating or turning to ash on the breeze.

The power of creation is also the power of destruction, he wanted to tell them. They had not counted on Pax and his kin being willing to sacrifice those they had sworn to protect. The light moved, fast and sinuous, as tiny bubbles of air surfaced from the sunken houses. Blue eels snaked through the alley ways. Then, from the windows, the people of his city emerged—no longer land-bound, they moved tentatively. Here were women and men with new gills open in their slender necks, with silvered tails in the place of their legs. There were children, with the tails of sea serpents, breaking the surface to take great breaths, then descending again to wind and wend along the streets.

Pax, as big as a mountain, watched from his place on the shore, blood from his wound inking the water, blushing the white foam horses of the waves. Day after day, the mermaids and serpent children grew bolder, more curious, swimming farther and farther out from the city each day, as Pax grew weaker. He watched for Evres and Abby, but there was no sign of them. Day after day, the bodies of those who hadn't survived their new shapes floated to the surface, bumping gently against Pax. Each one was a fresh wound. He was weighted to the earth, heavy with guilt and anguish.

Then came the dusk when Pax waited and waited, but the men and women and children turned sea creatures didn't return at all. Starfish made their home in the fountain of the city square and coral grew atop lampposts and statues. Fish slipped along the coral.

Under the light of the crescent moon, another two shapes, not quite men and not quite ocean-bound, slipped from a tiny building in the old market district, through the kelp and sea grass. The shapes flickered, seeming human-shaped one moment, then fading into pearled-Andromeda in which shells and fossils, leaves and skeletons and unnamed animals spiralled in star-paths. Then back to the shape of boys, making their way upward, towards the shore.

Pax wanted to jump up, to greet them. He tried to lift his head, but couldn't. Abby and Evres laid their hands against his cheek, tiny next to his mountainous form.

Always and forever, they said.

The two of them worked through the night and into the early afternoon of the next day, building a great pyre and gathering the bodies. It was Abby who guided Evres throughout the night, confident in the darkness. Abby who would occasionally whisper a quiet word to Pax.

As the pyre reduced to embers, Abby and Evres ran down the beach toward Pax.

"You've a tomato vine growing from your back."

They smiled as Pax heaved a rumbling sigh.

He could feel the rows of tomato vines growing down his spine, just as he felt the grass beginning to unfurl in the crevices between his armoured plates. The plates themselves turning into rocky outcrops, and his legs and belly growing roots deep into the earth. The curve of his back rose up in a great ridge towards the sky, while his chin rested on the shore. Pax, once a dinosaur of the in-between times, now a mountain overlooking the sea cove in which his thousand year city lay.

From the north, a cold river that had once been Aietha snaked, carving through the land and reaching the sea at Pax's Cove. Three winds blew in from the west, from a place where fast cities once stood, bringing tales of the great canyons of the south that held the secrets of the cities that the earth had swallowed up.

Then one day, sea birds, feathered and elegant, flew in on those winds. They had only a hint of the gliders about them, something of the span of wing, the way they caught the updrafts. But their morning calls, the way they speared into the ocean after silvery flashes of fish, was entirely their own.

They nested in a ridge on Pax's neck, among the rocks and the thorny salt bushes, bringing new life to the mountain inside which lay the remnants of another time and a beating, fiery heart of joy and grief entwined.

G is for Grief in the Thousand Year City

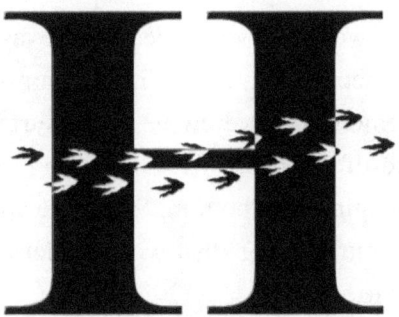

Megan Engelhardt

When there was water, we swam.

When there was not, we walked.

Swimming was better, was always better—oh, the dark cool depths, oh the whisper of deep currents—but there was not always water, and we can not swim on land, so we walked.

At first, we were clumsy. The change was...hard. Some of us learned faster than others. The slow ones, the half ones, the incautious and hasty and malformed ones, were caught. Mermaids and lizard men, freaks and sideshow wonders. Ah, my sisters. Oh, my brothers. Our tears for you leave salt trails in the dust.

We moved fast, on land, as fast as our clumsy legs could take us. We lingered when we found water. Days at a river, months near a pond, years and years in a lake, washing the dust away, letting the cool depths soak into every pore and gill, every dried inch of our malleable bodies. We allowed ourselves to be big, in the big lakes, and we fed and played and mated and birthed down where the secrets are kept, among rocks and shadows, caves and troughs. Years slipped by, twenty, forty, a hundred. What is time to us? What is time to the depths?

But always we would have to leave. Always someone came, someone saw, someone hunted. With spears—with guns—with cameras. With ceremonies that drew us to the surface, with boats that disturbed the peace of the deep, with technology that mapped every inch of the ever changing lake bottom. When we could hide no longer, we put on our legs, our two legs that were harder than fins ever were, and we began to walk again.

No language of man—and we have learned many—can tell the story as it is captured in our hearts. Mooned to us by our mothers when we and the world were new, when it was ours and only ours, before the fire and the ice and the sixth-day-man, the story floated among us like blossoms on the waves.

Once upon a time, it went, although there is no way to express the time-which-is-now-but-will-be, the time-that-we-dream-that-we-lived. Once upon a time must suffice.

Once upon a time, then, there was water, clear and clean, cool and comforting, crisp as creation in the dawn of the world. And the depths were a mother's caress, and the sunlight above the surface a warming song, and there was food and safety and everyone was together.

It was perfect.

For a time the story was our now, in the newborn days, before we were named terrible, before we ever saw the two leg form in which we would imprison ourselves. But fire came down to us, and ice came around us, and slings and arrows fell upon us, an outrageous fortune for we who were once the rulers of the world, we who were there before the rest. The story became our will be, somewhere not now and not here.

There must always be a will be. There must always be a not now and not here. A river must always flow to a sea.

So we began to search. We swam, and when there was no water, we walked.

Once upon a time which was then, men made monuments with our likeness in carved stone, and mounds of dirt, and lines carefully scraped away in the desert. Once upon a time which is never forgotten, we saw the bones of our lost in museums, on display, sinuous skeletons and screaming skulls made mock alive with wires, displaying our dead, oh my brothers, oh my sisters!

Once upon a time, we realized the story was just a story. The song our mothers mooned to us in the first five days of the world was not true. The world is smaller now. The water is not as wide, or clear, or welcoming. There is no paradise.

To stop swimming is to die. Some stopped with the song, oh my family, oh my friends, so many, so lost. Some left, to stay forever in one shape or the other, giving up the wandering to settle in lakes and bays, or in cities and towns. Their children never know of the challenge of two legs, or of the ease of fins.

And some of us go on, from year to year, generation to generation, down the path to the shore and up the road from the depths. We breech the surface, water rushing otter slick from our coils. We walk, the dust kicking at our heels. We bear the names man gives us— Morag, Memphre, Inkanyamba, Nahuelito. They sound nothing like our true names, like the names mooned to us by our mothers with the song that is no more.

The song may be over. The song begins again. The river flows to the sea flows to the river.

When the weather turned hot and the sun dried out the saltless skin I wear despite myself, I shed myself into the spitting cat lake, where the glacier water hides the land from shore to shore. I liked the way the round rocks rolled under my toes. I liked the way the unpredictable weather rolled my coils beneath the waves. I liked the glint of sea glass in the depths.

There was a storm, a sudden squall that kicked up the lake bed into a glittering, swirling cloud. I twisted and twirled in the gem-studded waves. I thrust my head above the water to catch a glimpse of the sweet summer lightning. After the flash, but before the crash that shadows the stormlights, I heard it.

Hark, my brothers! Listen, my sisters! It was the story! It was the song! That selfsame song that was thought long dead, from the then time mooned into the now by voices so like those of our mothers. Voices that could say our true names. Voices that were our then, and are our now, and could be our then again.

Somewhere there is water, clear and clean. Somewhere the depths are a mother's caress, the sunlight above the surface a warm song. Somewhere there is food, and safety, and everyone will be together.

It was—has been—will be perfect.

I go to find the paradise. Come, my sisters! Follow, my brothers! I bellow the song beneath the waves. I sing it softly on city streets. I moon the song of the story on bright moonlit nights when we break the surface, on cool foggy mornings when our fins form into limbs, when monsters become men, when terrible lizards shed scales for soft skin.

We will follow the song. We will find paradise again. We will walk, when we must, and when there is water, we will swim.

H is for Herpetomorph

Michael Fosburg

I cut across the meadow where the surviving horses graze, cropping new shoots with their old men teeth, tails flicking away flies. The warm wind stirs trees heavy with spring leaves.

The settlement still smolders. They slept through the fire, slept even as they burned, and now all we have known is in the wind. Smoke curls against the pale blue sky, and at irregular intervals cottages gnawed to nothing by flame collapse like pouches of blackened bones dropped across a fortune board.

But I do not need such to foretell that we are no longer fixed beneath this sky. Home lies elsewhere now, clear of the smoke and the rumbling mountains and the empty forest, somewhere beyond the Colossi and their titanic machinations. We must wander yet. The mandate is older than our blood.

But first I must take her beneath the mountain. To the Colossi that calls to her.

Kitarcha sways in her saddle. Dark shadows hang from heavy-lidded eyes. She is caught between this world and theirs, unable to wake for the strength of the creature's infectious dreams, nourished only by the honey and broth I rub on her cracked lips. Before she lost her speech she spoke of a whirlwind with teeth, of a place beneath the earth, of a great threshold there filled with the mind-murdering light of other suns. All her thoughts bent on that place, and she begged me to take her there. But I did not relent. We are of the Inaan—for all the good that did us.

Ashes reward my faith. Our blood is all but drained from the veins of the world, and if Kitarcha dies, the Inaan die with her. So I soil my hands with the char of the dead and wear them as an apostate's mask, for our destination now lies to the south, toward the ebon spine of mountains that mark the Colossi's foul nest.

Perhaps if I take her there, the dreams will relent. Perhaps she will wake from her stupor and greet me as her brother. Perhaps, through us, the Inaan will go on.

I do not look back. I carry our people in my blood, in the greasy ashes I wear. This has to be enough.

The Colossi sprang from the earth like a dark harvest and fell from the sky like profane stars. They erupted from mountains and bubbled up from beneath the sea, and all fled before them. With leathery skin hard as stone and jagged teeth long as broadswords, they broke our world and scattered the war-wracked kingdoms of men, and those who did not bend the knee were hewn into the soil.

But the Inaan revere only the Talus. The Prophet Khabris—when he divined the Forty Truths from the heart of a whirlwind—reckoned such devotion would not be tolerated by the worldly powers so for the survival of our people he decreed that the Inaan would have neither hearth nor home, and forbade the use of stone in building. We may settle in one location for two score years, but at the end of that span we must put to the torch all the work of our hands. Following the ashes on the wind, we must set off, again, to wander. Such is our

mandate until the Final Truth of the Talus is revealed to us.   So
the arrival of the Colossi changed little for our people. We still
wandered, still built our settlements, and still burned the work of our
hands after two score years. Beyond our ken another world was born
in blood and tribulation. The Colossi dissolved borders as though they
were drawn with mist and new kingdoms arose among men, ruled by
Colossi, who came to be venerated as gods.

We entered the realm of the Colossi I call the Dreamer after many
years of hard wandering, in the two-hundredth year of the Advent.
The wind had blown us north and west and north again into the lands
of Imhuin, and though we passed through seven villages and two
towns, no one came to watch our long train of caravans trundle by.
This was strange, for we could always count on urchins to throw
stones at our windows, or for cackling oldsters to shout age-old
accusations of blood magic and child sacrifice.

But the streets were empty. No watchfires burned on the ramparts
of the city walls. The air was flat and dread lay thick upon the land.
The dreams had all been drained away, like pus from a wound, but we
did not know this yet.

We settled in a fertile valley encircled by mountains, far from the
empty eyes of the abandoned cities. We built. We prepared the land
for planting.

And Kitarcha, my sister, began to dream.

She had always been troubled by terrors in the night, but *this* was
something new. She would thrash and moan and cry out into the herb-
scented dark of our caravan, plagued by visions of a whirlwind. The
elders rebuked me when I went before them for guidance, for they
thought her touched by the Talus, and one does not meddle with the
sacrosanct.

"The Prophet saw peace in the whirlwind," Kitarcha told me. "But
there is no peace in my dream. There is only a mouth with a thousand
teeth. It draws near to me and I can see that each jagged tooth is a

world, a terrible world. And such light! But the light is not good, Aron."

The elders thought her blessed. They told me Kitarcha was entering a sacred cycle, and that she was destined to be a great matron. But when I went to the matrons for guidance they declared her touched by the Wander, as a hard road can sometimes unseat the mind. Settle her, they said—build her a home and plant her a garden. So that is what I did. And still the whirlwind with a thousand teeth gnawed through her dreams.

"It's going to catch me," she told me in a small voice, her eyes haunted. "I can't run forever, brother—how can I, when my sleep is not sleep?"

Our scouts, long in returning, found the settlement the next day, ashen and half-wild with fright. The matrons gave them sleeproot and spirits to settle their nerves, and as we gathered around the nightfire that evening they told us of a ridge of dark mountains two days south of our valley, of the massive creature that wallowed there enormous and bloated, that wriggled wetly through caves like an enormous, mottled grub. A thing with no eyes and a mouth like a nightmare. A mouth with a thousand teeth.

One of the Colossi.

And while dozens of voices were raised in shock, in disgust, in fearful pleading Kitarcha ran from us. Only I saw her go.

But the Inaan are nothing if not contentious, and we debated long into the evening over our next course of action. The elders held that it was sacrilegious to break the settlement so soon after it had been established, while the matrons argued that the safety of the people came before all else. And all the while I thought of the whirlwind with a thousand teeth that pursued Kitarcha through her dreams, and feared for her. For us all.

In the end, the majority was with the elders, and it was decided that we would remain at the settlement for our two-score years. The land was ripe for cultivation and the Colossi to the south obviously preferred the dark beneath its mountain. So long as no one ventured near, all would be well. So we stayed and built and put down seeds in the land.

Kitarcha frayed like a poorly-knit garment. Every passing day saw her whirlwind draw nearer. She told the matrons of her dreams, but they chided her gently that her imagination had taken the reins. So she suffered, faded like the moon in the morning sky, became soft at the edges and pale, and began to speak of that watery door beneath the mountains—of sliding beneath its burning waters. She became convinced that doing so would stop the dreams. She begged and she pleaded and she threw her body against mine, but I could not allow her to go there. The very idea touched madness. After my third and final refusal, she cursed me in the tongue of Ezrihem and would not speak to me further. Her nights grew violent, and in the blush of spring after our third month of settlement she cried out one final time in her sleep and did not speak or wake again.

The whirlwind had caught her.

The forest is alive with secrets.

The wind steps lightly through the leaves. The earth mutters old truths through the creaking of each branch and brush. There are no animals here. They have left this forest, repelled, no doubt, by the presence that waits for us beneath the dark mountain. I can see them now, a tumescent rise to the south. The sky itself seems to shrink away from their jagged peaks.

Kitarcha is swaddled in silence. She barely stirs the air with her breath. Her long face is the gray of old ashes, her dark hair limp and greasy. She lists in the saddle, her body failing despite my ministrations. She takes food automatically, her dried tongue creeping out from between cracked lips to take in honey or broth, I fear that, too, will soon cease, yet I dare not hurry us through this forest. The land declines steeply and is full of hidden hazards, and a lamed horse will delay us further.

I talk to her as we plod along, describing the way the canopy shadows intermingle with the golden light of afternoon, or how wonderfully warm the spring air feels on our skin. I speak her name softly, insistently, as though placing a water-warped wooden peg back into a socket that it no longer perfectly fits. I've little experience with nursing a mind back to health, though I've seen it done before.

A girl named Saricha had been taken by low men in Solkshome, raped and brutalized, her lovely face sliced by their long knives. We found her clothed in naught but blood and dirt, her eyes blank as coins, and brought her to the matrons. After the insults done to her body were salved and bandaged, Mother Luma—who was the youngest and kindest of the matrons—stayed by Saricha's side for months, working to heal her wounded mind. She would speak for hours of inconsequential things, like the price of apples at the Khallistan Fair or the poor state of the roads into Vol Nuhgash. Saricha lay like a wooden doll made flesh, but mother Luma never faltered in her attention, and eventually Saricha came back to us.

But it came to nothing in the end. Saricha slept in fire with all the rest.

I tear away from the thought. The hurt is still too fresh, too *profound*, to safely approach, like a blaze that must first be allowed to burn down. I feel the loss of my people like a missing limb, am constantly thrown off balance by their absence. There is no one beside me when I face the rising sun in prayer; no matron to pour water over my hands when I perform evening ablutions. It is a hollow feeling, like starvation, being the last of your kind.

I take a moment to tend the horses. I cup my palm and pour some water there and hold it up to Kitarcha's lips, watching with some satisfaction as her tongue touches the water.

But as the black mountain grows and begins to fill the sky, good feelings shrivel like so much kindling tossed on a nightfire. I have yet to see the Colossi (*demon*, my mind whispers—*you bring your own blood to a demon*), but the air is charged with its presence. I invoke the Prophet Khabris and whisper the Forty Truths, but I still feel the blackness of the mountain infesting me like ticks. I flail myself with reproach until my spirit is as raw as a fresh burn. Tears cut clean streaks through the dried ashes plastered to my cheeks.

When the scouts fell into so deep a slumber that not even pins driven into their fingers could rouse them, I should have known.

The settlement grew uneasy when their unnatural sleep endured, bent beneath an unseen burden. Strange things lurched through our dreams. The forest beyond our borders grew dark and full of threat, and the mountains caged us in our valley.

We lingered at our rituals, felt the greasy tug of a presence that marred our familiar existence like a slash of storm against blue sky. We built the nightfires high and kept them blazing throughout the day. Fewer came to morning prayers, and even fewer made their sunset ablutions. Soon, when the rising sun threw down its golden light, long shadows stretched across an empty square, and the only ablutions made at dusk were by the stream itself, swollen from the spring thaw and overleaping its banks.

I found myself walking empty avenues where once there had been laughter and banter and stories, past gardens gone to seed and unfinished buildings gaping like ruins to the sky. Silence carpeted the mountain. Feeling an almost holy terror rise in me, I went from dwelling to dwelling, at first knocking on doors and then simply opening them, praying to find one soul—just *one*—whom I could rouse from sleep. But none woke. Their eyes flickered behind swollen eyelids but did not open. A plague of sleep had crept into our home like a foul fog off the mountain. Fear of falling asleep and never waking gnawed at me, but as I continued to arise each morning, I realized that I suffered a far worse fate.

There were now forty four souls in my care. The very existence of the Inaan—of my *people*—lay on my shoulders.

And may the Talus gird my soul, because I failed them all.

The trees have been gouged from the earth for as far as I can see. The land is a charnel pit of splintered wood and churned ground and scattered, rotting pieces of flesh. We are close. The tortured fundament rises to meet the black mountains filling the horizon, and I can feel tremors shudder beneath our feet.

It waits for her.

The atmosphere weighs me down like a wet woolen blanket, oppressive with the smell of dead flesh and thick with swampy heat.

Dreams swarm in the air around us.

At first I thought I was drowsing in the saddle—that the dreams were my own. But as they intensified (flesh of my forearm growing ever sorer from pinching), I was forced to admit that I remained in the waking world.

These dreams were not mine.

The winds of other lives howl through the air, tossing me like dust on a gale. My body is torn between realities as the dreams of others swarm and sting like hornets. Nameless terrors scissor long gray limbs through the stalks of winter-thin trees; my blood pounds as I witness my wife's rapist smile from across a crowded street, only to disappear as I approach him with my hands outstretched to strangle; my member hardens painfully as I melt into a velvet tangle of tittering, moaning bodies. A hundred, a *thousand*, different cuts of dream stagger my thoughts. But that is not the worst of it, for every tenth dream or so I stumble across an image or emotion I recognize, and my eyes burn with the realization that these are the stolen dreams of the Inaan.

Snatches of the tongue of Ezrihem flash into existence and are gone like the last fading chords of a bittersweet melody. Pilfered from their lives before they burned.

Kitarcha weeps softly beside me. But her eyes do not open, and her face remains slack with unnatural sleep.

The Talus protect her from what I cannot.

Distant gray columns rose into the clear sky and panic spread through me like brushfire. I dropped the basket of the blackberries I'd been harvesting and ran.

The journey back was the longest of my life. I crashed through trees and shrubs, cutting a desperate path through forest and meadow. Brambles tore my legs, branches whipped my face. I ran heedlessly, hot breath needling my lungs, the taste of copper hard on my tongue until I came to the edge of the meadow that bordered our home.

The settlement was a writhing animal of flame.

Kitarcha stood just beyond the conflagration. Her pale hands clutched a burning brand. Her eyes did not see. She swayed on her feet as I ran to her, grabbing her shoulders and shaking her.

"*What did you do? What did you do?*"

She did not flinch. She did not see.

"*I await you,*" she whispered, but her voice was vast and hollow, as though something with no throat and no tongue had spoken through her. The settlement withered around us and mair singed away as I fought to enter cottages that were not wholly engulfed in flames, but even these were lost to me. The sleeping pallets of wood and straw had ignited. Those upon them bubbled and smoldered.

I curled up on the grass and wept until my stomach clenched and my eyes were swollen and sore. I screamed into the smoke-filled sky cursing the Prophet Khabris and the Talus and the whirlwind with a thousand teeth. I howled my agony until I thought my throat would rupture and all the while Kitarcha swayed as though the sound of burning lives was a lullaby.

The winds fought over the ashes.

We have been swallowed by the earth and slide now down its dark gullet—a stony throat slick with foulness and the terror of others' dreams. Tarry black mucus films every surface and I struggle to maintain my balance while guiding Kitarcha away from the most treacherous patches of filth.

Hundreds of dark bores infested the base of the mountain. Each was taller than a cottage, perfectly round, sides striated with a thousand jagged lines. With a sick jolt, I realized that these had been *chewed* into the mountain—the ragged striations along the walls had been scored along the rock by *teeth*. So I chose one tunnel at random, the Talus fixed in my mind, and prayed that it would lead us true.

Now as we descend into the dark below the earth, a memory of a Wander decades past begins to crawl to the fore of my mind. We had stopped for provisions at a village outside of Solkshome.

I had been a child then, not yet riven by the winds of adolescence. The children had been kept close, still shaken by what had happened to poor Saricha at the hands of the low men with long knives. But the fool I was, I was having none of it. The air was touched by autumn, and a feeling of boundless freedom welled in my heart. I stole away from the matron tasked with minding us—our parents had succumbed to the wasting flux years earlier—and disappeared into the woods. I remember every crisp crunch of fallen leaves underfoot; every skirl of jackdaw and crow. I lifted my face and smiled, admiring the writhing fire of the wind-swept canopy.

Then the ground fell away. My feet trod empty air, my heart shot into my throat, and then there was unbelievable pain as my leg broke beneath me. I howled like a small thing caught in a snare, reduced to the shattered agony that had been my leg, and the only answer was my own cry caught and twisted by the old dry well into a mockery of my distress.

Ten feet above me, the sunlight and treetops swayed and danced. The day was drawing down and night would soon be upon me. The thought of being trapped here beneath the world filled me with a terror I could not encompass with thought, and spurred on by panic, I scrabbled at the old stone walls of my prison, only to vomit when the sudden movement put pressure on my leg. I lay in my own filth and wept, wept every prayer my panicked mind could muster, praying to the Talus for deliverance.

And through the tears I saw Kitarcha's small, worried face peer down from over the lip of the well. She had followed me through the forest and seen me fall.

I gaze at her now, asleep on her feet and stumbling wherever I lead her, her face waxen and gaunt. She saved me all those years ago. But now *she* has fallen into darkness. And it is my turn to save her.

I don't know if I can.

A pale coin of light shines in the distance and I see the first corpse by its watery glow, an old man thin as a bundle of reeds. The deeper we descend into the cave, the thicker the corpses become, until the tunnel is stuffed with them. Their bodies are the yellow of tallow and rasp dryly as we disturb them, rough as old parchment. Each face is a hollow mask, features exaggerations of mortal terror—eyes scored for shock, mouths twisted into toothy grimaces.

The people of this land. These tunnels must be filled with them. How many thousands—*tens* of thousands—are sealed away beneath the mountain? How many mothers and sons? How many brothers and daughters and elders?

The corpses grow in number as we move further down the tunnel, from a few scattered remains to inhuman heaps. Often I have to pause, murmuring a hasty *kadem* for the dead, and clear the bodies away. The corpses smell vaguely of cinnamon and dust and are as light as bales of corn husks. I have nothing to give them but old words of sorrow. There is no more space in my heart for them.

The light grows brighter, larger. Kitarcha seems eager now despite the slackness of her face—her shuffling footsteps are more hurried, her posture forward, intent. The coin of light in the distance grows brighter, and soon we are crossing the threshold.

We enter the foul nest of the Dreamer wearing the dust of the dead.

We stand in the heart of the black mountain—a vast, cold hollow. The walls are striated with teethmarks and rise beyond sight on all sides. The air is rank with the muck of centuries. The alien stink of it electrifies my body with terror and everything human in me wants nothing more than to bolt from this purgatory, Kitarcha's soul be damned.

But I hold the Talus in my mind, and gradually the terror diminishes. I stride forward, my sister's wasted arm in mine.

"*We've come,*" I shout, and my voice carries endlessly up into the stone hollow, echoing against itself until I have become legion. "*Now return her to me!*"

Skittering echoes reverberate throughout the vast chamber. A leaden presence presses against my mind, staggering me. Bile burns the back of my throat and goosepimples stud every inch of flesh. I lift my eyes to the unseen thing hanging above us, sense only a vastness defined as much by the *absence* it betokens as by the immense space it occupies.

Kitarcha's eyes have taken on an otherworldly light, caught from the pool before me—the same light-blasted portal that had haunted her dreams. I walk to its edge and peer into its still waters. It plunges deep, going on without end beneath the world. Kitarcha's mouth opens. The voice issues convulsively, as though struggling to articulate an alien tongue:

"*Disciple*," she says, lips curling around the word.

And lifting a wasted arm, she levels a finger.

At me.

"*Chosen*."

Like lightning from blue sky, its unclean mind is known to me. Kitarcha slumps bonelessly to the floor. And I see with awful clarity all the long years of the Colossi's life and the unnumbered dreams it has eaten, the peoples it has used and broken to achieve its unfathomable ends, the worlds left desolate in its wake. I understand now that only a certain kind of mind can endure its touch for long, and, in search of it, the Dreamer emptied this entire country of its people, entombing them below his mountain as a final monument to their inadequacy. It scoured Imhuin for years until tasting Kitarcha's mind.

And through her, mine. Cursed and cursed again.

And I comprehend the true nature of the Colossi: they are naught but warring locusts, descending on world after world to feed and plunder and feed again, waging ancient feuds across a thousand worlds, a thousand *stars*, a race of tyrants too large for kindness, too ancient for peace. Our world would collapse beneath them, and I would be used toward that end. My gorge rises, but I cannot escape the knowledge. It is branded against my mind now, as much a part of me as my own thoughts.

Kitarcha rises unsteadily to her feet, her dazed eyes finding mine.

"Aron?" she says, voice hoarse from disuse. My stomach flutters at the recognition that I hear. I smile and speak her name. But then her eyes roll to whites.

"*Leave us*," the Colossi says through her, *to* her, and suddenly as though by lodestones her eyes are drawn to the pool, to the vortices of light now dancing across its surface. On leaden feet she stumbles to its edge.

I scream her name and for a moment I think she hears me, but her eyes are filled with the light of another world. And then I hear them. Familiar as morning birdsong, sweet as my mother's half-remembered voice: the Inaan, alive and hale with the wind at their backs, caravans loaded for the Wander and a new world wide and wonderful before them. The light burns my eyes to look upon, and now Kitarcha is reaching out to touch them, our extinct people, her hand passing through the cold waters, the scene shuddering before me, and suddenly her feet are carrying her forward, into the fresh air of another world, the cold waters of the pool, down into its depths, into another life, a life that shouldn't be, a trap with walls of light and bars of song. She goes smiling to her end; such is her eagerness to greet our people, shedding the dust and memory of a dead world with every sloshing step. She disappears below the surface. I can hear her name being screamed in panic, in terror of loneliness, as she sinks. I cannot move, driven to the ground by the presence infesting my mind.

And then the ringing silence enfolds me, alone in the dark under the earth. But I'm not alone. And as I feel the Dreamer begin to chip away at my mind with a patience that eats mountains, I know that I cannot hold out forever.

Disciple, it wants of me.

But my feet are on a different path.

I hold the Talus in my heart as the whirlwind darkens my eyes.

I is for Invasion

Jeanne Kramer-Smyth

Bonnie Britewell was quite sure she wasn't turning into a dinosaur. The tiny bathroom's toiletry dispenser released another dollop of moisturizer and she reached behind her head and smoothed it across her shoulder blade. Twisting around she could almost see her back. It didn't look any different, but it felt like scales were just below the surface.

She pulled her beige jumpsuit back on. The fabric was soft, but it still seemed to scrape her skin when she moved wrong.

Her cabin wasn't much larger than the bathroom and the clock over the door showed ship-time. She did the math in her head. It was just past seven in the evening in New York. Right now she was supposed to be sitting on a very specific bench in New York City's Central Park. She imagined her contact checking their watch as twilight turned the park all dark blues and deep greens. Soon they would stand and follow a lamplit path into the darkness.

And here she was, stuck in outer space for at least two more weeks. She stomped her foot. It was entirely unsatisfying. No loud noise to speak of, barely a thump on the rubber floor.

Her favorite thing about being a smuggler wasn't actually the smuggling. It was the planning. Sure, she liked the adrenaline rush too. Slipping past security of one flavor or another was exciting, but much of smuggling actually just required patience and focus over the long haul.

She preferred the research—the details. Creating as many 'Plan B's as she could. Putting together the puzzle pieces of what was, in reality, one very long, slow magic trick. When she was six, her mother had taught her how to make a coin disappear. Sleight of hand was the first skill to master for a young smuggler-in-training.

Travelling via commercial space transport always made smuggling more dodgy. When Bonnie could fly a ship of her own, she was more in control. Or at least she could pretend to be. But the tiny ship she could afford to lease wouldn't move fast enough for this job.

She imagined she could feel the sample deep in her bone marrow, releasing its cargo into her body. The failsafe had been put in place to make sure she didn't abscond with the delivery and try to sell it to the highest bidder.

Bonnie slid the metal medallion side to side on the fine steel chain fused around her neck. It was stronger than it looked—virtually impossible to remove without special tools that she doubted were anywhere on the ship—and engraved with an intricate pattern, knotwork and helixes. The metal was thick and heavy, the edge inscribed with tiny leaves.

A cheerful voice over the ship's main speakers apologized again. It was all "please pardon our delay" and "so sorry for any inconvenience", followed by another slip in their arrival date. Inconvenience wasn't one of the words Bonnie was turning over in her mind. Infuriated? Doomed.

A small chime sounded on her armband. Her dinner shift was starting. She still went to meals in the low rent cafeteria a few corridors away from her cabin. Acting normal was important. The chances were slim that anyone was actually watching Bonnie, but there was a reason she commanded big bucks for a transport like this. Being invisible in plain sight was one of them.

Bonnie wove her way through the warren of bright hallways rapidly filling with passengers, sporting her best fake friendly smile. A wave to a tall man clad in techie green coveralls and a nod to another courier and she made it through the throng to the end of the line.

The ship was large enough that there was a fair bit of choice in the food. Bonnie took a big ship-grown salad, an apple, and a cookie. She filled a cup with lemonade at the drink dispenser. Standing with her tray she flashed back to middle school, hunting for a safe place to sit during lunch. The courier she had nodded to in the hall already had a table started, so she headed in her direction.

"Another day delayed, another free meal!" Marg was tall and slender. She could eat forever and somehow still make her lime green jumpsuit with "IntraPlanet Delivery Express" on the back still look sleek and stylish. "What sort of mouse food are you eating?" Marg pointed her fork at Bonnie's bowl full of leaves.

"Too much time sitting in my cabin. I'm trying to eat healthy." She clambered onto the bench across from Marg.

Marg talked. Bonnie nodded and shoveled the leaves into her mouth. She toasted to the delay when everyone else did. Inside she was screaming.

By the time a few of the other couriers approached with their food trays, Bonnie was back on her feet.

She had learned early that the gym was empty this time of day. Bonnie climbed onto a treadmill, picking a program with lots of hills. It felt good to move. The front of her pelvis wasn't sore anymore from the procedure. She sometimes thought she could feel a lump under her skin, but she knew it wasn't true. Even a bone scan wouldn't show anything more than a faint shadow in her bone marrow. Nothing to see here. Please move along.

The transport from Mars was supposed to have docked on Earth ten days ago—not two weeks from now. Her mission timeline had been 100 days from pickup to rendezvous and had included a ten day cushion. It was the most she could manage due to the timing of the commercial transport schedules and her window for acquiring the sample.

Her feet pounded on the treadmill's glowing track, the slope and speed adjusting automatically to her driving pace. Her thoughts raced as she ran.

The legitimate client she had waiting for an official courier delivery would be annoyed, but that wasn't what worried her. Her contact for the *real* job had explained that the sample had to be transported in a living matrix of bone marrow. Their clinic specialist had shown her 3D interactives of how it worked—though the biochemistry of it was all over her head. She'd paid more attention to the actuarial charts of predicted failure rate (low) and prior success stories (enough).

The extraction and cleanup had sounded simple, a standard bone marrow sampling followed by a selective cell-flush technique. The only wrinkle was the cellular fingerprint required to extract the foreign cells from wherever they settled in her system. That information was encrypted and encoded somehow into the design on the medallion around her neck. The decryption key was at the clinic on Earth.

Together, the key and the code would be used by the Earth clinic staff to clear out the non-native genetic material—assuming she made it there before she turned into a sample of the monster whose cells she was smuggling.

They were still too far out for a message to reach her contact on Earth. The window for delivery was closed, bricked up and boarded over, and there wasn't anything she could do about it.

The sample was too valuable for them to just let die, so they had built in the failsafe. Five days out from delivery, the sample had been set to go from dormant to active. Bonnie didn't think too hard about what that might look like if she actually became the creature whose DNA she was transporting.

The treadmill slowed through a cool-down program and Bonnie kept with it until she was standing still. She was exhausted and sweaty, her jumpsuit clinging to her skin, the itching nearly driving her mad.

She almost ran all the way back to her cabin, peeling off the jumpsuit as soon as the door clicked shut behind her. The sonic shower was efficient, stripping the sweat off her skin, but still she itched. She scratched everywhere she could reach, only forcing herself to stop when she saw blood in her nails' paths on her arms.

Standing naked in her cabin, forcing her breathing to slow and considering what medicine she could take that wouldn't raise red flags, she saw the radiation warning sign on the wall. It had been creeping up daily, but today it was in the red zone. Was the increased radiation causing the foreign cells within her to mutate and replicate faster?

She threw on a fresh jumpsuit and ran from the glowing radiation sign, out of her cabin. The hallway glare hurt her eyes. She squinted to let them adjust, then struggled to focus on a navigation panel map. She figured out the shortest path to the social club two levels up, her nose almost on the screen. Plan D required her to reconnect with the travelling cryptologist who she had befriended a week into the voyage.

Snyder was at the bar, nursing a drink and laughing at something the bartender had said when Bonnie slid onto the stool beside her.

"I have a trick to show you." Bonnie pulled out a deck of cards from her hip pocket.

"A new one?" Snyder looked suspicious. "I thought you showed me all the ones you knew already."

Bonnie smiled, shuffling the cards deftly. "A magician always has another trick up her sleeve."

"Is that so?" Snyder took another sip. "Okay, what's this one called?"

"The smuggler." Bonnie winked, then began laying out cards in a careful sequence of piles. The trick was easy, one of her early favorites, but she always saved it for when she needed a trick that didn't require her to think at all. For when the job was competing to make her heart race and her ears keen.

By the time the trick was done, Snyder was just a little drunker and just a little more impressed. Bonnie pulled her medallion out from inside her jumpsuit to fidget with. Snyder's pupils dilated a bit, taking in the details.

"New necklace too? Where did you get that?"

"Not new," Bonnie shook her head and looked down at the patterns glinting in the bar's faux candlelight. "I got this just before I boarded. Do you like it?"

"Yes." Snyder slid closer, teetering a bit at the edge of her stool. "It's very nice. Do the inscriptions mean something special?"

"I'm not sure." Bonnie had to play this just right. "The person who traded it to me really wanted my watch from Earth. He swore it had secrets encoded in it somehow," Bonnie shrugged. "But I don't know anything about decoding stuff." She let the heavy disc fall back onto her chest.

"Maybe I can help you?"

"Do you think you can?" Bonnie tried to look suspicious. Snyder was one of the best at decoding encryption that others didn't want to be broken and kept a hand in slightly unlawful activities.

"I might." Snyder finished her drink, her glass clinking to the bar surface, and leaned toward Bonnie, "May I?" she asked, her hand hovering just beyond the medallion.

"Okay." Bonnie angled herself forward, hesitating a moment before making it easy for the other woman to pick up the disc and get a closer look. Bonnie counted to ten very slowly. Time to set the hook. "What do you think? Can you figure it out?"

"I'm going to need a magnifier and my programs." Snyder mumbled, turning the disk over to examine the back. "It's more intricate than I realized." She pulled it toward her before realizing that there was no more slack in the chain.

"Umm..." Bonnie choked pulling back a bit until Snyder let go and sat back. "You want to go somewhere more private?"

"Yes." Snyder nodded and stood quickly, pushing her empty glass back further on the bar. "I've got what I need back at my cabin, do you mind?"

Bonnie fidgeted with the necklace. She glanced beyond Snyder to the bar exit.

"We can see if there's a hidden message." Snyder took two steps towards the door, then turned back toward Bonnie. "You coming?"

"Lead the way."

Bonnie knew where Snyder's cabin was but Snyder didn't know that, so Bonnie followed and made some jokes about how big the ship was and how far Snyder had to travel to get to her favorite bar.

Bonnie also worked hard to not scratch her skin and ignore how blurry Snyder's back looked when she got more than a few steps away. As they walked, she did a few little breathing exercises to quiet her heart rate. She didn't think she was going to start sprouting horns here in the hallway. Surely that level of genetic adjustment would take a lot more than five days. How much could the radiation speed it up?

"Hey Bonnie!" Marg from dinner was heading straight for them. She wheeled around and fell into step beside them. "Where are we going?"

"Snyder, Marg. Marg, Snyder." Bonnie worked hard not to sound angry. Afraid. This timeline didn't have much room for delays.

"Nice to meet you," they said at the same time, then laughed.

"Bonnie was just helping me back to my room," Snyder added, suddenly sounding quite drunk. "Right?" she slurred, stumbling toward Bonnie.

"Right." Bonnie smiled and got Snyder's arm over her shoulder. "Sorry we can't chat, time for Snyder to get some rest. Another time?"

"Oh." Marg smiled awkwardly as she stepped back and let them past. "Sure."

"Thanks. See you in the cafeteria." Bonnie gave her a tiny wave as they walked on, lurching a little artistically.

When they turned the next corner and the hallway was empty, Snyder stood straighter and they picked up their pace again.

Snyder's cabin was huge. Bonnie could have fit six or eight of her tiny space within it. Then Snyder opened a door that didn't lead to a bathroom and Bonnie realized that it had a separate bedroom.

"This is really nice."

"Thanks," Snyder said while shifting a chair over to near a desk in the corner. "Come sit down."

"I haven't been in a cabin this big before," Bonnie confessed sitting on the soft chair, "You have so much room." She knew she was laying it on thick, but it wasn't a stretch. So much private space on a high speed transport like this was extravagant.

"It's okay." Snyder acknowledged the compliments, then sat on the desk chair and shifted it closer to Bonnie. "May I take a closer look?" she gestured to the medallion.

"Yes, but I can't take it off."

Snyder was gentle and respected Bonnie's space as much as she could, aided by the fact she had some sort of augmentation for her eye. She winked and tipped the metal disc to catch the light. Then she winked again and Bonnie spotted a shift in Snyder's eye, some sort of lens sliding into place.

"There is definitely something hidden in there." Snyder said under her breath, nodding slowly to herself. She gently lay the medallion back down against the fabric of Bonnie's jumpsuit. "Would you let me scan it into my rig?"

Bonnie smiled a little. "I don't have anything to trade for you working on this. My advance for the courier gig barely covered my tiny cabin downstairs."

"No, it would be a treat!" Snyder dismissed Bonnie's protest, "I've been losing my mind with all the delays. I was supposed to start a new project the day after we got in, but now I've just been killing time. Hence walking to the farthest bar from my cabin."

"Alright," Bonnie scooted forward in her chair, "you can scan it. What do you think is?"

"I suspect some sort of key."

"A key?" Bonnie wrinkled her forehead and stared down at her necklace. She picked up the disk and mimed turning it in a lock like a physical key.

"No, not that kind of key." Snyder had a nice laugh, "An encryption key or maybe a code that unlocks something else. See if you can lay it on the desk."

It took a bit of awkward shifting to lay it flat and steady on the plastic desk surface. Snyder used a small hand-held scanner that was hard wired into her system. It took less than a minute to get each side. Then she gestured for Bonnie to sit back, and turned to her machine.

"How long does something like this take?" She thought she might have an idea, but this was high grade corporate encryption.

"I should know better in about an hour. Do you want to wait?"

"Yes please?" Bonnie looked around. "Do you mind if I sit on the couch?" She didn't want to be looking over Snyder's shoulder the whole time. That never made anyone work faster.

"Sure. Just relax and give me a little time to work."

"Okay."

Bonnie settled back into the soft cushions. The room was still and quiet and warm. Her limbs and eyelids grew heavy. She dreamed of running through thick jungle on all fours, being chased by customs officials.

When she opened her eyes, the cryptographer was looming over the couch.

"What time is it?" Bonnie lifted her head in an attempt to clear the cobwebs, then slumped back down in defeat.

"Time to talk." Snyder's arms were crossed over her chest. She was watching Bonnie very carefully.

"Yes." Bonnie nodded as best she could. She blinked her eyes and finally managed to focus on a clock on the wall over the door. She had slept through to morning. It was just past ship dawn. "Did you break the code?"

"I did. You want to explain what I just got myself involved in?" Snyder moved to sit beside her on the couch. ".. and how you knew what I could do?"

"Research. Deep dives into the passenger lists." Bonnie smiled a tiny proud smile. "I'm as good at what I do as you are at what you do."

"And what is it you do exactly?"

"Smuggling." No reason to hide anything now. If Bonnie had any hope of getting out of this with Snyder on her side, she had to come clean. "Genetic sample in live matrix in the bone marrow of my pelvic bone. You going to turn me in?"

"It depends." Snyder said after a moment. "What did you have me decrypt?"

"I hope it's the code I need to get this sample the hell out of me."

"So, what? I was your Plan B?"

"B?" Bonnie laughed, "God no. I'm better at my job than that. You are Plan D. Plan A was everything goes perfectly."

"How often does that happen?" Snyder turned toward her, her shoulders relaxing. She folded one leg beneath her.

"Everything going perfectly? Pretty much never. Depends on the complexity of the job. A really simple job, Plan A works about 50% of the time. Something like this," Bonnie waved her arm encompassing the ship at large, "maybe 5% if you're lucky."

"The delay."

"Yeah," Bonnie nodded, turning her body towards Snyder. The woman looked more intrigued than angry. For now. It felt like shop talk, but she couldn't forget that one word from Snyder and she would be in the brig the rest of the trip, likely delivered to Earth customs in the form of a dinosaur weeks from now. "The delay. I padded the travel time. I reviewed all the arrival logs for the past two years for this route, for this ship, even for every other ship in the registry files. A delay this long happens less than 1% of the time."

"Rare, but enough to demand a Plan D." Snyder tilted her head. "How many backup plans do you have?"

"For this job? Fifteen. But I only needed you for five of them." Bonnie's skin was itching again, this time on the back of her neck. "What did you find?"

"I found a few things. The part I got decoded looks like something to feed into a bioengineering module. Am I close?"

"Close. The containment capsule began to release the sample into my bone marrow about five days ago. I could try and wait until we arrive in port, then use my network to reach out to the delivery agent. I just don't know what the sample would be doing inside me in the meantime—what it is probably already doing. And I don't even want think about how the radiation levels are accelerating it." Bonnie coughed, choking on the words. "Water?"

Snyder jumped up and vanished into another room, returning with a cold metal tumbler which she passed to Bonnie.

"Thank you," Bonnie drank the whole thing in one go. The water felt like heaven. "Can you show me what you deciphered while I was sleeping?"

She had made the right choice. Snyder had extracted the encoded data from the medallion's designs and cracked the encryption for the cell cleanse. There it was, all on the screen—everything she needed. In theory.

"So what's the rest of Plan D?" Snyder prodded after seeing Bonnie's face light up.

"We need to get me into a Nucleotide Therapy bay."

"Like for cancer treatment?"

"Right," Bonnie nodded, "Exactly. Currently my bone marrow is cheerfully sending out signals all over my body to reprogram me into whatever they had me smuggling."

"It's turning you into something else." It wasn't a question.

"It's trying to. Don't worry, it isn't contagious."

"What's it turning you into? Do you know?"

"Not specifically."

"Generally?"

"Dinosaur."

Snyder burst out laughing. She clapped her hand over her mouth to try and stop but she couldn't. After a moment, Bonnie started to smile. Then she couldn't hold it back. They ended up back on the couch beside each other, doubled over laughing so hard they could barely breathe. Tears leaked down their cheeks.

"You..." Snyder tried to catch her breath, but then burst out laughing again. Then she shook her head and breathed in and out slowly, trying to regain control. "I know this isn't funny, but it has been a very long night. You are turning into a dinosaur?"

Bonnie couldn't stop laughing. All she could do was nod. It was ridiculous. Bonnie Britewell the Dinosaur.

"That can't be good." Snyder shook her head and patted Bonnie's shoulder awkwardly.

"No." Bonnie shook her head. She didn't trust herself to speak more words yet. She just breathed carefully.

Snyder recovered first. "So I have this code, but it isn't any use to me."

"I need the code, but I can't pay you for it. The code you hacked was customized for this job and my DNA. It wouldn't be worth anything to anyone else. The part you didn't crack last night—the generic code—is worth selling. It's tied to a full array of my biometrics. I think it's like a checksum for validating that the cell lines they extract haven't mutated."

"I like money, but I also don't really want a dinosaur in my cabin." Snyder choked back a giggle, then took a calming breath. "Look, I'm curious, paranoid, and maybe more than a little greedy—but I like to think I'm not stupid. The first step to any path forward for both of us is to stop your transformation—or at least remove the chance for a transformation." Snyder offered her a hand and Bonnie stood up. "One Nucleo-Therapy bay coming up."

Snyder transferred the code they needed onto a small transport key. Bonnie knew exactly where the bays were. They walked through the ship's central gardens, doing their best to look like they were out for a dawn stroll.

Bonnie was a night owl by nature. She'd always meant to see dawn in the gardens, but had never managed to force herself awake early enough. Now Snyder and Bonnie strolled together, following a path that led diagonally towards the medical self-treatment zone as the sky grew lighter.

A side path took them through the orchard. Bonnie had to stop herself from grazing leaves directly off a tree. Instead, Snyder picked her an apple before they continued to their goal.

"Self-treatment bays are available from 9am to 5pm. Please return later." Snyder read the posted sign out loud. "Now what?"

"Four branches to this plan," Bonnie ticked off quickly and quietly, leaning in close to Snyder's ear, "one, we wait. Two, we use force to break in. Three, we convince it to let us in early. Four, we 'gain access'," this with air quotes, "to one of the medical staff bays and 'convince it'," again with air quotes, "to do what we need."

"I vote option three."

"What time is it now?" Bonnie squinted at the panel, her eyes failing to bring anything into focus.

"6:15 AM." Snyder read off for her.

"So... we need the door to think it's 9:15. Can you manage that?"

"Sure." Snyder nodded. "Sure, that's an easy one."

Three minutes later they were inside and Snyder let the clock reset so that once the doors closed behind them, no-one could bother them. Not a bug, a feature.

The self-serve bays made it easy for anyone on these long trips who needed ongoing treatment. Bonnie sat in the treatment chair and fed her arms into the sleeves and Snyder loaded the code. Within minutes, the system was whirring and the sleeves were inflating to hold her arms in place.

"I'm going to at least owe you a drink." Bonnie admitted to the cryptographer. "Can you scratch the back of my neck?"

"Sure. How long do these treatments take?" Snyder reached under Bonnie's hair and scratched. Her hand froze.

"What? What do you feel?" Bonnie was trapped. The sleeves wouldn't let her move.

"Nothing." Snyder swallowed a laugh, but started scratching, "What did you think I was going to find? A horn?"

"Wouldn't it be a plate if it was on the back of my neck?" Bonnie glared at her. "Maybe I won't buy you a drink." she grumbled.

The first treatment took a full two hours. Snyder hacked the booth to disable the standard video recording devices, then stayed with her as they traded stories. They both had so few people to share their tales with, and they each enjoyed their captive audience.

"If your employer already has the code for cleaning this junk out of your system, what do they need the live sample for?"

"Theoretically they could grow their own cells." Bonnie pulled herself out of the sleeves. "But it takes a long time and has a high failure rate. The Mars' labs are just so much further ahead. Smuggling it has a greater ROI than building a lab program from scratch in secret."

"Still, the code itself must be worth something." Snyder turned back to Bonnie and leaned against the counter, watching the smuggler's face carefully. "I have connections for selling interesting information. Would there be a better market for the code on Mars?"

"Maybe." Bonnie's heart sped up. "But if it got back to my employers, it isn't going to help my reputation any."

"What if I assured you that they couldn't trace the source? I could wait a while, send it out to a totally different network."

"Do you have the tech for reading biometrics? Voice, cornea, dental, and saliva?"

"No, but I could get it. Probably in port. You going to go out for this job again?"

"Absolutely not!" Bonnie rolled down her sleeves. She stood up, wobbled and sat back down. "Can I get a hand?"

"Non-human cell lines detected, treatment bay quarantine required." An overly polite female voice came out of the speakers in the ceiling. "Appropriate officials have been notified. Please remain calm."

"Snyder?"

"I thought I would have time to purge the logs when you were done."

"Can't you do it now?"

"Did you hear the voice? Officials are on the way. Do you have a plan for this?"

"No." Bonnie's voice was quiet.

Snyder turned to the keyboard, but the screen only flashed the word QUARANTINE in bright red against a black background.

"I think the plan just became 'get arrested'." Bonnie wrapped her arms around herself. "And then turn into a dinosaur. A convict dinosaur."

"This is what you get from using tech that's tied to the network." Snyder slammed her hand on the console.

"Ok. Ok." Bonnie began pulling open drawers and unlatching cabinets.

"What are we looking for?"

"Anything that might be useful." Bonnie held up a vacuum-sealed package with metal tools gleaming inside. "If we can get out fast enough, we still have a chance. Well—you do anyway. They have my DNA print."

"I can get rid of that if I can get to an active terminal again." Snyder stared at the wall beside the door.

"What?" Bonnie stepped to her side, trying to see what Snyder was seeing.

"The control panel for the door has to be on the other side, right about here—don't you think?" Snyder was fighting to get her fingernails into the seam between the wall tiles.

"We need tools." Bonnie slid the vacuum release to the side and picked the sharpest implement from the neat array that unrolled onto the counter. "Move over."

Snyder shifted to give Bonnie space at the tiles. Bonnie half cut and half slid the blade between them, prying the one that Snyder had indicated off the wall. It broke free with a hollow pop.

Snyder reached into the wall and yanked out a tangle of wires, methodically separating them by color and pattern. Two minutes and some wire splices later and the door mechanism released. Bonnie and Snyder curled their fingers around the door's edge and slid it sideways far enough for them to slip out. Bonnie started down the hallway, but Snyder signaled her back to help slide the door shut again.

"No reason to help them know we aren't in there."

They forced themselves to walk, heading back to the winding paths of the garden. The ship was beginning to wake up. Children ran down the paths, sleep-deprived parents following along as best they could.

"How many more treatments do you need?" Snyder asked.

"Four more. They are supposed to be every twenty-four hours." Bonnie watched her face as she said it. Snyder didn't flinch.

"What happens if you can't continue?"

"With the radiation so high? I don't think I'll wake up a dinosaur tomorrow, but I definitely can't pass the genetic screening for Earth Customs."

"We can't go back to our cabins. The next step after that quarantine is following your DNA to your cabin. Then a full ship lockdown and cabin to cabin search." Snyder spoke under her breath.

"Anything in your cabin you can't walk away from?"

"No. All replaceable. I can re-decrypt what's on your medallion if I need to. A dead man's switch will wipe my tech after twenty-four hours. But where can we go?"

"Plan E. We borrow a long distance shuttle and I fly us back to Mars."

"Why *we*? What do you need me for? You have what you need for your treatment." She flashed Bonnie a glimpse of the transport key she clutched in her hand.

"I need your help to get past the security between us and a shuttle. Plus, I sincerely doubt that I will make it back to Mars before some sort of transformation takes hold." Bonnie scratched her arm, then pulled Snyder to walk faster. "You not only get a free shuttle adventure back to Mars, you also get shuttle pilot lessons."

"So I fly after you can't?"

"Even if I don't turn full dinosaur on you," Bonnie waved vaguely at her torso. "I bet I won't be feeling too good for terribly long."

"And I get you treatment on Mars."

"And when I wake up dinosaur-free, we take the cracked code and my biometrics to your best contacts."

"It's a reasonable plan. We might even make a good team for future projects. If you can get your 'dinosaur problem' taken care of." Snyder smiled and used air quotes. "And sooner is better than later for your issue, right?"

"Right. Mars has plenty of treatment bays that don't bother scanning for non-human cell lines. Four days back on-planet and I should be back to myself."

"And I can decrypt the data to sell once we have access to your biometrics and a way to read them. You might come out ahead on this whole disaster—even with the 70/30 split I'm going to insist on."

"Ha. Thanks for the warning. Maybe I'll be the world's richest dinosaur." Bonnie couldn't hide her smile. "Just please don't get me arrested. My grandmother would never let me live it down."

"Your grandmother?" Snyder barked a laugh. "She knows?"

"Sixth generation, right here." Bonnie pointed at herself with her thumb. "It's a family business. How about you?"

"They think I'm a stockbroker."

The shuttle bay security quickly fell to Snyder's magic. Their luck held long enough for them to find a long range emergency shuttle, stocked with food and fuel.

Snyder was working on getting the bay doors to the outside to release them when they heard the first official request for them to exit the shuttle and surrender.

"Do you have some plan for when we get to Mars?" Snyder's hands flew over the communication and security controls in the shuttle's cockpit.

"Mars will let us land. Their security folks will be grumpy with us right up until we officially vow to return the shuttle to the owning company, along with an exorbitant rental fee that includes the cost of fuel."

"You make it sound as easy as returning a rental shuttle late."

"It should be."

"I hope you're right." Snyder did something to silence the last alarm before turning to Bonnie. "You ready?"

At Bonnie's nod, the external bay doors yawned open and the shuttle's engines kicked on. Bonnie deftly boosted them free of the shuttle bay and the ship's gravitation field. The massive cruiser disappeared into the distance almost instantly as they began their slow progress back toward Mars.

Bonnie slumped in her chair. She looked over at Snyder who was grinning.

"I have a confession. I can barely see the control panel. Good thing those bay doors were opened so wide. The good news is that I've only been craving vegetables. If you're lucky I'll be a kindly near-sighted herbivore."

"Don't worry. If your inner dinosaur does come out before we get back to Mars, I'll lock you in the bathroom and feed you lettuce. Or sedate you—depends on what's in the first aid supplies."

"And here I thought you didn't care about me."

"You have a few weeks to win me over."

"Very true." Bonnie gave her a tired smile. "I bet you didn't think you were starting a new adventure when you went to the bar last night."

"I did not." Snyder shook her head. "I just wanted to get a closer look at your necklace. Any plans for the medallion? After we unlock all its secrets?"

"I think I'll keep it—something to remind me that I can even survive running out of plans." Bonnie fidgeted with it a moment before laying it back down on top of the jumpsuit's fabric. "It makes a nice piece of jewelry."

J is for Jewelry

Pete Aldin

"These damned rocks," Brynjar cursed.

He shifted position so that the rock impressed itself upon one buttock rather than further aggravating his piles. His companion, Gunnar, had caught a piece of wood from the ship to sit on, positioning it in the nexus of two ridges of pocked stone so it formed a kind of stool. A perch wide enough for one. No way for Brynjar to sit beside him. But the least the bull's arse could do would be to share it from time to time.

An evening and a day of this fidgeting had nigh on done him in. Exhausted, his woolen trousers stiff with dried sea salt, gut clenched in hunger, and shoulders trembling with cold, he was a prisoner of the ocean. He kept his arms wrapped around his knees and tried to return his mind to soothing blankness—the hopelessness of their situation was enough to drive even a grandson of the Vikings to weep.

Stubbornly refusing to be blank, his thoughts drifted to Gunnar's perch. The hardest of woods would feel like straw after hours on this rock. Why couldn't the bastard share? One hour for Gunnar, one hour for Brynjar. Something like that. Twas the very least a fellow sailor could do for another.

Particularly since Gunnar had been half responsible for the wreck.

At *least* half, maybe more.

It might have been Brynjar who convinced the captain to sail south of their normal waters—"Five hundred years ago, Captain, our forefathers did it and the Britons trembled along their coasts! We're missing valuable fishing opportunities!"—but it was Gunnar who'd suggested that the *best* fishing would be near this chain of islands. So it was Gunnar's idea—mostly—that had dashed the ship to pieces.

Islands! he scoffed. Mere stones poking like boils from the sea. Rookeries for gulls to roost and nest and shit. Nothing more.

Just one hour upon that wooden board. Just one.

"I said, these damned rocks," he repeated a little louder.

"This damned everything," Gunnar grumped. And that was that.

Brynjar wished he had the water to spit.

One night and one day spent in misery.

One night and day closer to a cold and wretched death.

At least the day was calm. Now. Not like the tempest of yesterday.

Perhaps it would do them good if he could find a bright side to this disaster. Buoy their spirits. "We survived the storm," he tried. "We got here with only a little bruising and scratching. And *can't you give me just one moment on that damned board?*"

He full expected argument—fisticuffs even. But Gunnar was staring hard out to sea, hand raised against the sun. "That's a ship," he hissed. "A ship!"

Brynjar followed his gaze, and saw it too. A spot, irregular, maybe a half league out. Gunnar clapped his shoulder and Brynjar slapped his leg. They rose and jigged the best they could without toppling or slicing their bare feet. They whooped... and then whooped louder when the dull shape became larger, a sign of it turning their way.

"They've seen us!"

The design reminded him of something, a story. That's right, old Grey Ulf had described ships like this over ales at the inn, Scots ships. Well, they mightn't speak the same language, but sailors were sailors and they'd help them for sure.

They might ask us to live among them. If they can't get us home, we might have to.

His gut dropped suddenly, but it was not at the prospect of never seeing the barren lands of his youth again nor of dying an old man among a foreign people. Rather it was at the prospect of *living* among others, others of the sea.

"There's a problem."

"What problem?" Gunnar squinted his way, then turned his squint upon their sanctuary. "These rocks? They get closer, we swim out before they breach. Simple as that."

"Not so simple. They'll take us on as crew, sure. They'll let us live among them. They'll teach us their language. And then one day they'll want to know what happened to *our* ship."

"Oh?" Gunnar scratched his head. Salt cascaded down like dandruff. And then his squinty eyes grew round. "Oh!"

"They'll think us gods-cursed. We'll be useless to them then."

"As valuable as maggots and wood-borers."

"Pitched overboard."

"Or left to live our lives on land."

They shared a shudder.

"What can we say happened?" Brynjar asked. "There are no enemies here: no one is stupid enough to fish this close to rocks in a high swell."

"None but us."

"We can't tell them it were our fault. Not and hope to be accepted."

Brynjar thought and thought but nothing came to him. The tiny ship grew larger until the moment drew near they would have to swim out to it. He was standing and rubbing blood into his bony arse when the surface of a deep rock pool rippled with movement. Brynjar took a shaky step and squinted against the diamond fragments of sunlight across the water's surface until the shape beneath broke that surface, came into the light of day: eight arms and a foot-sized body, pulling itself along the uneven terrain in search of its next meal. And the idea—the lie—came to him; it even had a fine and frightening name to match.

"Gunnar."

"Uh?"

"You know how the fish that got away is always bigger than the one you bring home?"

"What of it?"

Brynjar pointed at the octopus and smiled. "Behold the greatest story the sea has ever told. Behold, our destroyer."

K is for Kraken

Alexandra Seidel

The two suns were hanging near the horizon—two leviathans frozen in battle—and Corvy counted three moons climbing the crimson bruised sky. The other two would follow once the two battling stars had drowned beneath the horizon for good.

"Can we go home now?" Corvy asked her mother's turned back.

"In a minute." Corvy's mother was a geologist with a passion. She had been trained by her parents who had learned the trade back on Earth, in universities and lecture halls. As Corvy understood it, her grandparents had chosen to study rocks, and her mother had never even considered anything else, but Corvy didn't want in on the family trade. Not that she had a choice.

Her mother's short auburn hair bristled in the breeze, and goosebumps prickled Corvy's skin. "Mom," she said.

Her mother ignored her for at least another minute before replying with "Alright. These samples all look interesting,"

Corvy managed something like an affirmative grunt. *Although*, she thought, *Mother might just be talking to herself.* Corvy was used to that and preferred it to lectures about how amazing being a geologist would be for her if only she chose to embrace it wholeheartedly.

Her mother picked up the sample crate. "You take the rest of the equipment," she told Corvy without even sparing her a glance.

With practiced efficiency, Corvy collected her mother's set of tools and gadgets in another crate and followed her toward the rover. *Fuck spending all day out here in the middle of nowhere, and fuck all these rocks*, Corvy thought, her thoughts blurring inkily like the plum-colored sky at her back. They were walking toward the rising stars, and just for a moment, Corvy looked up to the scattering of light, something her mother had told her a million times not to do while working.

"Aah!" The tool crate went flying, and so did Corvy, before a hard landing. Her toe hurt from where it had caught on something. Then her knee hurt from where the ground had decided to take a sample of human skin. *Only fair,* Corvy thought, *considering what Mother scrapes away with her passion for rocks.*

Her mother stopped, put down the sample crate, and ran back toward her daughter bending to collect the tools that had spilled out of their container.. "Corvy, I told you to watch where you are going."

Corvy tried to force the tears of pain back into her eyes and suppress the tinge of pain that she knew had mixed into her voice. "Sorry."

Against the hard bite of the scrapes and developing bruises, Corvy picked herself up off the ground while her mother looked toward her, though not *at* her, scanning the ground for tools she had missed. "Oh! What's that?"

Following her mother's gaze, Corvy spotted what had tripped her. A triangular piece of rock was peeking out from the ground. And unlike ordinary rocks, it was *glowing*.

Corvy's mother bent down, examining, unearthing. "Wow, look at what you found. This is interesting, some kind of luminescence."

Corvy didn't care. She was bleeding. She hurt. She could feel the cold of the oncoming night, and she just wanted to go home.

Still, she stood by, watching her mother wordlessly and handing her tools and brushes when asked. Some time later, her mother put the glowing rock in her crate and carried it to the rover. Corvy followed after being told to *watch where you are going this time*.

Her toe hurt.

Her knee hurt.

Her heart hurt worse.

The nights here were very long—about four times that of what a night was back on earth. Story nights, the first settlers called them. And during their long dark hours, they'd tell each other stories of home and hauntings and happy endings.

But Corvy was not a first settler, she was a native, and she knew no other nights than these.

When they got to the surveying outpost they called home, the darkness was complete, only broken by five gemstone moons and a sprinkling of stars.

"You can leave the tools in the rover for now," her mother said, "just help me with the sample crate right now. And don't look like you've been dragged to a crater race without running shoes. No one has ever found something like what you did."

"Awesome," Corvy said, but her mother was not really listening anymore. She was out of the rover, all eager to get the samples in her home lab.

Corvy opened her passenger side door with a sigh. Just like the gemstone moons, she was caught in an orbit, and she felt like she would never escape it.

The crate was heavy, and Corvy was hurting but she helped her mother carry it inside and set it on a big work table.

"Hey, you two! You've been out late. What happened to your leg, kid?" Corvy's father said when the noise of the arriving duo drew him lab-wards.

"She fell when she discovered this! Come here, have a look at it."

How can they both enjoy this so much? What is so life-changing about staring at the dandruff of this planet's crust? Corvy sat on a chair, a little to the side. She knew she'd be able to fade in the background from here. She had done it before. Did it all the time, in fact.

"I think it's a fossil! I've only ever seen them in pictures, but look at it! That's what it is, isn't it?" Her mother looked younger. Like a girl almost, bouncing on the balls of her feet.

"But fossils don't usually display luminescence, do they?"

"Well, this one does."

Her father rubbed the stubble on his chin. "You know, everyone was always told that there was no animal life here. Not now, but not before either. This is very weird."

"Do you see this part? It's almost like a spine. We'd have to compare them, but these are similar to human vertebrae."

"True. But, I mean, they checked before they decided on settling this planet, didn't they? This should not exist."

"But it does." Corvy's mother ran a hand through her short hair.

"How old would you say this is?"

"Well, the area is pretty well surveyed by now. 100 million years. Pretty exactly."

"Mmh."

While she was sitting there, Corvy grew colder and more tired by the minute. It felt as if the darkness from outside was reaching in to grab her, pull her with it.

"I'm tired. I'm going to bed now," she said, getting up.

"Well, ok. But are you sure you wanna miss this, kid? Something like this is sure to happen just once in your life, you know."

"Yeah, dad, but I'm just really beat. G'night."

"Sweet dreams, kiddo."

Corvy walked out the door to the lab, but before it fell shut, she heard her mother whisper, "She's always strange like that, and growing stranger, not happy with anything..."

Corvy stumbled up the stairs to her room and into her bed where sleep grabbed her like a torrent and took her away with the tide.

The creature was beautiful. Long neck, long limbs. A beak made to carve bones from a living body. Not big, no. The skin on its arms was thin, it helped it glide.

And Corvy, sleeping Corvy, saw it glide through the night sky that was gem-hung with five moons. A soft glow, as soft as if it came from within the creature, helped it fade into the moons-lit night sky.

At first, Corvy was just watching the creature. It was a very strange kind of watching, almost as if she were a drone, following the moving creature, but the sense of movement just wasn't there.

Then, their eyes locked. The creature's eyes were shimmering, shining as if back-lit by blue fire, and full of intelligence.

Corvy thought they were saying why are you here, you shouldn't be here. *But maybe she was imagining things; dreams are incense for the imagination after all.*

But even if the creature really just looked, soon enough it came closer, and fast.

Corvy woke with a start. Her clothes were sweat soaked, and she was as thirsty as she had never been. In the darkness, for the night was still not done, she stumbled to the bathroom and drank straight from the tap. Swallowing, swallowing, it felt as if the thirst would never end.

When she had finally had her fill, she limped back to her room to change out of her wet clothes. In the moonlight that spilled in from her window, she could see that her knee was actually worse than she had thought—there was a deep cut—but it had bled less than she would have expected and looked as if it was well on its way to healing already. A thick scab had formed, and in the light of the five gem satellites, it looked almost shimmery.

Something was pulling at Corvy, and it wasn't tiredness trying to pull her back to sleep, no, something else. So she opened her door to the hallway and went outside.

The house was silent, and there was not even noise or light drifting over to the living area from the lab. *That's strange. It's a new discovery and all.*

Corvy went into the lab. It was noisy as a forgotten tomb and the lights were turned off but the fossil, still in its place of honor on the table in the center of the room, was glowing softly, a glow soft enough to paint the night sky.

Corvy walked toward it, and for the first time really looked at the creature caught inside the rock, so many million years ago.

This is what I saw, Corvy though. And it was, sure enough. Not whole. Not with wings of skin remaining after all these years, but the graceful neck, the vicious beak, those were all still there.

"Can you see its light?"

Corvy spun at the sound with a sharp intake of breath, banged her back into the table. Her mother was standing in the door to the lab, complete darkness draped around her. And something about her looked very different, very weird.

"Mom?"

"It is so bright. Your father couldn't really see it the way I do. I don't know why. He said, he couldn't see it move, and the sounds...he said he heard nothing, nothing at all."

"Mom, what are you talking about?"

"You never liked any of this though, isn't that right?" Her mother took one slow step into the room. She was barefoot, and her clothes were dirty, covered in earth and reddish brown mud.

"I sometimes wondered how you could be mine, you know. I mean, for research, they sometimes do things when they settle a new planet. Everyone knows. I just wondered; were you really mine, or did they put something inside me they mixed up in a Petri dish? You were ever such a strange girl, wanting to leave this place."

Corvy wanted to back away further, but the table was at her back so she moved sideways instead. "Mom, you are scaring me. Where is dad?"

Her mother sucked in a lungful of air. She lifted her head a little, and Corvy saw her eyes, pupils wider than wide, blackness so deep it swallowed the white.

"He is gone. And he is not coming back. He looked at the fossil and didn't see, so that's good riddance in my book."

I am still dreaming, still dreaming, just a dream Corvy thought, but she felt the reality of it. It reflected right off the screwdriver her mother was holding behind her body, its tip crusted in something dark. Corvy couldn't make out color in the blue luminescence, but the feeling in her gut made her cringe all the same.

Another step closer, and the blue light was hitting her mother straight in the face.

"I made him see, though. In the end, I made him see..."

They always teach you about contaminants, toxins. Watch out for odd things, odd behaviors. Act without hesitation.

"...I can make you see too, Corvy."

Corvy's eyes found the fossil, and instinct took over. There was a hammer on the table too, a solid affair, and Corvy grabbed it and brought it down on the stone-encased bones in downward strike that made up for lack in gracefulness with strength born of fear.

"*Nooo!*" her mother screeched behind her, and Corvy heard the screwdriver drop to the floor. She lifted the hammer again. Not even a heartbeat later, Corvy felt her mother lunging at her, but she brought the hammer down again, then let go of it and elbowed her mother.

The older woman let go of her daughter bent over the fossil's cracked and chipped surface.

"*Look what you did!*" she screamed.

Corvy ran out the lab and out the front door.

"Dad!" her father was lying on the ground, had either dragged himself or had been dragged toward the rover.

He was on his back, and Corvy bent over him and felt for his pulse. There wasn't one. She had started crying at some point, now she had trouble seeing because of the tears but his eyes were wrong and there was blood. The moonslight was dim, but there was blood.

Had Mother run the screwdriver through his eyes? Had she done that? She wouldn't. Corvy hated her mother, thought she hated her mother, but her mother would never—could never—do this.

In the lab, that was not her mother.

A sound was coming from inside the house. Corvy was scared. She moved even though she was scared. They were an outpost, and she knew she had to get to the nearest settlement, tell them. Get help. Save mom.

She stumbled toward the rover, got in, locked the doors just as her mother's face—not her mother's face—appeared at the passenger side window. Two seconds later, the hammer Corvy had used on the fossil smashed into the enforced glass. Another second later, and Corvy was driving away. Her mother was in the rear view mirror, a blurry image running after the rover. Corvy wiped the rear view mirror, but it was fine, it was the tears flooding her eyes that were the problem.

The settlement was dark. People were asleep or working indoors. *We are indoors at night because of the cold*, Corvy remembered. But tonight, she wasn't cold. Instead Corvy felt as if her body was telling her stories, as if her eyeballs were whispering secrets into her brain.

Cetnral building. Have to report to central building. The thoughts were like echoes. It felt so loud in Corvy's head, but the echoes were fading into the background. Still, she found the central building, spotted the antenna easily enough, and headed toward it.

She banged her fists against the door several times and kicked it with her knee. *It's no longer hurting, that's good.* Finally, she remembered the chip in her left wrist. *The computer will read it. Just swipe. See, easy.* Maybe she remembered her mother's voice, or her own. It didn't matter. The chip opened the door for her.

People were coming toward her already. A group of three, just the way protocol demanded. "Hey, you gotta tell me what a teenager is doing driving—oh my fucking stars!"

"What is with her eyes?"

"Security protocol C-83. Lock down central."

They all were moving so fast, so very fast, and Corvy found it difficult to see—the lights were so bright. Maybe she could make them stop and listen and turn down the lights.

When Corvy opened her mouth to tell them about everything, her voice was gone, but the voice of her dream creature was there, calling her into the darkness.

They kept her in a containment chamber. Her knee had healed completely, it was smooth and shimmery and whole. The smell of dust and soil was gone. The rocks that her parents loved were more than a lifetime away, and Corvy was almost content. The only thing she need now was the gem bedecked sky, but that would come. The noises from outside her chamber had grown first, then faded fast, and now, darkness was coming to take her home.

L is for Luminous

Michael B. Tager

"Besides wormholes, there's chemistry-," Eddy struggled for words. He was a small boy with dark black hair. He wore crisp khakis and his father's old Astros hat. "Imagine time's an ocean of chemicals and you can jump in with the right reaction." He tilted his head at the blue summer sky. "Swim around..."

"That's weird." Julia was also small, her skin dark, intricate braids pulled into a long ponytail. She smiled often, especially in class when she knew the answer. They were lab partners. While in class, he had initially proposed cloning dinosaurs from bone shavings, but she'd laughed, declared it impossible and said, "If it's that easy, why not just build a time machine?" They'd been discussing it since: he claimed time travel and cloning were possible, she laughed at everything he said.

"It's not weird, it's a theory," he stammered.

"You are too weird," she winked. "Time travel, dinosaurs; what's that about?"

He mumbled something about relativity and covalent bonds of chemical compositions but when Julia's eyes glazed, he picked at an imaginary spot on his khakis. "Besides, class is boring."

Julia laughed. "I'm just teasing. Class *is* boring. And I like my friends weird. Wait, hold on a second," she said when buzzing emanated from a pocket on her red skirt. She checked her little flip phone and hummed. "My parents just texted: they're running errands. You doing anything? We could get started on the experiment or whatever."

"Well," he said, surprised. Were they friends? "The only thing is that it's my birthday and I don't know if my parents have anything going on."

Julia clapped her hands. "It's your birthday? Did you ask for anything?" She patted her dress and her backpack. "I don't have anything to give you."

"That's ok," Eddy said. "I don't have anything for your birthday next week." When her eyes widened, he continued, "You mentioned your dad watched the Mets instead of you blowing out the candles last year. There were only two Wednesdays last year with Mets games around this time."

She laughed. "Wow. That's impressive."

He bit his lip. Sometimes, when he rattled facts off like that, people made fun. "I remember things?"

As Eddy led the way to his house, Julia punched his shoulder, not hard. "That's great. My dad says he has CRS disease whenever he forgets."

"CRS?"

"Can't remember ... well, sss." Julia blushed. "It's a dad joke. Is your dad funny?"

He told her that, his dad wasn't funny, but he wasn't un-funny. He mostly just worked and watched baseball. He had been a minor league player for the Astros. It was there that he met Eddy's mother, managing a ball park. She wasn't particularly funny either. They were both quite enthused with Eddy's school, though. They were professors at York College and "just knew that Eddy could do better in school, *if he just applied himself.*"

"Do you think they got you those worm homes?"

"Wormholes; collapsed stars. It's one theory about how time travel is possible. I read about it in *A Brief History of Time*."

"Right. Well. I hope you got something cool, regardless."

He smiled. Julia seemed cool. And she was smart, the top of their class. His mother always told him that he needed to make friends.

He figured that if he wanted to make a friend, he'd have to trust. "Well, I don't know if I should tell you this. I asked for something to help my experiments."

"I love secrets."

"Well, I got this dinosaur fossil online; I saved for three birthdays and Christmases. I know," he held up his hand as they passed beneath the shade of an elm tree. He smelled leaves and cut grass and roses, just now blooming, "It could have been bogus, but the dude used to be an archaeologist. It's small, but I got some great DNA samples. For cloning."

She chewed an errant strand of hair. "Cloning?"

Eddy stopped. "We're here." Their house had big bay windows and white paint, surrounded by sycamores and azaleas. Taped to the yellow front door was a note. He read it, sighed and handed it to Julia.

"Mijo,

Your Tia got in a little car accident. She's ok, but I'm at the hospital with her and Papi is with your little cousins. We'll be home when she's out.

I left your birthday present on your bed. Pizza money and cell in the kitchen. I wish we could be there on your special day, but time isn't always our friend.

Te amo,

Madre

PS: Please help with the Saturday crossword! It's killing me!!

Taped to the back was the crossword. Inside, he took his shoes off and motioned for Julia to do the same, brushing away her mumbled apologies. He ignored the pain in his chest. "It's not a big deal and besides," he continued as they went upstairs, "if they were around more, they'd find what I'm about to show you."

Outside his bedroom, he quickly marked the answers to the crossword with a pencil: Kumquat (genus Fortunella); Pagliacci (Sad clown) and once inside, he first positioned his dinosaur models *just so* and then showed Julia the experiments.

The perpetual motion Erector Set machine was beginning to fall apart beside his bed, his volcano with 1000 degree Fahrenheit lava barely bubbled anymore, and the less said about the rain forest inside his closet, the better. "These are amazing," Julia said, flicking the tiny, desiccated jungle that lay upon a tarp beneath his winter coats.

He muttered thanks and was beginning to regret inviting Julia home. He was about to invite her to leave when she saw the terrarium on his dresser and the vials of shaved dinosaur fossil beside it.

"What's in there?" She pounced over the small bed and tapped on the glass.

"That's William," he said, sitting on the mattress.

A small triangular head stuck its head out from beneath a fake palm tree. A thin neck, small feathered body skinny legs emerged. It, William, skittered to a small bowl filled with bird seed, snagged a few choice pieces and darted back into the safety of shadow.

Julia's flycatcher hung open. "That wasn't no lizard."

"Totally a lizard."

"It had *feathers*, Eddy."

Eddy shook his head, grabbed her hand and turned on the heat lamp above the terrarium. "I'm hungry," he said. He led her downstairs to the small, modern kitchen. As his mom said, pizza money was on the counter with a menu and cell phone. What she hadn't mentioned in the note was the ChemFit sitting beside it, a bow around it. "Happy birthday to me," he said.

"Oh neat," Julia said. "That must be the present you were talking about."

"I'll explain soon," he said with a grin and grabbed the cell phone. Julia nodded, picking at her cuticles.

Eddy ordered, feeling oddly electric, his eyes closing. He knew that his brain, if imaged, would be full of electrical impulses and neurotransmitter tidal waves. Thoughts of his stalled cloning experiment drifted away. Time as chemicals was an interesting notion … He closed his eyes as equations and covalent bonds danced in his mind.

After, Eddy said, "So, William is a lizard. But I was able to splice him, in the egg, with dinosaur DNA. I can't explain the science. My dad used to tell me about 'the zone' when he was a baseball player. Like, you get in this fog where everything makes sense and all your cells are working together? And you're capable of extraordinary. You know?"

Her head bobbed. "Like when I'm writing sometimes. Or when I'm batting and the baseball looks super big and I know I can't miss."

"I didn't know you played baseball." Eddy scratched his head. His dad wanted him to play, but Eddy thought smart kids didn't sport. "So I can't tell you exactly, because I was *in the zone*. I tried for months with this off brand chemistry set and failed over and over again. Failure and failure and then finally success."

"Like baseball." Julia grinned and offered Eddy the flat of her palm. He slapped it. "You can stop explaining. I get it." She turned her eyes. "What about that?"

Eddy opened the ChemFit and said, "This will get me to the next level." The set was basic, but high quality: glass pipettes, manuals, bottles of chemicals (Sulphur, ammonia).

Already lost in mental calisthenics, he started when the cell phone buzzed. "Hola."

"Eddy Vasquez?" a deep voice asked. "You just ordered a pizza?"

"Si?"

"I knew I remembered pizza." The deep voice sighed. "But what's the address?"

Julia mouthed at him, *who is that?*

Eddy put sunshine into his voice and mouthed *pizza man*. "36 Ash Street," he said.

"Of course. I'm a few houses down." Eddy grabbed the money and headed for the front door.

"There's no way the pizza's here already," Julia called.

Next to the door was a small white marble table, a pad of paper and pen on top. Humming, he grabbed and began sketching, trying to put the images in his head on paper.

Dad's favorite story was when he graduated to Triple A ball. His first game for the Grizzlies, he was so in the zone it was like, 'running through magic.' Eddy never understood it until William. Now, he was seconds away from being in the throes of it again. Atoms touched atoms on the page and chemical formulae appeared in margins.

When the doorbell rang, Eddy yanked the door open and blinked at the still-bright day. "What?" he asked, shoving the drawing into his back pocket.

"Evening, Eddy," a tall man said. Dressed in dirty khakis and a ratty t-shirt, he had hairy arms and a pot belly. Bald except for grey fuzz beneath his ears, he resembled a sad version of Eddy's father. In one hand, he held a carrier, large enough for a cat.

"Where's the pizza?"

"I don't work for Pizza Town, Eddy."

Eddy's hand tensed on the door. "How did you know my name?"

The man removed a folded, yellow piece of paper from his own back pocket. "Look at this," he said. "Look because it's your birthday, Tomas Edison Vasquez. Because I know you're curious and you won't let anything get in the way of that curiosity." The man hoisted the carrying case.

Eddy's neck heated. What could this be about? He took the paper.

It had a drawing and notes in the margins. He bit his lip, reached into his back pocket. His was only a sketch, the margins free of notes but at the top, he'd scrawled his name out of habit. The two papers were otherwise identical.

"Who are you?" Eddy whispered.

"Tomas Edison Vasquez. People call me Tomas these days." He invited Eddy to look inside the case. A feathered face stared back at him, talons scrabbling against plastic. Eddy blinked and saw the man's hand extended. He shook it. The man's palms were covered in sweat. "I'm Eddy from the future."

His brain shook. "Happy birthday?"

"Happy birthday. Now, let's go inside and talk about time travel."

After Tomas had used the bathroom and gone to see "our little dinosaur cloning experiment," they sat in the small dining room drinking: Eddy, a glass of juice, Tomas a beer. Julia sat between them at the walnut table, poking her finger through the grate of the carrier at the dinosaur. From time to time she muttered, "wow," and shook her head.

"Tomas" mumbled and stared at the ChemFit, then finished the beer, belched and grabbed another from the fridge. Dad always had a six pack on hand but Eddy had never seen him drunk. Tomas drank fast, his prominent Adam's apple bobbing. His skin was fish-belly white, his eyes bloodshot and streaked yellow. He smelled unwashed and sour.

Still, Eddy saw that their slender fingers, hooked nose, slightly pointed ears were all the same. Tomas was Eddy, no doubt, but an Eddy who grew up hard.

When Tomas hiccupped and wiped his nose with the back of his hand, Eddy realized why he wasn't scared. Tomas was pathetic, not frightening. It was disappointing; like any boy, Eddy *knew* that he was destined for greatness. "Why are you here?"

"You're direct." Tomas laughed, hard and bitter. Tomas twirled the pipette and the bottle of Sulphur, then lay them flat on his drawing of equations and formulae and took another draught. "I spent forty years on this paper. Dropped out of high school." He pointed at Eddy. "You know how you're friendless?"

"Um, I'm right here," Julia mumbled, her attention focused on the small dinosaur.

Tomas seemed to dismiss Julia. "I had no friends. After high school, I had less than no friends. All so I could work on time travel."

Eddy's belly flipped in excitement.

Tomas tapped the picture and scratched his pot belly. "I'd explain it all, but you wouldn't understand. You're a genius, but you're a kid. You need to study and read a bit more, but not as much as me. That's all I did for my whole life." He belched again and Eddy recoiled. "I know what you think. I'm ugly. I smell. I've been alone since mom and dad died."

"What?" Eddy blanched.

Tomas waved his hand. "Old people die, Eddy." He withdrew a roll of papers from his pocket. "These papers contain the answer to every question you'll ever have. Every problem that took a year to solve, every mistake that took months to fix."

"Why are you giving this to me? And what about the *dinosaur?*" Eddy whispered the last part as the creature chirped. He couldn't believe it was even here. It was so much more advanced than William.

Tomas waved his hand. "Forget the dinosaur. I'm giving you this because it saves wasted time. I want my childhood back. I want to prove I'm not a loser. And I can't," He grunted and finished the beer. "But you can. What's time travel for but to change the future? It all starts here," he said, tapping the ChemFit, "Everything proceeds apace."

Tomas stood and thrust the stack of notes into his hands. "Happy birthday. Read it." His eyes were liquid. He loomed over Eddy, casting a shadow from the fluorescent lights overhead. Julia murmured, but she was too absorbed to do more than that.

Eddy let curiosity take over. The handwriting was nearly illegible.

The first thing to do is think about time not as a river, but as a series of unconnected moments, bound together like islands in a sea of chemicals. Pick a chemical and cause the ripple. It's a simple thing to jump in! This is all theoretical nonsense of course. But the answer is there I must think more of this, get the right chemicals ...

He looked up. It was what he'd been thinking earlier. He'd vanished. Eddy's throat seized. Tomas was gone, like he'd never been there at all. "Where's Tomas?" Eddy blinked and shuffled the papers.

Julia shrugged. "No idea. I've been hanging out with Mortimer here."

"Who?"

"The dinosaur." She nudged the cage. It was currently sniffing her fingers. In the light, closer, Eddy could see that its feathers were brown and gold, tufted spikes, long talons on its paws.

"I guess I didn't see him leave."

"You're always distracted." She chuckled; Eddy liked that her dark eyes danced, mischievous. "Is Tomas your uncle or something?"

"I guess you could say he's a close relative." If Julia hadn't been talking about it, if the dinosaur wasn't there, he'd think he was going crazy. A quick glance around the kitchen and the white walls swayed. The papers burned in his hand. Someone knocked at the door. "Be right back." While he walked, he glanced through the notes. The equations, questions, diagrams, they set off detonations of insight. "This is what it's like," he whispered, "to know the future."

Eddy yanked the door open and thrust the money at the tall, good-looking man in the black suit who was standing there holding a pizza.

"Hey Eddy," Tomas said, holding the pizza. "I paid the driver. Why don't you step aside and we'll chow down?" Puzzled, shocked, Eddy let Tomas in, his heart pumping.

Where before Tomas had a belly, now he was toned, his shoulders broad. His hair was still sparse but it was manicured and clean instead of doing the mad scientist thing. His dark, pin-stripe suit and red silk tie looked expensive. Evidently just reading the notes had changed the future. Eddy said so.

Tomas-two dabbed a pizza slice with a napkin. "Life is much easier with a crib sheet. I came here today because I remembered my older self coming when I was you. It's confusing, I know, but I had to come *because I already came.* And believe me, I wouldn't be here otherwise. This place," he sniffed, "is the kind of hovel I avoid. And your little friend is the kind of person I stopped seeing long ago." New-Tomas's voice was strangely accented, like he held his nose.

Julia had put Mortimer under the table, away from Tomas-Two. While she also had a slice in her hand, she kept her eyes focused. Eddy didn't blame her; he didn't much care for Tomas-Two's sneer. "What about mom and dad?"

Tomas-Two shrugged. "Last I heard they lived in Wisconsin with sis."

Julia said, "You have a sister?"

"Don't interject, honey," Tomas-two said, "men are talking. As for our sister, she's a person. Boring. Her kids too. I haven't even met the last one." He checked his watch, a shiny gold Rolex.

Sister? Tomas-two was so arrogant. Was this the kind of man he'd become if he didn't work hard? He hadn't much cared for the pathetic Tomas-One, but this? Eddy dropped his slice into the box. "What did you want to tell me?"

Tomas-Two rapped the wooden table with a diamond thumb-ring and tossed something. "Catch."

Eddy inspected it. "A wallet?"

Tomas-Two smirked and rose, stopping to touch the ChemFit, a half-smile on his face. "I love this thing." Eddy followed him to the front door, turning and holding up his hands to Julia.

Parked partially on the curb was a black BMW. "Enjoy the wallet. Use it for your fifteenth birthday; you'll know why." He drove away, techno music blasting from open windows.

"That guy looked a lot like Tomas." Julia said. She had the carrier back on the table and frowned inside. Eddy rounded the table and looked over her shoulder. Mortimer was now a dark red.

"He's also kind of my uncle?"

"He's a jerk," she said. Distantly, muffled by sycamores, they heard the BMW roar away. Julia rolled her eyes. She grabbed another slice of pizza.

Julia ate while he inspected everything. Beside the ChemFit was Tomas-One's notes; on top of those, Eddy put the wallet from Tomas-Two. Inside were dozens of hundred dollar bills.

"Kind of a strange birthday haul?"

"My family's kind of-" There was another knock at the door. "Wait here."

A tall, bald, one-armed man in a brilliant white suit with a heavy gold crucifix around his neck stood outside. Tomas-Three dropped another crucifix into Eddy's outstretched palm. As he opened his mouth to speak, eyes pained, Eddy slammed the door shut.

Julia looked up from the carrier. "New present?"

The crucifix joined the wallet. "It's hard to explain."

She shook her head and reached into the collar of her shirt to remove a thin cross. "I have one too." Julia scratched her head and looked at Mortimer. "Is it my imagination, or are you growing?" The dinosaur was now almost too big for the carrier.

Eddy was about to speak when the knocking resumed. He glared over his shoulder. The knocking intensified, so hard that the door rattled in its frame.

Julia stood. "Should we see what it is?"

"Wait," he said, dashing away. He peeked out of the front window. There was another Tomas. Eddy knew that if he opened the door, this Tomas would walk in and there would be some new sadness. Tomas-four was painfully thin and ground his teeth, eyes puffy and red. Eddy didn't want to open the door.

He ran back to Julia "C'mon," he said, gathering his 'presents.' He thought about the pathetic version Tomas-One and the mean Tomas-Two. Was his future set in stone? "Can you grab Mortimer?"

They walked through the kitchen and outside. The back yard was a simple ten by ten space with a lonely chestnut in one corner. They set their loads on the granite patio.

"What are you going to do?"

"*We're*," he emphasized the word, "going to experiment. If you want."

Julia squatted beside him. "What kind?" Light freckles spotted her cheeks.

"Do you know how to make acid?" She shook her head. "You want to learn?"

"Heck yeah."

They spent the next few minutes mixing chemicals in pipettes. Occasionally they heard knocking, but they ignored it, talking quietly, the sun beating on their backs. Soon enough, a pipette was ready for action. Eddy proffered it. "Do the honors?"

She had one finger through the mesh carrier and Mortimer was licking it. She rolled her eyes. "Just get on with it, dude." He took a deep breath and said, "Can we pretend that time travel is real and there's a real dinosaur before us? And can we pretend that I got a glimpse of the future?"

"We have a dinosaur beside us, so I think I can pretend."

"Can we also pretend that I'm not very good at friends and maybe we can be friends?"

"I'm not either and we can totally be friends." She pushed him. "Go on already."

Mindful of spills, he poured the acid out. The crucifix sizzled, tarnishing and warping. The wallet hissed, a large hole widening in the leather. The notes were last, curling into itself in a flash. All told, it took thirty seconds.

The ChemFit, he decided, he'd keep.

A bird chirped in the distance. The wind blew remnants away. Julia laughed. "That was unimpressive. Fun though. And the knocking stopped too." She jumped. "Where did Mortimer go?"

The carrier was gone. "Maybe pretend he was never here?"

Julia's chin wavered, but she nodded. "Let's go back inside."

He ran his hands under water. He wondered about time paradoxes; if he never invented anything, could Tomas have come back and given the notes?

Julia interrupted his reverie. "Your birthdays like this a lot?"

"Gosh, no. Let's talk about you though. What do you like to talk about?"

Julia rushed to answer. "Can we go look at William again? I've been into dinosaurs since I saw *Jurassic Park* when I was a kid. And I miss Mortimer."

Grinning, he led the way back to his room. "Before William, none of my experiments worked. I didn't have much hope that the ChemFit would help, but now? Now all I need is a centrifuge. I made a crappy one from binoculars and walkie-talkies, but I need a real one."

She raised an eyebrow. "That's a spinny thingy?"

"For blood. The crappy one is how I got William. But it broke."

Eddy's mind wandered at his bedroom door. He imagined a series of equations and a diagram of linked molecules. He thought he heard something, a faint knock.

"What's up?" Julia asked.

"Nothing." He glanced outside the window above his dresser at the peaceful street. There was a car parked out front, a plain white van. A squirrel dropped an acorn dropped from a branch and chattered at nothing.

The image of linked molecules filled his head again. He reached into the terrarium and grabbed William. She punched his arm. "Let me hold him."

Outside, a large man emerged. He had evidently been knocking at the front door. He held a leash in one hand, though Eddy couldn't see what was at the end of it. Instead, he met the large man's gaze. It was Tomas. This Tomas looked, not happy, but content. He was a little dirty, a little disheveled. He waved.

The images in Eddy's head bounced, demanding attention. But he watched as Tomas shrugged and tugged on the leash. A small, feathered animal padded into view. It had an oblong head and claws on its bird-like feet. It looked like Mortimer, only much larger.

Julia noticed none of this; she faced away from the window, holding William. "I like your models, too," she said, pointing at the T-Rex. "I have one like it. Also, where's that centr-thing? The broken one."

Eddy knew—he intuited—that he had a choice. The new Tomas might be happier than all the others because he, Eddy, had changed the future, by letting someone into his life. But the Tomas out there, the one who had invented time travel and had a pet dinosaur didn't seem *happy*. His eyes were bleary, his clothes unwashed. He still seemed like a man who let life go for his science. Did Eddy want that?

He took a breath and shook his head at Tomas, turning his gaze to Julia fully and banishing the equations. He made his choice. One day he'd have time for science, but not today. He showed Julia the pieces of the broken centrifuge and told her about the barriers to cloning.

"You really think you can clone them?" she asked. "Like Mortimer?"

Eddy nodded. He knew he could. A few minutes later, when he stood to get them both a glass of water, there was no one outside. For all intents and purposes, there never was.

M is for Mentation

KV Taylor

Stomped ants littered the cement front stoop. Weeds sprouted from cracks on the sidewalk below, some temporarily flattened by the same boot that had squished the ants. The weeds would spring back. Unlike the ants.

Judy examined the bugs, wondering what had brought them to this unfortunate doorstep. A search for food, probably. Everything in the wild seemed to boil down to the search for food—fuel for life. Some nights, Judy could understand that. When she did the bad thing (that she didn't think was bad), Dad made her go a whole day without food. Sometimes longer. It was easy to lose track since Dad had nailed the plywood over her window. She'd loosened a corner so she could peek, but it wasn't enough.

Judy turned her face to the sun. The tiny trailers and scrubby, scorched earth beyond disappeared, leaving just her and the clear, blue sky. The light warmed her skin. Also fuel for life.

Poor ants. She shouldn't think about it or the bad thing might happen but it wasn't fair—they'd only been trying to exist. All the warmth bled out of her suddenly, and Judy sighed. When she looked down, the ants were scurrying busily around.

"Judy!"

She winced at the sound of Dad's voice, harsh and cold as a winter night.

"You want dinner, get in here!"

Judy stood, careful of the ants, and entered the trailer. The screen door smacked behind her, the linoleum floors squeaked, and a loose bit caught on her pink Velcro sandal. A cockroach escaped from beneath the tile, skittering toward the kitchen table.

Dad's workbook crushed it. "Goddamn creepy-crawlers. Whole place is infested."

Judy didn't look up past his knees. She never did, if she could help it. His eyes were always full of fear that turned to hate because he liked to kill and she liked things to live, and she was better at hers than he was at his.

Dad moved to the counter to grab the loaf of white bread with a clown face on it. Judy thought hard, what little warmth she'd regained since bringing the ants back dissipated and the formerly crushed cockroach stood and skittered away.

Dad paused, loaf in hand and the tops of his ears turned pink.

She prepared herself with a deep breath. It felt like her heart was going too fast, like it'd explode and send blood shooting everywhere. *Run, little bug, run.*

Dad turned slowly, movements controlled, but his knuckles were white, fingers crushing into the bread like a soft toy. "Where's the creeper?"

Judy fixed her gaze to the table.

Dad threw the bread; it hit the wall with a dull *fwap* and a crinkle of plastic, then bounced to the table. Dad took two steps in the direction of the torn linoleum, then squatted to examine it.

He had three days of stubble and black circles under his eyes. The whites were going yellow day by day, yellow like the whisky in his plastic jugs. They were darker than last time Judy had looked at them, maybe two weeks ago.

"You done it again," Dad said, then gave a little, animal growl. "You done the bad thing."

"It's not bad," said Judy under her breath.

"What?" Dad stood to his full height, looming in the tiny kitchenette.

"It's. Not. Bad." Judy enunciated each word as if she feared being misunderstood. She guessed she did. Dad was ignorant as hell. He was supposed to be home-schooling her, but Judy had learned everything she knew from old books and encyclopedias and the tiny lending library he took her to twice a month.

He made sure Mrs. Peacock, the old lady who ran the library, never talked to her. It had been three years since Judy had really talked to *anyone* but Dad. Since Mom died in the bath tub. (Judy hadn't tried to bring her back. Mom had begged her not to, in the note.)

Judy was only nine, with no friends and old books, and she knew more than Dad. That wasn't saying a lot, but it was enough to know that what she could do was the opposite of bad.

Dad turned red. "Get. Get, you Devil-child! Get to your room! Go before I introduce you to your real father!"

Judy got.

She shut the door to her tiny room quietly, since slamming it made the whole trailer shake, which made Dad angry. She leaned against the door, under the silhouette of a crucifix. After Mom died, taking her endless prayers with her, Dad had burned all the crucifixes and the pictures of white men with long beards praying. That much, at least, had been nice.

But it was obvious that Dad was her 'real father'. Not the Devil. That was just something Dad used to say to hurt Mom, and now said to try and hurt her. Even though it never worked. She'd rather her father was the Devil; he couldn't be much worse than Dad.

Judy slid down to sit on the floor and reached for a well-worn book about the fall of the Roman Empire. Her stomach grumbled as the heat returned to her middle once more, then spread through her limbs. She wanted the sun—it was summer, so it would still be up for a few hours.

Unfortunately, so would Dad.

Thunder rumbled overhead when Judy woke, still on the floor, book on her belly. She crawled to her window and pried loose the plywood; it was dark, now, but a flash of lightning lit up the barren landscape, all the way to the hills. She counted the seconds between the flash and the sound: *one Mississippi, two Mississippi, three—*

Crash.

The plywood wiggled. No screen, no glass—why bother when the wood was there? Now, Judy was glad for it. A wild idea came to her, and she wiggled the wood some more, loosening it as much as she could. When it wouldn't budge any more, she waited for another flash of light. Then, *one Mississippi, two Mississippi, three—*And she shoved as hard and sudden as she could.

The rumble of thunder covered the sound of the nails releasing and the plywood hitting the ground. Rain started falling outside.

Judy grabbed her raincoat, stuffed some books into a backpack she'd never used before, and jumped out the window.

The rain stopped after just a few minutes, and Judy moved fast to put the trailer town behind her and make her way into the hills. They were bleak, but Judy saw promise in them. Safety. She'd have to start her own search for food, but at least there wouldn't be the stupid bread with the clown face on it, anymore and if she didn't eat, it was because she didn't have food, not because Dad was being horrible again.

The clouds blew over fast, leaving starlight to keep her on her feet. Once she came to the rockier spots, though, she nearly fell and twisted her ankle—so she decided to wait for morning. She hunkered down between some oddly shaped crags and closed her eyes.

When she opened them again, it was warmer and the air was as dry as ever. Judy pushed herself up out of her sleeping crag and looked around. The rocks were strange and pale, not rock-like at all in shape. The one she'd leaned against was flat and hard, and long pieces jutted upward in rows nearby, like giant, ancient fingers clawing their way out of the earth, toward the sky.

Judy rubbed the sleep from her eyes and stood, backpack at her feet, then did a slow turn. The long rocks *were* a ribcage, they had to be. After a few long turns, taking in the rocky hills bleaching in morning sunlight, things became a little clearer: the long rocks weren't fingers, they were ribs. Huge ribs in two rows, broken off here and there, chipped and petrified.

Judy hit her knees and pulled her animal handbook out of her pack. She spent awhile looking for anything in the Dakotas that could be that big, but there was nothing. And anyhow, shouldn't bones be white? That time when Mom's arm broke after that fight with Dad, the piece that split out was bright white, glistening. Seeing it had made Judy throw up.

Seeing these big, old bones just made Judy feel... warm. Good, inside. Or like she could *do* something good. For the bones. For herself.

Judy smiled and focused on the bones. She'd managed it with a half-decomposed raccoon, once. Why not something all-the-way decomposed—and maybe a little petrified? It was weird, not knowing for sure what the animal was supposed to look like, but if the bones were rocky like this, it had to be *really* old. Dinosaur old.

Even though the sun beat down hot and hard, the warmth bled out of Judy's body. The ground beneath her shook, but she stayed on her knees. The flat bone she'd rested against all night propped her up as she swayed with power.

Ed woke just after noon, head throbbing, feeling like the room was shaking. Goddamn bottom shelf plastic bottle hooch wasn't what it used to be. He staggered to Judy's room.

He poked his trusty alun wrench into the keyhole and swung the door open just as the house gave a *big* shake. He hit his knees and fiery pain shot up through it and into his hip, sobering him unpleasantly. He swore in a long string, one hand on the door jamb. It vibrated.

He couldn't stand, his knee was frozen with pain, and the brat must've been hiding in her closet again. The bed was made, the room immaculate. Little freak got that from her mother, too. "Judy!" Ed shouted. "Judy, get over here and help me or I swear to god, I'll—"

With a deafening crack, the roof flew off the trailer and hot sunlight spilled in, blinding him. All he could see was a huge shadow above surrounded by a blur of brightness, like something heavenly and terrible.

"This is for Mom... but mostly all those ants." Judy sounded faraway.

Ed rubbed at his eyes and the shape hovering above his home came into focus: a giant skull, like the T-Rex at the museum when he was a kid. And then a huge, clawed foot kicked through what was left of Judy's window. And the world exploded in hot pain just before it faded forever.

N is for Necromancy

Amanda C. Davis

The air in Hazel's apparatus smelled like sweat and the stale city and her own fast breath. She clung to Zig's hand. Around them, the Machine whirred and hummed and then fell still. The fog lifted. Out from the mist rolled the jungle: the dense tropical swatch that would form all of everything from its air and water and molecules. She had known to expect jungle—she had known to expect *big*—but this place swallowed her whole.

"Did we make it?" said Hazel meekly.

Zig rubbed some condensate from a dial, frowning. "Close. Doesn't matter. It's close enough." He stood, dropping her hand. In two steps his feet crunched onto the undergrowth and sank into a young, spongy earth.

"Lana's mom said it could get us within a second," said Hazel, scrambling after him. "A microsecond. Hey—how much did it miss by? Cause it doesn't matter *this* way but—"

"Don't worry about it," said Zig. He pulled a machete and began to hack a path in the green barrier that cradled them like a basket.

The humidity sucked them deeper. Hazel stayed close behind Zig, trying to see it all at once. Zig forged ahead without paying attention to the fronds scraping his jumpsuit, let alone to her. Every time his boots crunched, she winced, and looked for butterflies in his footprint.

"We shouldn't have to go far," she said—whispered, really. She felt very small and her voice shrank to match. "Lana's mom says there'll be bugs everywhere."

Zig made a low, pleased growl in his throat. Hazel struggled through moss and ferns to his side. Against a rooty overhang nestled about twenty or thirty eggs, each bigger than Hazel's hand, in roughly concentric circles.

"Perfect," said Zig.

He sheathed the machete. With a vicious grin over his shoulder at Hazel, he sent the composite tip of his boot into the closest egg.

It crunched like candy. Thick milk welled out of the cracks, mixed with gummy clear albumen and spindles of blood. An embryo flopped into the puddle of prebirth, trailing gooey strands. Hazel could tell what it was trying to do, what it would be doing if it had been formed and born. The struggle broke her heart.

"That's enough," said Hazel. Her nerves screamed up her back and into her shoulders—it should be dead! Why did she have to watch it twitch and die? "You only have to do one little thing, right? Lana's mom says then everything afterward—"

Zig stomped on the next egg.

Hazel flinched. Pieces of shell and little crushed limbs followed his boot to the next egg.

"Stop it," she hissed. "That's *enough*."

"Got to be sure," growled Zig. He crunched on to the next egg. With a wicked mischievousness, he jumped and landed with both feet at once. The sprawl of embryos shivered in his path. He pulled his machete and began whacking at the rest of the eggs like a hatchet, spinning in place, raining carnage.

"Stop!" said Hazel.

Zig looked up sharply. He drew his gun.

She staggered, seeing things in his face she hadn't seen in the camp, but that she should have known were there. He aimed past her and fired. An unearthly shrieking squawk shook the leaves of the fern; something fast, something half-feathery, something *big* crashed away. And Hazel remembered what to be afraid of.

"Zig," she said. "Time to go."

Zig stomped a last egg. "Then go."

"Zig."

He fired into the air. This time a long, sonorous trumpet replied. Thunder calling to thunder. The rustling of the jungle resolved into purposeful thuds, in steady time, coalescing and approaching.

Hazel backed away. She turned and, following the torn-up trail, ran to the Machine.

It was gone.

"Zig!" A shriek, almost not his name. She turned and collided with his back—he had both machete and gun extended toward the ravaged nest. Toward the trumpet, the thunder. "Zig!"

"Get ready," said Zig. He had not always looked so dead in the eyes, so alive in the cheeks.

Hazel grappled out her gun. She fumbled with the safety, and it seemed so *small*—the gun and the safety and her hands, all of it insectine under the looming trees. The same world she'd left, the same air and water and molecules—but this one was green, and so old, and it wasn't going to turn into the same world now, was it? Her world had built a Machine...

"We broke it," she said.

"It was already broken," said Zig. "Maybe next time we'll do better. Maybe we got all us dumb monkeys out of the way somebody smarter can try. Get ready."

The safety clicked. She put her back to Zig. She felt sick and dizzy, exhilarated, like jumping off a cliff, watching the rocks grow and sharpen below.

A butterfly flickered across the barrel of her gun. She stopped herself from firing. "Next time," she told the butterfly. "Do better."

Shadows fell over Hazel from behind. Zig opened fire.

Hazel turned and finished shattering the world.

O is for Open Season

Beth Cato

The moms retreated with chatter about coffee and TV shows, leaving Carmen to face her cousin Reina, two strange neighborhood girls, and a translucent rainbow-flickering velociraptor.

"We're going to play house," announced Reina. Carmen opened her mouth to speak but Reina cut her off with a slash of her hand. "No, we're not playing with you. You're just here. You can go play with your pet *dinosaur*."

One of the other girls giggled. "You have an imaginary friend? You're like my age, right? Nine?"

"Maybe Carmen should play the baby!" said the other girl. All three laughed.

"You're at a disadvantage here, Carmen," said Vincent. His voice reminded her of the ice cream-thick tones of Vincent Price, which was why she had dubbed him Vincent when she was about three years old; her mom's year-round favorite song was the old Michael Jackson tune "Thriller," and Vincent's lines were the best part of the whole thing. Carmen could barely remember a time before the dinosaur had attached himself to her. "Reina has already made up her mind. You must learn diplomacy and tact, and when you must concede defeat. You cannot win here."

Carmen flushed as she granted the shimmering velociraptor a tiny nod to acknowledge she had heard him. She should never have told Reina about him years ago, but as Vincent frequently pointed out, everything is a lesson.

She couldn't bear to think of how she would soon go blind and deaf to his presence. How was she going to get by on her own?

The girls whispered something in a little huddle and burst out in unabashedly cruel laughter. Carmen's fists balled.

"Go ahead and play house," she said. "Reina, why don't you pretend that your father didn't leave your mom for his secretary?" The words slipped out, cold and sharp, and Carmen turned away before she could see Reina's gutted reaction as she stalked away.

"That," said Vincent, his clawed feet silent on the carpet, "Was uncouth and cruel, though relevant to the conversation."

Carmen slipped into the household library and leaned on the shut door, eyes closed. Shame formed a sick knot in her stomach. Reina hadn't deserved that. The girl's whole life was in turmoil. Her obsession with houses was what kept her going—playing like she had her own house, drawing house plans, going on home tours. On Saturday mornings, Reina watched *This Old House* on PBS the way most kids watched cartoons.

Carmen opened her eyes to take in the library. It looked worse now than it had only a few weeks before. Reina's father had removed about half the books. The remaining volumes leaned at hard angles or sat in haphazard stacks. Dr. Seuss mingled with law reference texts and stained Betty Crocker cookbooks.

Vincent walked around the room and inspected the shelves. His scaled hide was like a shifting rainbow—it was part of the illusion that hid him from the sight of most people and many animals. He could pass through furniture and walls, but he usually didn't—those actions had really bothered Carmen when she was very young.

It bothered her to look on him now, too. She could read whole book titles through him.

Vincent was quiet as he completed his circuit of the room. "You're not simply upset about Reina, are you?" He was like the Vulcans in Star Trek, in a way. Logical and cool. That was fine most of the time.

"You're getting fainter," she blurted out.

"Well, yes. We've talked about this before, Carmen. It's inevitable that my physical apparition will fade away, as will my voice. It's part of your brain maturation."

"I don't want my brain to mature that way. I don't want to question if you really *were* just an imaginary friend that I envisioned to cope with my 'genius.'" Carmen's lips turned in a snarl. Her mom had already dragged her to psychiatrists because of Vincent. Carmen had learned how to engage in more subtle conversations with him after that. "I might be smart, but I didn't learn quantum physics and the grammar structure of the Qaal'tath by age eight on my own."

Vincent sighed. He folded his long three-fingered hands together across his chest. "You're going to learn a great deal in the coming years without hearing my voice. You're not going to forget I existed. I simply won't matter as much. That's fine. You have proof of our conversations in your journals, even if you have no proof of *me*. No photographs, no video. No footprints. No other witnesses, as our other chosen ambassador children are scattered across the planet."

Carmen tried to memorize him as he was at that moment—as tall as her, his hide favoring shifts between yellow, turquoise, and magenta. Vincent was from the Kawlin race on a planet dubbed Vallia. His ship was traveling toward Earth and wouldn't arrive for another twenty years. His projection had formed the shape of a velociraptor because she had a thing for dinosaurs from an early age. His real form was much more alien.

Her fingers glanced the shelf and found Stephen Hawking's *Brief History of Time*. The binding was perfect, unread, unlike her copy at home with its bowed and whitened spine.

"What if I'm not ambassador material?" she whispered. "What if I don't make it through college?" That seemed appalling and unthinkable, since at nine she was already using independent study to work on high school material. "I might end up at McDonald's or something."

"Whatever you are, wherever you are, you are representative of your people," Vincent said, tone patient. "If you work for the United Nations, that is fine. If you are cooking French fries at McDonald's, that is fine. All work is relevant. Your brain and your imagination aren't bound by your employment or your degree of education. You know that. You don't judge other people that way."

"Maybe my faith in you isn't what scares me the most," she whispered. "Maybe it's that you shouldn't have faith in me."

"Ah, Carmen." Vincent looked on her as tenderly as a velociraptor could.

"How am I supposed to be a diplomat when I can't even make friends with other kids my own age? Everyone else seems so... stupid."

"That would have been an issue even if I hadn't attached myself to you. You're brilliant. You don't fit in. That is one benefit of me retreating from your life soon. Your brain has stored vast amounts of data to be tapped when the time is ripe, but you need to socially develop as well. I can't rush that."

"Socially develop." Carmen cringed at the memory of what she had said to Reina and how Vincent had chided her. She looked at the broad wooden desk in the center of the room. "Maybe I can start on that now."

She rummaged in the drawers to find a notepad and pen, and spent a few minutes at work. The weight of Vincent's curious gaze rested on her, but he didn't come close or question her actions. She folded up the sheet origami-style, the way other girls passed notes in school.

Carmen gave the library a final glance. She could easily, happily, pass the next hour in there reading. Cowering, really. But no. She couldn't. She might feel better for a while, but shame and misery would make her feel worse and worse, like an infection setting in.

She followed the girls' voices out the sliding door. Reina had a plastic playhouse angled to receive the full morning shade of the slatted patio. One of the neighbor girls pretended to water real flowers. She shot Carmen a glower, which she accepted with a nod.

"Mail delivery!" Carmen knocked on the hollow front door.

Giggles evaporated inside the playhouse. "Go away," snapped Reina.

"I'm sorry." Carmen put full meaning into the words. "I shouldn't have said that, no matter how much my feelings were hurt. It was mean of me." She pushed the letter through a mail slot. "Tear this up if you want to. I understand."

"I wish you wouldn't come to my house." Reina's voice was muffled.

"Yeah. It's stupid that our moms try to make us be friends when we don't even like each other. Maybe we can start to tolerate each other, though. Just to pass the hours."

"I hate you. Go away."

"Okay." Carmen was surprised at how Reina's words didn't hurt—maybe because she reciprocated the emotion. "I'll go over to the yard. At least it'll look like we're playing together." Carmen was yelled at a few visits back when she was caught in the library.

She retreated past the flower pots and began to walk, quietly naming each plant in Latin as she made her way around. Latin was the first language Vincent had taught her when she was little because it provided a good foundation for learning so many of Earth's languages—and some alien languages as well.

Vincent followed her like a rainbow ghost. How would she fall asleep without his gentle voice telling her stories of the Grand Horribleness of Hanahana or how light travels through space or of the chemical reactions in the brain that made fresh chocolate cookies taste so glorious?

Carmen waited until she was at the far edge of the yard until she spoke again. "Vincent, when you finally arrive on Earth, will you introduce yourself to me? The real you?"

She knew his people didn't outwardly promote individuality on their bodies. They believed in personality expressed through creative action.

"Of course." He sounded surprised. "I'm already tasked to lead your team."

"It will be odd to be with a you that isn't a velociraptor."

"I can regulate my voice to sound like this when I'm physically present."

Tears filled her eyes as she breathed in the perfume of *jasmine mesnyi*. "I'd like that. I'd like that a lot."

"I'm aware that this is akin to a cycle of grief, as if I'm dying—"

"It's worse than that, really," she whispered. "You'll still be there, but I'll be blind and deaf to your presence. I don't *want* to ignore you."

He was quiet for a moment. "I know. I won't hate you. I won't be disappointed in you, whatever happens. Even if you deny that I ever existed. Even if you burn your journals and try to forget all I have taught you. There are many other things to fear about the future, but don't fear that my feelings for you will change."

"Carmen?" Reina called. Carmen hurriedly pressed tears from her eyes before she turned. Her cousin stood at the edge of the lawn and held up the unfolded paper. "You drew that?"

Carmen nodded, still not trusting herself to speak.

"You did that here, just a while ago?"

"Yeah."

"Wow. This is... this is cool."

Carmen had drawn the full plan of Reina's house down to estimated square footages of rooms and the full backyard. It had been pretty easy compared to the fission drive schematics that Vincent had her working on all year.

"Well, I know you like houses, and I wasn't sure if you had actually seen a plan for your house, so I wanted to give it a try."

The other two girls lurked back by the playhouse, unsure of this change in relations.

Reina glanced at the paper. "This is more than a try. This is *good*. I can't even draw lines that straight on grid paper. Do you want to see my house plan magazines? I keep telling my mom that after she gets money out of Dad that we need to redesign the kitchen by removing the wall with the dining room. You could draw that. You *owe* me, for what you said." Her eyes narrowed.

Vincent stood off to one side, flickering hunter green, baby blue, and violet to an unheard rhythm. He laughed. "If you can succeed in diplomacy with young human children, you can engage in diplomacy with alien beings. They're not so different, really."

He gazed on her with what could only be described as pride, his lips parted in a toothy smile.

Vincent believed in her. She wanted to live up to his faith. She wanted to be everything his people believed she could be, everything humanity would need when first contact occurred in twenty years' time.

Carmen was destined to be an ambassador for humankind, but she could choose the kind of ambassador she could be. That began now.

She walked toward Reina. "Sure. Those house magazines sound fun. Do they show pictures of houses at the coast?"

"Yes! From California and all over, even log cabins. Come on, I'll show you, but don't you dare mess up the pages, okay?" Reina dashed toward the sliding door and waved the other girls to follow.

Carmen glanced back at Vincent. He flickered gold, turquoise, and pink as he trailed her. His clawed feet were soundless and trackless, yet bound to follow her, no matter her path.

P is for Pet

Lynn Hardaker

The summer promised to be an amazing one. It sure lied.

But at the time, John and I were totally looking forward to spending the summer holiday in the city in a big, old house. Without our father and our stepmother.

Neither of us wanted to be at home that summer. And we weren't particularly wanted there. Our stepmother's baby was due part way through July, and she hadn't exactly been subtle about wanting to enjoy the time. Just the three of them.

Our mother died when I was six. John was three. He doesn't remember her at all. Two years ago, father married again. She never really took to us and things started to change at home pretty much from the start. She pulled father away from us. Of course, he's every bit as much to blame: he let it happen. Too easily. Soon it was clear that Father and she were one family, and John and I were another. The baby would balance things out: it against the memories of our mother.

The other thing I had been dreading about the summer was that my best friend, Zeenat, had just moved away. So unfair. And on the last day of grade eight too, meaning we didn't get to spend any holiday time together.

Anyway, off we went to Uncle Mitch's for the summer.

I should mention, he's not our real uncle, just an old friend of father's. They're both stupidly old fashioned about kids calling grownups by their first name, so, Uncle Mitch he was. He had no kids. No partner. Father had known him for years, although they didn't see each other very often and John and I had only met him a couple of times, and never in his home.

The house. Well, it's pretty amazing. It's old, made of red brick, with a peaked roof and even a turret. Just like out of a book. When he dropped us off, John and I ran from our father's car as though a starter's pistol had gone off and stood side by side in front of the door. I let him ring the bell. I wanted to put my arm around his shoulder—I often found myself wanting to make motherly gestures to John—but knew that would embarrass him.

John.

What happened to him wasn't my fault.

How many more times do I have to say that before I begin to believe it?

Alright. Back to the summer.

As soon as our father's car drove off, Uncle Mitch took us on a tour of the place. From his study at the very top, which was a small room with a tiny window to the street, to the living room on the ground floor.

He didn't say much as he showed us around, just enough to let us know which rooms we'd be sleeping in and where the bathroom was. It was an old fashioned bathroom with tiny black and white tiles on the floor and walls, and a huge tub with clawed feet. No shower.

Many of the rooms were mostly empty, except for maybe a small writing desk, or an armchair and Uncle Mitch said we were free to explore them. It was sort of like The Lion, The Witch, and The Wardrobe. I was so excited.

As we headed to the living room for the first time, he asked us a bit about ourselves and we answered politely, but not too enthusiastically. He was practically a stranger to us.

The living room was incredible. The walls were wrapped in built-in shelves full of books: heaven for a bookworm like me. There were a couple of old fashioned armchairs and a sofa, two small round wooden tables with what looked like African violets on them. Off to one side was a table with a large terrarium on it, the kind you keep lizards in. John, being a twelve-year-old dinosaur-and-lizard-freak, went right over to it.

The terrarium had pieces of driftwood and slabs of slate in place to create caves and crevices where a creature might hide.

"What's in it?" John asked. I recognized the excitement in his voice.

"What's your favourite type of lizard?" Uncle Mitch asked.

"Bearded Dragon. By far."

He'd been bugging our father for one for ages, but our stepmother had said no way. Too much like dinosaurs, which she was afraid of. Which is exactly what John liked about them. One time he brought home a live chicken from a friend's farm and let it run around the house. He told her that he decided to have a chicken for pet since they were an even closer relative of dinosaurs. He was grounded for a week, but we agreed that it was totally worth it.

John and Uncle Mitch stared in through the front panel of glass.

"Take a look."

Slowly, a Bearded Dragon walked out from the slate cave. John smiled an insanely huge smile. I had to smile too. Perhaps our father had told Uncle Mitch. And in that moment, I felt slightly guilty for the nasty things I'd been thinking of him for, well, for a long time.

I should have known.

"Would you like to feed it?" Uncle Mitch asked John.

John nodded and took the small tub of live crickets handed to him.

"Drop his prey out of reach so that he has to hunt for it," Uncle Mitch said. John dropped one in.

"Give him another one. He hasn't eaten for a while."

I turned in time to see Uncle Mitch's smile. It made me feel suddenly cold. He met my eye.

"I'll just go and take care of dinner now," he said and left the room in a hurry.

On that first night, we sat around the oval dining room table eating the Chinese food he'd ordered in. It was all fairly formal with upholstered wooden chairs and linen serviettes, which looked silly with the steaming aluminum and Styrofoam food containers. It was awkward, but at least the food was good, and I wondered whether maybe our father had told him that Chinese food was our favourite.

John nibbled on an egg roll. Uncle Mitch spoke, but in that forced way that people who aren't used to being around kids speak to them. His voice got higher and his mouth bent into a fake sort of a smile. Like he was trying too hard.

He asked us questions. Stupid ones, mostly. What's your favourite book? Favourite colour? Type of music? As though kids are just buckets full of favourite things.

Still, there we were. Away from father and our stepmother and whatever little troll-baby they were about to bring into the world. We had more books than I'd ever seen outside of a library, and a Bearded Lizard for John. Chinese food for dinner. And Uncle Mitch didn't even say when we had to go to bed.

We went to bed early, anyway. I think we were exhausted by the newness of everything.

John wanted to sleep in my bed that night. For once, I let him.

"This is like a dream," he said with a sleepy, smiley voice.

'Yes.'

I was relieved that he was happy. He'd been upset for months, ever since our stepmother announced that she was going to have a baby. Not that he told anyone how he felt. But I knew. The feeling that we'd lost our father as well as our mother was harder on him than it was on me. I'm the big sister. I have to be strong for him. To look out for him. That's how it should be.

That's how it wasn't.

Stop, stop, stop, stop, stop.

The next couple of weeks were good. The only time that I felt uneasy was when Uncle Mitch was with us. Luckily, he spent a most of his time up in his study.

Before arriving, I'd had all these plans for spending my time wandering the city: going to Ontario Place, exploring downtown, maybe even going up the CN Tower. But once there, I lost interest in all of that. At the time, I thought it was just because we were staying in the coolest house I'd ever been in. And in a way I was right.

John and I spent most of our time in the living room. I spent hours looking through the books, reading their spines, pulling one down. It was strange. On that first day there, I looked at the books for one that sounded interesting. At first none did; they were mostly old historical books about the kings and queens of Europe. Not my thing. But then as soon as I'd think of a particular book or topic, I'd suddenly find a shelf full of books I wanted to read. It was funny, the books seemed to appear according to my wishes, but what was funnier was that I didn't think there was anything strange about it at the time.

Just as there was nothing strange about the Bearded Lizard.

Or, about what was to come.

So, I'd spend my time sitting cross legged in one of the armchairs with a book, and John would spend his time with the lizard, watching it and feeding it live prey from the plastic box.

It's strange. I'd never been squeamish about things like that, but as I watched him, day after day, dropping the helpless crickets into the terrarium, seeing them sit there, startled and waiting for the lizard to hunt them down, I started to get to me.

I'd hear the crunching once they were caught. I hated it. I'd sit in the chair with my fingers in my ears until they were done.

A couple of weeks later I woke up in the middle of the night. John was still sharing a bed with me and I realized that he wasn't there. I assumed he'd gone to the bathroom down the hall, so I closed my eyes again and fell asleep. When I woke up next, sunlight was shining in and John was next to me, sleeping. I didn't think any more of it.

Until the next time.

That was a couple of nights later. I awoke again to find him gone. This time, since I had to pee anyway, I went down the hall to the bathroom. Only he wasn't there. A tickle of fear went through me. When I'd finished in the bathroom, I went downstairs to the living room thinking maybe he was there watching or feeding the lizard, although I had noticed that he'd been spending less time with it over the past couple of days.

I opened the living room door. He wasn't in there either. My bones felt like they'd turned to ice. Where was he?

I went back upstairs and looked into my room. He was lying on the bed. I went in, shutting the door behind me. Quietly, I walked over to the bed. John was breathing the deep, regular breaths of someone sleeping. Or - I was convinced - of someone pretending to be sleeping.

"John," I whispered. I noticed a slight tension in his body. "John," I said again.

He turned and groaned and played the part of someone waking from a deep sleep.

"Wha—what?" He opened his eyes.

"Where were you just now?"

"What do you —"

I smacked his arm. Hard.

"Ow! What's that for?"

"Where were you?" I demanded.

He didn't say anything. I was so angry I couldn't speak. I crawled under the covers. He kept quiet. So did I. My anger was irrational, I knew that even at the time, but I couldn't help it.

With our backs to each other, we eventually fell asleep again.

The next day, as he and I ate our Cornflakes alone in the dining room, I asked him where he'd been in the night. His hesitation was slight, but I knew he was preparing to tell me a lie.

"Sleepwalking. It was so weird, Margaret. I woke up standing in the hallway in front of our room. Crazy, eh?"

John had always been a good sleeper. I'd envied that about him. I poured more milk over my cereal and attacked it with my spoon.

The next couple of days were fairly uneventful, though I was starting to get tired of Chinese food; something I never would have thought possible. I tried to ask John again about that night, but he continued to play dumb. That was what angered me the most. John and I had been a team for years. We'd had only each other, and now, now he was turning away from me, keeping secrets from me, lying to me.

I spent my time immersed in my books. Meanwhile, John spent some of his time with the lizard, but more and more, he would wander the house. I asked him about that once. He said that there were things more interesting than lizards, then walked away with a funny grin.

John announced that he wanted to start sleeping in his own bedroom.

I don't know why it bothered me as much as it did, but it did.

I brought a long book to bed that night. I had always been able to stay up for hours. And I wanted to know if he got out of bed, and if so, where he went.

But that night, I slept like the dead.

I didn't wake up until ten the next morning.

It was a horrible day. I felt like I was alone, truly and fully alone for the first time. My family, meaning John and me, didn't feel like a family and I was desperate to find out what was going on with my little brother.

There was something else bothering me, though I kind of thought I was being paranoid at the time.

At dinner that night, I didn't eat any of my Chinese food. I'd had a lot of practice hiding things like brussels sprouts and fried liver in my serviette from years of father's pre-new-wife cooking. It was a bit harder with shrimp chow mein, though.

I lay in my bed trying to read, but feeling too anxious to absorb any of the words. Finally - finally - I heard John's door and his footsteps in the hallway. One of the good things about old houses, only ghosts can sneak around unheard.

I listened for where he was going, hoping it was just to the bathroom. It wasn't. Quietly, he climbed the stairs to the top floor.

I waited, not even breathing.

A door opened and shut. Uncle Mitch's study.

I sat up, my heart pounding like a fist. Getting up as quietly as I could, I went up the stairs to the closed study door.

I walked in.

They were there. John was sitting on Uncle Mitch's lap and they were both looking at the table in front of them. On it was a nest made of pieces of slate, like the ones in the terrarium. There were three huge eggs in it.

Uncle Mitch turned to me slowly. He smiled.

That smile.

"John," I said, "what are you doing?" My voice trembled.

John looked at me.

"Watching them hatch."

I was torn, so torn between curiosity about what they were doing and a feeling that this was wrong. All wrong.

"Come back to bed," I said.

"Can't," he said, looking back at the eggs.

"Come join us," Uncle Mitch said and patted the chair next to him. For a moment I couldn't move. Was I just over-reacting? Was I getting worked up about nothing? As I questioned myself, I felt deflated, like a paper egg collapsing in on itself.

I walked to the chair and sat down feeling cold and numb and still strangely dizzy. I looked at the eggs. They were bigger than ostrich eggs.

"What are they?" My voice now sounded flat.

"You should know that, with a brother who's practically a dinosaur expert."

I looked at John. He was staring at the eggs with an expression of wonder on his face. He seemed so happy. I wanted him to stay like that.

I guess that's why it was easy for me to believe that they actually were dinosaur eggs. John believed it, so I allowed myself believe it too. For him.

"John's been coming up to watch them hatch. It's a long process. Not one I've ever witnessed before. Been going on for days."

Apart from some slight quivering from one of the eggs, nothing more happened that night. As soon as the sun started to rise, Uncle Mitch sent us back down to our rooms.

The next day, John spent more time with the lizard in the living room, dropping the live crickets into the terrarium. I tried to talk with him about the dinosaur eggs, but he was strange. Like he didn't really want to talk about them with me. He did answer my question about why he had to go up in the middle of the night to see them, though.

"They have to stay covered during the day. Away from the sunlight."

What did I know? It made sense as he said it. So many crazy things made sense in the house.

The next evening, I actually found myself feeling excited about seeing the eggs again, to see if they were going to hatch.

And I ate a ton at dinner that night.

Too much. I made myself sick, which is probably the only reason I was able to wake up that night.

I went to the bathroom, sweating all over, my entire body shaking. I retched into the toilet bowl I don't know how many times. I hadn't yet figured out that it was the drug that had made me so violently ill, not the quantity of food. I rinsed my mouth with water over and over, I left.

And heard the noise from upstairs.

I fumbled with the handrail as I tried to get my feet to work the stairs. I heard a voice.

"You realize that if you don't, I'll destroy the next one."

Uncle Mitch.

"No. Please."

"You saw how easily I did it."

"No!"

"I will do it with all three of them if you don't. Come now, I'm asking much of you. You did promise me."

I forced my trembling legs up the last few steps.

'You're acting ungrateful.' His voice turned nasty. 'I let you stay in my home, I feed you, I give you everything you could want. And when I ask the smallest thing of you...'

I reached the top and charged in.

John's pajama top was open. He looked startled, relieved, embarrassed. Uncle Mitch was next to him, next to the nest. One of the eggs was in his hand. On the floor, lay another. It had obviously been crushed under a shoe.

Uncle Mitch turned to me. He smiled. As he did, he threw the egg against the wall with more strength than I thought he had. It exploded with a pop. Whatever tiny life had been growing in there, slid slowly down the wall.

John looked devastated. Uncle Mitch turned to me.

"Shame you've let your brother down like this. You should have looked after him better. Seems neither of you are much good at caring for a small and fragile life."

He picked up the last egg. And gave me a smile.

His smile slowly became a grimace. For about two seconds, I was completely confused, the sort of confusion that seems to freeze time.

John reached around from behind Uncle Mitch and took the egg from his hand. I still didn't know what was happening, until Uncle Mitch's legs folded and he dropped to the floor. In John's other hand was a piece of slate from the nest. Its tip was sharp as a spear. His fingers were running with blood.

He stepped over the body and came to me. Neither of us said anything. We hugged for a long, long time.

It's funny. We thought that the magic in the house would vanish with Uncle Mitch's death. But we were wrong. The magic didn't come from him, it came from the house itself.

And now, the house is ours. We're still figuring out how it works.

For example: all of the books in the living room are now ones I want to read. There must be hundreds. The Bearded Lizard is still in his terrarium, but now there's another terrarium next to it—John just had to sort of think it into existence and there it was—the last dinosaur egg is lying in it.

Also, we told the house that we didn't want to be bothered by police or anybody about Uncle Mitch's disappearance. And we haven't been.

I called my father - for the first time since we arrived - to tell him that Uncle Mitch had decided to let us stay here and go to school in the city. I'm not even angry that he didn't ask to speak to Uncle Mitch to confirm this. Or that he didn't sound the littlest bit upset. I didn't even find out whether they had a boy or a girl. Whichever it is, I wish it well. It's an innocent in all of this.

For now, we've got our own little one to think about. The egg's been moving all morning and a tiny crack has appeared. I'm dying to know what will come out. John is convinced that it's a Compsognathus. I have no idea what that is, I'm just so happy that John seems okay.

Seems okay.

We're sitting together on the sofa. I don't even stop myself from putting my arm around him now, and he doesn't seem to mind. We're watching as the crack in the shell keeps growing. We've already discussed feeding it, if it is what John thinks it is. Will it like the crickets? We'll see. If not, there are different types of prey. So many different types. We'll find something, I'm sure.

Q is for Quarry

Sara Cleto

For Jared and Krupal

The bones broke the dirt and met sunlight on a summer afternoon. The air felt heavy, more likely to compress and conceal than reveal, but the bones had waited too long as it was, and they had grown impatient of their solitude.

Two sisters lay by the stream behind their house. One held a sketchbook, idly smudging charcoal with her thumb as she coaxed the shadows to lie flat, the other half-hidden behind an open novel about ghosts, Victorian ladies, and other things long dead. The one with the sketchbook would sing a few bars of different songs as the shapes solidified under her fingers, and the other would occasionally chime in with a harmony. They sang more than they didn't, much to their mother's chagrin—Disney songs, sixties Motown, any pop hit they heard play more than twice on the radio. But today, it was ballads— their grandfather was visiting, and he sang them unthinkingly as he washed dishes and checked his inbox. The one holding the sketchbook settled in on a particularly morbid ballad, and her sister wove a descant in a minor third, their voices twinning, twining:

"I'll do as much for my true-love

As any young man may;

I'll sit and mourn all at her grave

For a twelvemonth and a day."

The twelvemonth and a day being up,

The dead began to speak:

"Oh who sits weeping on my grave,

And will not let me sleep?"

The bones had been waiting more than twelvemonth and a day, but they liked the girls' sweet, uncanny voices and the way they sang about old things. They let the dirt fall back from them like a too-warm blanket and waited for the girls to see them, and remember.

Lizzie saw them first. She looked up from her drawing as she wiped charcoal from her hand onto the grass and saw an edge of white cresting from the dirt. Dropping her sketchbook, she pushed off the ground, shaking loose leaves from her skirt, and wandered to the stream's edge, still humming.

The white thing, half submerged in the dirt, gleamed at her in the buttery light.

"Lizzie, what are you doing?" her sister Laura called, but Lizzie could barely hear her. There was a thrumming in her ears, not quite a melody. No distinguishable words rose up from the rolling sound. More than anything, what she didn't-hear was like the memory of a song, her mind straining and stumbling after a cadence with a ghostly familiarity to her ears, to her fingers and legs. She wanted to sing along, to dance, but the tempo and the notes remained elusive, the phantom melody haunting her as she swayed slightly over the white thing in the dirt.

"Lizzie!"

Lizzie jumped as she felt Laura's hand close on her arm, freezing cold despite the warmth of the afternoon.

"What are you looking at?"

Lizzie gestured at the white ridge, her hand fluttering over it like a bird without a place to land.

"Well, what is it?"

Lizzie shrugged at her sister.

Rolling her eyes, Laura knelt down and smoothed away the crumbling earth, dirt clinging to her fingers. A long, curved arc of ivory appeared in full under the sweep of her hand. "It's a bone," she said calmly, though she snatched her hand back and pretended that her fist was not opening and closing in an effort to push away the sensory memory of it.

"Oh God, it's not... it's not human, is it?" Lizzie whispered.

"No, it can't be," Laura said. She was proud of how steady her voice sounded. "It's much too long. Maybe some kind of animal, like a deer or a moose or something."

"A moose? We live in Ohio."

"Well, maybe Ohio used to have moose."

"Ohio did *not* have moose." Lizzie was indignant.

"It doesn't matter! Anyway, I guess we should tell Mom that there's a giant bone in her backyard. She's going to *hate* it."

"As long as she doesn't dig up the garden again."

"She probably will, and make us help. Let's go get it over with."

After repeating themselves several times, with increasing volume, the girls finally convinced their mother to follow them through the garden and to the stream in the back. Her expression shifted from absently disbelieving to incredulity to amazement as her daughters pointed at the gleaming curve rising from the earth. They called the police, who called the coroner, who called a friend from med school who worked in a museum, and soon the bone and the other shining tips that had revealed themselves upon closer inspection of the cleared ground were surrounded by yellow tape and dozens of pairs of boots.

Lizzie and Laura watched from the trampled garden as people with official looking name badges came and stared and poked at the bones with different instruments and took notes.

"They weigh too much! Far too much," a young woman in a lab coat exclaimed as she tried to pick up the largest bone, the one that Lizzie had first seen.

"There's really no 'normal' for this kind of thing, you know," the man behind her said, rather pompously, Laura thought. "Think of how light hollow bird bones can be, how heavy the bones of a rhinoceros!"

The woman rolled her eyes. "Fine, Bob, *you* try picking this up."

The man casually grasped the end of the bone with one hand, and the woman released her grip on it. The bone fell to the ground, dragging the man with it. "Shit! This thing is way too heavy!"

The woman snickered and typed something onto her phone while the man stared at the bones, dumbfounded. Lizzie laughed, too, and she thought her heard a low echo, rumbling under her feet.

Finally, hours later, the team of people in lab coats finished inspecting the garden and the riverbank. The girls sang softly as they watched the bones vanish into long, padded boxes and then into the back of a truck.

The bones sang back, remembering the sisters even as they vanished behind closing truck doors. They remembered their poise and humor in the midst of strangeness, remembered what it was like to be young in an old world, how it felt to be so sure and so uncertain all at once. The bones reached for the girls, willed them to remember, too.

That night, Laura dreamed of dinosaurs. She imagined how their huge bodies roved over the earth, their proportions jarring against a landscape in which trees were smaller than the creatures that moved through them. She saw teeth, some blunted, some sharper than her mother's best kitchen knives, and she knew they were just as hard as the bones that she and her sister had seen behind their garden.

She dreamed, too, of small, bird-like creatures, feathered and winged, their bones hollow or heavy or vibrating with vaporous music. If she concentrated, she could almost hear the melodies they exchanged as they danced along the horizon's bright edge. The smallest of the creatures, small enough to fit in the palm of her hand, seemed wreathed in fine, grey tendrils that dispersed with each winged flex. When they opened their mouths, to chirp or cry or sing, Laura thought she could see embers pulsing in their throats, sparks wreathing their heads like starry, avian crowns.

In room across the hall, Lizzie dreamed of dinosaurs. She dreamed, and remembered, how it felt to be the smallest, quietest person in the room, to be hollow and feathered in the midst of a lumbering crowd full of teeth. She dreamed of the first day of school, the collision of elbows and barely retracted claws in the halls as students lumbered or scampered to class. She remembered how the onslaught of faces blurred together, leaving only the impression of blinking eyes and clicking tongues. How she had stood alone for too long in the cafeteria, holding a shaking tray with clenched hands, until she sat down abruptly in the nearest chair. A girl with nails curled into talons glanced up at her from a book before sticking her nose back into it. Lizzie sighed in relief and pulled her own book from her bag, losing herself in the story as she nibbled at her sandwich.

"You know you're both reading Jurassic Park," observed a boy as he sat down between them, nothing but three apples on his tray. He brushed dark feathers away from his face and grinned at them. By the time Laura found her at the table, Lizzie was gesturing wildly with an apple between bites as they talked raptors and bones and chronostratigraphic music. As she dreamed, she remembered what it was to go out into the world and find other people your size, to know your bones were not so fragile even when they are sunlit and bare.

When she woke, she felt heavy and light all at once. An echo resonated through her body, as if her bones, too, were singing.

R is for Remember

Jonathan C. Parrish

This was the place she liked best, in all the world, in all her time. Specifically this room, and the rooms adjoining. It wasn't quite right, some subtle things didn't quite match with her ages old memory, but they were close enough that she wasn't sure if it was this thing or the memory that made the incongruence. Maybe both. A shade of green, the shape of an eyebrow scale, the particular shape of that grass being trampled. Still, it was close enough, and close enough was far closer than anything else had been. Everything except the smell—she knew that was wrong, even if it had been so very long since she had inhaled.

She would stand for days just staring at the scenes in these rooms. Time meant very little, now. Once it had been a much more pressing concern; seconds meaning the difference between breathing or not breathing. There was that period where she wandered anxious about passing time—seeking, exploring and longing—but hope and desperation had settled to a low monotone of unease instead of being quite so pressing.

Sometimes she would wander outside or into the other rooms, but very little of that made sense even though some of it was familiar. The little houses that appeared—long after she needed to breathe—she remembered, both in memory and in some of the other rooms;

however, the ones in her memory were filled with life and movement, they were not so still. Outside, everything was a blur of motion, there was a stillness and a slowness at the core of it all but everything vibrated in a way that made her feel anxious all over again. So now she went inside more often than not.

She didn't sleep—but she would dream. She dreamt of the breathing urgency, reliving the fear. Screams, decisions, regrets. Teeth, terrible teeth; tiny eyes, pleading and terrified; tails torn and broken. And under it all the longing and the seeking.

Then the stillness was disturbed—a shift occurred in the room about her. She found her path obstructed and altered; barriers appeared, others vanished. She maneuvered her bulk easily; frills and tails no longer caught on the world, obstacles weren't really obstructions anymore. As she explored the new space she found the same things in new places.

And new things in old places. One thing in particular.

It was tiny—the size of her back leg. She sniffed it, it still smelled wrong, but it looked right enough. Tiny eyes that made her heart almost beat again. Tiny horns, tiny frill, tiny intact tail. Seeing it, she knew what to do. This time, she would not fail.

She curled up around it, exhaled and fell asleep.

S is for Spirit.

Samantha Kymmell-Harvey

Maebelle hummed as she snipped the silk yarn. The freshly tatted dragon wriggled and snapped at her fingers, but Maebelle had grown quick in her knot-tying. She flipped the dragon on its belly, inspecting the lacy knots ensuring she hadn't dropped a stitch. It beat its wings in protest. Satisfied, she added her newest creation to her shelf of tatted lace creatures. The cats, dogs and dinosaurs teetered on lacy paws and claws to meet their new friend. Maebelle smiled, forgetting her fanciful tune. In the song's absence, the creatures fell limp, draped like cobwebs on the shelf's edge.

She put her tatting shuttle and needle into her satchel and dragged her wooden stool over to her dresser where her terrarium of silkworms sat. She had built it with her father a few months ago, much to the delight of her mother who took it as a sign of her daughter's interest in engineering.

"Be sure to make a tintype of the process, dear," her mother had said to her father. "We'll need it for Maebelle's application for the Youth Federal Academy of Dino Sciences." While her father carefully measured the wood and secured the glass, Maebelle had mostly just watched.

Peering through the glass, Maebelle spotted a few conical white cocoons, like little tufts of fairy floss tucked into the twigs and mulberry leaves and clapped her hands. More silk to be spun and tatted.

"Maebelle!" Her mother called from downstairs. "Fetch your bonnet and gloves. The triceratops skin ones, they are the finest. We cannot be late to this interview."

Ignoring her mother's pleas, Maebelle unlatched the terrarium lid. As she scooped up the first cocoon, she began to sing the same lullaby she'd been singing to the worms since her father had first brought them home from his lab months ago. The cocoon gently pulsed to her song, until the worm emerged. Gingerly, Maebelle unraveled the silk, the worm seemingly lulled to sleep by her tune. From the shelves above, the silk tattered creatures also swayed, their wings fluttering, heads bobbing to her music.

"Maebelle! Now!"

Maebelle twisted the last of the silk around the cone and as she put the worm back into the terrarium, she said, "Thank you! Sleep well, my friend." The tatted creatures instantly slumped where they had once walked about.

She shoved her newly spun silk thread into her satchel and hurried downstairs.

Her mother tapped her hard soled heel on the floor. "We are going to be late! This is your future on the line, young lady. And don't forget to put on your gloves, no daughter of mine will be so improper."

Maebelle took her tatted lace gloves from her satchel.

"Where are your triceratop skin ones?"

"I'm wearing these ones instead, mother." Maebelle crossed her arms.

Her mother firmly planted her hands on her hips. "Fine, let's go."

The coachman helped Maebelle step down and avoid the muddy dino-dung that encrusted the street gutters. Maebelle approached the raptors who impatiently pulled at their bits and reigns. Their scales shimmered green-brown in the sunlight, their eyes amber slits. People said they were just work animals with no feelings, perfect for pulling carriages, tilling fields, or becoming garments and sports ball skins. But Maebelle disagreed.

"Come on, Maebelle," her mother said. "We have three minutes." She grabbed her by the hand and hurried her up the Academy's steep marble steps. Maebelle stared up at the gold-painted block lettering engraved across the architrave: Youth Federal Academy of Dino Sciences. This was it. Her future.

"Good morning, Miss Littleton, Maebelle Hart is here for her 10 o'clock interview with Dr. Perkins," her mother said to the secretary.

She dipped her dino skin wrapped pen into the ink well and made a firm check beside Maebelle's name in the appointment ledger.

"Perfect, Maebelle, please come with me." She held out a gloved hand. The scaly glove shone green-blue under the flickering gaslamps. Maebelle didn't want to touch it.

"I could make you gloves," she said to Miss Littleton. "Out of silk. Here I can show you." Maebelle opened her satchel and fished around for her spool of silk, but her mother snatched the satchel away.

"But Mom!"

She gave Maebelle the wild-eyed look she uses when she's about to send her to her room without dessert then turned to the secretary. "I apologize, Miss Littleton. Now please, show us to Dr. Perkins' office."

Miss Littleton smiled. "Thank you, Mrs. Hart, but I will bring her back when the interview has concluded. We have the latest magazines for your perusal while you wait."

"I don't understand," said her mother. "I thought we were interviewing together."

"Dr. Perkins likes to interview perspective students on their own, but don't worry. She'll be back very soon."

Maebelle waved goodbye to her mother and reluctantly took Miss Littleton's hand.

"Right this way, Maebelle," said Miss Littleton as she pushed open the heavy wooden door leading to the classrooms and offices.

Strange yipping and barking noises echoed down the wood-paneled hallways as they approached Dr. Perkins' office. Maebelle jumped. Miss Littleton chuckled.

"There is no reason to be alarmed. These are the dino labs. Maybe you'll get to take a class in one if you are accepted into the honors program. It is only for the Upper School though, so you have a few years yet."

Maebelle nodded, swallowing hard. She clenched her fists, trying to force the queasiness in her stomach to settle.

"I know what you'd like to see—the dinosaur nursery. I'm sure Dr. Perkins won't mind. It is, after all, the first thing you'd learn if admitted into the fifth grade." She inserted the skeleton key into the brass lock and twisted.

The thick humid air saturated with a pungent scent. Maebelle's eyes watered. There were dozens of terrariums on the lab counters, much like the one she and her father had built for the silk worms, but larger. Each had a handwritten label glued to the glass.

"V. mongoliensis, V. osmolskae," Maebelle read aloud as she peered in at the giant eggs.

"Do you know what they will hatch into?"

Maebelle shrugged. "Dinosaurs of some kind."

Miss Littleton furrowed her eye brows. "Raptors. What's a Brachiosaurus altithorax?"

Maebelle strode to the next terrarium. This one had a newly hatched dinosaur. It was chewing on the pre-ground bloody meat mix in its bowl. "I don't know."

"A brachiosaur," said Miss Littleton.

"Ah, yes, the ones with the long necks." Maebelle pointed at the baby dino. "Is this a tyrannosaurus rex or an allosaurus?"

"I must say, Maebelle, normally our applicants know the scientific names of dinosaur species. And they certainly can recognize the difference between a t-rex and an allosaur."

"So what is it? It looks sad."

"Allosaur," said Miss Littleton.

"Do you have any silk worm labs?" Maebelle instinctively reached for her satchel, only to remember that her mother had confiscated it.

Miss Littleton shook her head. "No need for silk worms here. We only have the essentials in dino studies here. Well, I am sure Dr. Perkins is ready for you now."

Maebelle sat on the chair opposite Dr. Perkins' desk, swinging her legs back and forth. I wish I had my tatting, she thought. I'd like to make an allosaur next, that little one could use a friend. She began to hum her lullaby as she imagined her lace creature comforting the baby dinosaur.

"What a pretty song! It's too bad we don't have any music classes here." A woman's voice startled Maebelle.

She jumped to her feet. "Good morning, Dr. Perkins, my name is Maebelle Hart and it has been my dream to dedicate my life to science and math for the future endeavors of our dino-technology." Maebelle was pretty sure she'd remembered everything her mother had told her to say.

Dr. Perkins' smiled. "I'm Dr. Victoria Perkins and I am happy to have you here today. Please, sit down."

Maebelle laced her fingers together. A warmth tingled on her cheeks and spread to the tips of her ears. She gulped.

"Maebelle, why don't you tell me about why you'd like to attend our Academy's junior secondary school?"

Maebelle's mom had warned her that this would probably be the first question she'd be asked. They had practiced over and over again, including at last night's supper. Maebelle took a breath. "I would like to attend the Youth Federal Academy of Dino Sciences because math and science are the future. Without math or science, we would not have been able to harness the awesome power of the dinosaurs in order to advance our own society. It is essential to being useful to our society."

"I see." Dr. Perkins jotted a few notes down into her dinosaur skin bound journal. She set her pen in the ink well and leaned forward. "Maebelle, did your mother and father help you think of that?"

Her mother would not have liked that question, but her mother wasn't here to be contrary. "We talked about it together."

"How about you tell me in your own words why you want to study science?"

"Well, I like science. I built a terrarium with my father for my silkworms."

"You have silkworms? How interesting! And what experiments do you do with them?"

Maebelle giggled. "I don't do experiments, I use their silk to tat lace animals, and gloves, and other pretty things. My grandmother taught me."

Dr. Perkins added more notes. "So you haven't studied them?"

"No, my father tells me what to feed them and how to treat them."

"Then what happens when you have to extract the silk? Does your father kill the larvae for you, too?"

Maebelle clasped her hands together. "Kill them? No! We don't kill them."

"Then how do you extract the silk? The worms don't want to give up their silk."

"I sing to them and they let me. They like my music. It calms them. I've been singing to them ever since the day I got them. I sing to them every day. They trust me."

Dr. Perkins dipped her pen in the inkwell. "There's a little bit of science in what you've just said. Maebelle, the Youth Federal Academy of Dino Sciences is famous for its advancement of technologies. Our best known invention is the aerodynamic dino skin lacrosse ball. We've also pioneered firefighting garments and gloves thanks to stegasauraus plates and skin. What new dino technology would you hope to start during your studies here?"

"I'd propose a swap from dinosaur skin to silk instead. It's not fair to raise them and earn their trust only to skin them." Maebelle sat up straight. Dr. Perkins' glossy lips press together in a half-frown. Thank goodness her mother wasn't here.

Dr. Perkins removed her spectacles and rubbed them with a leather handkerchief. "This concludes the interview, let me escort your back to your mother."

When Dr. Perkins pushed the door open, her mother stood up.

"Finished so soon?" she shot Maebelle an accusatory glance.

Dr. Perkins patted Maebelle on the head. "Mrs. Hart, thank you so much for bringing us Maebelle today."

Maebelle tried to pry her satchel from her mother's hands, but she only gripped it tighter. Defeated, she sat and crossed her arms over her chest.

"Mrs. Hart, Maebelle is a lovely girl, but I don't think she is Dino Sciences material. Have you considered the Visual and Performing Arts primary? She seems to have a real passion for arts and music."

"I studied math and science, her father studied math and science. This is in her DNA."

"As far as I can tell, Mrs. Hart, she possesses neither the interest nor the talent to succeed in a scientific school."

"Good day, Dr. Perkins."

Maebelle felt her mother's firm grasp on her arm. "Come on, we are leaving right now."

Her needles and shuttles clattered against one another as her father carelessly tossed them into a box. Maebelle screamed.

"Daddy, no!" She lunged for the box, but her mother intervened.

"You can't get any of it back until you fix this, Maebelle. Your father and I have done all we can do."

Her father wadded up the lace dragons and cats and dogs and tossed them into the box. Next, he swept the tatted deer and squirrels and foxes as if they were dusty cobwebs in need of cleaning. Then he picked up the terrarium, wood creaking in his arms. The white cocoons swayed. This time, her mother couldn't hold her back. Maebelle grasped the terrarium and tugged.

"No! Stop!" Maebelle cried. "Who will sing to them? You don't understand."

"No more tatting, no more needles, no more silk, no more singing," said Father, whose grip was none the looser. "You have to earn these back."

Maebelle sunk to the floor, fists balled in defeat.

"You should've thought about the consequences, young lady," her mother said as she shut the door behind her.

Sobbing, Maebelle rubbed her eyes. The lace gloves she still had on from her interview felt smooth against her puffy skin. She flexed her fingers as she thought. If the lace animals came to life when she sang, what would the lace gloves do?

Maebelle took a deep breath, combed her hair, and pinned her bonnet atop her brown curls.

Her parents never heard her soft steps on the staircase nor the front door gently close. Maebelle kept her head down as she walked past the raptor carriages lining the rowhomes of their city streets. No dinosaur was going to be put to work on her behalf. Instead, she hurried down the sidewalk, her boot-clad feet wobbling on the uneven bricks.

The church clock tower chimed 4 o'clock as Maebelle found herself standing once again on the Academy's portico. A few students clad in their navy blazers still sat on the steps waiting for their parents or nannies to arrive.

"It's closed," one of them said to Maebelle as she reached for the door.

"I don't care," said Maebelle as she pulled the doorbell cord.

A few minutes passed and Maebelle pulled the cord again. This time, she rang the bell incessantly. The door swiftly opened.

"Miss Hart!" It was the secretary, Miss Littleton. "Where is your mother? Does she know you're here?"

"I have something important to show Dr. Perkins. Is she still here?"

"I'm afraid you cannot come in without an appointment, Maebelle. Go home and have your mother write us a letter. Have a nice evening."

Miss Littleton slammed the door closed. Maebelle grunted in frustration and gave the door a swift kick, thus breaking the heel off her boot.

"Maebelle!"

She looked up from her busted heel to see her mother getting out of a raptor carriage.

"I was worried sick on account of you!"

Maebelle folded her arms across her chest. "I'm making things right."

Her mother grabbed her arm and pulled her to her feet. "Get in that carriage, we are going home right now!"

"No!" Maebelle pulled free and started to pound on the Academy's door.

Swiftly, her mother caught her hands and took the lace gloves from them. "I thought we'd taken everything, but I see we missed your unseemly gloves!"

Maebelle reached for them. "Give them back!"

"Not until you get into that carriage!"

A long high pitched shriek echoed from inside of the Academy. Maebelle tried the door knob and it clicked open. Miss Littleton had forgotten to lock it in her haste to shoo her away.

"Don't go in there!" her mother grabbed her by the shoulders.

Another scream echoed from within. It sounded like Miss Littleton.

Maebelle snatched her gloves back from her mother and darted inside the school.

The lobby was dark but the flicker of the gaslights emanated from under the wooden door that led back to the classrooms. Maebelle pushed open that door to find Miss Littleton poised at a laboratory door, revolver in hand.

"Maebelle! Do not move!" said Miss Littleton, her eyes wide.

Maebelle's mother still lingered on the Academy's threshold. "You are making this worse! Come home!" "Don't kill the dinosaur, I can help!" she said, taking a step closer.

Children's screams pierced the stillness. The nursery door's window shattered as glass shattered and a brown-yellow dinosaur barreled through.

"The lab!" Miss Littleton yelled. "Get the children to safety!"

Dr. Perkins emerged from her office. "What is going on?"

The tick-tick of claws tapped against the tile floor. Maebelle and her mother watched as a small creature barreled its way toward them, the science teacher waving her arms behind it.

"Stop it!" the teacher screamed. "Stop that allosaur, please!"

As she neared, Maybelle saw the teacher's arms were dotted with something red. It ran down her arm in thin lines. Blood.

"On the count of three, Miss Littleton!" Dr. Perkins said as she removed a small metal object from her belt loop and pointed it at the infant allosaur.

The cat-sized lizard sprinted, its mouth open and full of pointed teeth, saliva glistening on its lips.

"Wait!" Maebelle screamed, waving her hands. "I can help. Don't hurt it!" This is my chance, she thought.

Maebelle held out her lace gloves and began to sing. The gloves shook and shivered in her palm as they came alive and then sprang from her hand and chased the infant allosaur. Fingers outstretched, they pounced. The dinosaur and the gloves slid across the tiles together before thudding against the wood-paneled wall. The gloves laced their fingers around the allosaur's mouth. It tried to wriggle free, but the gloves held.

Maebelle didn't stop singing until she'd scooped up the infant allosaur and replaced him in his cage. Dr. Perkins reholstered her weapon.

"That's amazing, Maebelle!" she said.

Miss Littleton and Miss Hart said nothing but their mouths were open.

Maebelle shrugged and handed Dr. Perkins her gloves. "As you can see, the silk held. There are no holes or tears. And I believe them to be more stylish than any dinosaur skin gloves I've seen."

Miss Littleton peeled off her dino gloves and tucked them into her pocket. "And that thread would take up dyes easily."

"Exactly," said Maebelle, smiling.

"And how does it come alive?" Dr. Perkins turned the gloves over looking for some source of magic.

"It's the song I've been singing to my worms, it builds trust. It builds a relationship. That makes the thread unbreakable and yet flexible. And it doesn't cost any lives."

"This has such potential, I can't believe I never considered any other possibilities before." Dr. Perkins returned Maebelle's gloves to her. "You know, I think there might be space for you at the academy after all, Maebelle!"

Her mother clapped her hands together. "That is wonderful news! Thank you! What do you say, Maebelle?"

"I will accept on one condition," said Maebelle.

"Name your condition, young lady," Dr. Perkins returned her gloves to her.

"That the dinos in the lab are set free and that my silkworms take their place."

"I would only ever agree to such a condition if the results could be revolutionary," said Dr. Perkins.

Maebelle gripped her mother's hand and they started toward the door.

"Excuse me, Maebelle," said Miss Littleton. "I'd love a pair of those gloves."

Maebelle smiled. "You can have these ones, Miss Littleton. I can always make more."

She put them on and held up her hands. "These fit nicely! And they are warm, too. What do you say, Dr. Perkins?"

Dr. Perkins nodded. "Those gloves are revolutionary. Your silkworms are revolutionary. Welcome to the Academy, Maebelle. I can't wait to see what your future has in store."

T is for Tatting

Michael Kellar

Raymond always credited his grandfather for cultivating his interest in dinosaurs. It was Grandpa who introduced him to stories as "A Sound of Thunder" and "The Fog Horn" by Ray Bradbury and movies by Ray Harryhausen. "The Valley of Gwangi" and "One Million Years B.C." had made an indelible impression upon him as a child; sure the plots were somewhat improbable, but the important thing was that they brought dinosaurs *to life* for him. (And he came to consider it an act of fate that he shared the same first name as his two early heroes.)

His early passion eventually dictated his choice in careers. He earned a degree in paleontology despite continuing opposition from friends and family. Truthfully, his first position after college , as an environmental consultant, was somewhat lacking in excitement or personal fulfillment but he felt that he'd finally found his true calling when he began to publish a series of alphabet-based science titles for children. ("A is for Allosaurus" was popular and "B is for Brontosaurus" became an Amazon best-seller.)

On February 12th, 2045 contact with the inhabitants of a new planet was announced. The planet, named Crichton after the author of "Jurassic Park",

paralleled Earth's prehistory with a major difference. There, the dinosaurs had escaped extinction and evolved into the dominant, intelligent species.

Ray followed every bit of news about Crichton and was in awe of the images as direct feeds began to be transmitted to Earth. By August, linguists had functional translations of their major languages, and socialists had begun to grasp the intricacies of their social structure. And then, in the last week of October Raymond received a life-altering invitation. Considering his background as a paleontologist, paired with his communication skills as a popularizer of science, would Mr. Barron be interested in serving as Earth's first ambassador to Crichton?

Mr. Barron wasted no time in indicating that he would, indeed, have such an interest.

When Raymond reported to NASA's Diplomatic Training headquarters, he was greeted in the reception area by Marilyn 975 and led into the main office by Madonna 637. (Ray had a vague idea that the original Marilyn and Madonna had some connection with popular culture, which was a weak area for him, but he could tell that both had expected more of a reaction from him.)

One of the most popular imported alien technologies to date was a body-morphing system. Through a rather surprisingly simple procedure, anyone could have themselves transformed into their own ideal image. While this practice was condemned by a vocal minority as excessively vain, it would actually play a vital part in preparing Raymond for his role. In order to visit the dinosaur planet, he would have to learn to appear and behave as one of the natives who'd exhibited a disdain for the human form. Paleontologist Stephen J. Gould 37 was in charge of helping Raymond select his morph form. Ray initially embarrassed himself by declaring that he would like to arrive as a T. Rex.

"I'm afraid that would be quite impossible. Not only would it be ill-advised to present yourself as one of the most prestigious members of their social order, but the procedure itself cannot increase your mass. You will be limited to a selection somewhat in proportion to your own size and weight range. I've taken the liberty of sorting through possible candidates and the very best match would seem to be a psittacosaurus..."

"You want me to become a parrot lizard!""I see you are familiar with the genus. While you would not walk completely upright, the psittacosaurus could achieve a length of nearly two meters, which nearly matches your height. They weighed in somewhat lower than you do, but we can work with that."

In rapid succession Raymond voiced a number of objections to the proposal and suggested a number of alternates, but before long he realized this meeting was merely a diplomatic gesture towards him and his 'choice' had already been predetermined. He would just have to get used to having a beak and probable back issues.

In truth, Ray would have accepted *any* form offered to him. Not only was he interested in dinosaurs, but he *identified with them* and had for far longer than any type of transformation had ever been possible.

He never would have dared to express to anyone that he had always felt like a very old soul and that he should have been incarnated in a different form had they not met with extinction. He essentially considered himself a dinosaur which had mistakenly been born in a human body. And now, this error of nature could actually be rectified!

The next six months involved intensive training in a wide variety of areas, including Crichton etiquette, religion, language, and speech.

When the day arrived for his transformation, Ray could barely contain his excitement. The closest existing analog to the device itself was the 3-D printer, although that comparison would be like suggesting that a pirate's iron hook had anything in common with today's highly sophisticated brain linked prosthetics. Flesh and bone were dissolved while almost instantly (and seamlessly) rebuilt with a rapid layering of tissue according to a preselected pattern. While no foreign materials were introduced into the process with ordinary humans, in this case such considerations as scales, a beak, and quills required the addition of collagen tissue fibres, a significant amount of keratin, as well as other minor embellishments.

While a certain number of human morphs had elected at some point to reverse the procedure or choose another model entirely, Raymond was made to understand that in his case the transmutation would be irreversible - only his mind and memories would remain unchanged. This was his dream come true, and he was amused that everyone who prepped him had expected him to react as though this were some insurmountable obstacle!

He was instructed to lay face down on a specially designed table filled with depressions which - he was excited to realize - bore no relation to his human form. His head dangle loosely over an inverted curved cone, through which he heard a hiss of gas, followed by a near immediate loss of consciousness.

After a period that seemed but a few seconds, but which he knew had to have been much longer, he awoke to the sound of someone speaking his name.

"Mr. Barron. The procedure was successful. You can try to get up now."

Ray attempted to push back from the table, but his thumbs wouldn't respond to his efforts. Actually, he no longer appeared to have thumbs.

After much awkward and uncomfortable fumbling he stood partially erect and gazed down to see his body covered in green and brown scales.

"Sir, you might want to step onto the mirror."

He allowed himself to be led onto a holodisk platform, and was amazed at the 3-D image that began to materialize in front of him. He was covered from head to...tail...in a pattern of predominantly brown and green overlapping flaps of scales. His forearms were much shorter and while they did not end in fingers, the digits he now possessed were responsive to opening and closing in quick, grasping motions.

His center of gravity had drastically shifted and only the counterweight of a long, magnificent tail which formed the last third of his body length, ending in rows of long lime green quills, kept him even semi-upright.

He tried to *do something* with this new appendage, which at first was unresponsive to any mental commands. It was only after he made a movement which formerly would have led him to clenching his buttocks that the tail suddenly swept into a circle and nearly knocked over one of his attending doctors.

He thought a word .

"Sorry."

What he actually heard was some sort of clicking sound.

The nearly assaulted doctor - who was also a linguist - assured him there was no problem, and requested that he calm down so that they might settle into a lengthy process of evaluating each of his new body parts and their function.

Weeks passed, during which time Ray continued to marvel at the power and energy inherent in his new body.

As his orientation and flight preparations neared completion, he found that he spent more and more of his spare time on the holo mirror doing nothing more than basking in amazement at the splendor of his new self, and finally admitting how disdainful he had been of his old body.

On the day of his journey Raymond was led aboard his vessel by an escort of medical and navigational robots. This was to be a solo mission, and - although rather short in duration - would be passed in a state of assisted hibernation.

Unlike the instantaneous feeling associated with his morphing surgery, Ray believed that he did sense some passage of time during his journey. As he began to drift off he found himself reviewing the environment which would be encountered upon his arrival.

While the planet's inhabitants had, indeed, evolved, Crichton itself remained a raw, primitive world. A large percentage of its four continents consisted of primeval forests, natural asphalt lakes and tar pits, and hundreds of (primarily) dormant volcanoes.

They did not live in cities as we would define them, but instead gathered in artificially created cratered areas, surrounded around the rims by entrances to cavernous dwellings.

As Raymond's own robotic assistant stimulated him into a state of complete wakefulness, Ray wondered if dreaming was a vestige of his human form and would fade away or whether it was natural to the dinosaurs as well? If the former were the case, then he would be happy to have the ability fade away, as had most other human feelings and practices.

His transformation during the past months had exceeded his hopes and expectations. Truthfully, he had been concerned that a vegetarian diet of leaves and grains would be boring, but was pleasantly surprised to discover that his sense of taste had been greatly enhanced. His modest diet now possessed an unsuspected degree of variety and subtle texture.

Likewise, his vision was sharper and he had learned to identify his doctors and instructors by their sense of smell the moment they entered a room.

His emotions had grown raw, wild and free. He hadn't suspected the broad range of feelings that could be expressed in a nuanced swipe of his tail.

It was growing increasingly difficult to focus of his mission. He knew that was his sole reason for visiting Crichton, but as his transformation had grown complete, he found that he wanted nothing more than to be let loose on the planet and allowed to "go native".

His introverted tendencies had been swept away and he looked forward to at last being able to roam free amongst his people. Even if most of them were reptiles. Ray's detachable living pod was met by a mechanical crew and transported directly to a guest chamber in a cavernous pocket of the unpretentiously named city of Rim #2.

As he was being moved into his carrier, he caught a brief glimpse of a bubbling tar pit to his left, and thought he saw the head and long, elegant neck of a plesiosaurus emerging from an ocean-like body of water at his distant right. He could barely contain his excitement, and was not looking forward to the week long period of containment which must be endured while it was determined that he had made the adjustment to Crichton's denser atmosphere and higher temperatures.

On the morning of his summoning Ray's door was unsealed. He glanced down at himself and laughed to realize that this was an instinctive lingering urge to check the appearance of no longer existing clothing. He made certain he had his gift to the Crichtons - a carved rod that was half coal and half stylized digital components which some committee had determined, erroneously he felt, to represent a joining of cultures - and cautiously lumbered forward.

He emerged from the shadows into a marbled semicircle of jade platforms, lit from the rays of a sun's light filtered through a thick atmospheric haze. As his vision adjusted he began to recognize the living counterparts to bones he had curated in his museum work.

Shadows cast from the upper area of the arena coalesced into the form of majestic, perched pterodactyls. Their wings were formed of a combination of skin and muscle membrane, and were of a color which he could now perceive but as yet had no name for.

An upper tier was populated by a row of dryopithecus, which appeared more prehistoric monkey than ape. Ray wondered if this were the closest to humanity that was approached on this world's evolutionary scale as he shifted his gaze to a grouping of glyptodons. They resembled rather stoic, contemplative armadillos, and barely seemed to notice a pair of giant flightless phorusrhacos hopping about them in an excited, vaguely predatory manner.

At lower levels a trio of duck-billed iguanodons mingled with what must be a very immature megalosaurus. Finally, as anticipated, Ray found himself standing directly opposite a magnificent allosaurus, which towered over him at nearly three times his height.

It radiated force, power and what could only be described as an unconcealed hunger. In this society carnivorous urges were now satiated through synthetically-produced meat, and he marveled that it could possibly keep its primitive urges in check.

The reigning allosaurus remained still and silent as most of the other dinosaurs descended to the main level and began to assemble around the visiting representative of Earth. They sniffed and poked and prodded at him while they clicked and roared and swished their tails.

Raymond assumed this was all part of a formal greeting process until they began to speak.

"What is this frail being?"

"Where is our ambassador? They assured us that we would be greeted by one of our own!"

"Is it wearing a zippered suit?"

"Its flesh reeks with the smell of rancid pink meat."

Raymond was stunned.

Didn't they understand that he was now no different that they are? He was one of them!

Ray offered his planet's gift to the allosaurus.

The creature regarded it for a moment, then lurched forward and snapped the rod between his jaws before issuing a bone-chilling roar and storming out of the amphitheater with all the others following close behind.

Ray stood alone in the massive space. Lost. Dejected. Soon, four of his automated attendants appeared with his transport pod in tow.

The implication was obvious.

He was being dismissed and about to be led back to his vessel. Not only had his mission failed, but so had he.

But what was left for him? In this form there would be no place for him back on Earth; he would be rejected there just as readily as he had been dismissed here.

As he left his transport platform he once again had a view of the plesiosaurus swimming in the distance, as well as the tar pit bubbling a few feet from his landing area and instead of entering his ship he stepped forwards towards the heat.

He'd made his decision.

Even if he wasn't accepted by his chosen creatures, he knew that he could still have at least one last truly authentic dinosaur experience.

Extinction.

U is for Unwelcome

Cory Cone

The orange glow of Michael's cigarette vanished in the van's headlights. He had been sitting in darkness on his front porch with his lunch box in his lap when I arrived, and now walked toward the van like an apparition. I pointed to one of three coffees in the cup holders. Michael took it as I backed out of the dirt drive, and his house sank into the morning black.

"What's for lunch today?" I asked.

"Roasted veggies," he said and looked out the window. Steam rose from his coffee cup.

"Sorry for the early wake up."

"I was up anyway," he said. "Harrison's teething."

Michael had been working with me for twelve years—he'd been my first apprentice and I was glad he'd never left.

I got to the new kid's apartment in ten minutes.

Jessi was leaning against a street sign at the corner of Elm and Chestnut. It was his first job as my new apprentice. He'd been the first kid I'd ever interviewed who wasn't at least a little freaked out by my left hand; my middle and ring fingers were eaten when I was a kid but people always think it happened on the job and I let them think it.

Jessi didn't care about any of that and even looked at me like I was beneath him for having gotten my fingers eaten by a dinosaur. He was the sort of guy who liked to get in your face. Fight you for the sake of fighting.

But I take what I can get when it comes to help.

I pulled the van to the corner and Jessi squeezed in beside Michael and grabbed a coffee. He didn't have a lunch.

A block away there was a cop car sitting in the shadows. I could see the blue dash lights on the cop's face.

"Good morning," I said.

"Fuck yeah, it's a good morning," replied Jessi.

Michael said nothing.

I pulled away from the curb and we headed toward the job.

The cop did not follow.

We got to the site and the dash clock blinked from 5:59 to 6:00. Our headlights flooded the front porch and made the house look fake, like a doll house or a diorama or something from a dream. Mrs. Wexler was sitting on the stairs with the baby asleep in her arms and she shielded her eyes. The baby was so soundly asleep in his mother's arms he looked like a rag doll, just dead weight. Meanwhile, Mr. Wexler was pacing the length of the porch with a shovel in his hands as if something might leap from the yard or from inside.

I waved to the family and then noted our time of arrival in my log. Beside me, Michael yawned while Jessi glared at the family illuminated in our headlights and said, "Are they really so scared of a couple of *raptors*?"

"They were a breath away from losing their baby, kid," Michael said. He already looked close to bashing Jessi's head through the passenger window.

"Horse shit," said Jessi. "If it were me—"

"It's not."

"*If* it were me, I'd have stomped that fucker to death in the nursery. A dino in *my* kid's crib? No way, man."

"Do you even have kids? What are you, nineteen? Have you had a velociraptor in your house, your room? How about a half-dozen Western Claws creeping under your covers, nibbling at the gunk between your toes before making their way to the arteries in your leg?"

"Of course I haven't. I don't live like a disgusting pig. But I wouldn't wet my pants over it. What did these two do, huh? Cower in a corner?"

I said, "They called us is what they did." I put my log book down beside me on the seat and turned off the van. "And now we're here, so don't let me catch you talking that way where they can hear you or I'll rip your tongue out and feed it to a raptor. Got it?" I stepped out of the van and slammed the door.

Jessi tossed his cup to the floor and got out and lit a cigarette. Michael had shimmied his way from the middle seat out of the van by the time I came around and leaned in close to Jessi. "Got it?" I asked again.

He blew out smoke and it was thick and gray and whipped away into the morning blackness around us. "Yeah," he said. "I got it."

The Wexler's porch light was on and the scene looked more like a depression era painting now than a diorama. We walked to the porch and Mr. Wexler ceased his pacing a moment to shake my hand. He was limping and his pants were covered in blood from where the raptor had taken a chunk of his leg.

"Thanks for coming so quickly."

"It's what we do," I said.

Jessi brushed passed the family and into the house. The screen door slammed behind him, startling the Wexlers. The baby stirred but did not wake.

"Little guy's all right, then?" I asked.

"Yes," said Mrs. Wexler. "He's all right."

I eyed Mr. Wexler's leg wound. "You should get that looked at."

"I will, when this is taken care of."

"It's not always fast. It can take a few hours, a few days sometimes. There a place you can stay if that's the case here?"

Mrs. Wexler said, "My sister's?"

Mr. Wexler seemed to shudder. "If we have to, yes."

"And get that leg looked at," added Michael from the edge of the porch. He was looking over the side, scanning for signs of dino footprints. "Sooner than later. These things carry disease. You're liable to lose it."

The color drained from Mr. Wexler's face.

"Sometimes they don't though," I said, to calm him.

But they usually do.

Mrs. Wexler stared off toward nowhere and said, "We knew there might be a few of them…you know, nothing so bad. We thought it would sort itself out. We…we had no idea…"

"Listen," I said. "These situations get out of hand very quickly. I've raised a kid and my partner here has got a six month old at home right now. We get it. You're tired, delirious and everything about your life is changing. Times like that, things can spring up on you. But that's why you called us. That's why we're here." She met my eyes then, came back to us a little.

"Come on," I said to Michael. "Let's get our stuff and get to it."

I called in to Jessi to help grab the gear and he bounced back out of the house with an excitement reserved only for the green in this job. Mr. and Mrs. Wexler hobbled toward their hatchback as we walked back to the van. Looked like they were off to her sister's after all.

"We'll call you around lunch with an update," I said to them as they packed the baby into the car seat. I looked to Mr. Wexler. "And get yourself to a hospital. Today."

They drove off.

Michael, Jessi and I grabbed our nets, knives and stethoscopes from the back. I took the sledgehammer, in case we had to get into the walls. The van also has six cages and a flame thrower. Hardly ever get to use the flame thrower.

The Wexler hatchback's taillights blipped away in the distance and then we headed into the house.

We stood a moment in the foyer and Jessi said, "It's bad."

I could smell them, a nauseatingly thick stench like wet dog covered in shit. And the walls were alive with rustling and scratching and short manic chirps. The air vents along the upper wall were clogged with red and blue feathers. This supported the Wexler claim that they were infested with velociraptors as did the fact they had gone for the baby first. Velociraptors are not fantastic hunters, and prefer small manageable prey, hence the meaning of their name, 'Speedy Thief." They'll lacerate your Achilles and then your throat in two seconds flat, but they'd prefer to simply steal your eggs and bring them back to safety.

Or your baby.

I leaned the sledge against a wall and slapped Jessi upside the head. "Don't just waltz into a house before we've spoken with the family. What the hell is the matter with you?"

"I was getting an idea of what we're up against."

"We *know* what we're up against. I get it, you're new, but there's a way things are done. Those people out there were scared and our first job is to make sure they are okay. Respect the client, and more than that, respect the *danger*."

"What danger?"

Michael rolled his eyes and headed up the stairs to the second floor. "I'm going to assess the upstairs." He brandished his net, patted his knife. "I'll call down if I need you, Archer."

"You got it," I said then turned to Jessie. "He respects the danger. He doesn't walk unprepared into a house he's unfamiliar with."

"Raptors are what, two feet tall? I can handle them."

"Sure you can handle one of them. Maybe two. But ten? If you've get ten raptors around you, don't look to me for help, because I'm not helping. You're dead meat then. Nothing you can do about ten."

"There weren't any."

"Lucky you."

He leaned against the wall and stared at me.

I said, "So you got one thing right."

"Oh yeah?"

"Yeah. It's bad in here, but it's manageable. While Michael's checking out the upstairs you and I are going to hit a few hot spots and see if we can't put down or capture a few on their own."

"You're not worried about him up there alone?"

"He's been doing this a hell of a lot longer than you. Come on."

The first floor had a kitchen, a half bath, a small study and a living room. There was a door in the kitchen that led to a back yard. The sun was coming up now and light shined in through the door and cast long shadows along the kitchen's wood floors. The half bath was in the hallway between the foyer and the kitchen and that's where we went first. The door was open and Jessi walked inside ahead of me—

—and was immediately knocked to the ground. The force of the velociraptor's attack slammed the door shut and both their bodies wriggling on the ground kept me from easily reopening it. The creature shrieked so loud my ears felt like they might bleed. Jessi was screaming too.

Michael bounded down from upstairs.

I pushed as hard as I could against the door with no luck. "Jessi, listen to me!" I hoped he could hear me over his screaming. "Keep your hands around its neck and push. Do not let it bite you. If it bites you, it's got you."

"*Get in here, man!*"

"Roll away from the door!"

"It's going to kill me!"

"Throw it and roll!"

I heard a thud, and a screech of annoyance from the raptor and I pushed. The door swung inward just as the raptor lunged a second time. I had my net out in front of me fast enough that it leaped right into it, snapping its jaws like wild and getting just bits of net for its effort. Within moments it had knotted its legs and tail in the net.

Michael took his own net and we double wrapped the son of a bitch. "What the hell happened?" he asked.

Jessi was on his feet and out of the half bath. My arms were shaking from the effort of stopping a full on lunge from a raptor and I was feeling a bit dizzy from the sudden change of pace so I didn't see Jessi unsheathe his blade until he was standing over the netted dino and plunging it into its throat.

"Fucking monster!" he said, and twisted the blade.

Michael dropped his net's pole and shoved Jessi away from the dying dinosaur. "What the hell is the matter with you?"

"It almost killed me!"

"It was caught! You…you can't just…" and Michael turned away and clenched his fists.

The raptor jerked around a moment more before going still. Its blood pooled out around it, shiny and slick in the hallway light. I leaned over the corpse, yanked the knife out of its neck and handed it, still bloody, to my young apprentice. "Put this back on your belt, you imbecile," I said.

He took the knife and looked at the two of us like we were nuts.

We all stood quietly for a moment, catching our breath. Then I lifted my left hand up in front of Jessi's face and spread my remaining fingers wide, so he could get a good look at the gap between my pointer and pinky. Then I lowered my hand again.

We could hear the velociraptors scuttling about beneath the floorboards, anxious and agitated in the basement.

I said, "When I was five years old, we had a nest of these fuckers in our house. The day my dad found it he went into the shed and got a hammer and bashed the brains in of the mother, right there on the cold cement basement floor. Then he took the hammer to the eggs. One, two, three, four eggs broken to bits, spewing their insides around the nest. Just before he broke apart the last one I snatched it up and held it to my chest and told him to stop. Not this one, Daddy, I said. This one is good.

"It took some pleading and some tears on my part but he didn't think the thing would live without its mother anyway so he let me keep it. I'd be damned if that thing wasn't going to hatch so I got myself a heat lamp and built a nest out of twigs and set it up all cozy on a chair beside my bed. About a week later it hatched. Tiny little thing scared about the world and I scooped it up and loved it to pieces right away.

"Dad told me I was an idiot for keeping the thing, but if I was going to keep it I had to respect it. Velociraptors, he said, were not my friend. They were *dangerous*, and if I didn't respect the danger, I was going to pay for it. And you know what, Jessi? Five year old me didn't know jack shit about respect, or danger, or putting the two together.

"It grew up fast, and before long I was feeding it half a chicken breast four times a day just to keep it happy. But I was playing with it, too. The way you play with a cat, I guess. Fetch. Petting it. I loved the damn thing. Then, one day, when he was about the size of a cat actually, he up and bit me. I was so surprised that it didn't hurt at first. He got my middle and ring fingers square in his jaws and chomped. And squeezed. And then the pain set in. And the blood started flowing. And my little friend the velociraptor, he stared growling.

"I screamed as long and as loud as I could and my dad eventually came into my room. When he saw what was going on he crossed his arms. Jessi, he crossed his arms and he stood there. He stood there and he said, "What did I tell you, son?"

"That's all he said, over and over again. "What did I tell you, son?" until I heard the bone and cartilage rip away and I fell back onto my bed and my hand was spurting blood like a fire hose."

Jessi looked at my hand now where it hung beside me. "Jesus..." he said.

"I didn't respect the danger, Jessi," I said. "And I paid for it."

In the kitchen the fridge was wide open. There was plastic on the floor from some wrapped deli meats beside a busted open carton of milk. Three-pronged milk prints led to a gaping hole in the wall beside the fridge.

Michael cautiously approached the hole in the wall. "Wonder how long this has been here."

"Not long," I said. "Could have happened when we were outside. They know the family is gone."

The house was theirs.

I used the sledgehammer to bust the hole wider. A few babies fell away from whatever they'd latched onto within the wall and back to the basement below. Adolescents would be too large to crawl around in the walls, so I wasn't concerned with any serious attack.

"How did the upstairs look?" I asked Michael.

"It's clear. I think the rest are all down there."

"All right," I said, and looked at Jessi. "Let's head down stairs. Jessi, I want you in front."

The door to the basement was beside the kitchen pantry. With my hand on my blade I opened it slowly but there was nothing on the stairs. A smell like shit and bad breath wafted out from the doorway. Jessi coughed. Then he took the lead.

"Take it one step at a time," I said. "Anything lunges at you, I want you to get it in your net."

"Okay," he said.

"You get anything in your net, you come back upstairs and we get it into a cage. If you can't get it into your net, then you can put it down."

"Okay," he said.

"Net first, knife second."

"I got it," he said and looked back at me. "Okay? I got it."

We descended the stairs in a line with Jessi in the lead and made it all three of us to the bottom without any sign of a raptor. This did not sit well with either Michael or me.

"Be careful," I said.

"There's nothing down here," said Jessi, and he lowered his net. Then he stood frozen, listening. "Over in the corner," he said.

There was a single dinosaur, not quite a baby and not quite an adolescent, curled up there, squeaking quietly. It had tiny brown feathers along the ridge of its head and along its tiny stick like arms. It reminded me of the one that had taken my fingers.

"Stay where you are," I said.

"It's all alone," said Jessi, inching toward it.

"No, it's not," said Michael.

Jessi shook his net. "I'll use this, don't worry." The attitude had returned to his voice. "I won't hurt your little friends."

Michael took a slow step forward, but not much farther than the stairs, in case he had to run. "Jessi, for God's sake get back here. We haven't gotten a good look around. We—"

And then they crept out of the shadows, out from behind boxes, behind the water heater, the furnace. More than I could immediately count. All sizes. Some were larger than I'd ever seen before, as high as my hips. They growled in unison, the sound vibrated in the air.

Jessi was so focused on the little one he hadn't even seen them yet. But Michael had, and he was already moving. The look on his face was the same one I imagine Mrs. and Mr. Wexler had when they found one of these raptors leaning over their baby boy, its breath steaming his flesh, its feathers shuddering with anticipation.

Michael grabbed Jessi by the shirt collar and threw him back toward the stairs. He turned to run back as well, but one of the big ones got his Achilles between its jaws and Michael fell hard to the concrete floor.

And then they were on him, all of them. The whole family was there, and dinner was served.

Sometimes it only takes a moment for a hard lesson to sink in, and Jessi's first glimpse of what was happening just might have been that moment. I don't know. I don't care. The kid made to run for the throng of raptors that had engulfed Michael and were tearing the clothes and flesh from his body, but I got my forearm around his neck and dragged him half way back up the stairs, growling in his ear, "There's too many, you fuck, there's too damn many…"

I can't describe Michael's screams. I don't think I have to. But they were there. They are always there for me now, really.

I loved the guy.

When we were halfway up I stopped, kept my arm around my new apprentice's neck, and twisted him around. He struggled against me. I held him firm.

"You watch," I said.

"No…,"

"You look and you watch what you've done."

"We can help him!"

"Think about what he did for you."

One of the raptors made its way from the throng with Michael's arm in its jaws.

Jessi vomited and it burned my forearm. I squeezed him tighter.

"Think about his baby boy, at home, in pain because he's teething."

Jessi began to cry.

I squeezed him tighter and put my mouth against his ear and my own tears washed from my face and into Jessi's hair. "Think about that baby boy and what you did to his daddy, Jessi!"

Let me tell you, that kid thought about it. He thought about it long and hard. And I imagine he still does, every time we're out on a job together, every time we're interviewing for a new apprentice. He looks at the green kids and remembers what it was like to watch Michael get eaten alive.

He learned to respect the danger.

A few of the raptors looked up to the stairs.

It was time to leave. I let Jessi go and he raced up the stairs and I followed. I slammed the basement door and we made our way past the dead raptor in the hall and out to the van. Jessi fumbled with the door handle, sweating, frantic.

The sun was fully up.

It was a cloudless, beautiful morning.

"Where the fuck do you think you're going?" I said.

"He...he..."

I took my phone out of my pocket and threw it at him as I walked to the back of the van. He caught it. "Call the Wexlers," I said.

Jessi turned on the phone and opened the recent calls list. He took a breath. Collected himself. "What do I tell them?"

I swung open the doors and wrapped my mangled hand around the flame thrower. "Tell them we'll be done before noon after all."

V is for Vermin

Hal J. Friesen

For Lisa Cranston, the battle for the Earth-spirit started in the zoo. Not in the ferns and amidst the dinosaurs, but in the four-story complex that stuck out of it like the hilt of a knife.

She crept beneath ten-foot ceilings in a maze of empty cubicles that all looked unused. On the far side sat a wide-bordered office in a corner of the EnBio corporate building. Ornate drapes hung behind glass walls but muffled shouts snuck through the folds. There was a faint smell of fresh paint.

Next to her a floor-to-ceiling glass window looked out on the sea of protesters. They girded the building, held back by security guards with raised arms and batons. Behind them the dense tropics of the zoo waited for salvation.

Lisa knew her sister Dana's protesting wouldn't save the dinosaurs. EnBio's CEO was too good a manipulator to get anything but what he wanted. That's why Lisa had needed to get in and under the veil, to record the side he never showed the public and force EnBio to keep feeding the dinosaurs to save face.

She hadn't realized her real motivation until she'd snuck in through the underground shipping tunnel. When her resolve had been tested in the face of true action, she realized the dinosaurs she'd nurtured were mirrors of herself.

Both of them were genetic abnormalities no longer wanted by the world, who needed to plead their case for existence. Both victims of CRISP-R. The dinosaurs, brought back by the genetic modification technology, would die simply because the people holding the reins had lost interest. Lisa and her sister might die because they were born naturally with a disease a genetically modified CRISP-R society could not abide.

And so, Lisa was not only fighting for the dinosaurs' lives; she fought for her own, too.

She had no idea what would happen if she got caught, but the risk was worth it. She'd shoulder that risk alone, though—Dana had no clue she was here. It was better that way.

Creeping closer to the glass door, in the hall between cubicles, she checked to make sure her phone was still recording. She'd been recording everything since she came into the building, partly out of terror that her body would give out on her at the worst time.

"I tell you, they're bloody real."

Lisa swallowed. The voice belonged to EnBio's CEO, Rick Morter, who appeared in countless ads. Her hands shook. The ever-present ache in her gut tightened.

"Do you think it's a coincidence the mudslide happened the day we set foot in that abandoned area of the zoo? No geologist would have predicted it. The Earth is fighting back. And I've got your ticket to listen.

"Yes, they talk. They feel. They think. These wights—these demon spirits halting progress in the natural world—can be defeated. Yes, I said wights. No, not ghosts. Ghosts can be innocent. Wights are not. Demon spirits—are you listening to me? They have a network they communicate on, and with this new technology, we can listen. We can be ready next time they try to stop us. Development *will* happen here. This is prime real estate that's being wasted on the stupid dinosaurs."

Lisa jerked. She'd expected the latter part of the conversation, but nothing else. She thought the company would discuss the starvation of the dinosaurs, maybe the latest fads in marketing, market share—but not demon spirits. Wights? Lisa considered going away with what she had as proof of Morter's mental instability but there was a chance it wouldn't be enough. She had come too far to leave without an iron-clad case.

"You're sure?" A guard's rough voice creeped behind from the far hallway.

"Things were jostled in the basement," another guard said.

Lisa squeezed her eyes shut. She'd left a trail.

"Nothing on the other floors?"

"Nope."

"He needs to know *now*."

"Mr. Morter!" the guard shouted. "Sir! Are you all right?"

Feet padded toward Lisa on the other side of the glass door. Her heart hammered. She surged into the nearest cubicle, darting beneath the desk.

Black leather shoes stepped into view, stretching up into pinstripe pants.

"What is it, Roderick?" Morter's Hollywood voice boomed baritone, rich and hearty.

"There's someone in the building. We're searching every floor."

The feet moved out of sight. Lisa closed her eyes and mouthed a thank you.

Then her phone buzzed. She tapped frantically to get it to stop popping up with error messages, each one wrenching her gut. It had run low on memory from all her recordings. No no no—

The leather shoes came back. Rick Morter crouched down, a giant barely confined to a suit.

"She's right here."

Lisa was too cramped to do anything but stare.

Morter's square jaw moved beneath a long face with curated lips, the lower a slight fuller than the upper. The eyebrows neat but thick, flat with a touch of roundness, and sky-blue egg-shaped eyes. His wavy black hair in the perfect brushed-back arch. Tough but tidy, announcing strength but gentility. Skin white, of course.

He looked the same as what Lisa had seen plastered on ads in every form of media, all touting the same message a thousand different ways: everyone had things CRISP-R could fix.

CRISP-R, the gene modification technology that could save everyone and even bring back dinosaurs, but only for profit.

Morter clamped a thick hand on Lisa's shirt and hauled her out. Her feet dangled. He handled her, a grown woman, like a child. His eyes held a vista of sky painted onto a hollow shell. "Well," he said, his smile reaching just as deep, "we'll have to tighten protocols."

Lisa thrashed. Her clothes tightened around her throat but words tumbled out of her nonetheless. "If you hurt me, EnBio is finished."

Morter smirked. "I haven't hurt anyone. I'm defending myself against an intruder. A non CRISP-R, probably anti-CRISP-R, am I right?"

How could he tell? He carried too much power; it practically dripped off him. She would take as much from him as possible, or make him share it.

"I wouldn't be anti-CRISP-R if you invested in curing Wilson Disease."

Rick Morter laughed. "Wilson Disease? That's archaic, too low percentage, too low return. Barely worth talking about."

Lisa spat, but only a sprinkle of saliva reached his unblemished cheeks.

"Anti-CRISP-Rs usually do that, too," he said. "Always from powerlessness. Did you really come here to convince me to cure Wilson Disease? You should have brought the other—what, five people—with you." He dragged her into the board room and tossed her like a rag doll onto a couch. She was grateful for the extra cushioned leather as her face landed in it.

He shut and locked the door behind him.

Lisa's throat tightened. When she spoke, her words carried small and trembling. "You can't get rid of me like you're doing to the dinosaurs. People will know."

Morter laughed. "I don't need to get rid of you. Your body will do that for me." He rolled out a chair and sat. "We're just going to sit here and talk until the protest is over."

"Let's talk about that cure, and how you're going to save the dinosaurs."

"First," he said, giving no sign he'd heard her, "give me your phone." He held out a hand as he leaned back.

Lisa swallowed. "I left it at home. I didn't want you to have any information on me."

He laughed. Lisa swore the glass panels shuddered each time.

"Do you have any idea what we do?

"I could find out where your ancestors were buried, and what genetic predispositions led to their pathetic demise, all with an overnight test. I could clone you—a better version of you—without your sickness, and your parents would be overjoyed with their *perfect* bundle of joy. Do you think there's anything I can find on *your phone* that will be more powerful than what I already have?"

Lisa crossed her arms, hiding trembling hands in her armpits. "If you can do all that, a cure should be no trouble. Nor would feeding the dinosaurs."

"I've devoted myself to this work for years," Morter said gesturing to the portraits around the room, always two children, two parents. "I can spot weakness from a mile away. I can see how close people are to death as though it stands in the room with them. I know you have your phone as clearly as I see your Wilson Disease and the fact you've sided with the hopeless dinosaurs. Hand it over."

"If you're so powerful, you don't need my phone," she said. "Nothing I have on there would interest you anyway."

"You're right; nothing on there interests me. What you have on there interests *others*."

"Feed the dinosaurs, cure me and I'll give it to you."

He sneered. "I've asked nicely more times than you deserve. You've trespassed on my property. You have no power, and the sooner you recognize that, the better off you'll be."

The moment Lisa gave him the phone, all her work would be for nothing. It was now or never. She reached a hand into her pocket, and swiped the passcode into her phone.

"Stop. Now," Morter snarled.

Lisa stood. "I'm calling—"

He vanished the space between them. Giant fingers reached in and threatened to crush her phone. He held her aloft once more, and ended the call before it started.

Lisa's heart turned to sand as Morter did a factory reset on her phone.

"Roderick!" he shouted.

Roderick came in, eyes hungry for blood. Lisa went limp in Morter's grasp.

"Get her out of here, same way she came in." He tossed the phone to him. "Give her this as she leaves." He turned to Lisa. "This will be the last time we see each other. Enjoy what's left of your life."

As the glass door closed on Rick Morter's perfect face, Lisa saw the dinosaurs' salvation and her own vanish into the black.

#

Months later, Lisa stood on a cracked sidewalk next to the river, staring through the window into a drug store. She hunched and cradled her belly.

Her sister Dana coughed beside her. "Let's go home," she said, laying a hand on Lisa's shoulder.

Lights inside painted the interior a pasty white and jagged EnBio advertisements poked out of the shelves every few feet down the aisles, bold fonts clamouring for view.

Pregnant? Ask your doctor about CRISP-R! Give your baby the best.

Lisa took a deep breath. If she had a baby, she could save it with the gene modification—but not her or her sister. She wished, not for the first time, that she could transfer her pain to Rick Morter.

"We have to try one more time," Lisa said. The partial reflection in the window showed her narrow face, eye bags and sallow skin.

Dana hobbled a few feet over to a bench. "All right. But promise you won't make a scene."

The ache behind Lisa's eyes pulled at her patience. She couldn't promise that. Let the pharmacist eat rice, bananas and white bread for a month, the diet she'd been on for longer than she wanted to remember.

Dana stared across the river. Her voice softened. "I can't believe the zoo's... over."

"I can't believe EnBio got the support they needed from the media," Lisa replied. "If they couldn't plan for the entirety of the dinosaurs' lives, why did they bring them into this world?"

Lisa followed her sister's gaze. Beyond the river, dense verdant foliage began, where dinosaurs had once roamed. Thanks to EnBio, no more.

"I miss them."

Faint lines drew across Dana's forehead. Half-moons hung beneath her almond eyes.

Lisa extended a hand.

"Let's try one more time."

Inside, as Lisa strode toward the pharmacy desk at the back of the store, she tried but failed to ignore the ads. No one could.

Rick Morter stood in a suit holding a perfect baby. Beside him: *Buy the Standard Package and get Elite Enhancements at no extra charge! Make sure your beautiful baby is healthy.*

Lisa closed the distance to the pharmacy counter. Beside it the sign said CASH OR INSURANCE ONLY.

She went through the same routine she'd tried at other pharmacies and hospitals. She tried her fake prescription for peritonitis antibiotics, which she and Dana genuinely needed, and proceeded to bribe the pharmacist.

She got the same disgusted remarks, threats to call security, all parts of a mechanical dance she'd somehow only learned to lose.

This time, however, when Lisa headed out with her bribe money and fake prescription, she found Dana sprawled on the store floor. It was suddenly all too real—the constant plodding not a pointless grind, but an absolute necessity as her sister's mortality stared her in the face.

They should have gone home. They should have quit after the first few pharmacies. They should have recuperated, saved their energy. Dana was always too kind to speak up when she was on the edge—

In a second Lisa crouched beside her, touching and checking neck, cheeks, shoulders—everything seemed okay—

"I can't feel anything below my waist," Dana whispered.

Lisa poked and prodded, gauging her sister's reaction.

"Nothing."

"Did you feel it coming?" Lisa asked, fighting to keep the panic from her voice.

Dana nodded.

"Why didn't you tell me?"

"Because there's nothing you can do about it," she said, closing her eyes.

Lisa called out for help and heard sounds of disgust from the pharmacist at the end of the aisle. "Fake prescription, no insurance," he muttered. "Bunch of parasites."

Knocking over bottles of shampoo and body soap, Lisa maneuvered with Dana to drape her over her back. She didn't feel her sister's weight, but her gut stretched with each step she took toward the front of the store.

"It'll be okay, Dana," she said. "It'll be okay."

They passed another Morter ad: *Ask your doctor what illnesses can be prevented by CRISP-R.*

Dana hung on Lisa's back as they made their way home. Lisa's thoughts churned, fuel to keep her strength up. If only they had seen the insurance cut-off coming, and had stocked up. Feigned injuries. If only they had thought to fake Dana's identity as a CRISP-R baby—for she looked the most picture-perfect of the two of them—then they could get insurance. But the policy changes were subtle, a few at a time, FDA inconveniences that combined until they were out of options. In a starving world where babies could be made perfect, there was no room for Wilson Disease or its complications.

Lisa thought she'd prepared herself for the end, but there was nothing she could do to prepare to lose her sister.

Death took Dana later that year, and then came for Lisa.

Lisa awoke, or rather didn't, as a ghost. She knew from the translucent sheen on her skin and the lack of moving blood in her veins that made everything feel in stasis.

Her ethereal body grew feverish, as though she were as sensitive to the winds of the spirit world as dinosaurs were to sunlight. She ran to enhance the sensation of branches pushing past and through her skin. The faster she ran, the more she felt, and the more she closed her eyes and pretended she was still alive.

Within minutes she recognized the paths of the zoo. Was she dreaming? Her spirit didn't have a reason to drift back to this place, did it?

She wanted to scream out for Dana, but didn't want to show death any more weakness. It had already taken too much from her.

She didn't stay with her thoughts long before she halted. Her feet sank into the mud beneath the sun-roasted grass.

A Utahraptor stood half in the bushes, its neck bowed low to the ground, its mohawk of feathers camouflaged like a tuft of grass. It growled, razor teeth barring blood-red gums. A festering scar ran the length of his neck, the unmistakable mark of Pisos, one of the earlier raptors she'd nurtured.

Lisa knew Pisos was dead; he'd been one of the first victims of EnBio neglect. A chill ran through her. Was this all a dream, or something worse?

The translucent sheen on the parts of Pisos's skin uncovered by feathers gave her the answer: Pisos was a ghost.

He growled again.

Lisa didn't know what could hurt her as a ghost but if the scratches she'd gotten from running through the bushes were any indication, then Pisos attacking her would be agony, if it didn't kill her again.

"Pisos," she whispered, struggling to keep the tremor from her voice. "Are we going to be okay?"

Pisos let loose a caw-croak. Lisa flinched, fighting the urge to turn and run. Her zoo training was kicking in. To run would send him the wrong message of dominance over her, and any respect or fear keeping him from attacking her would be destroyed.

"Come on, Pisos, calm down," she said, extending her arms. She'd never been this close to a raptor before, even with an enclosure separating them.

Pisos flapped his protowings, the feathered foreclaws that now grazed the ground. He cocked his head and readjusted his tree-trunk sized hind legs, half-moon claws tearing up the dirt. He grew still.

She'd seen the same pose before, but usually she watched from high atop a concrete enclosure.

He's going to jump at me. She took a few halting steps backward.

Pisos launched at her. She rolled to the side as one of his claws grazed her back. The cut sizzled and burned with vaporizing air. All Lisa could think was how she would be torn apart without seeing her sister again.

She couldn't outrun or overpower Pisos. There was only one thing to do.

Lisa scrambled up and onto the raptor's back, narrowly missing his snapping jaws, and tugged on the feathers of his neck, making his muscles jerk and twitch. She stood on his back with her head pressed next to his ear, a handful of feathers balled in her fist. "Listen, Pisos," she said, "I don't want to hurt you. We were friends, remember? I used to bring you your meals every day."

Pisos snarled and tried moving his head, but Lisa just pulled tighter.

"You know me," she said. "Pisos, you know me." Her eyes burned, wanting and failing to flow tears. "If the after-life is as full of as much hate as life, then maybe I should just let you tear me apart." The words made her chest ache. "But not until I see Dana."

Pisos sniffed, his nostrils twitching while the silence thickened. Eventually, his nose lowered as much as it could under Lisa's grasp. She relinquished and sat down on his knobby back.

Pisos shook his neck, then craned to look at her. The weight beneath her eyes lightened. "Friends," she whispered.

Pisos trilled and leapt into a sprint. Lisa clutched his feathers. They wove through dense foliage, the leaves alternately scraping and passing through Lisa as she ducked and bobbed with the raptor's insane pace.

They pushed out into a field where golden grass swayed in the wind. A luminescent figure sat beneath a tree, a Triceratops beside her.

Lisa's heart raced, and she dug her heels into Pisos to try and make him move faster. Her sister looked up, smiled, and waved.

Pisos closed the gap before Lisa knew it. She threw herself off and to the ground, accidentally taking a tuft of feathers with her. He groaned but otherwise bowed his head low so Dana could scratch it.

"You brought me the best gift ever, Pisos," Dana said.

Lisa stared between them. None of the reasons or explanations mattered. She jumped up and embraced her sister.

"I don't know what we are," Dana said later. "Maybe part of the Earth-spirit. Maybe we're haunting the zoo."

They sat in front of each other in the grass beside the mother Triceratops, while the wind made the grass shimmer in the sun.

"We can move through things like ghosts," Lisa muttered.

"You can feel the connections to everything, can't you?" Dana glanced down at the awakening baby Triceratops. It blinked its eyes, then turned toward her, one horn leaving an indent in her arm.

"A little," Lisa said, noticing the Triceratops glowed with the same faint light that shone in Dana. She reached across and patted the baby's belly, half expecting her hand to go through, or for the dream bubble to burst. Terrified that it would. Instead she felt soft wrinkled skin, the rise and fall of breathing. "They're ghosts too, right?"

"Yeah. But it's... more. I realized after a while... they're part of us, and we are part of them." Dana met Lisa's gaze with glistening eyes. "I'm so glad you're here."

"I was scared I'd never see you. That I'd be alone."

"I *was* alone."

A sharp pang stabbed Lisa. "I'm sorry."

"No, I'm glad you had more time than I did," Dana said. "I just... expected to see Mom or Dad, or anyone. But it was just the dinosaurs. They needed me to help them understand and protect them when EnBio came to develop this area. So far we've managed to keep it. Learning to be a deep part of them, of everything, has helped a lot."

The wind blew tufts of grass through Lisa's fingers, several blades at a time trickling out to the other side and away. They tingled as they went.

Though overjoyed at her reunion with Dana, Lisa couldn't accept or wrap her mind around their new existence. What did Dana mean to be a deep part of the dinosaurs?

"There are more dinosaurs than I thought there ever were at the zoo," Lisa mumbled. "Some I've never seen before."

Dana nodded, mouth drawn in a line. "Not all of EnBio's creations were made public."

"Bastards."

Dana nodded again.

"Are we cursed?"

"I don't know."

Lisa firmed her lip. "Maybe we can curse *them*." That was something she could wrap her head around. That, at least, made sense.

Dana shook her head. "The best thing we can do is stick together, Lisa. They can't fight us all at once. It's worked so far."

Lisa didn't think so.

As though reading her mind, Dana got a far-eyed look and described what had happened before Lisa got there.

EnBio had begun expanding its development into the zoo, sending in equipment to start turning the abandoned zoo into a corporate campus.

When Dana described the pain she felt whenever an artificial construct cut into the zoo's habitat, her face grew older, the years flitting by with every branch snapped along the path of destruction.

Dana had rounded up the dinosaurs and defended against the interlopers by smashing the soft soil near the river, and toppling the equipment into the river.

After that EnBio had started using electrified fences to delineate areas to clear-cut. Dana lost many dinosaurs in subsequent battles, and barely slowed EnBio down.

She and the dinosaurs had been moving farther into the hills, and they'd maintained a slim advantage from the fact EnBio never saw them coming.

But it was just a matter of time, Dana said, stroking the baby Triceratops. Lisa saw the creatures as Dana's new family, and knew she would let nothing come between her and her children.

Lisa resolved then to sneak her way into the EnBio compound. She knew they'd need to fight eventually, and that by waiting they gave up a huge advantage. How could she force her sister into a conflict-ridden carnage? They'd both gone through so much, and now that Dana had some measure of peace, Lisa would do nothing to threaten that.

Lisa would need a bit of help, based on what Dana'd told her. If Pisos came along, she'd make it past the defences, and wouldn't have to burden anyone else in order to tear down EnBio.

Lisa curled her fingers around Pisos's feathers. They raced through the dilapidated gates of the zoo toward the EnBio complex.

Rolling hills stretched out below them, a criss-cross of paths and roads all-too-familiar to Lisa. Black glass obelisks of EnBio's expanded complex jutted out of the rainforest at the edge of the man-made island.

Nothing moved. They'd made it past the electrified fences, and it was the perfect time to get in and disable EnBio's technology. Lisa didn't know how much influence she could exert once they got there, but the important thing was that she was doing something, and that she had a purpose she could wrap around herself like a cloak.

Pisos kicked up again and they surged through the parkways, along narrow strips of grass gilding a shallow stream winding its way through the zoo. Pisos leaped over the stream, landing in a whoosh of air. They wove back into the zoo's maze. Lisa knew they approached the main complex by the appearance of concrete paths, which Pisos avoided like hot lava.

Pisos slowed as they neared the edge of the grass pathway, a parking lot filled with dozens of cars. The air reeked of engine oil. Dana had told her about a cold static that lit her body when she touched artificial materials, but Lisa reasoned she'd tolerate the ghostly pain for the right reasons.

Lisa dismounted. The grass welcomed her like a warm cushion. When she reached the boundary separating nature from the manufactured reality of EnBio's domain, Pisos growled.

"It's okay," she said, stroking his feathers. "I'll go the rest alone." He twitched, his wide, wild eyes flitting about.

Lisa stepped onto the pavement. A chill snaked up her legs like a tundra and she lost all control. She slammed down, her head smacking the pavement. Electricity reignited pains from memory that wormed up her spine. She jerked and shuddered against the contact. Everything froze until it burned.

Dana had described nothing like this.

Lisa crawled, her limbs twitching and failing, breaths acid. Her left hand touched soil, and she felt tugging. *Pisos.* The word came through delirium.

Pisos pulled gently on her hand with his teeth. But the force that rooted her to the pavement gripped tighter and drew her closer. Pisos tugged harder and his teeth dug in, distant pinpricks compared to the consuming pain. Plasma's electricity, white and blinding, made up for the lack of blood.

She wrenched her arm until it shook, but it remained glued to the pavement.

Footsteps approached. "Wow, I never thought it would work so well."

Lisa stilled. She recognized that voice...

"Run Pisos. Get out of here. Now!"

Lisa shoved Pisos again and screamed at him. The raptor fled without a glance back.

A shadow snaked along her body. "The signal's saturated. It should be right here. I told you the new measures would pay for themselves."

Lisa craned her neck, and stared up at Rick Morter.

His suit blotted the sky. He beckoned some guards over. They had long rifles with electricity crackling at two-pronged ends.

The men fired their guns, and Lisa jerked upright. She twitched and shook as the lightning drove deeper.

"We only got one," Morter said from somewhere far away. "But this is a great start. Good work, everyone."

Lisa moaned. She thought Rick Morter had already taken everything from her, but even in death, he still held all the cards.

White tendrils snaked off Lisa's body. Blue bindings strapped her to a chair rocking in the back of a van.

Her ineffable connection to the Earth had become a hot line driving up her spine. And somehow, Morter squeezed it.

Morter sat in front of a screen taking up an entire side of the van. Readouts and numbers bobbed in crisp lines and clean graphics scattered over the display. The one thing of any real meaning was the map, which showed the zoo and its outskirts. The air reeked of solder and electronics.

Lisa wanted to tear off the restraints and smash through the back doors, but she shuddered with the pain of each effort. It was just as bad as when she'd been alive. Eventually she sat as still as stone in the chair, determined to simply avoid further torment.

A grip squeezed her tether to the Earth. Vibrant colours popped into focus. Leaves rustled and the sun's light blinded as branches parted to let the rays through. Lisa drew herself toward the light, a warm blanket sliding around her shoulders.

The wind quieted. The leaves reformed the canopy of shade. She stood amongst the herd of Titanosaurs, ankylosaurs, raptors and Triceratops. Lisa had never felt so relieved to see them. Some of the raptors nipped at the Titans' heels, but mothers halted and stayed their childish wrath.

Dana marched with spiked shells covering her forearms, batting away and disciplining dinosaurs who didn't exercise control for the common good.

Lisa wanted to wave at her sister, but the restraints...

Dana frowned, looking through Lisa as though they didn't have a lifetime of shared experience together. Lisa knew with sudden clarity she wouldn't get a chance to reach the zoo haven in front of her. Morter still had her in the van.

"Dana, get out of there!"

The grip on Lisa's spine tightened, and all the colours drew toward her in star bursts. She cried out as the colour burned away into the grey of Morter's van.

"We traced them," he said, turning to the driver. "We know where they are. For once, we'll get the jump on them." He walked over to Lisa, where the white tendrils cascaded off her like tears.

"You're the first one I've seen, you know that? Yet you seem familiar. I can't count the times I've wanted to tell you how you were ruining my business. Can demon-spirits understand the bottom line? Millions of dollars wasted, all of the friends who thought me insane for thinking you real? I'm grateful you are real and alive—in some sense of the word. You know what's the best part about you being real?"

Morter held up a fist clutching a remote. Lisa fell forward in the straps, pulled by invisible strings, hair dangling at his knees.

He leaned in until his lips tingled her ear. "Because you are part of reality, you can be ruined."

A chill creeped up Lisa's spine. She wanted to retreat, get as far away as possible, but she couldn't move. She thought of her sister's advice that they should stick together. She would give anything for someone to face this megalomaniac with her, but there was no one.

"Fascinating, your connection to the rest of them," Morter said. "If I got some of our scientists involved, they'd be chewing this for years before we did anything. Years before we made progress. They can keep their data points and technobabble. I'll keep the money."

Lisa's eyes burned. Tears would have helped, but she had none. Fighting against the restraints caused nothing but pain, and it seemed whenever she sank into the dream-vision of being with her sister, Morter honed in to the dinosaurs' location, if he didn't already have all the details.

Morter would seize her sister and all the dinosaurs, all because of Lisa doing what she'd always done: go in alone and try to take care of things herself. She'd done it during the protest, and she'd done it again by trying to outsmart EnBio. She should have known better. She should have listened to Dana rather than her stupid self. Her inward focus would leave her twice-dead and alone.

The only thing she could do now was avoid going into the dream-vision and making things worse. Lisa took in the details around her, trying to stay grounded in the horrible reality.

Framed pictures buffeted against the walls of the van. The family photos all showed two parents and two children, one boy, one girl. They bore the same poses, the father's hands on the son's shoulders, the mother's on the daughter's. The perfect-teethed smiles were all identical, pasted on from one to another. Lisa recognized them from the board room in EnBio.

The family pictures had slightly different facial structure, different hair colour, but in essence they were the same. A very narrow slice of what a family could be.

She'd thought they were propaganda, but this was Morter's personal van...

Dana and her dinosaur family were all Lisa could think of. She prepared to throw herself into the fire to stave off Morter's approach to the colony, where he would capture and hurt Dana, or worse.

The family images flashed in and out of focus. Fleeting memories pulsed with the pain, reminding Lisa of a time she had ignored her sister in favour of studying for exams, even when Dana had ended up in the hospital. She'd been determined to maintain her GPA, and things with Dana had never quite been the same for years afterward.

Lisa had to gamble on her assessment of Morter, but there was no other option.

"Where's your sister to celebrate this victory with you?" she said.

Morter's sky-blue eyes could have melted glass, but his face remained impassive. "What are you talking about?"

"Your sister. Your parents. They're obviously important to you."

A flinch betrayed the truth behind his cold expression. "EnBio seeks to bring out the best in families."

"Good marketing line, but that's not why those pictures are up."

He stalked over to her, hand on the remote. The tendrils tugged and squeezed Lisa, burning white spots into view. She heaved, collapsing again in the restraints.

"Be quiet," he said. "Your part's done."

Lisa dragged her gaze up off the floor. She smelled burning metal and the artificial sweetness of esters. "You can't have them, can you?" she said. "You want them but everything you've done chased them away."

Morter's cheeks grew red. "I hold myself to a higher ideal," he snapped. "I do what they can't. I devote myself to bringing in a world, the right world, they deserve to have. A world they will have. Every step of progress of EnBio brings me closer to that world."

"And you think it brings you closer to them."

Morter's jaw worked.

His psychology was a painful reminder of Lisa's regrets, all the selfish things she'd done to push Dana away, including her ignoble quest to take down EnBio alone.

Morter pulled on the tendrils again. Lisa craned her back as lightning arced up her spine.

Flashes of family portraits alit. Whispers accused, said she was capable of becoming Morter should she continue along the path...

She tried to deny the accusations but knew the truth. A few whispers snaked up from the connection to the Earth—past the pain—and rebutted the self-loathing.

A whisper spoke of a release from the pain if only she would let go of her attachment to the ghostly facsimile of her body. If she would let go of the inward focus that had gotten her into this mess, the same need for self-definition that drove Morter into the depths of evil. Lisa drew toward the voice, then retreated back into herself. Letting go felt like jumping into an abyss, but the alternative was to be electrified until she felt nothing at all.

She twitched on the edge of a precipice, her feet dancing a rhythm of indecision. Through all the pain, all the transformations and changes beyond comprehension, she was the one constant. She had remained intact despite it all. No way was she going to lose that.

But as she clung, the ground turned into quicksand, and she sank, cold wet stickiness groping up her legs. Everything she clung to pulled under, and soon enough there be nothing worth holding onto.

She heaved to pull her legs out of the muck, but it bulged over her kneecaps. She screamed, desperate for an exit, and stared into the abyss.

Lights twinkled on the boundary of the void, and Lisa strained to discern what lay in wait.

Riding atop a Titan, Dana sat in the bottom of the darkness. The nearby lights glinted from other ghosts and dinosaurs, their details blurry.

Lisa might lose herself by casting into the abyss, but her network would catch the pieces and remind her who she was, wouldn't it?

She owed it to Dana to get back and help, at any cost, even if they didn't catch any pieces of her at all. Next to EnBio's threat to her sister, Lisa's self-preservation didn't matter.

Lisa burst from the mud and cast down into the dark. Her body turned to smoke, the tendrils sizzling as she vanished into the connections, accepting her place as a linkage rather than separate from it. A linkage to her sister, her family of dinosaurs, and everything.

Far away, Morter shouted in surprise.

Lisa drifted through the spaces between, feeling nothing but intervening forces binding the community of dinosaurs and spirits together. She was nothing but a collection of emotions, tenderness and shared experience. Nothing could be a separate entity from anything else. Spirits floated in and out of the transient variances, rippling like pebbles dropped in a pond. Their translucent faces shimmered to be replaced by another's. The palpable thing lay in between the figures.

Lisa was nothing, less than the fleeting glimpses of players doing their part in the stage play of the Earth Spirit's drama.

And that was okay.

If Lisa never found herself again, she'd be content with that ineffable softness, that transient glint as part of an ebbing tide. For the first time in her life, she didn't need to feel separate, different or special. The grandness of the web more than made up for that. She didn't need a perfect image of herself distinct from the rest of the world. Strands of the web caressed, comforted, gave security. They coaxed the fragments she'd forgotten about back together, lightning converging into a single point of impact. Thunder shook the sky.

Dirt poured off of Lisa's skin smelling sweeter than honey. Clouds shifted above the treetops of the rain forest.

Dana rushed toward her, surrounded by Titans and raptors. Her family. The web incarnate.

After they embraced, Lisa said, "They're coming."

Dana nodded, and Lisa realized this level of connection must be what her sister had felt all along.

They scrambled to prepare for battle.

Titanosaurs formed a ring around Lisa and Dana, their long necks low to the ground.

Dana went over to one and patted the bump on its head. "They can hear the machines, the infrasonic rumble," she said.

They held the high ground atop rocky slopes.

"Maybe the Titans can't crush them," Lisa said. "But rocks can."

With Lisa on Pisos, and Dana on her young Titan Kirby, they readied to herd the Titans. Lisa swallowed, remembering the very real pain when Pisos had attacked her, and how they could hurt each other easily as ghosts. If one of the Titans didn't like being herded, she'd be crushed underfoot or maimed by its tail. And there were at least forty of the great beasts. She wasn't sure if she could die again, but knew the pain would be very real. Maybe second death would be better than an eternity of pain.

Lisa and Pisos moved around the periphery, nipping at the Titans' heels. The Titans bellowed and swung their tails around, Pisos dipping and narrowly avoiding them. A few of the other raptors weren't so lucky, and flattened against trees.

The Titans turned away and Lisa had to weave through their legs to head them off. Pisos nipped as they went, and a lumbering foot tried to crush them on their way past. The hornbill-elephant bellows and groans filled the forest.

Then Lisa heard the rumble. Machines—bulldozers, diesel trucks, excavators—approached. At this rate, when the destroyers arrived Lisa and Dana would have just gathered the dinosaurs for slaughter.

"We need that avalanche ready," Lisa said, tightening her grip on Pisos. "They'll be up here soon."

She and Dana frightened the Titans near the edge, who reared up on their hind legs until their heads dusted the clouds. Lisa and Pisos leaped away as the Titans' legs crashed down, air thundering.

The ground trembled, but the rock didn't break. The machines had started knocking over trees. All the machines turned and pointed up the hill and excavators clawed their way up toward them, carving a sloped path of destruction.

Lisa and Dana got the Titans to stomp again, in unison. The rock trembled but didn't break.

The machines didn't slow their advance.

Lisa wove her hands into her hair and pulled. No, no, no!

They stomped until it seemed the sky would fall.

The bucket of an excavator poked above the peak. Soon an avalanche wouldn't matter.

The machine crawled higher, the Titans recoiling from the diesel fumes. The cabin and operator showed, the driver another close copy of Rick Morter's facial type, as though he himself had come to do the work.

If she got the creatures to land on the same rock at the same time, Lisa felt certain the avalanche would begin.

Pisos nuzzled her and gave a gentle bite on the hand. She understood *him* well enough; the Titans, on the other hand, seemed braindead.

But she'd never tried. She'd put the time in with Pisos, but not with any of the other dinosaurs, the ones she'd just worked with but feared the entire time. Once more, she had been so focused on her own pain she'd made no effort to understand the creatures on their own terms.

There wasn't enough time to do what she'd done with Pisos. There was only enough time to take herself out of the picture.

Lisa closed her eyes and relaxed her grip. Delving into the spiritual darkness, she found the abyss. She leaped, her ghost vanishing into the space between.

She felt the Titans' urge to help, their helpless confusion as they sensed Dana's need with no clue how to respond.

Lisa flickered in the connections, and realized she could nudge, influence. She tried to bridge the gaps, act as a hand that pointed at what lay there already. She did this for one, then another, and another Titan. Her influence blew like a breath of wind bending the grass to uncover a gift buried in the weeds.

The Titans understood, and a moment later, two of them reared up and came crashing down on the same large section of rock.

Thunder resounded as rock split, and the excavator creaked back and away. The Morter lookalike screamed in the cabin, moving frantically to twist the gears.

The Titans stomped again, the shock nudging the excavator backward and down. As it fell, the rock crumbled apart like a sandcastle in the tide. Boulders smashed through operator cabins, collapsed digger buckets, tipped dump trucks. The shattering continued for several minutes, until the air thickened with dust and burnt metal. Leaves rustled in the treetops, a distant aftershock.

Lisa, drifting as nothing, would have been lost if not for Pisos's insistent tugging at hints of her.

She landed back in her ethereal form with a gasp. Pisos crouched, ready to pounce, and then nuzzled her.

Dana ran up beside her. They both took a few minutes to embrace and catch their breaths, while the dinosaurs around dispersed in slow herd movements.

"They think we're wights, demons sent to wreak havoc upon them," Lisa said.

Dana surveyed the dinosaurs. "I don't think they're wrong."

Lisa smiled at her sister's glowing figure. She was the best demon spirit anyone could have. Pisos and the Titanosaurs weren't too bad, either.

They'd won this battle, but many more would come. For Lisa, the battle for the Earth-spirit had become a war, and if the Rick Morters of the world hadn't yet perished, they soon would.

And they would fight together.

W is for Wight

BD Wilson

The waiting room was full when Victor arrived at the medical bay. He stood in the corner and fought back a yawn. It was still two hours to his shift, which meant he was up at least an hour and a half earlier than he wanted to be. He scratched at his arm, all the while telling himself to ignore the itch and failing.

Victor was relieved when the monitor in the corner switched from the recreations to the morning address, Dr. Rumsfeld's image fading in to provide a distraction, his warm voice greeting them as he always did.

"Good morning, Sentinels. I know that you, like me, are looking forward to the work of the day." Today's was the one in front of the beach, with its bright blue sky, deep dark water, and almost white sand. The sun was soothing and bright, and Victor wished he could feel the warmth. "I know you are eager to continue our quest to make a difference for this world. We are so close to our break-through. I know today is the day we will see it through to fruition."

Victor had been in the Institute for two years, and every day from his first to now, Dr. Rumsfeld had known it was the day they would see it through to fruition.

Still, every day he felt the hope rise in his chest, the possibility so close he could feel it on his skin like the light of the sun on Rumsfeld. They had been working on this for so long, surely they really *were* that close.

"Say it with me, Sentinels," Rumsfeld continued, "I am looking forward to the work of the day."

"I am looking forward to the work of the day," Victor said, in time with everyone else in the waiting room, including the medical staff.

"I am eager to continue our quest to make a difference in this world," Dr. Rumsfeld said, his arms raised and fists tightening to reinforce the image.

"I am eager to continue our quest to make a difference in this world," they repeated. Victor tried to say it with the sincerity and commitment of the doctor. He was never certain it came through in his voice, but he could feel it in the movement of his muscles as he repeated the gestures he saw on the screen.

"I am a dedicated member of the Institute, and I will not allow anything to stand in the way of our great work."

"I am a dedicated member of the Institute, and I will not allow anything to stand in the way of our great work." He said it with firm resolve, but that part was easy.

That was why they were all here, after all. If they did not believe it, they would leave.

"Excellent, brothers and sisters," Rumsfeld said, and pressed his hands together in front of him. "Now go forth and do good work, Sentinels. Namaste." His image flickered off the screen, which returned to showing the usual video of how illness affected a system, how injury and weakness from sleep deprivation or drugs could accelerate it. Victor sighed and shifted on his feet.

"Victor," the nurse called, "we have a room for you now."

"Thank you," he murmured and followed the other man down the narrow, door-filled hallway.

The nurse, who he thought was Collin and felt terrible for not knowing after so long, opened the door of a room at the end, the last one before Quarantine. "Doctor Yari will be with you shortly."

"Thank you," Victor said again and slipped into the room. The door closed, and he felt an irrational sense of relief. Even though he knew it was important to have one in a facility like this, he hated the quarantine room. It was too much like having a prison, though he supposed they had one of those too, on the security level somewhere.

The examination room was small, just enough space for the table, a chair, and a small shelf with the more typical treatments, depressors and things. Victor hopped up on the examination table, making the paper crackle. On the wall, a monitor showed the same video that had been playing in the waiting room. He didn't quite know this one by heart, but he'd been in the medical bay often enough over the past month or so that he was coming close.

"Be sure to take care of yourself," he said along with Dr. Rumsfeld's narration, trying to capture the concern in his tone. "Your health is vital to our mission, and illness thrives on weakness."

The door opened, and he felt himself flush at getting caught reciting along with the video. Dr. Yari didn't seem to notice, or if she had, she was kind enough to continue without mentioning it. "Victor, back again. What can I do for you today?"

"Still the same rash," he said. "I used up the cream you gave me, but it doesn't seem to have done anything."

"That sounds like a persistent one. Let me take a look."

He pulled up his sleeve, exposing the skin he'd pretty much scratched raw. The rash was scaly and rough, with faint lines running through it, but most of the details were lost in the red splotches, and the marks his nails had left.

She shook her head. "Really Victor, you should have come back to see me before it got this bad."

"I didn't want to be a bother," he said. "Plus, nothing was really helping, so I thought it would just stay the same anyway. It's just that it itches."

"Sometimes change takes time," she chided. "And sometimes, it takes trying a number of different things. Isn't that why we're here?"

"I guess you're right," he said with a chuckle. "I'll come in sooner next time."

"See that you do." She finished the examination and then sighed. "You're right that it doesn't seem to be any better, though. I'm going to try you on a stronger cream. Give it a couple of weeks, and if there still isn't any change, come back." She made a note in his chart, and then pulled a tube of the cream from the top of the small cabinet.

"Thank you," he said, once again glad that one of the Institute's benefits was medical coverage. She made him put some of the cream on immediately, and he felt a little sheepish as he laughed and did as she ordered. The itch subsided, and he was hopeful this one would work. He tucked the cream into his pocket, following a few other patients as they also left. He wasn't the only one with the same tube, but then, that was one of the drawbacks of working for the Institute. With so many people in the underground facility, it was almost worse than a daycare when it came to illness.

He was one of the last people to the cafeteria for the morning meal. He preferred getting there early and finding a seat while there were still plenty available. At least it didn't take long to fill his tray with the prescribed meal of fruit, tofu, and a green smoothie. When he scanned the room, he quickly found Kayla sitting at a table with a free seat, maybe even a saved seat, and joined her.

She handed him the salt and pepper shakers as soon as he sat down. "The tofu is even more tofu-y than usual today."

"Thank you."

She held up her smoothie glass and turned it in her hand. "I miss food that has colour. Other than green."

"Hey," he said as he pointed at the cantaloupe, "orange is a colour."

"In that shade, barely. But fine, I miss food that has colour and flavour. I would kill for a piece of bright yellow pineapple."

"Maybe they'll have some next week."

"You always say that," she said with a sigh, and then grimaced before she chugged the smoothie.

"Stranger things have happened."

"Especially around here."

"What do you mean?"

"Don't worry about it. Are you still in Lab D?"

"Yup, fungus, fungus, and more fungus." He'd been assigned there six months ago, and it didn't look like he was going to be reassigned anytime soon. Based on the logs, the lab had high turn-over. They were probably happy to have someone who didn't mind the repetitive work.

"Well, it's probably more interesting than weather disbursement patterns from millions of years ago. No matter how much intel we have, we're still just guessing." She shook her head. "It's all estimated data anyway. It's not like anyone had sensors in the Cretaceous period, right? So, ice shelf analysis, fossil records, glacial striations, all the stuff we can't really say for certain recorded what we think."

Victor shifted in his seat and focused on his food. They weren't supposed to talk about the experiments in other labs. It might cause problems with studies later. Still, he never liked to ask Kayla to stop talking about anything, especially not when it was him she was talking to.

"But estimates are good, right?" he asked, trying to bring her back to more generic terms.

"Good enough for horseshoes, but that's not what we're playing." She put her empty smoothie glass down and began tidying up her tray. "Have you ever been in the room with Dr. Rumsfeld?"

"No," he said and felt a slight shimmer of jealousy. But Kayla was one of the scientists, and he was just a lab tech and an Institute-trained one at that. "He usually talks to Gerry."

"He's pretty demanding." She sat up and her eyes widened. "I mean, don't get me wrong. He's the same motivational guy who got us all here, but it's just that he expects everything to be perfect."

"What we're doing is important."

"I get that, but what I'm doing is based on estimates and flat out guesses. There is an inherent margin of error, and it's big. He needs to understand that." Kayla sat back and sighed. "Sorry, it isn't fair to dump all that on you."

"I don't mind."

"That's because you put up with way more than you should." She smiled at him, and he was pretty sure there was genuine affection there. "Thank you, though, for listening. I better get back to it."

"Have a good day," he said as she packed up her tray. She returned the greeting on her way out, calling it back over her shoulder.

Victor reached the first set of doors and scanned his key card. It took a few seconds before he was authorized, his ID flashing in the display window before he was let in. From there he walked the fifteen steps to the second set of doors, and entered it with his key card and thumbprint. At the third doors, it was key card, thumbprint, and voice sample.

Every now and then, he thought the security in the lab was perhaps a bit over the top. After all, it wasn't like anyone could enter the

Institute facility itself without authorization. Why did they need security doors to keep out other Sentinels?

The third door opened on the locker room. His personal locker only had a three digit combination, but it wasn't like anyone would steal anything from him. He didn't have anything to steal. He changed out of the Institute-issued casual clothes and put on scrubs. Over those he slipped on the protective suit, covered his shoes in the paper slippers, secured his face mask, and fixed on one glove.

The lab door required the key card, thumbprint, voice sample, and a blood sample. After it pricked his finger, he wiped on the disinfecting sealant, and secured the second glove before entering the lab proper. Gerry was already there, a tray full of samples in front of her, checking their growth progress, and recording data in the computer system.

"You're late."

"I'm sorry. I had to see the doctor and the only appointment time available was this morning and then I had to make it for the meal."

"Victor, take a breath. I was teasing." She looked up and smiled at him, though it was hard to see through the mask. "You're the most punctual person in the whole place. I think you've earned a few minutes tardiness."

He looked down at his paper-covered shoes, and then forced a chuckle. "Sorry."

"No, I'm sorry. I know you take your job seriously. Too seriously, but seriously." There was something off in her voice, a raspy sound that wasn't usual. Behind the mask, he thought her eyes looked red, and her skin a little pale, but she carried on like nothing was wrong. "Speaking of, we're going to need another tray prepped. Can you get that ready?"

"Of course." He relaxed as soon as he had the day's task, and let Gerry continue cataloging the samples, but he noticed her hands seemed to be shaking. He ignored it for now, and began to prepare the

Petri dishes for a new batch. "We've been making a lot of these lately."

"I know. Dr. Rumsfeld has increased the number of experiments using them. I wish I knew why."

"Maybe we really are getting close," he said as he took the initial fungus sample from the storage container, and carefully transferred pieces to the new dishes.

"I hope that's it," she said, a touch of excitement entering her tone, audible even though the raspiness. "Can you imagine? I mean, how long have you been here?"

"Five years."

"Five years, I've been here two. When he hired me for the job, Rumsfeld promised we were going to change the world. I wasn't sure it would actually happen in my lifetime, but if we pull it off? That would be incredible." She broke off, coughing, and then groaned. "Right, coughing in a protective suit sucks, in case you're curious."

"It looks pretty terrible. Are you sure you're all right to be here?"

"I'm not sure, actually. I cut my damn hand on a broken glass this morning, and now I'm getting a cold. I'm going to give it another half-hour, and then make up my mind."

Their conversation trailed off as they both got caught up in their work again. In the background, the monitor played the session on prehistoric plants and animals. There was a bit about the food chain, about carnivores eating the herbivores who ate the plants. Then a piece that always caught his attention.

"Our worlds were not so different," Dr. Rumsfeld said. "The dinosaurs were the largest animals, by all appearances ruling over the Earth. And yet, they could be felled by viruses and bacteria, by the smallest of creatures. The true survivors of that time, the real strength, was found in the meekest of them all. Ever humble fungus—a species that spreads unnoticed by most—managed to outlive the dinosaurs. Or more to the point, it slept, waiting to be uncovered."

He continued, describing the discovery of the fungus spores in preserved samples, the tiniest particles recovered in the imprint of a dinosaur's hide, and placed in a lab. Described how they discovered the ancient specimen was indeed still viable when a curious assistant attempted to grow a culture from it. Like a time traveller, it was an ancient species in a new age, and Dr. Rumsfeld believed it was vital to their cause.

As Victor loaded tray after tray of that same fungus into the culture bath, he wondered how it could help them. Was this the cure for cancer? To some other disease? Could they uncover the ability to regrow brain cells or repair spinal cord injuries? It was a lot of expectation to place on the back of a fungus, but each one of those Petri dishes held his hopes for a better future, even if he didn't know how they would bring it about.

Gerry began coughing again, attempting to cover her mouth, even though she couldn't through the mask. "That's it," she said, and began to pack her samples away. "I need to go see the doctor."

"Let me take care of that," he said. "I know the procedure."

"Thanks, Victor." She unclasped a card from her belt and handed it to him. "Lab's yours for the remainder of the morning, at least. I'll let you know how long I'll be out once I know, but Jason should be in for the afternoon shift."

He took the card, somewhat uncomfortable as he added it to his credentials, and watched her leave the lab. She slumped on the bench in the locker room as she stripped off the suit. Her skin was flushed, she was sweating, and her eyes were bloodshot. He hoped it wasn't serious. She waved her bandaged hand at him, and left the locker room. When she was out of sight, he packed away her samples, and returned to making more.

It was repetitive work, the same motion dish after dish, but he didn't mind that. He listened to the video in the background, and imagined what the world would be like when it was cured of all diseases. What it would be like when people no longer had to worry about family members dying and leaving them all alone.

A couple hours later, Gerry called to say she'd caught something contagious enough to be put into quarantine for a few days. Victor shuddered and told her to get well soon.

Quarantine was probably the worst place in the entire building, and he really hoped Gerry didn't have to stay in it long.

The lab video reached the first of the computer-generated simulations. The style was something Victor would have expected in a museum or an educational program. It had always seemed odd to him to have it in the talks for the Sentinels, though he supposed those were, in their own way, an educational program.

There were three dinosaurs in the scene, ones he couldn't identify. (Dr. Rumsfeld never seemed to include those who had ruled Victor's childhood: Brontosaurus, Triceratops, and of course, Tyrannosaurus Rex.) These were large and small, with bright colours and frills, walking together or fighting as the scenes shifted and Dr. Rumsfeld's calming narration played over all.

"We are not, no matter how much we would like to think so, the only, or even first, masters of the planet. There were many before us who lived across the vast surfaces of our world, who co-operated or fought as they and their natures saw fit. The difference, I believe, is the amount of damage we have been able to do. The dinosaurs did not deplete the ozone layer, they did not pollute the waters and the air, they did not weaken this precious planet as we have."

As he worked, Victor glanced now and again at the video, though this was the one he knew by heart. All this time, though, and he could still find new points to ponder in what were before just words. Most recently it had been something about the plants that had grown back then, the ones the herbivores fed on, and how they were now extinct as well. It wasn't just the animals, it was everything. Somehow, while he had been presented with the information constantly, it had never quite resonated that way before.

"What can we learn, brothers and sister, from these masters of the past?" Rumsfeld's voice raised here, taking on the cadence and volume of a preacher more than a scientist. "We can learn from their example, from how they lived and how they died. We can take it as instruction for how we should move forward ourselves. It is a warning, and we will heed the lesson it teaches."

This was the point Victor spent most of his days pondering, but he still did not know what lesson they were supposed to take from the dinosaurs. They were killed out through a meteor, weren't they? Or some environmental event? He supposed that last was a lesson, in that they were changing the environment so much through their actions, they might bring about a similar event, but it didn't seem to fit.

At least the puzzle gave him something to think about in the quiet lab, as he finished up the new samples and left them to grow. It had been a productive morning, and with luck, in a few days, Dr. Rumsfeld would have more samples for whatever research was being carried out. Victor was preparing an additional tray, just in case, when the klaxons began to sound.

He froze, his hands in the air above the tray, still holding a Petri dish. His mind went blank.

Instinct, or more precisely, training took over.

He put the Petri dish into place, and then put the entire tray into the fridge and locked it. He went around the lab, quickly but methodically, locking everything within. When he'd made the round, he let himself out, shut the door, and used the card Gerry had given him to initiate the lockdown. The credentials and security level that flashed across the screen were not ones he should have had, and again he felt the uncomfortable stab of doing something wrong as he put the card away. It wasn't exactly against protocol to hand off the lockdown card to a lab tech, if they were the only ones available, but it wasn't encouraged either.

When he had started working at the Institute, when they still ran drills like this every few days, the wrong person having the cards on them would be grounds for a talking to by the security forces. It had been so long since they'd run a drill, though, he'd almost forgotten what the klaxons sounded like. Now, as he pulled off his mask and suit, dropped them into the receptacle before leaving the lab, he listened to the pace and the pitch, watched the lights flash, and tried to identify the problem.

The Institute had five categories of alarms. The first was a typical fire drill, the same sort you'd find in any organization that needed to move a large number of people out of a building quickly. The next was a breach of the internal security doors, and accidentally setting that one off was common in the days when everyone was new and no one knew where they fit. The third was a containment breach in the labs, to be expected given the different substances they were working with. Fourth was a computer systems breach, which usually only concerned the IT staff. The fifth was a facility breach, someone who did not belong getting through the outer doors.

A cold chill settled in Victor's stomach, as he realized this was a category five alarm. The halls were crowded with people attempting to get to their designated muster points, and marching through them in the opposite direction were the security forces, fully outfitted with riot gear and guns.

He reached the mess hall, the muster point for lab technicians and scientists, and slipped in, drifting through people who didn't look as lost as he felt. Instead, most of them looked bored, and some annoyed. The alarm sound changed, sped up and yellow lights turned to orange.

Category five, level two, something he had never seen before. Drills only ever reached level one.

Victor searched through the crowd in the mess hall, and realized Kayla wasn't there. She should be there, unless something had happened to her. Something had to have happened to her.

He shifted his weight from foot to foot, watching the doors and hoping she would appear, hoping she had just been late, but none of the stragglers were her. His arm began to itch as nervousness set him on edge, and he realized the cream was still in his locker. He bit the inside of his lip to keep from scratching, and focused on the door, but Kayla still wasn't there. Murmurs began to flow through the crowd, as people searched for everyone they knew. No one was watching him, and he drifted back near the doors.

Before he could think about what he was doing, he slipped out.

The corridors were empty now, though he could hear the echoes of the security forces calling out, confirming their locations and clear halls. He walked as fast as he could without making a sound, turning at the corner that led to the analysis labs, following the markings on the floor. He wasn't supposed to be here. He wasn't assigned to these labs, and he didn't have clearance to be in this part of the Institute, had not been in it since the tour when he first arrived. At every corner he peered around, checking to see if the security teams were there, he expected to hear someone yell at him, order him to get to the ground.

No one did, and he reached Kayla's lab, only to find the door open, unsecured. Inside the orange lights reflected off the monitors of the workstations, everything still turned on. Victor didn't know the protocols for this lab, but he knew this was wrong. He crept through the room, looking for some sign of what had happened.

The monitor on the wall was still playing this lab's talk, the speech Dr. Rumsfeld thought would best inspire Kayla and her co-workers. It was one Victor had never heard before, and for the first time since he'd taken the position in the fungus lab, he heard Dr. Rumsfeld speak unfamiliar words.

"There is an order to all things in life," Rumsfeld said. In this presentation, he was standing on a mountain cliff, overlooking an ocean. His hair, what was left of it, blew in the wind as he faced it. "To our lives as we progress through them, to the animal kingdom, to the cycle of the seasons, to the hydrologic cycle that sees our water recycled and replenished. Nature is order, and so often, that order revolves, everything that existed taken up to become all that is now."

Diagrams replaced him, showing water evaporating and raining down and weather patterns around the Earth. The change broke the spell that held Victor motionless, and he continued his search as the presentation went on.

"Time, too, is a cycle. It is not trite to say those who forget the past are doomed to repeat it. In fact, it is one of the most accurate proverbs we have. We must all learn from the past." The image switched again, to the more familiar recreations of the dinosaurs. "If we forget, then the lesson must be learned anew."

The monitors around the room were showing simulations, some similar to the graphics that had so recently been in Dr. Rumsfeld's talk. Weather patterns, for the most part, and Victor remembered Kayla talking about migration, plotting it, trying to guess at it, when she was telling him things he should not have been hearing.

A few of them had simulations that looked to him like population patterns, which he'd seen once in a presentation Dr. Rumsfeld had given at his University, before Victor had joined the Institute. There Rumsfeld had been talking about how the population of the world had increased over the years. Here, it looked like it was running in reverse. On the next screen he found another weather pattern map, only this one wasn't like the others.

He frowned, turning from one to the other, until it clicked. Most of the monitors were running the simulations Kayla had talked about: estimates from the past, based on whatever information they had available. All the continents beneath the weather were wrong in those ones, too close together and unfamiliar shapes. The last one, the odd one out, had the modern map, exactly as Victor would have expected it to appear. The world they were here to save.

These were not things he was supposed to be seeing. He stepped away from the monitors, and spun around, only to jump at the figure in the doorway.

"Victor!" Kayla said, holding her hand against her chest. "What are you doing here?"

"Damn it!" Without thinking about it, he mirrored her movement and could feel his heart pounding against his palm. "You scared me."

"You're supposed to be in the mess hall."

"I know, but you weren't there. I thought something had happened. So I," he felt silly now, seeing her standing there, still dressed in her lab coat with a pen tucked behind her ear, "I came to find you."

She smiled, just a little, and then jumped as Rumsfeld's speech started over. "I'm fine. I'm sorry I worried you," she said, as she rushed around the room, locking the workstations. "I was out of the lab checking on some records when the alarm went off. It took me longer than it should have to get back here with everything shutting down."

"The alarm is at level two," Victor said, and then kicked himself. She might not have been here as long as he had, but it was in the manual, after all.

"I know. We're going to have to be careful as we go back. They'll all be on edge, even if this is just a drill. We don't want to get in any trouble."

"We should go."

"Then hurry up," she said, though not unkindly, and hustled him out of the lab. She ran the lockdown key over the system, but the wrong way around.

"You have to turn it," he said, after she tried the second time. "They're different from the others on purpose."

"Why would they do something so stupid?" she muttered as she turned it around and watched the security information flash on the screen.

He shrugged. "So you have to know how before you can do it?"

Kayla grinned. "Well, good thing you were here then. Let's get back."

The mess hall had gained even more people in the time he'd been gone. The monitors in the wall here were still playing the daily speech, though at the bottom was a banner that said: CATEGORY FIVE ALARM ISSUED: LEVEL TWO, REMAIN IN DESIGNATED AREAS OR FACE DISCIPLINARY ACTION. If anyone had expected them to feel safe here, he didn't think that helped. In fact, just looking at it added queazy to the cold in his stomach, nerves churning the acid and threatening to make him ill.

He followed Kayla as she found a place near one of the opposite doors, where they could lean against the wall. "Everyone's terrified," she said.

"Aren't you?"

"Yes," she gave him a weak smile, "to be honest, I am."

He smiled back, but a hush filled the room before he could say anything more, and when he looked up, the picture on the monitor had changed. The daily video had stopped playing for the first time in five years. Instead, it showed Dr. Rumsfeld, sitting at a desk in an office. He was never in an office. He was never inside. The videos always showed them the world.

"Brothers and sisters, my devoted Sentinels of the Earth," Dr. Rumsfeld said, "today I greet you with sadness. As you are all aware, the Institute has been infiltrated. Not just one facility, but all of them. Our security forces have been deployed to meet this threat, but even we were not prepared for the coordinated assault they are carrying out."

Victor slumped against the wall and forced himself to continue breathing.

"If they breach the upper layers, if they continue to the heart of the Institute, our life here has reached its end." He rested his elbows on the desk and steepled his fingers. "We have always known there were outside forces working against us. We have always known the closer we were to achieving our goal, the greater their response would be, and we have always known they would stop us, if they could, on the day of our greatest achievement. We now face that very day."

This couldn't be happening. They couldn't have spent all this time, only to lose it now.

"We have done our very best work," Dr. Rumsfeld said. "We have stood fast before the rising tide, and achieved greatness. We have sought the mysteries of the past to save the planet's future. Those that take stands as we have do not always get to bear witness to the results of their achievements."

Victor closed his eyes. It was happening. It was happening, and they had all pledged to do whatever was necessary, to give everything for their goal.

"But do not fear, brothers and sisters, I do not ask you to give your lives, not on this day."

He almost sank to the ground as the relief weakened his muscles.

Dr. Rumsfeld smiled. "It is not because I doubt your devotion, never that. It is because I know our greatest chance of success is for you, my Sentinels, to go forth into the world to spread the result of our work. It is better for you to be living and breathing, to be the embodiment of the change we have worked so hard for." He sat up in the chair, and placed his hands on the desk. "Today, our security forces will do what they came here to do. They will stand fast within the Institute, and will play the hand fate delivers us. But. If our facilities fall, I want all of you to surrender to the intruding forces, and ensure what we have worked for is not lost."

Surrender. Victor closed his eyes, shame joining the relief he felt at this being all that was asked.

"I will not be able to go with you into this changing age, and so this is the last thing I ask of you: bring my work to every corner of this world I love so much. Go in peace. Namaste."

The screen clicked to black.

"Shit," Kayla muttered, as the crowd began to react to the unexpected news. Some were upset, some were angry, all were confused.

This wasn't what was supposed to happen, and it was upsetting, though Victor still felt that shameful relief. They didn't have to fight. They could wait here, wait for the security forces to handle it or surrender if they couldn't.

Kayla strained her neck, peering around the room.

"What's wrong?"

She didn't answer.

He tried to figure out what had caught her attention, but other than the number of people, the alarms, and the blank monitor, the mess hall was as it ever was. Except, of course, none of the security forces were present, not even the ones typically assigned to watch over mealtimes.

Kayla bit her lip, and then gave him an apologetic smile. "I just realized I've forgotten something. I'm going to make a run for it before things get worse."

"We're supposed to stay in the mess hall," he said. "What if they catch you this time? We were lucky before." The manual had never been clear on what exactly disciplinary action was, but some of the guards had hinted it could include anything up to shooting people, if they felt it was required.

"I'll be fine. They're all occupied with the fight on the upper levels. I'll be able to get there and back before it moves down here, if I go now." She patted his shoulder. "Just wait here, and don't worry."

She was out the door before anyone else noticed, and he did exactly as he was told, waiting in the mess hall with everyone else, while she went out alone, into a facility under attack.

It wasn't that he didn't think she couldn't take care of herself. In fact, she could probably do a better job of it than he could, but what if she needed help? No one was out there, and the facility was in lockdown. There weren't many options if something happened.

Victor stared at the door, wondering why he was still standing here when he had clearly made up his mind. All he had to do, was go. He looked back up at the monitor where there was a black empty hole where he was used to receiving instruction and guidance. The cold feeling left his stomach and travelled to his limbs, but he still forced them to move.

His exit from the mess hall was not as subtle or quick as Kayla's had been, in fact, he stumbled over his own feet and almost fell before leaving, but it didn't seem as if he'd drawn any attention to himself, not enough that anyone followed him or asked what he was doing. Outside the halls were unnaturally quiet, the klaxons turned off even as the lights still flashed, red now instead of orange.

Victor hadn't thought it was possible for the Institute to be this quiet. Sure, they had noise dampening in the walls, but with so many people in one space, there was always the sense that someone was nearby, that there was a conversation happening you couldn't quite hear. Now, the space felt more like a warehouse, vast and uninhabited.

Kayla was already out of sight, and he didn't know where to start looking. He could try her lab again, but she had done the rounds there. If she had gone after something forgotten, it might be somewhere else, could be anywhere else. He glanced back at the doors of the mess hall, where he was supposed to stay, still close enough to return. He shook his head. He would try Kayla's quarters. If she had realized they were going to be leaving the Institute, she may have gone after some personal effects, though they weren't supposed to have any.

Victor found the lines on the floor that would lead to Kayla's block in the personal quarters. He'd been there once, when she'd invited him over, but it hadn't happened again. He'd spent weeks wondering what he'd done wrong. That had been right before she started to get annoyed at Dr. Rumsfeld, more than impressed by him, and no longer seemed enthusiastic about the work they were doing. That had also been when she'd started complaining about her work in the lab, letting details slip.

A flash of guilt hit him. He should have asked her to stop. He should have refused to listen. It was the nature of people to talk about their day, to complain about the things that made it difficult or frustrating, but it was the duty of their friends and colleges to keep them from revealing more than they should. He had failed her.

He was so caught up in his thoughts, he almost didn't register what he was seeing when he turned the corner that led to her quarters. Four people in tactical gear, similar to the uniforms of the security forces, but without the Institute's crest on their arms, and they weren't wearing the berets. Kayla was standing with them, talking.

"—got the codes, but Gerry wasn't in the lab." She was just standing, one of them, not a prisoner, a co-conspirator.

One of the intruders raised his weapon and pointed it at Victor's chest. "Contact."

Victor raised his arms. They were supposed to surrender, that was what Dr. Rumsfeld said. Wait, that was after the Institute fell. As far as Victor was aware, it hadn't yet. The fighting hadn't even come to the lower levels. Did that mean he was supposed to resist, report them? He didn't know what he was expected to do.

"Oh, Victor," Kayla said. "Why didn't you wait in the mess hall?"

"It's dangerous out here," he said, glancing between her and the four intruders. "What are you doing with them? Kayla, what are you doing?"

"I'm trying to save people."

"That's what we're all doing. Us, not them. They're trying to stop us."

She raised her arm and motioned at the one intruder to lower his weapon. "They have to stop us, Victor."

"I don't understand."

Kayla walked toward him slowly, and none of the four interfered. "Dr. Rumsfeld isn't going to save the world, Victor. He hasn't even been trying."

"That's not true."

"It is."

He shook his head, but she kept talking, and even now he couldn't stop himself from listening to her.

"Victor, think about what he has us doing."

"I'm not supposed to know what he has you doing."

"But you do, just like I know what you're doing. Did you forget you told me about it? When you came over after your shift, still wearing your scrubs?"

Had he told her? He couldn't remember. He did remember forgetting to change, remembered being embarrassed by it, but he didn't remember a word of what he'd stammered out while hoping she wouldn't think he was an idiot. He only remembered that she hadn't cared.

"What we're making here, Victor, what you're making here, it's dangerous, and it will mean the end of the human race. That is what he is trying to do."

"I don't believe you."

"You're growing a fungus, right? A prehistoric fungus?"

"Yes." He wasn't supposed to tell her things like that.

"And I'm studying weather patterns—not *just* weather patterns, distribution patterns. I'm studying what happens if you release a chemical, or a bunch of spores, into the atmosphere. I'm studying how long it would take it to travel all over the world now, compared to how it would have, must have, travelled then. Have you considered what would happen once that stuff you're growing gets out into the atmosphere?"

"It's not going to get out. It's impossible. There are three security doors and a lab between it and the Institute, and the Institute is underground. There's nowhere for it to go."

"Not yet," the intruder who'd pointed the gun at him said. He was tall and broad, and had a patch over his heart with the name Dolan in capital letters. "But once he decides it's time to let it out, he's made sure this place is in the best position to take it wherever he wants. He's just been waiting for the right time."

Victor shook his head.

"Look," Dolan said, "we just need to destroy that shit before it can happen. That's all. We need to destroy it before we start accepting surrenders and letting anyone out of here. If it's still in the facility, our work isn't done."

"Please, Victor," Kayla said. "We need your help."

"My help?"

"You said it yourself, the lab is behind three security doors and that's before even trying to get in. You can get us there before the fighting moves down this far. We have to beat that, and we don't have time to do things the way we planned."

"We don't have time for any of this," one of the other intruders said, a woman with a brusque tone and air of command, patch reading Shevchenko.

"If I can prove it to you," Kayla said. "Would you help us?"

"We don't have time," Shevchenko repeated, but Kayla just kept looking at him, eyes passionate and earnest as they hadn't been for months.

"Show me."

She took him to the medical bay, empty for the first time ever. No one was waiting in the small room, bored and hoping they could get through this in time for their shift. No one was behind the desks, calling outpatient names and prepping examination tables. Kayla led them back into the little hallway, all the way to the end, to the door marked Quarantine.

"Wait, what are we doing?"

"I told you I can prove it."

"Everyone in there is sick."

"I know. They tell us they've got regular old viruses, maybe the flu at most. Just like they tell us people sometimes choose to leave. It's not, and they don't." She entered a code on a keypad, and pushed open the door.

The quarantine wing was bigger than he expected, bigger even than the hallway for the regular rooms. There were individual cells here, the doors solid metal, except for a small window in each. Kayla didn't open any of them, thankfully, but she pointed in.

Victor stepped up to the first window. Bile rose at the back of his throat as he pieced together what he was seeing: a figure on a bed, pale fibres that he himself had seen in grown cultures, fibres let loose to cover the figure, fill the bed. In some places, he could see where the fungus was eating away at the body, replacing the skin with more of itself. He was certain he could see exposed ribs through the strands.

"There are no machines," he said. "Where are the machines?"

"They don't need any," Kayla answered as she joined him at the window. "Whoever that is in this room, whoever they were going to tell us had decided to go home, they're dead. They're all dead. This is what Rumsfeld wants to release into the world." She flipped down a keypad beside the door, entered another code. The room lit up like a flare, and when he looked in again, everything was burnt to a crisp, the body and the fungus just ashes on the metal frame.

"This can't be real. It can't." He continued to walk through the hall, and in each lonely room it was the same. If she was right, they needed to destroy it all, not just what was in these rooms.

He felt the familiar stab of guilt at being in a position he should not have been in. He wasn't supposed to be the one in charge of the lockdown card, much less opening the lab up again. That was supposed to be Gerry. Gerry.

Victor ran from window to window, searching for something, anything recognizable. In every single one he saw the same fungus-covered bodies, but in the one at the end he found someone who wasn't quite dead yet. Beneath the fibres starting to crawl up her arms and legs, he recognized Gerry, her face still flushed and glassy with the illness. She was still breathing, still sweating, still feverish. He pulled at the door. "We have to get her out of there."

Kayla grabbed his arms and pried his hands off the handle. "We can't. She's as good as dead now. We don't have a way to stop it, not yet. There's nothing we can do."

"There has to be something. We have to do something. We can't just leave her here."

"There's nothing we can do for her, Victor. It's too late." Her words were firm, but there was compassion in her eyes. "All we do is stop this from happening to anyone else. This is what he has planned for the entire world. We, you, can stop that."

He turned away as she hit the button on Gerry's room, covered his ears with his hands and told himself he couldn't hear screaming.

"I'll open the labs," Victor said when it was done, the words taking everything and leaving him hollow.

They encountered a security force team in the hallway before the first of the security doors. It was a small deployment, three people, not even as many as the team of intruders who had come to stop them. Victor and Kayla pressed against the walls as the bullets fired and shouts rang out. He didn't know if the security forces team knew they were there, but he didn't think they would have changed their actions if they did.

Disciplinary action. He'd never been in trouble with the security forces, not once in five years. Now, even if they escaped from this, there would be evidence. There would be security recordings, videos from the cameras in every room. If the security forces won the battle on the upper floors, there would be no escape.

A shot splintered the wall beside his head, plaster spraying forward and brushing his cheek. He didn't move.

"One more," Shevchenko called, and after another flurry of gunfire there was a silence that echoed in the halls and in his head. "Dolan?"

"Be good in a second." Dolan was being patched up by one of the others, bandages holding his arm tight to his chest as blood from the gunshot in his shoulder spread through the off-white fabric. He switched his gun to his other hand as they continued, stepping past and over the three bodies in riot gear, Institute badges on their arms, berets lost.

The lab was still in lockdown. Of course it was. Gerry was ashes on a bed in quarantine after being consumed by the very thing they had been working on, and the lock card was at his waist. He ran it through, the wrong way around, and typed in the code the cancel the security shutdown.

As it processed the request, he stepped back and waited for an alarm to sound, waited for the code to be rejected even though he knew it was right, waited for something—anything—to stop him from betraying Dr. Rumsfeld.

The light went from red to green, and the display became active. He took his key card out, and entered it.

Key card for the first door; key card and thumbprint for the second; key card, thumbprint, and voice sample, for the third. The locker room still empty, still with his and Gerry's suits in the disposal bin. Only the door to the lab itself was left.

"Brothers and sisters," the painfully familiar voice said from behind him, "this is indeed a sad day. To think, all your dedication and devotion has ended in this."

Victor turned around, and found Dr. Rumsfeld standing in the door behind them.

Dr. Rumsfeld, in real life.

Victor expected him to seem smaller, shorter, somehow diminished by the knowledge of what he had done, but he was exactly the same. The same strong stance, set shoulders, intense gaze. The same fierce confidence that had first convinced Victor to join what had seemed like a hopeless cause. This was, however, the first time he had ever seen Dr. Rumsfeld's eyes filled with disappointment, and he felt the shame of his betrayal all over. He folded in on himself, back pressed against the door, holding onto his arm, which still itched underneath the light fabric of the lab scrubs.

"Why are you here, brothers and sisters?" Dr. Rumsfeld asked, though he must have known the answer.

"We're here to stop you," Kayla said.

"Stop me? Everything we have done here, everything you have ever done here, has been to bring about this glorious end. This is the culmination of all our years of work. This is the change we have been striving for. There is no other way."

"You told us we were going to save the world," Victor said, and he felt about five years old, telling his parents they had promised to take him somewhere, when of course they couldn't.

"Don't you see, brother," Dr. Rumsfeld said. "That is what we are doing. Humanity cannot be saved, not if we wish to save the planet. We are parasites."

"You've been crazy this whole time," Victor said. "We've been following you, doing everything you asked, and you just wanted us to kill everyone."

Rumsfeld shook his head, and the only thing in his eyes now was compassion. "No, brother, this is not what I wanted. I worked for years to find a way to change that relationship, to ensure it was symbiotic, but it all failed. You have to understand, sometimes sacrifices must be made. When an invasive species, when a pathogenic parasite attaches itself, you need to make a choice. Either the host survives, or the parasite does. There is no in between." He motioned at the lab behind Victor. "What you have been growing in there teaches us that lesson clearly."

"The fungus is a parasite."

"Exactly. It attaches itself to a host, as we have to this planet, and when the host is weakened it turns pathogenic. Without intervention, the parasite always wins. This will be the cause of our mass extinction event, as it was the one before. It was no comet that cleared the Earth of the dinosaurs, no great environmental event. If this humble fungus, this brutal parasite, can wipe those majestic beasts from the face of the Earth, think of how easy it will be for it to remove us. One parasite to cure another, one from which we know the planet can recover. Elegant, don't you think?"

He pictured the bodies in the quarantine wing, he pictured Gerry's eyes still open. "No, not at all."

Rumsfeld nodded. "It is all right, brother. You don't yet understand and your vision is clouded, but it is not too late. I can show you, I can teach you, if only you step away from the door."

"Shut up!" Shevchenko said, raising her weapon as the others followed suit, even Dolan despite his injured shoulder.

Victor stepped forward, positioning himself between the guns and Rumsfeld. "Stop this, please."

"Get out of the way," Dolan snapped.

"Don't," Kayla yelled. "We need him to open the door."

A stab of pain went through Victor at the practical statement, and Rumsfeld nodded with sympathy.

"I understand, brother. I know what moves you to turn your back on us, but you can see it, can't you? You can see the pain we cause without thinking, the injuries we have done without knowing. It's just our way, our nature. It cannot be changed, it can only be accepted, and dealt with. Return with me, and we will save the world."

Bodies in quarantine, mass extinction events, parasites, cycles, hosts.

"I'm already saving it," he said, finally meeting Rumsfeld's gaze. "I'm sorry."

He stepped out of the way.

"No," Rumsfeld said, as Victor turned his back to the doctor.

"Gun!" Dolan shouted.

Gunshots rang out, beside him, behind him. He braced himself to feel pain through his body, but he didn't feel anything except a shove and numbness. He stumbled forward, to the lab door. Key card, thumbprint, voice sample, blood sample. The lab door opened as the gunshots ended. His ears rang, and he couldn't feel his left arm. It hung limp at his side, and he realized there was blood seeping into his scrubs, and was distantly glad the bullet wound had only destroyed the disposable clothes.

"Shit, Victor, let me help you," Kayla said as the intruders rushed into the lab to finish their mission. Three intruders. The last one, Dolan, lay collapsed on the floor.

Across the room, Dr. Rumsfeld had propped himself up against the lockers, bleeding, but alive.

Flares of fire and light began to go off as they activated the emergency protocols in all the fridges, storage units, and baths. Victor took the medical kit from Kayla, and knelt beside Dr. Rumsfeld. "I don't think this will be much help," he said, trying to figure out how he could get his one hand to do all the work.

"Let me," Kayla said, and took over. "Though we should just let him die."

"It is all right, brother, sister, I do not blame you. I know you need to try. Even in the face of overwhelming odds, we always have to try."

Victor could hear the intruders destroying the equipment in the lab, before stepping out to seal it up. They entered the emergency code to destroy everything in the room, a category three alarm joining the one already active. It seemed like it might be over-kill, but Victor could understand. His skin crawled, itching all over now, as he thought of what he had been nurturing there. "I wanted to help."

"You have," Dr. Rumsfeld said, "never doubt that you have."

Kayla turned her attention from Dr. Rumsfeld, and this time Victor let her see to his arm. He was beginning to feel it again, every movement sending sharp pain through the numbness. As she worked and the intruders confirmed the destruction of the lab, a new team burst through the door to the locker room.

"Hands in the air!" one shouted.

"He's injured," Victor said, trying to keep pressure on one of the wounds with his good hand, even as Kayla was attempting to do the same for him. "He needs a medic."

"Hands up!"

Victor closed his eyes, but did not move, and waited to be shot, again.

"Stand down," Shevchenko said, and they complied. It was over. "Get them evacuated with the others, and make sure someone sees to their injuries."

Everyone was being loaded into buses. Kayla had said they wouldn't be put in jail, that it was understood they hadn't known what Dr. Rumsfeld was doing, but Victor didn't really believe that. All in a line, being shuffled into the vehicles with their hands restrained, they certainly looked like prisoners. Besides, people liked having someone to blame, someone to punish, and it didn't look like Dr. Rumsfeld was going to survive to be their target.

Victor had already given his report—Kayla was giving hers now—and was sitting in the ambulance as the paramedics worked. They were talking as if he weren't there, comments about the world being better off, running a fever, got what's coming to him, possible infection. It was a strange mix of professionalism and hatred, but Victor didn't really blame them, even if he couldn't summon up the same animosity now that everything was destroyed.

Dr. Rumsfeld really had wanted to save the world, even if he hadn't wanted to save the people in it. Victor could understand that, on some level. Just like he could understand how Dr. Rumsfeld could have thought they were parasites, no different from the one Victor grew every day.

He grew more of the parasite every day.

Things slowed down as they forced him out of the ambulance, closing the door on Dr. Rumsfeld. The doctor's skin was flushed, he was sweating, and he coughed, difficult in an oxygen mask, though not as difficult as in a protective suit. The doors closed, and Victor could no longer see his eyes, but he knew they would be bloodshot, just as Gerry's eyes had been when she'd left the lab that morning.

She had cut her hand. Dr. Rumsfeld had been shot.

When the host was weak, the parasite turned pathogenic.

He pulled up his sleeve and looked at the fine lines almost invisible under the raw rash of his inflamed skin. The faint, almost insignificant fibres embedded in the surface, and he imagined them growing as his system weakened, creating an illness that forced him to stop moving, that left him stationary as they took over his entire body, hollowing it out.

"Move them out!" Shevchenko ordered, and the buses and ambulance began to pull out of the yard, through the last thing that separated them from the outside world: the Institute gate. All those people, in the same space, at least some of whom he knew had received the same treatment from the doctors, for an infection they all shared.

"You have to stop them," he called. "You have to bring them back!"

He ran to Shevchenko, saw Kayla coming for him, concern on her face, but the buses kept pulling away. Shevchenko grabbed his arm as he tried to chase them. "What the hell are you going on about?"

"We have to bring them back. They're infected."

"What are you—"

He held up his arm, pointing at the rash. "It was never isolated in the labs. He didn't plan for it to spread through the weather patterns. I mean, not to start. He just wanted to make sure it would be carried far enough away once we got to the cities." The maps weren't to find out how it would spread from the Institute facilities, they were to figure out how it would spread once it was free of them. When Sentinels spread the message, across the world. "Oh God, this wasn't the only facility."

"We hit all of them," Shevchenko said. "We didn't know which one he would be in, but we knew they were all growing that stuff. We couldn't risk him getting it out."

Victor laughed, a harsh, panicked sound. "We have to go into quarantine. Back into it. The entire facility was quarantine." It had been contained, and in trying to destroy it, they had set it loose.

The buses had already left, were driving farther away even as Shevchenko called into the radio they needed to be stopped, to be kept from populated areas. As he stared after them, he could still see the ambulance lights flashing, bringing forth Dr. Rumsfeld and the end of the world.

X is for Xenoparasite

Andrew Bourelle

"What's the Y stand for?"

We were staring at the package on Fender's glass coffee table, a quart-sized zip-lock bag full of gray-white powder. It looked like cocaine cut with fireplace ashes. There was a red sticker on the package with a black "Y" scrawled with a sharpie.

"I'm not sure," Fender said. "That's just the street name."

Fender said it was the newest thing in Asia, some kind of opiate mixed with cocaine alkaloid and crushed dinosaur bones. Not just any dinosaur—one specific skeleton that was stolen from a Hong Kong museum. Fender couldn't remember the name of it. He said it was supposed to be like China's version of the Allosaurus, but I didn't know what the fuck that was either.

Because Y came from only one skeleton, that meant it was just short of impossible to get. Which is what made it attractive to Fender—who was a collector as much as he was a dealer.

"Have you tried it yet?" I said, but I could tell from the package that he hadn't touched it.

"Nope," he said. "I'm a business man. Each snort is probably worth ten grand. But I am curious," he added.

Fender and I were sitting in the living room of his spacious penthouse apartment. He had a nice view of Lake Erie out his window. The sky was overcast, the water gray.

Collector guitars decorated the walls of Fender's apartment. An acoustic guitar reputedly owned by Johnny Cash. An electric from Eddie Van Halen. One with burn marks on it that was supposedly from that Great White concert where the pyrotechnics got out of control and killed a bunch of people.

Fender once joked that it was hard to know what was more valuable in this apartment: the guitars or the drugs. But I was as skeptical of the stories about the guitars as I was about the origins of Y.

We shared a joint and each had a bottle of beer, and talked about whether we thought the dinosaur-bone story had any truth to it. Fender said he believed there were real dinosaur bones in there—that much was probably true—but he doubted they contributed to the high.

"It's like a rhinoceros horn," he said. "People think it contains magical qualities, but that's all bullshit. The real rush is that you're snorting something rare. Exotic. We're talking about a supply so finite that it's practically nonexistent."

Fender was wearing a silk robe with silly leather slippers, and his shoulder-length hair was pulled back into a pony tail. He had a soul-patch and hoop earrings and looked quite a bit different than the kid I shared a room with when we were freshmen in college.

I told him I didn't think the drug was going to go over well here. This was America. People here didn't believe in that crap about rhinoceros horns, and they wouldn't buy any mumbo jumbo about mystical dinosaur bone dust.

"I already got a buyer lined up," he said. "We're just haggling over price."

"Speaking of buying things, I need to get a move on."

He took me back to his study and unlocked the safe. I turned away so I wouldn't see the combination. It made me uncomfortable how leisurely he was about opening it in front of me. Did that mean he was like that with other people? I hoped not.

The safe was the size of a small refrigerator. A series of shelves lined the left side, some stacked with cash, others with every kind of drug you could think of. On the right side were guns: a shotgun, some kind of military rifle, a handgun. There was also a pearl-handled switchblade, which I'd seen Fender open lots of bags of drugs with.

Fender reached in and brought out a brick of marijuana.

I handed him a stack of bills.

I shoved the marijuana into my knapsack, and we headed back to the living room.

I excused myself to his restroom before I left. When I came back, Fender and my backpack were sitting on the couch, but the bag of Y was gone.

"Why isn't there a Chinese symbol on the package instead of a Y?" I said.

At the bar I managed, I used rat poison that was from China— poison that I'm sure was illegal as hell here in the U.S.—and there were Chinese symbols all over the packaging. I would think that whether Y was the real thing or someone was just pretending it was an exotic Chinese drug, either way it would make sense to use a Chinese character instead of an English letter.

"Beats me, man. Maybe they're trying to Americanize it."

I smirked at Fender and shook my head.

"I think you've been had," I said. "Someone cremated a fucking dog and put it in a bag and you just paid God knows what for it."

"Ye of little faith," Fender said, clapping me on the back.

He opened the six deadbolts on his door, led me into the foyer, and opened the six deadbolts on the exterior door.

"See you," he said.

"Wouldn't want to be you," I said.

"Bullshit," he said, just like every time we said goodbye. "You wish like hell you were me."

I went directly to the bar to open up. It was important that I get there before Theresa because I had to clean up the dead rats before she arrived. She'd come in once before me and was gagging her whole shift.

Each night before I left, I'd set out the poison in the storage room. Each day when I came in to open, I'd find three or four dead rats. Today, there were only two, which meant maybe I was finally making a dent in the population.

They were lying on the concrete, their bodies twisted into stiff, strangely contorted poses, like they'd been convulsing until their muscles finally locked up. Their tongues hung out of their mouths, clamped between their teeth, and a strange bloody foam spilled from their clenched jaws like dyed beer froth.

I always wondered if the rats ate the poison at the same time, or if they were so fucking stupid that they went ahead and ate it even after they could see that one of their brethren had died. I'd considered hooking up some kind of camera to watch, but that was too much effort. I didn't care that much.

I put the two dead rats in a plastic bag and was outside tossing it into the Dumpster when Theresa came walking up.

"Hey, handsome," she said, and gave me a smile that was better than any drug.

"Hey," I said.

I wanted to call her beautiful or good looking or something like that, but I couldn't bring myself to do it. I wasn't sure what Fender would think about me flirting with his kid sister but I didn't figure he'd be too happy about it.

I was a decade older than her for one thing. And I wasn't exactly what you'd call a good catch. My name was on the bar's deed, but it was really owned by Ramzen Akhmadov, the head of the Chechen mafia in Cleveland.

That's what happens when you borrow money from the mob for your drug problem. The vig is too steep. You get in over your head. Instead of getting your legs broken, you make a deal.

And then you're stuck. You can't walk away. Ever.

"Did you go see my brother today?" Theresa asked as she started taking chairs off the tables.

"Yep."

She grinned. If I saw Fender, that meant I had dope.

"You want to smoke a jay before we open?" she asked.

Theresa was a cute girl—how could I say no?

I didn't tap into the new brick of marijuana. I left that in my backpack behind the bar and went to the stash I kept in the freezer. I rolled a joint while Theresa finished setting up the chairs.

We sat at a table like a couple of regular customers and passed the joint back and forth. The funny thing about pot is that the best stuff in the country comes from Colorado, where it is legal. I figured it was just a matter of time before it was legal everywhere and my little side business would be defunct. I was trying to figure out a plan to get out from under Ramzen by then, but I hadn't come up with any ideas yet.

I'd been smoking so long now that smoking a joint was kind of like smoking a cigarette to me. I didn't get much of a buzz. Theresa had done some hard drugs in her day, but she didn't have as many years of smoking weed on her resume as I did. Her eyes quickly turned glassy and she couldn't stop smiling.

Theresa had dirty blond hair that wasn't nearly as well cared for as her brother's mane. She wore low-slung jeans, a tight tee shirt, and no bra underneath. Her breasts were small, but I liked looking at her nipples poking against the fabric.

I was sure she noticed.

I was sure she liked me looking.

It was just a matter of time before we hooked up. That would probably mess things up with Fender. And if I didn't have him supplying me anymore, then that would mess things up with Ramzen, who expected the cut I gave him every week and wouldn't like it if I went back to just being a bar manager.

In other words, hooking up with Theresa wouldn't just risk my oldest friendship. It might risk my life.

But I had a tendency to not think with my head. A younger version of me would have made my move already. Theresa and I would be fucking in the back room instead of sharing a joint up front.

But I was trying to be smarter these days.

Trying.

Two unusual things happened that night at the bar.

We were doing moderate business for a Tuesday night, enough that Theresa and I were busy but we could handle it ourselves. I worked behind the bar and she spent most of her time on the floor.

When customers came to the bar and ordered the special, I'd take them into the storage room and sell them however much pot they were looking for. I was always careful. I knew everyone I did business with.

The first surprise was that Ramzan Akhmadov and his henchman Zakir came in.

Ramzen never came himself. He always sent Zakir, or someone even lower on the food chain. So when Ramzen showed up, I got a knot in my stomach and started to sweat.

"Hello, Charlie," Ramzen said, sitting on a bar stool across from me. "How's things?"

He and Zakir both had thick accents, like a couple of Russian terrorists in a bad action movie.

"Good," I said, wiping the bar off as if I was a character in such a movie.

Ramzen was in his fifties, with a face like a boxer who retired well past his prime, with lumpy, ruddy patches of skin and a mouth full of crooked teeth. He had a head full of silver hair and eyes that looked black in the bar's dim lighting. Zakir was in his thirties, maybe a few years older than me, and he was handsome, with slicked-back hair and a mouth full of straight white teeth. While Ramzen looked like a dock worker trying on a nice suit, Zakir looked the part of a gangster.

I made myself put the towel down and just stand and talk with the men. Stop pretending nothing was weird.

I asked Ramzen if he wanted anything, and he declined.

"You?" I said to Zakir.

Zakir always took single-barrel bourbon, and I would normally pour without asking, but with Ramzen here, he might not want to be seen drinking on the job, so I figured I better ask.

He shook his head no and came around the bar like he always did and went into the back to the cooler. There was a case of Budweiser that was always in the same place. There were twenty-three bottles of beer inside. In the one empty space was an envelope of cash that I kept up to date for these visits.

"Did you catch the game?" Ramzen asked, making small talk.

"No," I said. "I missed it."

I had no idea what he was talking about, not even what sport. It was summer, so that meant either the Indians or, if they were still in the playoffs, the Cavaliers. I didn't give a shit about professional sports, and I'm sure Ramzen didn't either, except for the betting that went along with it.

I figured the game, whatever game it was, had something to do with why he was here. Maybe he wanted me to start taking bets like a bookie.

I didn't want to do that. I didn't want to get any more involved with him than I already was.

"Have you seen your friend Fender lately?" he said.

"I saw him today," I said.

Honesty seemed the best policy here. I didn't want him to find out later that I was lying.

"And how was he?" Ramzen asked.

I shrugged. "Fine."

I was doing my best not to look over Ramzen's shoulder at Theresa out on the floor. As far as I knew, Ramzen didn't know that Fender's sister worked for me. She was just another cute waitress. I had a few of them. Call me sexist, but good-looking girls help with business.

"Did Fender tell you about a new drug he has?" Ramzen asked. "I think it is called Y."

Zakir came out from the back and sat next to Ramzen. Both of them stared at me.

"He mentioned something about it," I said, again choosing honesty. "Some new thing from China."

"Did you try it?"

"No," I said. "You know me. I stick with naturals—no pills, no powder."

Their eyebrows raised in unison, and that made me qualify my statement.

"No powder anymore," I said.

"This is from the bones of a prehistoric animal," Ramzen said. "What is more natural than that?"

I forced a laugh.

Zakir spoke up for the first time. "Did you see it?" he said. "The Y?"

Now I chose to lie.

"No," I said. "He knew I wouldn't be interested in something like that."

Now things were starting to make sense. Fender said he had a buyer lined up. They were just haggling about price.

Ramzen was his buyer.

Fender paid his cut to Ramzen just like everyone else. But he didn't work for Ramzen. He was never in debt, never needed Ramzen's money (unlike me), so he was able to operate more or less without any oversight.

Still, Fender needed to be careful.

Ramzen Akhmadov wasn't someone I would haggle with over a price. Fender had bigger balls than I did.

Ramzen and Zakir were boring into me with their stares. I could feel Theresa doing the same from across the room.

"If you find out anything you want to tell us," Ramzen said finally, "call this number."

He set a card on the counter. It was blank except for a handwritten number.

I frowned, hoping my expression would say, *I don't know what you're talking about.*

But I did, and they knew I did.

After they left, Theresa came over, her face full of worry.

"What was that all about?" she said.

"Do me a favor," I said. "Call your brother and see if he's okay."

That's when the second surprise of the night came: a police detective walked into the bar.

He was in street clothes, but I could tell he was a cop. For one, he had the air of scumbag smugness that cops have.

For another, he had a pistol strapped to his hip.

He came up to the bar, his eyes focused on Theresa, not me. He introduced himself as Detective Sean Williams.

"Are you Theresa Matthews?" he said.

She nodded, her eyes confused.

"And your brother is Glen Matthews?"

She nodded again, her eyes changing from confused to scared.

"I regret to inform you that your brother has been murdered."

I closed the bar, told all the remaining customers that their tabs were on the house tonight, and then Theresa sat down with Williams at the same table where she and I shared the joint a few hours ago. She was in shock. She hadn't cried yet. She had a dazed look on her face, a little like she was stoned but without the pretty smile that usually accompanied her highs.

Theresa asked if I could sit with them, and when I explained that Fender—i.e. Glen—was my college roommate and a longtime friend, Williams agreed.

He asked her questions about when she'd last seen Fender, if she was aware that he was a drug dealer. I knew which answers were lies and which were the truth.

When he came to me, I told him that I'd seen Fender earlier that day, that we'd each had a beer. I figured my fingerprints would be all over the place: the bottle, the bathroom faucet.

"What was the nature of your visit?" Williams asked.

"Just visiting," I said. "We're friends."

"And were *you* aware that your friend was one of the biggest drug dealers in the city?" he said.

"We didn't talk about that stuff," I said.

"What kind of stuff did you talk about?" he said.

"The girls we slept with in college," I said. "The time we stole a ceramic cow head from a fraternity party. Classes we failed. Stuff we did when we were eighteen and drunk and stupid."

This was all true. Fender and I had very little in common these days. I sold dope, and he sold it to me—and I gave his kid sister a job when she needed one—but that was pretty much it. Otherwise, we lived worlds apart. We talked about old times—*remember that one time?*—and that was usually it. Discussing his latest boutique drug purchase was out of the ordinary for us.

"Did he mention a drug called Y?" Williams asked.

"Look," I said, "Theresa and I don't know anything about what Fender did. We don't know what the hell is going on. What can you tell us?"

"The investigation is ongoing," he said bureaucratically.

"Cut the shit," I said. "Either you tell us what happened or we won't say another word until we get a lawyer."

Williams took a deep breath. He turned to Theresa.

"Your brother's throat was slashed," he said.

She gasped, bringing her hands to her face.

"But he was tortured first."

She started sobbing. Then she rose from the table and ran into the back room.

Williams turned his stare to me.

"His apartment was ransacked. His safe was emptied. His guitars smashed."

For some reason, that last bit hurt me the most. Fender loved those fucking guitars.

After the cop gave me his card and left, I found Theresa sitting in the cooler, her arms wrapped around her, covered in goose bumps. Her cheeks were streaked with tears, which had started to crystalize in the cold.

"I came in here because I wanted to feel some kind of pain besides what's inside of me," she said, her lips quivering, her teeth beginning to chatter.

"Come on," I said. "I'll walk you home."

I didn't bother to put out rat poison that night. Didn't balance the books. Didn't even take the tips out of the tip jar. I just grabbed my knapsack and locked the door.

On our walk, the warm summer air erased the goose bumps on Theresa's arms.

"What's this Y he was talking about?" Theresa asked.

"Some new drug," I said. "Your brother said it was super rare."

"Do you think they killed him for it?"

"I don't know," I said, and I didn't ask her who she meant by "they."

She lived in a small one-bedroom. There wasn't much to it. A thrift-store futon that she used for a bed and a couch. An old box TV. She had some movie posters on her walls from back when she used to work at a theater.

Back in her heavy drug days.

Fender had introduced her to the hard stuff when she was a teenager, then paid for rehab when she was out of control. He asked me to hire her when she was out, told me to keep her away from anything stronger than pot. Since I didn't deal in chemicals—and because I'd been through something similar to her, back in my own dark days—he thought I was the right person for the job.

She sat down on her futon and pulled her legs up underneath her. She hugged herself like she had in the cooler even though her apartment was stuffy.

"Do you have anything stronger than pot?" she asked.

"No."

"Let's smoke a bowl then."

I opened up my backpack to get the new brick that Fender had sold me.

The bag of Y was inside.

I didn't tell Theresa the Y was there. I pretended like everything was normal. I pulled out a pinch of dope, packed her pipe, and passed it to her.

I took a couple hits, but that was just to give her the impression she wasn't smoking alone. My mind was reeling, reliving my last conversation with Fender.

Had he acted unusual in any way? Had he seemed scared?

No, he seemed perfectly normal. Yet, when I went to take a piss, he slipped the Y into my backpack. It must have been an impulse move. He wouldn't have known I was going to pee before I left.

Still, he must have feared that someone would come looking for the stuff. I wondered if they'd tortured him for the combination to the safe, then killed him, only to find out that the safe didn't have what they were looking for. Or did they know the combination and torture him afterward when they didn't find what they were looking for?

They probably smashed every guitar looking for a secret hiding spot.

Theresa lay out on the futon and put her feet in my lap. I rubbed them. She had delicate feet, perfectly smooth, her nails painted an ugly purple color.

She groaned, "God, that feels good."

"I need to get going," I told her.

"No," she said. "Stay. I'm afraid of what I might do if I'm alone."

I was afraid of what I might do if I stayed. But I told her I would.

She sat up onto her knees and put one hand on my shoulder.

"This dope isn't strong enough," she said. "I need something else."

I stared at her, knowing what she was going to ask for.

"Make love to me, Charlie. I know you want to. The only thing stopping you was my brother."

"It doesn't feel right," I said.

She put her hand to my crotch, where my cock was hardening like quick-drying concrete.

"It feels right to me," she said.

We never bothered to fold the futon out. We spent the night curled together, cramped on the couch cushion. No sheets or blankets. Just our skin, clammy in the humid air. We talked for a long time. I knew she needed to be distracted, so I filled the silence with talk about my life and how I didn't know how I'd ended up where I was.

I should have been thankful, I guessed, that I kicked the coke that once brought me so close to ruin. But the cost was a partnership with the Chechen mob—a lifetime contract unless I could think of a way out.

"Why didn't you ask my brother for the money?" Theresa asked.

"Pride," I said. "Fender and I were friends back when we were nobodies. He was a somebody and I was back on track to becoming a bigger nobody than ever. Besides, Fender touched more drugs in one day than most people do in a lifetime, but he's never really been hooked on anything. The willpower that son of a bitch had. I was embarrassed to admit I needed help."

"I know the feeling," she said. "But I always hated him for introducing me to the stuff. What kind of brother does that?"

She was right: Fender was no saint. He was a narcissistic drug dealer.

But he was my friend.

When Theresa drifted off to sleep, I lay awake, staring at the water spots on the ceiling, listening to the sounds of the city coming in through the open window. Voices. Music. Sirens.

I felt antsy, unable to lie still. Finally, I untangled myself from her and started to dress. Streetlights through the window illuminated her milk-white skin, her pink nipples, her lovely face, which looked incredibly young while she slept.

"Sorry, Fender," I whispered aloud.

Theresa's eyes opened a crack and she muttered in a dreamy voice, "Where are you going?"

"I've got a few things I need to do today," I said. "Go back to sleep. I'll call you later."

"I don't want you to go," she said, but she was already closing her eyes and drifting away.

"Theresa," I said. "Don't go anywhere. Don't trust anyone. Don't answer your door. Not until I call you."

"Okay," she said, but she seemed asleep already.

When I left, I locked the door handle but had no way of locking the deadbolt unless I woke her up to do it. I thought about it, and decided to let her sleep.

My apartment lived somewhere in the world between Fender's and Theresa's: not as shitty as hers, not nearly as nice as his. It was a modest two-bedroom with a nice TV and decent furniture.

I opened my backpack and put both bags of drugs on my wooden coffee table.

I stared at the Y.

Did Ramzen kill Fender?

Probably.

That meant the smart thing to do—smart for me but also smart for Theresa—was to hand the stuff over to him. That was the easiest way to stay safe, and to keep Theresa safe.

But Fender was my oldest friend, which pretty much made him my best friend. We didn't have much in common anymore, but I liked him more than most people.

And I was in love with his sister.

I admitted that to myself at that moment, with the dull dawn light coming in through the window making the powder in the Y bag look even more gray and ashen.

I told you before I often did stupid things, impulsive things. You could say sleeping with Theresa hours after her brother was killed might be one of them.

But there was an even dumber thing I felt like doing.

I wanted to try the Y.

I kept telling myself that I would be able to think better if I knew what I was dealing with. Was this some great revolutionary new drug? Or just ordinary coke with a made-up story to go with it?

I wasn't sure how knowing the answer would help me, but I felt like it would.

Or maybe I was just rationalizing. I wanted to try the Y, and so I convinced myself it was a good idea.

I got a drinking straw from the kitchen, cut off an inch section of it and went back to the living room. When I opened the bag, there was a peculiar smell. Like a dusty book sitting on a shelf for a couple decades, with another underlying scent barely hidden—a rotten smell, like road kill.

I stuck the straw into the bag, put the other end to my nose, and snorted a good, hard pull.

The effect was instantaneous.

It felt like I'd inhaled fire, and the flames spread through my skull and down into my limbs. I thought I was going to die, and then the pain turned into a soothing warmth. I sank back into the couch like I was falling into an ocean of pillows. I just kept sinking and sinking, my fingers and toes numb, the rest of my body nonexistent. I closed my eyes and began to dream.

I wasn't human. My heart was pounding, my breathing coming out in raspy, ragged bursts. I had big powerful legs and tiny little arms, and a long tail that balanced the weight of an enormous skull. I had a massive snout and teeth the size of kitchen knives. It felt natural to have this body, to have this balance.

I was running through a jungle of exotic plants. My sense of smell was stronger than any human's, and I inhaled rich, wild scents that I'd never experienced before.

It was intense, this dream, so lucid that I didn't want to open my eyes and risk dissolving it.

I don't know if it was the power of suggestion making me see what I was seeing, and feel what I was feeling. Just knowing the story behind Y could have been enough to tell my brain what dream to have. Opiates can work that way.

But it didn't feel that way at the time. I felt like whatever was in the Y had transported me back—mentally, telepathically, supernaturally—to a time millions of years ago. When the world was embryonic, and the animals were primal, instinctual, murderous. I could feel the stardust in my bones, the atoms that were once plants or animals or water. I was the world and the world was me.

In the dream, I killed some smaller creature, a feathered, four-legged little dinosaur. I ripped it apart with my sharp teeth, and I woke up with the coppery taste of blood in my mouth.

I staggered to the bathroom, unsure how to walk without a tail. I slurped water from the sink and looked at myself in the mirror.

There was a little splotch of dried blood around my nostril.

I checked the time. Six hours had passed.

I rushed out the door and headed for the bar. Theresa and I were both scheduled to work tonight, and I needed to find people to cover for us. The employees' numbers were tacked up behind the bar. I didn't have them with me.

There was no way I was working, and I wasn't leaving Theresa alone either.

I didn't feel any closer to having a plan about what to do, and I wasn't sure if it was a good idea to tell Theresa how powerful the stuff was, given her drug history. But I felt like I should tell her. Her brother had died for this stuff. She had a right to have a say in what happened. And if I'm honest, I pictured us snorting the stuff together. It was that good.

I called her, but there was no answer.

When I walked into the alley behind the bar, Zakir's black BMW was sitting there idling.

His arm was sticking out the open window, holding a cigarette.

"Hey," I said, acting as if nothing out of the ordinary was happening.

"Where've you been?" he said. "You need to open soon."

"Having a rough morning," I said. "You heard about Fender?"

"Yeah," he said. "Tragic."

He said the words as unemotionally as if he was reporting on some crime on the other side of the planet.

He pitched his cigarette into the alley and followed me inside.

I poured him his single-barrel bourbon on the rocks, like always— when he wasn't accompanied by Ramzen, that is.

He threw it back and slurped it all down.

"Another?"

"No."

He reached into his sports jacket. I thought he was going to pull out a pistol, but instead he pulled out a switchblade.

The same pearl-handled one from Fender's safe.

He poked around in the ice of his glass. There was blood on the blade, and tendrils of red spread into the liquid remnants at the bottom of the glass.

He fished out a piece of ice and popped it into his mouth. He crunched on it like candy. Then he folded the knife and stuck it back in his coat. His hand came out with a plain white envelope.

"Open this after I leave," he said.

"What is it?"

"I'll be back when you close tonight," he said. "You give me what I want. I give you what you want."

I scrunched my nose to pretend that I didn't know what he was talking about.

As he walked toward the door, he called over his shoulders. "Don't get any smart ideas. Don't call the cops. Don't call Ramzen."

I said nothing. But I understood. He was going behind Ramzen's back.

When he was gone, I tore open the envelope. Inside was a small plastic sandwich bag, and inside that was a tiny severed toe.

With ugly purple paint on the nail.

I called in a waitress and a bartender, and I made them do most of the labor while I sat in my office. I let them each go an hour early, and then I told the few remaining customers that I needed to close early.

When Zakir came in with Theresa, I was sitting at the table she and I had used the day before, first to share a joint, then to talk to the cop.

Theresa was limping. She had on black Nike running shoes, and it looked like the toe area on one foot was wet.

Zakir shoved her roughly into a chair and sat down across from me.

His bourbon was already poured, sitting next to the bag of white powder.

"It looks like you opened it," Zakir said as he took his seat.

I nodded.

"And?"

"It gave me a bloody nose," I said. "It burned like a son of a bitch. But it was the best high I've ever had."

No need to lie about that.

He grinned widely. He picked up his bourbon and twirled it around, spiraling the ice cubes, which had started to melt while I waited.

"You didn't think of poisoning me, did you?"

"I thought about it," I said.

He laughed. Then he threw back the glass and slurped out the bourbon. Like before, he pulled out the switchblade and dug around in the glass. He fished out a piece of ice and crunched it in his teeth.

He left the switchblade sticking out of the glass, the tip bleeding into the puddle of bourbon at the bottom.

"So what happens now?" I said.

"What do you mean?" he said. "You get the girl. I get the Y."

"I mean with you and Ramzen. You trying to take over? Coup d'état?"

"Just a little side business," Zakir said. "You can keep your mouth shut, no?"

"Yes," I said.

"And you?" He looked at Theresa, his eyebrows arched.

"She can," I said.

"Good."

He grabbed the bag of powder and headed for the door.

"What do all these Chinese letters mean?" he said.

"I think it's supposed to be the name of the dinosaur whose bones are all busted up in there," I said.

He gave me a hard stare, and I wondered if he could see my pounding heart shaking my chest from where he was. His eyes drifted over to Theresa.

"You coming?" he said.

She looked at me, and, in a second, her demeanor changed from fear to a look of guilty pleasure. She gave me a smile that was part apology, part delight.

She stood and kissed me on the cheek.

"I did have fun," she whispered, and walked toward Zakir with no limp.

Zakir was grinning, his mouth full of white teeth, so pleased with himself that he couldn't contain his elation.

I glowered at Theresa. "You should have just taken it from me this morning after you fucked me."

She shrugged. "I was going to check to see if you had it with you. But you wouldn't fall asleep."

She turned to go and I didn't know what to say, so I blurted, "Your brother loved you."

She huffed and said, "My brother loved his stupid guitars."

They left and I sat alone in the bar for a long time. Then I collected the switchblade and my backpack and walked home. On the way, I took a detour down to the lake's edge and tossed the baggie with the toe—whoever it belonged to—into the gray water.

I locked the door and spent the day with the switchblade in my hand, nodding in and out of sleep.

When evening came and no one had broken down my door, I went over to Theresa's apartment. The door was unlocked. She and Zakir were both there, Zakir doubled over on the futon, Theresa lying on the floor. The bodies were contorted, frozen in positions of agony. Their noses had hemorrhaged a pink foamy blood. Their eyes were bloodshot and bulging from their sockets, their faces locked in a rictus of pain. Theresa had bitten her tongue between her clenched teeth.

I had hoped that Zakir would go first and that Theresa would be smarter than the rats. But they must have done their lines together.

I took off Theresa's shoes just to be sure. She had all ten toes.

There was a framed photograph on the counter of Fender and Theresa. They were a few years younger, both smiling enthusiastically. I wondered if they were actually happy or just acting. I'd never really known Theresa at all.

"See you," I said to their smiling faces, my voice a hoarse, haunted whisper that I didn't recognize. "Wouldn't want to be you."

I called Detective Williams and spent the rest of the night at the police station answering questions.

"Turns out this drug called Y is nothing more than Chinese rat poison," he said.

He looked at me skeptically, wondering what I knew and wasn't telling him, but he seemed to be satisfied that the case was closed. He never searched my backpack.

I walked toward home, a zombie, in the early morning hours. I had hardly slept in three days. I'd lost my oldest friend and a girl I loved, even if only briefly, even if she never really existed. A fog rolled in and I stood at the edge of the lake, looking out into the smoky gray air, imagining a world on the other side with dinosaurs running around with eternity pulsing through their veins.

I called Ramzen.

"Zakir tried to blackmail me for the Y," I said. "He was going behind your back."

"You had the Y?"

"I gave him rat poison," I said. "He's dead."

Ramzen was quiet for a long moment, then he said, "Someone else will be making the collection next week."

"I figured."

"And what of the Y?" he asked. "Where is it?"

I knew the Y would buy my freedom. I had been looking for a way out for years, and this was it.

"I don't know," I said, and hung up.

In my apartment, I pulled out the bag of Y, opened it, breathed in its primordial scent.

I wanted to escape.

To disappear.

To go back in time to a prehistoric world where Fender hadn't died yet and Theresa hadn't revealed her true self.

I poked the knife, sticky with dried blood, into the Y and came out with a heap of bone dust on the blade. I lowered my nose to the tip and inhaled as quickly and deeply as I could.

Y is for Yangchuan Lizard

Laura VanArendonk Baugh

"The jaws are wide enough to swallow a man, the teeth are large and sharp, and their whole appearance is so formidable that neither man, nor any kind of animal can approach them without terror."—Marco Polo

Brianna tipped her head back against the seat rest and closed her eyes. She always meant to drink more water to help offset the jet lag, and she always forgot. "How far to Zunyi?"

"About three and a half, maybe four hours," answered the man behind the wheel. "Feel free to nap if you like." He had a pronounced accent but the syntax of his English was perfect. Brianna wondered if he'd learned it working as a professional driver for visiting academics or somewhere else.

The legendary Chongqing heat was in full force and man, she was tired. She really ought to stay awake, reset her internal clock by going to bed by local time, but she had stayed up to watch all three *Iron Man* movies on the plane and it was catching up with her….

The hills and curves settled the question for her. Brianna slept.

She woke with a dry throat and a sense that she'd overslept. "Are we close?" she asked.

"Not so far," answered the driver. "About two more hours." He had a nice smile, making his face look younger than the early thirties she supposed he was. He reached behind his seat and passed her a bottle of water, warm with summer heat despite the car's struggling air conditioning.

Brianna cracked the lid gratefully. "I'm really sorry, I've forgotten your name."

"Xiaolang," he supplied. "I am Li Xiaolang."

"Nice to meet you," said Brianna automatically. "Again." She took a long drink.

It was a bit cooler here in the mountains. Brianna casually glanced at her watch and swore. "I was asleep four hours!" She frowned out the window. "Shouldn't we be close to Zunyi, then?"

"We aren't going to Zunyi."

Xiaolang said it very calmly, very matter-of-factly, so that Brianna struggled to grasp his meaning. "I—where are you taking me? Who are you? What do you want?"

For a moment she could hear her mother's voice warning her against traveling, especially warning against traveling to all those countries where they didn't like Americans, where she'd be murdered or kidnapped or put into prison, and now she was right, Brianna was kidnapped, and her mother would be so smug as she cried at the press conference, and who even kidnapped a paleographist anyway—

"My name is Li Xiaolang, as I said, and I will take you to Zunyi when we have finished. But first, I have something to show you in Zhenyuan."

Brianna's mental carousel of weeping mothers and presidential interventions slowed. "Um—okay. Will it take long?"

"That depends on you." Xiaolang looked from the mountain road to Brianna and back. "Are you fit to climb mountain stairs?"

"I run two days a week."

"Good. Then we will be able to move more quickly." Xiaolang smiled. "I apologize for the inconvenience, but we had only this one chance to speak with you, and we have been turned down twice before by other academics."

Crackpot theorist, then. Brianna's abductor/rapist-filter went down and her wacko-filter went up. "You found the holy tablets Jesus inscribed during his lost years visiting China?"

Xiaolang laughed, which Brianna considered a good sign. "Nothing like that, no. But we are going to a temple."

Okay, then, at least she'd get a nice temple tour out of this, and maybe a good story. Nobody really abducted paleographists, anyway. Not enough publicity in it.

"So," she said after a moment, "what are we going to look at? Or are you being careful not to influence me in advance?"

Xiaolang smiled. "I fear any prejudices you have may already be set," he said, "My task is to open your mind to let you see beyond them."

Definitely a crackpot theorist. "So have these inscriptions been published before? What's the subject?"

"No." The SUV jolted on the eroded road. "What do you think of dinosaurs?"

"No, no," said Brianna. "I see the mistake. I am a paleographist. Paleography is the study of ancient writing. Paleo, ancient, graphy, writing. Paleontology is the study of dinosaurs and things. I can see where the error might happen, but they're not the same thing at all."

Xiaolang laughed. "It is no error," he said cheerfully. "I am quite aware of your specialty, Dr. Allen. As I mentioned, we have previously asked two paleozoologists to come, and both refused. But we have recently found something which may be a written reference, and for that we are most interested in your paleographic opinion and of course in your academic reputation to lend validity."

Oh, definitely a crackpot. Not only did paleography and paleozoology share nothing more than a tab in the dictionary, but Brianna's doctorate was barely a year old, and her academic reputation nearly non-existent. She didn't dare publish anything too controversial yet or her career would be over before it began.

"So," Brianna asked, trying to stay positive, "what's your field, then? Because you're clearly not just a driver." She gave what she hoped looked like a friendly smile.

The SUV jolted again. "I am a driver, licensed and professional," he said. "But that is not the only way I occupy my time."

He was playing coy, was he? "*We*," she said. "You said *we* earlier. Who else?"

He hesitated a bit too long. "I am a cryptozoologist. You know, Bigfoot, Loch Nessie, Ropen, Yeti, that sort of thing."

Brianna slammed the water bottle to the dashboard. "Oh, no. He sent you, didn't he? The answer is no. Turn around."

"I can't turn," said Xiaolang a bit apologetically. "Not here."

That was true; the narrow and rutted mountain road would never permit it. "He told you to ask me, didn't he? Brandon?"

Xiaolang had the grace to look embarrassed. "He suggested you, yes." He cleared his throat. "Brandon is at the temple."

Brianna stomp-kicked the dashboard and swore. "He's here?!"

Xiaolang said nothing.

Brianna took a long breath and looked at Xiaolang. "He, um, probably didn't tell you how I'd react."

Xiaolang's head bobbed from side to side as he considered his words. "He, er, suggested it would be best if I met you with the car, as your expected driver."

"Because he knew if I spotted him I'd be right back on that plane, Zunyi or not." Brianna sighed. "It's not your fault. Probably not, anyway. I'll try not to kill the messenger."

"I appreciate that, Dr. Allen."

She huffed out a breath. "Cryptozoologist, eh?"

"Yes. As a hobby."

Of course it was a hobby; looking for Bigfoot rarely paid the bills. "And you think there are dinosaurs in the temple?"

"No, of course don't. That would be ridiculous." Xiaolang used both hands to jerk the car away from the mountain road's steep edge. "We think there used to be."

The SUV jolted to a halt beside a dusty grey-brown bridge, and a dusty figure emerged from a dusty grey-brown building. Brianna got out of the car and slung her backpack viciously over one shoulder. "We thought you were dead."

Brandon was as good-looking as ever, deep brown skin over strong bones and melting-chocolate eyes which had always looked better on him than her. He shrugged one shoulder, grinning like a toothy display would somehow pacify her. "Nah, not yet."

"Obviously. I didn't expect this trip to be so disappointing so quickly."

"Well, you know how travel can be," Brandon countered cheerily. "Did Xiaolang tell you about the temple?"

He would never, never grow up enough to face his own mess. Brianna gave up. "No, not really."

"Well, I'll fill you in on the way. Let's go."

He pointed back to the car, and she turned to get in. As he circled to enter the back seat, Brianna pulled her phone from her backpack. She should probably tell Mom she had seen her twin brother, and also that she'd made it safely to China. Mom would be equally happy at each piece of news, which showed there was no accounting for a mother's love.

But her phone was completely dead. How? She thought she'd turned it off during the long flight, but apparently she'd forgotten that, too.

She quickly shoved it back into her pocket before either of them could notice the blank screen and know she was out of communication. It wasn't that she distrusted them, not exactly; Brandon would never harm her. But it was always best to keep one's cards close with Brandon; he wouldn't hesitate to use her lack of phone to coerce her into something else.

"So, cryptozoology," she said to Xiaolang, to fill the air. "I don't know anything beyond the most famous hoaxes, like Nessie's photo and the Cottingley Fairies and whatever sob story Brandon's telling Mom to get more money this time."

"It's not all hoaxes," Xiaolang said, as if she'd never mentioned Brandon's name. "Some are, of course. And there are always some who will fabricate evidence to try for their minutes of fame or grant money. But most of us who are honestly pursuing knowledge are not featured in the news."

Most of Brianna's colleagues were not in the news either, because the media found paleography too boring to compete with supermodel squabbles and politicians' tantrums and sports speculations, so it was hard to muster much sympathy for the overlooked cryptozoologists even without the complication of her deadbeat twin.

"So," she said, "dinosaurs."

Xiaolang visibly brightened. "We have long known that dinosaurs did not die out in a day, whatever the tragic romantic appeal of a single cataclysmic event."

"Some species lived longer than others," volunteered Brandon, "and some lived on to become birds. We think some lived on into ancient China, and were venerated here."

"Thus the temple."

"Exactly."

"But I haven't seen a lot of dinosaur statues in the travel brochures," Brianna said. "Seems like that would be a thing."

"Ah, Dr. Allen, you are a scientist," said Xiaolang. "You know you must piece together the evidence, that is it never sitting before you in glorious color waiting to be noticed."

"Still, dinosaurs seem like kind of an obvious thing to overlook."

"Who says they have been overlooked?" Brandon leaned into the front seat. "Look, sis, I know you are not too keen on my calling, but—"

"Your calling is bilking Mom out of money."

"Don't change the subject. Tell her, Xiaolang."

Xiaolang was amazingly good at ignoring interpersonal conflict and speaking as if he were giving Brianna a guided tour. "It's astonishing, really, how late dragon lore persisted in the humanist literature. I'm not only talking about the Anglo-Saxon Chronicle, though it's clear on several occasions, but scientific works like bestiaries and early encyclopedias."

"Naturalists described them as real creatures with actual specimen examples even into the eighteenth century," contributed Brandon, "and folk references persist into the nineteenth and early twentieth."

"Several accounts are recorded of flying lizard-like creatures in your American Wild West. And Western consultants in the South Pacific were told stories of bat-winged creatures as recently as the 1980s."

"There are always stories," Brianna countered. "You said yourself people make up stories about Bigfoot and Nessie. Doesn't mean they're out there, just means people want on the talk show circuit."

"No one has matter-of-factly cited specimens of Bigfoot," Xiaolang said, "or written as if his readers have of course also seen him and are familiar with him. Always it is a breathless tale of a rare and secret glimpse, not a mundane report alongside a citation of rabbits."

"Those specimens aren't preserved or described today."

Brandon held up a finger. "The Barbary lion was one of the most popular zoo exhibits for centuries, kept by several royal families, and popularly hunted. Yet just half a century after its extinction, we have only nine skins and a single skeleton preserved. Do you expect more from an era without taxonomic or conservation standards? If those skins and skeleton were lost by fire, theft, or accident, would you be justified in saying the Barbary lion had never existed and those who described it were mistaken or lying?"

Watch out, Brianna, she told herself, *or they'll start making sense.* This was how crackpot theorists—and Brandon in particular— worked; they got you agreeing first, and then believing, and then in Brandon's case, finally opening the checkbook.

"A species can survive without a large population," Brandon continued encouragingly. "The Devils Hole Pupfish has less than two hundred individuals and the entire species lives on a ledge of less than a hundred square feet. The Lord Howe Island tree lobster had just twenty-four bugs living in a single bush before conservationists created insurance populations. It's unlikely such a population would leave many natural traces, and they're not statistically likely to fossilize, but they could be real just the same, and noticed and venerated by humans."

Brianna was saved from responding by Xiaolang's announcement. "Here is Zhenyuan."

The town was astounding. The river snaked through the center in a picturesque curve, dividing Zhenyuan into two. One part looked like a quaint, neat city, bright in the sun, and the other—the other was a preserved vision of a past China, all sweeping roofs with upturned corners and stone and tile reflecting in the slow water. A set of matched traditional buildings ran up a steep hillside, marked by a large gate.

"That is Quinlong Dong," said Xiaolang, pointing. "It is the temple complex."

"In English they call it Black Dragon Cave," Brandon said as they crossed an ancient stone bridge. "But it is only partly a cave, enhanced with the temple architecture."

"And we're here because of the black dragon."

"It's not an exact translation."

"So, it's really Black Dinosaur Cave?"

Xiaolang smiled patiently at her sarcasm. "*Long* is dragon," he explained. "*Qing* is... a color. It's not a color you have a word for. You would call it blue-green, or perhaps azure."

"Oh!" This time Brianna did not feel stupidly adrift. "Like the Japanese *aoi*. The color of nature. They didn't really have separate words for blue and green until World War 2 or so."

She had surprised Xiaolang. "I think so, I'm not sure of the Japanese. But it is likely."

Brianna nodded. She'd briefly dated a grad student working on something about linguistics and cognition. She hadn't paid much attention to his droning endlessly on about his research—there was a reason the relationship had been brief—but that tidbit had stuck with her. She was grateful for it now; she was starting to feel a bit slow under their patient examples, even if she thought the guy a brilliantly educated crackpot, and it was always good to know something Brandon wasn't expecting.

"You might know the Azure Dragon from *feng shui*," continued Xiaolang. "Are you at all familiar with *feng shui*?"

"I had a roommate who subscribed to it," Brianna said. "Briefly. He kept yelling at me about my desk facing the wall and stifling the phoenix."

"The phoenix is a word from western mythology," said Xiaolang. "We call it the *fēnghuáng*. It has appeared in our artwork for eight thousand years." He gave Brianna a significant look, waiting.

"And?"

"And, it is indisputable that we are losing known and unknown species at an alarming rate, and have been for some time. Is it not possible that eight thousand years ago a bird existed which no longer exists today?"

Brianna thought of the dodo, the aurochs, the Tasmanian tiger, the passenger pigeon. "Not only possible, but likely."

"And if a bird might be known and then be lost, why not a relative of a bird?"

Brianna raised a warning hand. "Oh, no, I won't follow you over that bridge. Dinosaurs and birds are cousins, sure, but they're not that close a family."

Xiaolang smiled and shrugged, unruffled by her skepticism. "You prefer your dinosaurs with scales instead of feathers?"

"I'm a traditionalist, I guess."

They entered the temple complex, Xiaolang flashing some sort of ID to speed them past the entry, and started uphill. The temple was set into the side of the mountain, each building linked with steep stairs studded with panting tourists.

Xiaolang led her into a hall, and Brianna protested immediately. "No, no. These are fakes." She crossed to the large Buddhas, running her hand over them. "And not particularly good fakes at that, though they might fool some tourists."

Xiaolang followed her and shook his head. "No, they are not intended to pass for original. The antique statues were destroyed during the Great Proletarian Cultural Revolution."

Brianna's breath caught. She knew only the vaguest outline of it— universities were shut down as Mao Zedong, weakened by socialism's failure to bolster the economy as promised, sought to regain control, and the dismissed students were encouraged to form paramilitary units to attack intellectuals and academics. Millions were imprisoned, tortured, or executed. Mao's personality cult left little room for history and heritage, and many cultural treasures were destroyed.

It wasn't a unique story; the Khmer Rouge did much the same a decade later, torturing and murdering the educated and systematically destroying "impure influences" such as religious objects or buildings. The so-called Islamic State was doing it now, brutally murdering Christians and Muslims alike and smashing ancient historic sites to rubble.

It was hideous to Brianna on every level, academic and humanitarian.

"I'm sorry," she said. "I should have guessed."

"The inscriptions we want you to see are not in the more visited areas," he said. "Come this way."

Stairs. So many steep stairs. Brianna jogged only on the flat, and her legs were burning.

Acka lacka lacka boom, she chanted to herself as she climbed, trying to keep her pace steady. A dinosaur. In a Chinese temple. How crazy was this? Brandon had taken things to a whole new level.

When was the last time she'd seen him? About eight months ago, maybe. Yes, it was Great-Aunt Patricia's funeral. Brandon hadn't made it to the service, but he'd appeared at the family dinner and sweet-talked Mom out of several thousand dollars. He was gone by dessert.

They had not seen another tourist in the temple for about ten minutes; Xiaolang and Brandon had led her through narrow passages and half-concealed doors, and she suspected they had left the part of the ancient temple generally open to visitors.

Xiaolang spoke to her from a few steps above, still climbing. "*Qinglong* is the dragon of *feng shui,* as we have said already."

"The Azure Dragon, yes."

"One of the *sì shòu.* There are white tigers to be found, you know—perhaps not so readily today as before, but they are indisputably real. And dark turtles are not a thing of imagination. And—"

"And you're going to tell me that *qing*-colored dragons and phoenixes are a thing?"

Xianlang smiled and took a small notebook from his inner pocket. He opened it almost without scanning, as if he knew the contents of each page and exactly where to turn. *"There are also certain other creatures which, being as big as rams, have wings like dragons, with*

long tails, and long chaps, and divers rows of teeth, and feed upon
raw flesh. Their color is blue and green, their skin painted like scales,
and they have two feet but no more."

Brianna sighed, beaten. "Who is that?"

"Filippo Pigafetta. Sixteenth century explorer."

"It doesn't mean it's a dinosaur."

"Is that what you think?"

Brianna realized she'd been played smoothly into his argument.
Drat. But she could not stop the mental image. Two legs, wings, tails
and teeth and carnivorous.... It did sound something like a dinosaur.
Would they appear scaly or feathered, if they had—no, no, she was
buying too much into this already. Modern paleozoology was still
sorting out feathers on real dinosaurs, and it was far too early to start
speculating about their presence on something which couldn't
possibly be a dinosaur.

These two were making her crazy.

Xiaolang gestured at a painted ceiling above them. "Look at the
shēngxiào, or you might call it the Chinese zodiac," he said. "What do
you know of it?"

"There are twelve animals," answered Brianna, "and each year has
an animal. Brandon and I are the year of the Snake, if the buffet
restaurant placemat didn't lie to me when I was a kid." She glanced at
her twin. "The snake shows more in some than others."

"Zodiac hours as well," prompted Xiaolang. "What animals?"

"Snake, obviously, monkey, rat.... Dog." She was straining now,
and they'd passed out of the room with the ceiling cheat sheet. "Cat?"

"No cat."

"No cat, then.... Cow or ox or something. I dunno."

"Also horse, tiger, rabbit, goat, rooster, pig... and dragon."

"Okay."

"Does it not strike you as interesting that eleven of those twelve
creatures are common, everyday beasts which certainly lived and were

certainly known to the scholars? Why would such educated men place a wholly imaginary creature among them?"

"I don't know." Brianna considered. "Maybe it was symbolic. The future is unknown, or is full of potential beyond our imagination, or something like that."

"The Dragon is fifth in the cycle. Neither first, nor last, nor central. Perfectly ordinary."

Brianna climbed another dozen stairs and let her panting excuse her from answering.

"Kazahkstan also has an animal zodiac," Xiaolang said, "only it has a snail in place of the dragon. Perfectly ordinary, a common creature they saw every day."

"Well, there, see—"

"There are one hundred thirty eight species of dinosaurs currently identified in Chinese fossil beds, and new ones yet being discovered," Xiaolang continued. "Kazahkstan has had only four."

The implication was heavy in the air, and Brianna did not respond.

"It's not far now," said Xiaolang. "Then you can read for yourself and tell us if this writing is authentic, and if these people really venerated a living creature instead of an imaginary one."

"Even if the writing is authentic, I can't tell you if an animal was really there."

"You can tell us if the people of the time thought it was real," Brandon answered. "And then you can help us publish."

"What? No!" Brianna shook her head. "No way."

"Come on, Brianna, you already know all that stuff about how to write it up and where to send it. And you're so much better at writing than I ever was."

"Because I did it," she snapped, "instead of whining that it was hard until someone else took care of it. Like you've done with your entire life."

"That's cold, Bri."

"I've brought the flashlights," interrupted Xiaolang. He handed Brianna a small, heavy model. "Freshly charged."

Brianna looked at the flashlight and then at her twin.

"We're going back into the mountain itself," he announced gleefully. "Xiaolang and I found an old, old passage back. We think it predates the Ming construction by quite a while."

"How much?"

"No, no, that would be influencing you. I heard academics need open minds." Brandon knelt and felt along the wall, probing with his fingers. "We had to block it up again, lest anyone else find it before we were ready."

"Go ahead and start on the passage," said Xiaolang. "I'll take Brianna a bit further up this corridor and show her the bridge."

"Right," said Brandon. "Go ahead."

Xiaolang's fingers brushed Brianna's forearm as he passed. "We can look down on the city below," he said. "This way."

Brianna looked at her forearm and then followed him.

They crossed a sky well, an open courtyard, and Brianna squinted up at the hazy blue. Then they went through to a window cut into the stone, and Xiaolang pointed far below to the bridge they had crossed before. "Wow," she said, looking at the brown river curving through the ancient city. "It's really amazing from here."

"Look to the left," he suggested. She did, her eyes almost immediately picking out the carved stone figure. It was greatly eroded, fading into the stone; it would be nearly impossible to distinguish from below. But from here, she could clearly trace the outline of a *fènghuáng*, slender neck and outstretched tail feathers and folded wings.

"It was probably painted once," she said. "It would have been beautiful."

"I think it is beautiful now," Xiaolang said. "It has aged, but it still carries power. If you understand me."

"I do."

"Dr. Allen," he said, less certainly, "I can see the past actions of your brother weigh upon you. And I am not going to defend him; I can pretend to no knowledge of your family, and I myself know he can be... insistent in his enthusiasm."

She snorted. "You put it so prettily."

"I only wish to say, he may mean no harm as he does it. But that is not an excuse for him."

Brianna tipped her head to regard him. "You're the first person to ever tell me it's not an excuse."

Xiaolang turned up a palm. "Intent and effect are not the same, and we as adults should see that."

She turned to face him. "You know, I wish I'd met you anywhere else. Someplace where you weren't working with my deadbeat con-artist brother."

Xiaolang smiled. "I'm not sure he's a con artist. He really does believe in his work."

She sighed. "I know. That's the worst part of it. He absolutely believes it, all of it. That everyone else has just had better luck than him, or more privilege, or that he would have made a real go of things this time if the refrigerator just hadn't gone out that week." She shook her head. "He believes it, and that makes him believable."

"Your mother believes him?"

"Oh, yeah. Every time. And not just Mom. Three times he convinced school administrators to waive a failing grade for 'extenuating circumstances.' Once he even got a scholarship to help retake a semester of classes he'd been too sick to test in."

"And was he sick?"

"Oh, sure he was. A little mono, a little affluenza, a lot of *Call of Duty* with his feet on a heating pad. It was rough."

Xiaolang smiled reluctantly. "He does believe in the *fēnghuáng*. And I don't think this is merely a convenient fiction."

She hesitated. "I wish I could believe he was really pulling himself together, but.... Our freshman year, I got a massive eye infection and had to wear an eye patch for a week. Not only is that not exactly *haute couture* among the high school set, but it was harder to read and concentrate, with only half as many eyeballs. But one of my teachers told me, 'When the going gets tough, the tough get going.' I didn't know it was a cliché, I hadn't seen it before, and I took it to heart. I wrote a paper that week and aced a huge exam.

"A month or so later, Brandon broke his ankle playing football. He ended up with a few days off school and Mom went in to talk to his history teacher about how it was hard for him to concentrate with the pain, and so he got a pass on the test that week. And I was like, Why did I do my work instead of getting off like him? But I don't know if I could have gotten away with it like he did. It was always like that. I guess she thought she was doing him favors, taking care of him. But now he's got a string of fed-up ex-girlfriends, a massive credit card debt, and a perpetual coprophagous grin."

"And what do you have?"

"Me? I have a PhD."

"Sounds like you did the right thing that week."

She stared at him, stunned and embarrassingly grateful for the praise. She was so accustomed to hearing it was wrong to resent her brother's failures, wrong to show him up, wrong to criticize his endless second chances.

"Maybe," she conceded. "And it really would be great if he'd get some traction this time, even in a... less traditional field."

Xiaolang laughed. "Less traditional, yes. But don't worry, you have your safe, conventional academic research still waiting for you tomorrow in Zunyi. I'll drive you there in the morning." He hesitated. "I will be driving to Zunyi several times over the next week or ten days. I will not be far from the institute."

It was a soft pitch, well-aimed. "Is there a coffee shop near the institute?" asked Brianna.

"I believe so."

"Drivers need a lot of caffeine, to stay alert on the road. Especially mountain roads." Brianna tipped her head, nodding thoughtfully. "And academics need a lot of caffeine, to stay alert over their research."

"Maybe we could get some coffee at the same time."

"Maybe."

Brandon, as always, ruined everything. "Guys! Hey, guys! I'm through!" He came into the doorway, waving them away from the stone window. "Come on!"

The passage Brandon had cleared was only about eighteen inches high, and narrow even for Brianna's slim shoulders. "We crawl through?" she asked skeptically. "I didn't bring my fedora and bullwhip."

"You'll be fine."

"Brandon, you had me kidnapped straight off the plane. I thought I was going to meet Dr. Wang in these clothes. I'm not dressed for crawling through centuries of dirt."

Brandon, crouching in the low tunnel, leaned out to regard her. "You're offered the chance to crawl through a secret passage in an ancient temple to look for dinosaurs, and you're balking because you're worried about *clothes*?"

Brianna made a small, strangled noise in her throat. She hated it when he was right. How could he be right so often, when he was always wrong? It was infuriating.

The passage was too low to crawl comfortably, so she had to lower herself to her elbows. Grit bit at her forearms as she wriggled after Brandon and Xiaolang, grateful to be last so they could not watch her flopping like a walrus. Her flashlight illuminated only Xiaolang's legs and a short stretch of the narrow, unfinished arch of the passage.

"Brandon?" she called. "How far is this?"

"Not too far," he called back, muffled by Xiaolang between them. "About a half-mile or so."

"Brandon!"

"I'm kidding, I'm kidding. About twenty meters." He was still crawling. "Here, I'll distract you with background. Did you know that three different languages in pre-Columbian Central America named a deity the 'feathered serpent'? They trace back to a thousand years before the Spanish arrived. Have you ever looked at the statues depicting Quetzalcoatl? A reptilian head with a ruff of protruding feathers." His flashlight bobbed. "Meso-American archaeologists have always said it was a blend of rattlesnake and bird. It's only been in the last few decades that we have accepted the idea of feathered dinosaurs."

"And you think it's the same as the *fènghuáng*?"

"Not necessarily; the art is recognizably different. But we are talking different hemispheres; it'd make sense to see different species."

"Uh, huh," she called. "So you guys believe in a, what do they call it, a young earth?"

"I never said that," Brandon corrected her.

Xiaolang said, "We believe in the long tail of a declining species. It is not that we think dinosaurs did not exist during the Jurassic age or that there was no Jurassic age; we only suggest that some may have persisted, albeit in small numbers."

"There are lots of references to creatures which might be dinosaurs, or something like them," Brandon said.

"So you keep telling me," grumbled Brianna, but she wasn't as irritated as she sounded. There *were* an awful lot of instances, Quetzalcoatl and dragons and the *fènghuáng*. How much was reliable?

"Did we mention Marco Polo yet?"

"What?"

"I guess not. He described dinosaurs right here in China."

"I disagree," said Xiaolang. "What he described are not consistent with current dinosaur theories. They may have been heavier reptiles, similar to crocodiles or Komodo dragons, but they are not likely to be related to what we seek as the *fènghuáng*."

"You can't argue with Marco Polo, Xiaolang."

"It weakens the argument, as I've said. The other references are consistent with birds and dinosaurs. Polo describes something like a crocodile."

"We're here," Brandon said, his voice changing as he left the passage.

Brianna crawled out after them, getting to her feet in a domed chamber which faded to shadow all around them. Brandon swung the beam of his flashlight overhead, briefly illuminating a low, curved ceiling, and then pointed the light forward.

"Oh, wow," breathed Brianna.

The statue was ancient and intact, nothing like the tourist-worn examples in the public temple below. Smoothed stone formed a tall, lean bird, head extended forward and mouth closed, feathers streaking back from its head and half-tucked wings and then gliding back into a long plumed tail which disappeared in the darkness.

"It's a beautiful piece," Brianna said, moving toward it. "Oh, you sexy thing."

Fragments of color clung occasionally to the carved *fènghuáng*, but the stone was mostly bare. A few flakes of oxidized paint lay about the base and floor; victims of time.

"There's an inscription wrapping the four sides of the base," Brandon pointed out. "We need the period confirmed. Authenticity."

Brianna squatted to look at the square pillar, turning her flashlight on it. "This is old," she said. "What period is the temple?"

"Qinglong Dong was begun in the early Ming Dynasty." Brandon glanced sideways at Brianna. "That is not so long after Marco Polo described his great lizards."

"Oh, shut up about Marco Polo already. He didn't write this."

"No. But what I meant was, Qinglong Dong could have been constructed on a more ancient site. The *fènghuáng* has been venerated for thousands of years."

"Well, this is definitely pre-Ming." She frowned at the stone. "More light, please. All angles, no shadows."

They turned their lights on the inscription, and she began examining it.

"Also," began Brandon, a touch of embarrassment in his voice, "if you could, you know, tell us what it says…."

She pulled her head back and stared at him. "What?"

"You know. Translate it."

She stared at him in speechless incredulity. "You—you—you don't even—you just—my plane—"

"C'mon, Bri, this is what you do! You're good at this!"

"Flattery will get you a punch in the teeth," she snarled. "I can't believe you dragged me out here to verify something you haven't even identified yourself." Brandon started to answer, but she held up a warning finger. "Punch in the teeth," she repeated. "Shut up and hold the light."

He did.

"Well," she said, "I can't possibly translate this off the cuff. Not my period, for one thing. But I'll tell you it can't be that ancient."

"What? Why not?" they both cried.

She pointed. "See these characters? *Fengfeng laklak.* That's an onomatopoetic reference to the sound of a bell."

"And?"

"And that means this can't possibly predate the casting of bronze bells. That's going to be Zhou dynasty, or about tenth century BCE at the very earliest."

"Tenth century!" Brandon and Xiaolang looked at each other, faces splitting into delighted grins. "That's almost twenty-five hundred years before Qinglong Dong was started! It's definitely a more ancient site!"

"Hold on," cautioned Brianna. "That's not how it works. That's the earliest possible date, but it could be much later. I'll need to analyze the characters used, the shape of the strokes, the—"

They weren't concerned with her caveats. They were jumping and slapping backs and bouncing the flashlights everywhere but the inscription. Brianna sighed and gave up, rocking back onto the floor in a more comfortable position.

Her eyes slowly adjusted to the dark, now that she wasn't focusing beneath the flashlights' combined beams, and she looked away from the statue and about the room itself. It was large, the edges shadowed beyond the light's reach, and the floor was of packed earth, not stone. The ceiling was roughly domed. Shaped by human hands, probably, though from solid rock or using a natural fissure or cave, she couldn't guess. Geology wasn't her thing.

There was another statue across the room, she noticed. It was barely visible in the dark, and—

Suddenly she reached out to seize both men by the ankles, gripping tight. They stopped, looking down at her. "What?"

She couldn't say it. "There—over there—it's moving. It's real."

They looked where she was staring.

It was a bird. Only it couldn't be a bird, not really—it was the size of a turkey, maybe, or an eagle, but with a plumed tail which stretched far behind like that of a phoenix or a peacock. It was perhaps as long as Brianna was tall, nose to tail tip, and it was covered in glorious blue-green feathers which gleamed in the dim light like an ocean.

The creature blinked in their direction and cocked its head, listening. Brianna held her breath, though clearly it had perceived them already. It was waiting to see if they were a threat, now that they had perceived it. Suddenly she hoped they weren't. "You aren't going to kill it, are you? For a specimen?"

"Kill it?" Brandon repeated as if she'd suggested eating a child. "After thousands of years of holding it sacred? Are you kidding?"

"We didn't come to collect a specimen," whispered Xiaolang. "We didn't know there would *be* a specimen."

"There are more passages," whispered Brandon. "We haven't explored them. But they must go on—maybe to a mountain valley, somewhere where a tiny population has survived. Like the Lord Howe Island insects."

The not-a-bird stepped forward, apparently dismissing them for the moment, feathers reflecting blues and greens as the faint light moved over the slim body. It paused, lifting one foot, and stared intently at the ground, eyes riveted forward. For a long moment it stood motionless, and then it snapped the foot down lightning-sharp, tearing back the packed earth floor and darting its slender muzzle into the opening. It pulled back with a squirming furry creature struggling and squeaking.

"Predator," observed Brandon gleefully. "A surviving theropod."

Brianna shook her head. "But it can't be a—it can't be a dinosaur."

"Then don't call it a dinosaur, if that makes you happy."

Brianna flailed for words. "But…."

"It is the *fènghuáng*," breathed Xiaolang. "It is not a myth. It was never a myth."

The creature shook its head, snapping the body of the small creature about its narrow muzzle.

Brianna reached for her phone and thumbed the button to bring up the camera. Nothing happened. She swore, remembering the dead battery.

"Don't worry," said Brandon, grinning at her. "I've got this." He held up his phone. A flash of light burst from it, and Brianna recoiled, shading her eyes. "Brandon!" she snapped.

The bird—dinosaur—theropod—*fènghuáng* leapt backward, dropping its limp prey. It stared in their direction a moment, chattering quietly. It did not seem afraid of them; perhaps it had not seen humans before. Perhaps the two species had not seen one another in centuries.

Brandon frowned at his phone. "Nothing," he said. "Can't see a thing."

He was so excited. His hands were actually trembling a little as he fumbled with the phone. She had never seen him so intent on anything.

Go easy on your brother, her mother's voice repeated in her head. *It's harder for him.*

Brianna wasn't sure it *was* harder for him, but she could hear her mother say, again and again, to give him one more chance. And maybe this was that chance he needed and could use. He had researched, he had acted, he had actually stayed on a project long enough to accomplish something. And what he had accomplished— they had found a *dinosaur.* Not just concrete evidence of an allegedly-mythological creature, but the creature itself. If he could take back proof, present his findings properly…. He could get a grant to study, make some money on talk shows and a mass market book, maybe pay Mom some of what he'd borrowed over the years—no, maybe just get himself a steady apartment and that'd be fine to start.

Brianna took a deep breath. One chance. He was her brother, after all, and her twin. One more chance. "Brandon, you did it."

"I'm going to get a better shot," he said.

"What?"

"Nobody will believe a blurry long-distance mass in the dark," he said. "I need a close-up." He started away.

"Brandon!" she whispered too loudly. "Brandon, no!"

"It's fine," he said. "It's like a turkey or something."

"I don't think you should get close to it."

"It eats rodents or whatever, little things. Not people. I just need a clear picture. Otherwise it'll be like the Bigfoot or Nessie pics."

She bit her lip, disagreeing but unable to argue with him. Always the charm and the seeming logic, with Brandon. Always the same.

She looked to Xiaolang, but he was fascinated by the creature and only nodded in distracted half-agreement, hardly aware of their conversation.

Brandon eased across the open space, and she saw him start the video function on his phone. "This is it," he whispered to the phone. "This is the *fènghuáng*. This is our first sighting; we thought we were coming for a statue. But this is no statue."

The *fènghuáng* lifted its head from the dead prey it had been eying and chattered again, its eyes on Brandon. Brianna didn't like how it seemed to go still. "Brandon," she called. "Don't get too close. The video is good enough. Come back."

But Brandon shook his head. "I'm fine. It's okay. As you can see, it's aware of me, but that's okay. Look at the feathers! They're so colorful! You can really see how this became the phoenix of mythology. I'm going to get a couple still photos."

He was close now, maybe fifteen feet. Too close. "Brandon—"

"It's fine."

The plumed tail rose a few inches higher, feathers spreading slightly.

Now Xiaolang was concerned, too. "Brandon."

"Brandon, stop!"

He ignored her. Always the same with Brandon.

The phone flashed brilliant light, blinding in the darkness of the cavern. The *fènghuáng* shrieked and sprang forward, winged forearms and clawed feet extended.

"Brandon!"

The first foot struck Brandon in the groin, shoving him backward and tearing into him. He screamed as he fell backward, and the phone clattered to the side.

The *fènghuáng* kicked with the second leg, clawed foot catching Brandon across the neck this time. He struck at the bird, shielding his face with his arm. But the *fènghuáng* was already moving backward, having successfully neutralized the threat. It retreated to its prey, looked back at Brandon, and then picked up the dead animal and jogged back into the darkness.

Brianna scrabbled to her feet and dashed to her brother. "Brandon!" she screamed. "Brandon, are you all right?"

He was not all right. The front of his khakis had been torn open and flesh gaped through his boxers. Brianna jammed a hand into the wound, wishing she had supplies. Why didn't she keep a first aid kit in her backpack? Even on a plane? She was so stupid, and now Brandon was counting on her to save him from his mess again, and she wasn't going to be able to do it.

"Brandon!"

His shielding arm drooped, and she saw his face and neck. Her body twitched as an electric shock seemed to pass through her. The gash across his jaw and throat was wide and bleeding fast.

Brianna tore her shirt over her head and stuffed it into the neck wound, as if it could dam the flow. "Oh Brandon," she breathed. "You idiot. You stupid, stupid idiot. I'm so sorry."

Xiaolang was behind her, pressing his hand into the wound she had abandoned. He was speaking, but Brianna couldn't understand him, couldn't make out his words. Somewhere in the back of her mind their mother was already screaming. Brianna could hear her voice. *Why didn't you save him? Why did you let this happen?*

I didn't, Mama. I told him to stop. He didn't listen.

You know what he's like! You know you have to take care of him! He's your twin, Brianna, and you let him down!

She was crying now. "Brandon, hold on. Hold on."

But he was wheezing, sucking air through his own blood, his eyes wide and white in the dark. He tried to speak and choked.

Poor, stupid Brandon. It wasn't his fault. He knew it would be all right, it had always been all right, and now he was dying.

He grabbed her arm, leaving bloody marks. She couldn't understand what he was trying to say, and that upset her. "I love you, Brandon," she said, and she meant it. "I was only angry with you because I loved you and I wanted you to succeed. I'm so sorry. I'm so, so sorry."

She wasn't sure of the exact moment he died. That seemed wrong too, as if she should have known, should have paid more attention. But she had never taken her eyes from him, never loosened her grip on his neck and his hand. When it came to her that he was dead, that he had been dead, she still couldn't let go.

Xiaolang found her hand, squeezed it tightly as he knelt beside her, looking down at his colleague.

They had to work him through the low tunnel, Xiaolang pulling backwards and Brianna pushing, and Brianna knew no matter how long she lived and what else she lived through, there would never be another task as awful as trying to shove her twin's utterly limp body before her, crawling through his cold spilled blood.

Xiaolang went down bare-chested to call for help; he had given his shirt to Brianna. When he returned, he came and stood beside her at the stone window, shoulder to shoulder.

"Sorry," she said. "I just couldn't look at him anymore."

She was leaning on the stone, staring down at the ancient town. The *fènghuáng* statue was visible to her left.

Xiaolang nodded, rubbing tears from his eyes.

"I'm sorry," she said again. "You're his friend. You don't have to hold back. I was his sister, but… we weren't close. We hadn't been for a long time. But you worked with him."

"He was… distractable," said Xiaolang. "But he was enthusiastic. And he was a friend."

There were voices on the stairs below them. Brianna couldn't understand them, but she supposed it was the coroner or mortician or whoever handled these things here.

"It wasn't your fault," said Xiaolang softly. "For any of it."

She looked at him. "We haven't known each other long enough yet for you to know that."

"It was obvious from the first," he said. "You would not have been so angry about his shortcomings if you did not care."

She began to cry again, and they turned in to one another, pulling each other close.

Something hard pressed into Brianna's ribs, and she drew out the phone. Brandon's phone. With the video.

"I can't watch it," she said. "Not now. Maybe not—maybe not ever. But I can give it to someone in a research department. You can tell them what you found. I'll help write it up." She choked on tears. "Stupid Brandon. You got me to do it after all."

Z is for *Zhenyuanlong suni*, "Zhenyuan's Dragon."

Thank you for reading

D is for Dinosaur

We would appreciate it a great deal if you would leave an honest review on Goodreads and wherever you purchased this book.

Your stars and a couple sentences mean the world to us!

Truly.

The importance of reviews cannot be overstated—they often make the difference between a book's success or failure.

Always Be The First
To Know!

Whether it's a new release, a call for submissions, cover reveal, super sale or I just want to share a new story I've written, you will always be among the first to know if you sign up for my newsletter.

I promise to respect your privacy and your inbox. I will only email you when I have something exciting to share, probably about twice a month.

Subscribe now and you'll receive a free download of my award-winning post-apocalyptic short story, "Starry Night" as a welcome-to-the-newsletter present!

Subscribe to Rhonda's Mailing List!

http://bit.ly/StarryStory